A BARGAIN WITH THE FAE KING

MEGAN VAN DYKE

Published by Megan Van Dyke

www.authormeganvandyke.com

Editing: Jeni Chappelle of Jeni Chappelle Editorial

Proofreading: Portal World Publishing

Cover & Interior Design: Megan Van Dyke

All images licensed appropriately.

Print Edition ISBN: 978-1-955532-15-0
Digital Edition ISBN: 978-1-955532-14-3

Author's Note

A Bargain with the Fae King is an fae fantasy romance aimed at adults, and contains material that some readers may find distressing or objectionable including: violence and blood, adult language, drinking, consensual sex, poisoning, kidnapping of a child, car accident, child injury, war, struggles with grief and guilt, death of a parent (off page/remembered), and parental abandonment (off page/remembered).

Please specifically note that the prologue and first chapter include brief descriptions of a car crash in which a child was injured. This event is also mentioned multiple times throughout the book.

To my younger self and everyone like her.

This was the book I wanted—needed—and nothing else would satisfy. But it didn't exist yet. So, I wrote it.

PROLOGUE

ALL I WANT TO do is run to the woods and never look back. I've done it this time. There's no coming back. No apology will ever be good enough.

My foot taps against the floor of the rideshare as I choke back another sob. It's winter, but a temperate one for Tennessee, and no matter how I hug my arms around myself, I can't get warm. The driver has the heater on full blast, and it's not helping either. Oh, the air hits my feet all right; those are on fire, but the rest of me? Cold as death. Icy as my little sister May could have been right now, thanks to my foolishness.

The driver turns onto the gravel drive leading to my family's cabin, and finally, I can breathe again. I unbuckle my seat belt and reach for the handle before the car is ever parked. It doesn't matter if I fall out. No one will care. But the door is locked and doesn't budge. Panic wells up as I wipe at my eyes.

"Now, darlin'." The southern drawl is thick in the air. "You sure you'll be okay?"

"Yeah," I manage. I jingle my key to the house for emphasis. Somewhere deep down, I'm thankful that whatever-her-name-is is worried about me, but all I can focus on is how I want to crawl under a blanket and never come out.

"If you're sure..." She picked me up at the hospital. It doesn't take a genius to know everything is not all right, but I'm not about to tell a stranger about the car accident. One moment, everything was fine—me driving along the winding country road like I had hundreds of times with May in the passenger seat. She kept asking me to look at something, and I turned to yell at her. One moment. One heartbeat too long. I missed the turn, sending the car off the embankment and tumbling down the slope.

My hand slides against the door as I search for the unlock button. Where the hell is it?

"I'm fine." The greatest lie of them all.

She sighs. "Okay." The door unlocks with a click.

I fly out. My boots crunch onto the gravel and fallen leaves. I don't even manage a thank you. I can't. The tears started to flow the moment the cool air hit my face. My heart pounds in my throat, and if I'm not careful, I might vomit right here on the drive.

This cabin was my special place long before Elise came into the picture when I was eleven. Then it was mine and Dad's. And Gran's too before she passed. I suppose Mom came here once too, but I don't remember her. She was my first failure. I made people want to abandon me long before I could even speak properly.

But that was before. Dad and Elise aren't going to want someone who almost killed their precious baby girl by being an idiot. If they did, they wouldn't have let me call for a ride instead of staying at the hospital with them.

How could I stay there under their scrutiny and judgment? How could I just watch my sister lie injured and unconscious? I had to leave. I *had* to.

I planned to beg.

I only asked once.

The car doesn't leave immediately, probably waiting to see if I make it inside. So, I rush up the stairs to the front door, fumble with the damn key that always sticks, and go inside. It's dark except for the lamp Dad always leaves on. Too bright for the darkness threatening to swallow me whole.

The familiar twang of old-person house and cedar hits me square in the face, and everything hurts so much worse.

May.

I run my hands down my face, probably dragging the last of my mascara with them. The unlit Christmas tree in the corner mocks me. How can we celebrate the holiday now? One day home from college, and I've broken so much—everything.

My fault. All my fault.

The room is comforting, familiar. And I hate it. Suddenly I'm gasping for air as if I've stepped into space. I lurch for the back door across the wide, open bottom level.

It's unlocked. Probably my fault too. I jerk it open, falling out into the night, but that doesn't help. I don't think—can't. I'm off and running down the back steps and out into the woods like I'd longed to from the moment my head stopped spinning and I stumbled out the driver's-side door of my car. Stumbled and fall because the whole thing was on its side, smashed up against the tree. And May...

Roots reach up and trip me. The pain is almost sweet. I deserve it. How could I escape with minor cuts and bruises when my sister is so much worse?

I shove to my feet and keep running. Branches tug at my clothes. Another scratches my cheek. If there was a path, I've lost it. I run until I literally can't breathe other than sharp, painful gasps of cold air that burn my lungs.

A clearing opens up among the trees. Soft-looking grass glimmers in the hint of moonlight from above. Nothing has ever looked so inviting—lush and green like summer. It's all I can do not to collapse face-first as I crumble to the ground. My arms hug my knees to my chest. Cold seeps through my sweater. Somehow, there are tears left, a well of pain that never runs dry. They're still leaking down my face when the crickets stop chirping and the scent of honeysuckle—so out of place on this December night—tickles my nose. It's distracting enough that I wipe at my face and force myself to sit up.

Breath catches in my throat. I'm not alone.

"Wh—who are you?" I scramble backward across the grass. My hand slips in evening dew, and I whack my head against the ground.

I sit back up, and he's gone. It was a he, right? *Doesn't freaking matter, Lia.* I've cracked. I'm so broken I'm imagining things now. "Come to drag me to hell?" It's no less than I deserve.

"Is that where you want to go?"

A scream rips from my throat as I rocket to my feet. I twist toward the voice at my back. It is a he, but the man is unlike any I've seen. Not in real life. My heart thunders in my chest as I take in the warm brown hair cascading down his shoulders and the clothes that, though shadowed, aren't something anyone would wear outside a cosplay convention.

Only two things I know for sure: The devil has come to drag me away, and the devil is hot.

"N-no."

His lips pull up in one corner. He's grinning at me, and I can't look away. "I'm glad you stopped crying."

Saw that, huh? I wipe my cheeks again. The heat that rushes there reminds me of how cold I am. Cold, and let's be honest, probably looking as dead and miserable as I feel. What does one say to the devil?

Of all the things he could do, he sits. The cross-legged position, hands on his knees, reminds me of my yoga instructor, and somehow his presence is just as calming.

I copy him, leaving a good fifteen feet between us. Only now do I notice the trees around us and the almost perfect circle they form. Nothing about any of it makes sense, so it can't be real.

"What do you want?" I ask. It's clear he wants something. Otherwise, he would have left or never come at all. Perhaps he'll be like the ghost of Marley and take me on a tour of all my misdeeds. Only, I don't need another reminder to know how horribly I messed up.

"If you want to leave, I can take you away from here."

A humorless laugh slips through my lips. To the afterlife? I'm not ready.

His head tilts to the side. Something about the motion is other-worldly—wrong. "You don't want to leave." It's not a question. He knows. "Why are you sad? What happened to you?"

Ah, time to confess my sins. I fall back onto the cushion of grass and gaze at the stars. My breath fogs the air as I begin. "I didn't mean to hurt May." Already my throat is closing up and the tears are crawling back to the corners of my eyes. But I want to tell him. No, something in me *needs* to. "I never wanted to hurt. I had to go pick her up from some stupid party because it would be too much to ask to have one night to myself with friends when I literally just got home from college yesterday." I taste the bitterness of the words on my tongue. It's cool. The devil knows everything, anyway, right? "She kept wanting to show me something, but I was driving. What idiot would take their eyes off the road?" My chest shakes. My fingers clench at blades of grass.

"So, I look. And then I yell at her for making me look. And the whole damn time, I'm not paying attention because I'm so mad. Then I—" I choke on a sob. "I've driven that road so many times. I missed the turn somehow." Can't even blame it on ice. Freaking global warming. The crash is one big blur. There's a crunch of metal. Screams. My body jerks. The seat belt digs into me. Then a sudden halt. It plays over and over like some kind of horror movie I can't leave.

A warm hand encompasses my own. It should be odd. I should pull away. There's a distant part of my brain telling me this is wrong, but the louder part embraces the comforting strength. I turn my head to the side, and he's lying next to me. Green eyes, a little too bright, stare into mine. When did he get so close? I never even heard him move.

Everything about him is odd. His cheeks are a little too sharp, eyes a little too big, hair far nicer than a model's. And his ears—I didn't notice them before—are pointed. My imagination is really working hard on this one. The warmth though... I don't care if he is the devil or some hallucination, it's all I want—someone to hold my hand and not look at me like the horrible person I am.

"What happened to her? To May?"

I sniffle. The side away from him is cold. So cold. How did I not notice it before? I'm freezing out here, inside and out.

"She...her arm and her face..." The doctor said her arm was broken. Compound break. And the cuts on her poor face... She'd bare those marks her whole life. How could I ever face her? Who could take one look at her and not remember what I've done?

Suddenly, I'm in his embrace, pulled up against a solid chest. Honeysuckle swarms my senses. I could stay here. Warm and sheltered. But he's not real, no matter how I want him to be. This is some trick my mind has conjured to cope.

"She lives?"

I nod against him, not trusting myself to speak.

"And you?"

Long fingers thread themselves through my hair. Am I alive? I hurt so bad inside that the bruises don't even matter. They're nothing compared to what happened to May anyway. The fact that it's my fault and she's the one who got hurt... "It should have been me."

"You can't blame yourself. You can't always protect the ones you love, even when you're with them." There's a slight tremor to his voice that almost makes me think he's talking about himself. But of course, he's my imagination, so that makes sense.

"Do you have a name?" he asks.

Such a weird question. He should know. I give it anyway. "Lia." Technically Amelia, but Dad only calls me that when he's pissed. Like today.

"Lia." The way he says my name is everything—soothing, comforting, and sensual in a way that slides down my spine and nestles deep within me. "It's cold. You can't stay here."

His hands brush through my hair again, and it's all I can do to stay awake. I'm so tired. Goosebumps cover my skin. The world is blurry at the edges. Darkness tugs at me, so inviting and welcoming. "You can come with me."

I stiffen, and so does he. A twinge of fear, of something wrong, jolts me awake.

"Or I can take you home," he offers.

That's right. This is a dream or something anyway. I sink back down into the edge of oblivion. It's nice there. "The devil knows where I live?"

"I'm...not sure," he says, almost as if he doesn't know who that is. "But I can follow your scent."

"Mmmhmm, okay." That makes as much sense as anything else.

Everything is fading. I can barely feel or hear, but I think I hear something else, something that doesn't quite make sense. "I'll see you again, Lia."

I jolt awake. The offending droplet of water that shocked me into consciousness slides off my nose.

"What? Where..." All my bruises and scrapes make themselves known. Everything aches. There's a terrible crick in my neck, and my whole face is puffy and swollen from crying.

My brows scrunch together as I take in the back porch of our cabin, the woods beyond sparkling with the early rays of dawn against morning dew. Birds chirp, greeting the new day. Memories of the night before flash through my mind. Was it really a dream? Running through the forest? That man?

The crash sure wasn't. My body, no worse, my soul, remembers it all too well. Nausea rolls through me, threatening to spill me off the cushioned chair. Blankets cocoon me, keeping away the chill, but I shiver from the memories alone. I stare at the plaid blanket. These weren't out here before. Did I drag them with me? They fall away as I slide my feet to the ground.

Then I see it.

Clenched in my hand, near flattened, is a section of honeysuck-le vine, its yellow flowers in full bloom, in December.

The world tilts, or maybe I do.

I didn't get these from the hospital or the house. There's only one explanation—whoever he was, whatever he was, he's real, and these flowers are a promise. I haven't seen the last of him.

Chapter 1

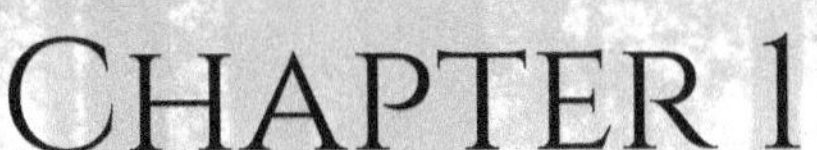

S OME PLACES ARE MAGICAL.

Not the pixie dust or golden sparkles kind of magic, but the kind that sinks down into your soul and blossoms in a shimmering rainbow only for you. Our cabin is that place for me.

Most people might look at it and just see its flaws—the faded wood, patched metal roof, and the third step that's bound to give way any day now. Don't even get me started on the musty smell that no amount of cleaner can purge, the creaky stairs, or the lack of air conditioning.

But they don't remember nights spent curled up on the couch with Grandma watching bad TV long after Dad went to sleep. Bacon cooking on the stove in the morning and smelling up the whole house. Hikes through the woods or down to the lake to go fishing. We never caught much, but that wasn't really the point. Or so Dad likes to say.

It's those things that matter. They ignite my soul and fill my heart in a way nothing else seems to.

I thought it might be lonely after Grandma passed, that it'd lose its magic, but it never did. Not when Dad married Elise a year later or even after they had my little sister, May. I suppose Mom probably stayed there too, but I don't remember her.

She was my first failure. One I managed to make before I could even speak properly. At least memories of her never touched the cabin.

None of the bad stuff did—until this past winter when I nearly killed my little sister.

Now, each moment increases my desire to run for the woods and never look back.

I no longer hear my dad or Elise as they rattle on like this is some normal, happy getaway to our favorite place. Like we aren't really here to fix the cabin up and sell it.

My fault. Another thing I've ruined. My hand clenches.

They wouldn't say that, but they don't have to. The taint of misery hovering over everything is worse than the summer heat and just as punishing. We haven't been back here since the accident. Too many hard memories, probably. And we need the money. Even me dropping out of college and getting a job didn't make much of a dent in all we owe. Medical bills, physical therapy for May...

I kick a stone with the toe of my boot and watch it tumble into the lake, sending up little ripples. It doesn't satisfy, doesn't ease the guilt trying to drag me into the water and drown me. If I had a boulder or half the dang hill to chuck into the water, maybe it'd make me feel better.

Dad mumbles something about scaring off the fish, but I ignore him. Not like they're biting anyway.

He and Elise could be a postcard, sitting there in their coordinating plaid with brimmed hats and fishing poles in hand. A happy mockery of my misery. How can they be so...so fine with everything?

May bounces into my line of sight, humming some song from her favorite cartoon. If anything was going to scare the fish away, it'd be that. She stumbles over a stone and I make to rise, but she's already skipping ahead, unbothered.

"Lia, Lia, Lia," she chants my name to the tune.

I cock a brow her way, waiting for the inevitable question to follow. Nothing dims her spirit. If only I could be like that.

She latches onto my arm, almost pulling me off my log and onto the dirt. "I want to walk. Come with me."

"All right. All right," I sigh. Anything to get away from this... I glance at Dad and Elise before rolling my eyes. Whatever this hell is.

May releases me and bounces through the air with all her six-year-old joy. I rise, dusting off my pants and freeing little bits of bark that cling to my legs.

"Where are y'all going?" Elise's pale brows crease in concern as she slips into mother mode.

I shrug, but the casual act belies the emotions twisting through me. Can't be any worse than here. Besides, I'm not letting May out of my sight. Already, she skips away from camp toward one of the pathways leading into the surrounding oak and pine. I say, "We'll be back soon."

"Don't go too far," Dad calls as I follow my sister into the woods.

I savor the breeze in my hair, the earthy scent of the forest. Each breath, each step away from the lake, calms me. Sunlight dapples through the trees. Birds chirp overhead. If I close my eyes, it's like stepping back in time. For a brief moment, I can delude myself that everything is happy and wonderful. This is a long weekend trip to our favorite place, complete with fishing, cookouts, hikes, and building blanket forts with Grandma's old quilts.

My whole body goes light and loose. I spread my fingers, trailing them through the air.

I'm still in college, thinking about applying for internships and the parties I'll go to with my friends. May is happy and healthy. My parents aren't burdened with medical debt.

Concern snaps me from my daydream as I hear May skid to a stop ahead of me.

"Lia?" She twists around.

"What's up?" I tuck loose hairs behind my ear and grimace at the perspiration already dotting my skin. It's not even noon, but that's summer in the South for you.

Her gaze darts around, focusing more on the rocky ground than me. A question lingers just behind her pinched brows. I suck on my teeth and pray it has nothing to do with the Christmas tree that still occupies the corner of the cabin's main room. My stomach bottomed out the moment I laid eyes on it. Elise's pale complexion showed just as much horror. We hadn't taken it down after the accident. That was the least of our worries, and because we hadn't been back since... Well, it was no wonder Dad turned right back around and grabbed the fishing poles from the car, insisting we walk down to the lake before it got too hot. No doubt one of them would slip back early and take it down before the rest of us returned.

"Are faeries real?" May's steady big-eyed gaze says she hopes so.

Faeries. My breath escapes in a huff of relieved laughter. "No, don't think so."

Her shoulders droop, and instant regret settles in my chest. Maybe I should have told her yes. I mean, just a few months ago, I told her multiple stories about the Easter bunny.

May's head tilts to the side. "Then who makes the flowers bloom?"

"Mother Nature?" My lips quirk up on one side. I flick her ponytail as I step around her on the trail.

"Hey!" She swats at my hand.

I dodge. "Too slow."

Laughter shakes my chest as I skip ahead, leaving May chasing after me while talking nonsense about the fairies in some show she watched and how they tend to all the plants in the forest.

Days like this—having fun with May, enjoying nature—are my favorite, the kind that make my worries slip away. But there won't be many more soon. Something tight and terrible wraps around my chest, and it takes everything I have to suck in one breath after another as I skid to a stop.

"Let's go up there." May points off to the right.

She doesn't notice my mood. Thank God for that. How can I tell her that this isn't just a fun family visit? That we'll be selling the place? I give myself a shake. Later.

"Up there?" I follow the angle of her arm into the trees. "The path goes that way." I hike my thumb toward our cabin.

"But look how tall that hill is." She bounces on her toes. "We could see everything."

Tall trees reach toward the sky, stretching above the others nearby. I squint, tilting my head to see between the limbs blocking my view. A tingle crawls down my spine. Yeah, it's the top of the hill and all, but something is off.

Weird. And familiar. But it shouldn't be. We pretty much always stick to the trails. The air around me chills as if a cloud has passed overhead, but the sky is clear and blue.

May pushes through the underbrush before I have time to argue.

"Not too fast." I reach toward her as she rushes ahead. Her slight limp—a result of the accident—adds weight to my shoulders with every step. It doesn't slow her down though. Not a bit. She's strong like that. Determined.

She could be my younger self—dreamy, playing outdoors, full of energy. Except that's about where the similarities end. She's the blond, bubbly one—Elise's looks, and God only knows whose personality.

Me? I'm all Dad. Brown hair, brown eyes, and a personality eternally battling between fire and rainclouds.

May doesn't stop until we're more than halfway up the slope to the hill she spotted. Good thing too. Something keeps drawing my attention, but I can't quite place it. I rub my hands up and down my arms, chasing away the goosebumps. Just shadows. Birds. Squirrels. Totally normal.

I glance back over my shoulder and scan the forest. Nothing out of the ordinary.

When I turn back, May is waiting for me, hands balled on her hips. The light catches the scar on her face, a jagged line running from temple to chin. The sight stabs me straight in the chest with regret. She'll have it all her life thanks to me.

"Slow poke." May sticks out her tongue before twirling around and bolting up the hill.

She doesn't notice the breath catch in my throat or the way my shoulders hunch in like I've been punched. Déjà vu locks me in place and refuses to let me go.

I've been here before, on that horrible night.

I know it in my bones, as if my body remembers being here and the despair I felt.

My head spins just like it did when I stumbled out of the driver's-side door of my car. Stumbled and fell, because the whole thing was on its side, smashed up against the tree.

I only took my eyes off the road for a moment.

Just long enough to yell at May for something stupid that I don't even remember. Couldn't even blame it on icy roads. Afterward, the hard half-looks from Dad and Elise were horrible. The silence was worse. Yelling, I could've handled. I deserved it. But nothing? My throat closes up just thinking about it.

They still love me, but sometimes I see it, a fog behind their eyes, a laugh a little too loud, comments that lack solid sincerity.

That night, with May in the hospital, the cabin felt too comfortable, too familiar, too special. Every moment made my skin crawl and my stomach turn until I couldn't take it anymore.

And so, I ran into the woods, down the path, away from the lake then up a steep hill.

My gaze pans up the slope. Empty. Worry stabs into my chest. "May?"

"You've got to see this!" Her voice carries down to me and I can picture her bouncing up and down, pointing to something, but she's out of sight.

Shit.

I sprint up the hill as fast as my legs will carry me, slipping on old leaves. My heart pounds. Can't let her out of my sight. Can't let anything happen to her. Not again.

Sunlight catches on blond hair. A heavy sigh bursts from my lips as I near the crest, and my whole body sags in relief.

May spins in a circle, her little arms reaching for the sky.

"They're so tall," she squeals.

Breath catches in my throat so hard I choke on it.

The trees she dances between aren't just tall; they're massive. Too big for this forest. But that's not what has my legs shaking. Verdant grass spreads in an unbroken carpet amidst the trees ringing it in a perfect circle on top of the hill.

Not natural. No way.

But this grass... I step inside the tree circle and kneel, running my hands along the soft blades. So lush.

A hint of honeysuckle teases my nose.

That scent.

On that horrible night months ago, I ran until my tears drowned me, and I collapsed onto a carpet of fresh, green grass, so out of place for the forest in December. It didn't make sense. Neither did the honeysuckle scent.

But the most unusual thing of all was the man who found me there.

His warm hand in mine was solid, comforting. Green eyes, a little too bright in the darkness, gazed into mine as I sniffled and spilled all my sorrow and guilt over the accident.

He didn't judge. Didn't shame.

But when I woke the next morning, I was tucked under a blanket on the back porch of our cabin. I was sure I'd dreamed it all. Some traumatic hallucination or something.

Until I opened my clenched fist to find a strand of blooming honeysuckle vine. Impossible in December.

That was only the first time I saw him.

Riven. That's his name. He appears as shadows, my own friend-ly ghost who visits my dreams from time to time. I know he isn't really there. Freshman year of high school taught me that sneaking a boy into the house without Dad or Elise finding out was literally impossible.

But whatever, whoever, he is exactly, I didn't care—I don't care.

He was my rock when the rest of my world fell apart, someone I could talk to about my guilt, about dropping out of school and getting a job to help pay the bills, about the days I just wanted to lay down and give up.

He never lets me. Riven insists I'm important. He tells me I can help him and his people.

Yeah right.

I'm not sure why my brain made that part up. It's been almost two weeks though. I've counted. Way too many days since he said his people were in trouble and asked me to come back to him.

Back to him, as in here?

My heart clenches, and I rub at my chest. Maybe my inner consciences thinks I'm healed enough not to need him anymore, but I—

"Oh, wow!" May grabs my arm and nearly pulls me over. If I didn't still crouch on the ground, she probably would have.

My fingers dig into the grass as I steady myself. "What is—"

A shadow spills out under trees on the far side of the circle, mottled by thin strands of light. My heart picks up its pace, pounding like a hammer in my chest.

Not a shadow at all. A great beast of a thing with dark fur.

A bear.

The fine hairs on the back of my neck stand on end. There's not a sound. No birds chirp, no cicadas hum, and even the breeze has gone utterly still.

Wrong. All wrong.

I swallow, my throat suddenly dry. The bear looks our way, entirely too much awareness in its face.

"Think it wants to play?" Mays says.

"Let's go." Where her voice had been loud, mine is a whisper. I tug at her sleeves.

She digs her heels in. "But it looks so friendly."

I stand with a grunt and shove her behind me. We are definitely going to have a talk about befriending wild animals when we get home.

"Now, right now." Each word wobbles with undeniable fear. I watch the bear from the corner of my eyes and murmur silent prayers as I wrestle May toward the edge of the hill.

A deep whine splits the quiet.

May and I go utterly still, frozen by the bear's cry. Its lumbered movement urges me into action.

I don't wait, don't speak, don't look, before I scoop May into my arms and sprint toward the lake. My pulse thunders in my heart, drowning out May's protests as she squirms in my arms to glance behind me.

Does it chase us? Can I outrun it? A scream climbs up my throat, and I swallow it down. My muscles do plenty of shrieking. May's so much heavier than I remember, and I'm not *that* strong.

My boots slip in the decomposing underbrush. I wobble, nearly sending us both tumbling down the hill.

"Let me down! Let me down!" May hollers.

I do, almost dropping her before her feet touched the ground. My arms cry in relief.

May takes off down the hill, me tight on her heels. She doesn't look back again. Neither do I, not until we're back to the path.

A whisper on the soft summer breeze teases my ears. It tugs me to a stop. My brows furrow as I strain my ears, filtering through the bird calls and rustle of leaves that's returned to normal. The whisper comes again, and this time, I can just make out what it says.

Lia.

Goosebumps race across my skin. I'm not afraid, or it's not just that. The breathless whisper yanks on me like an invisible string. A plea.

"Riven?" I can't say why his name climbs to the tip of my tongue. Maybe it's because of that first dream, but he was never a bear, never terrifying. I squint, looking back at the hill, trying to see beyond the leafy trees blocking my view.

Nothing.

May still races on ahead of me, and without another backward glance, I chase after her.

Dad and Elise hurry to meet us, eyes wide and brows furrowed as we near the lake's edge. May virtually collapses on the ground—a mix of actual fatigue and obvious acting. My heart pounds as my mind races in far too many directions.

"There was a bear," I say between breaths filled with the tang of algae and fish from the nearby lake.

I don't mention the whisper on the breeze. Probably just my imagination again. What would I say? I snort air through my nose and glance away. They don't even know about the man I see in my dreams.

Elise cuts my dad an alarmed look and brushes her blond ponytail behind her.

"John..." Her voice is a plea.

Dad shrugs, looking for all the world like the Brawny paper towel man in his red plaid. "What? It's just a bear. Ain't the first, won't be the last."

Just a bear. Right. I shift on my feet and stare out over the water. Except, I'm not so sure. Not anymore.

Something about this place is unique, and maybe it's not just my love for it.

CHAPTER 2

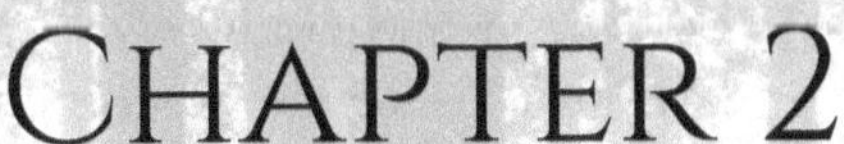

M Y FAVORITE PART OF the day is the end. It's the time when I can snuggle down under too many blankets and drift away to a place where I'm not the girl who almost killed her sister. Or the one who had to drop out of college to help with the medical bills.

Okay, maybe 'had to' isn't right. Actually, Dad insisted I not drop out. Can't blame him for not wanting me around the house. But what was I going to do? Show back up after Christmas break, force a smile, and answer the "how was your break?" question over and over? There're only so many times I can lie. Eventually, I'd end up saying, "Oh, it was great, until I almost killed May in a stupid car crash and made my family hate me." Yeah, that'd go over great. Wouldn't have gotten spread around campus at all. Though truthfully, they probably knew already. Small town and all. The pitying looks would have been even worse.

Making coffee is infinitely preferable. I take an order. Fill it. My paycheck goes toward May's physical therapy, or as much as Dad will let me, and I'm there for her. Somehow, she still wants me around all the time, even after what I've done. Like tonight, May insists on snuggling under my blanket, her head on my shoulder, as we watch her favorite animated movie for the hundredth time.

But honestly, there's no place I'd rather be. One perk of putting my future on hold is all the time we get to spend together now. She won't be young forever, won't want to hang out with her big sister who, frankly, could pass for her mom.

By the time I fall asleep, I've almost forgotten about selling the cabin, the bear—everything.

I wake with a start and jerk upright in bed.

The room is awash in gray and not just from the moonlight spilling through the window onto the green-and-yellow quilt Grandma made for me as a little girl. It's not a dream, but neither am I awake.

My heart leaps. My skin tingles.

"Riven." Without error, I find him in the shadows.

"You're here." His voice cracks, raspy and willowy as his shadowed form. But beyond it, I taste the richness, the strength of the man who held me on that terrible night. "You came back."

"Back?" My brows furrow. To our cabin? I can barely process his words. He's here. He's the one who came back.

He steps into the stream of moonlight, which pierces him like a fogged window. Even so, his form is vivid, colorful, so much more *real* than he's been over the recent months. Pointed ears poke out from the long, brown hair trailing down over his shoulders. Sharp cheekbones accent a strong and balanced face. Proof that no matter how bad I want it, what he says, or the flowers I found in my hand that morning, he can't be real. No guy looks like that.

And, oh, how I wish I could touch him. I can lose minutes, hours, thinking about the feel of his hand in mine that first night or the strength of his body when he pulled me close. I want that, crave it. Until this moment, I didn't realize how much I missed him, how much I'd come to rely on our stolen moments together—whatever they are.

Riven sits on the edge of my bed, and I'd swear I feel the mattress dip. "To the forest. To the door."

"The door to where?" I rub the quilt between my fingers. Solid. Comforting.

The hint of a smile flickers on his face. "To my home. Come with me, Lia. Please, we need you." He unfurls his palm. "*I* need you."

That open hand could be holding a diamond the size of my fist for the way my throat goes dry and my heart skips a beat. It's all I can see, all I want. I reach for him.

Our fingers touch, solid as the bed under me. My eyes fly wide. A shiver races across my skin. And then my hand slips through his, washed in cold emptiness. My own personal friendly ghost—like always. I called him Casper once, but he just looked at me funny. Figures he wouldn't know who that is.

"How can I find you?" My whispered words are too loud in the hazy silence.

One moment he's sitting on the bed; the next he's right next to me, inches from my face. A gasp lodges in my throat as the scent of honeysuckle swarms my senses.

Riven leans in, his lips a breath from mine. "Come to the circle on the hill."

The dream pops like a bubble as I wake, gasping for breath in my room. The spot on the bed where he'd been is smooth and flat. Not even the smallest wrinkle mars the green leaves sewn into the little quilt squares.

My fingers dig into the sheets as I anchor myself, panting.

The room is empty. I don't even need to look around to know. It's always the same after his dream—or visions or whatever—leaves me. Color has returned to my room. Bugs hum outside my window. An owl hoots. It could be any summer night.

I turn my palm over, staring at the tips of my fingers where we touched for the briefest of moments. He's gone, but my body, my soul, remembers. If I close my eyes, I can almost feel the brush of his hair falling across my cheek.

The circle on the hill.

There's only one place it can be, and no bear is going to scare me away this time, not until I get some answers.

Some hours later, my door crashes open. I barely register the rapid thump of footsteps across the floor before a form leaps onto the bed, lands directly on my chest, and knocks the breath from my lungs.

My gasping groan shifts into a cough as my sleep-blurred eyes adjust to the light streaming into the room.

"Wake up. Wake up." May chants in time with her bounces on the mattress.

"Go away." I roll over, taking the quilt with me. If only it could block out the *squeak, squeak, squeak* of the mattress as May continues her antics. How on earth do kids have so much energy?

The bouncing stops. Her feet thud onto the floor. "Supposed to tell you you're going to miss breakfast."

I sigh and peek out from under the covers. "Message received."

She skips off without another word, leaving my door wide open.

Aren't I supposed to get a break from this mess until I have my own kids? *If* I have my own kids?

Conversation drifts up the stairs with the smell of freshly cooked bacon. My mouth waters, and my stomach gives a little rumble.

Now that's a wake-up call.

I shouldn't have slept in this morning. A wiser woman would have gotten up early and left at the crack of dawn to go investigate the doorway Riven mentioned. I'd considered it last night, been so tempted, but venturing out into the woods at night isn't a great decision. It was a miracle I didn't twist my ankle in a hole or tumble down a hill during my emotional flight months ago. Didn't have to worry about the bears then either.

Besides, slipping out in the middle of the night would raise too many questions I couldn't answer if Dad and Elise caught me. It doesn't matter that I'm old enough not to need to explain my actions. When I'm under their roof, I'm under their rules.

I sigh in frustration and finish changing clothes. Any illusion of freedom I had vanished the day I quit college—or rather, took a leave of absence—and moved back home.

The stairs creak and groan as I hop down the worn wood into the main room that's kitchen, living, and dining room in one. May stretches on her toes, reaching toward the paper towel-lined plate in the middle of the small kitchen island that bears a few strips of crispy bacon.

"Nuh uh." Elise waves at her from behind her laptop where she's stationed at the kitchen table. How she managed to spot May when she's practically behind her can only be described as one of her many mom superpowers.

May frowns and drops back onto her feet but leaves the bacon alone.

I swipe two pieces off the plate on my way through the room and pass one off to her before crunching into the salty, meaty deliciousness that nearly makes me groan in pleasure.

The click of Elise's fingers on the keyboard stills as she shoots me a hard, flat look.

I shrug. What can one more piece of bacon hurt? "I'm going out. I'll be back in a little bit."

"Out?" Her brows rise as she lifts the reading glasses from her face. "We were going to paint today. Your dad is on his way to the hardware store right now."

"Yeah, just a quick jog. Get a little exercise before it gets too hot?" I gesture to my attire. "I'll be back in plenty of time to help with the painting." Maybe.

I don't give her time to argue before I scoop up my shoes from their home near the back door and throw it open.

"May, don't climb on the sofa."

My lips quirk up in the corner as I catch my sister using the sofa like a jungle gym. With Elise distracted, I slip outside. *Thanks, May.* The cool morning air sends a little shiver over my skin, but I savor every moment of it as I lace up my running shoes. It won't last. Never does in June. I hop down the back stairs, an extra bounce in my step.

Morning light glints through the trees, sparkling off the dew still clinging to their leaves. I'm not twenty yards from the cabin when the back door flies open to crack against the wall. The sound freezes me in place and has me spinning around on the balls of my feet.

"Wait for me!" May calls as she sprints for the stairs, leaving the screen door still swinging on its hinges.

A deep groan slips from my lips. Having a tag-along was not part of the plan.

"Did you even ask Mom?" I ask.

"Uh huh." She nods with enthusiasm. "She told me to go with you."

I pinch the bridge of my nose. Of course she did. "Well, you have to listen to me. And stay close."

"Can we go back to those cool trees?"

A soft breath catches in my throat. All I do for a moment is blink. Too easy, but I'll take it. "Yeah, sure."

"Yippee!" She's off and skipping toward the woods, her pigtails trailing behind her like little streamers.

I'll seriously never understand where she gets so much energy. I haven't had my morning coffee—or three—and boy, do I feel it. That hint of tiredness lingers behind my eyes that only that magical brew can cure. Wasn't time for that this morning though.

Our trek is full of laughter, which perks me up almost as well as caffeine. The odd shadows and whispers of the day before don't follow me. Nor do we see any bears—thank God. I'm almost convinced that whatever I felt yesterday was just another figment of my imagination until we reach the circle of trees.

The moment I pass by the massive trunks, chills skitter down my spine.

Riven? I fight the urge to call out to him. No one else is with us in the clearing, yet something tells me we're not alone. There's an otherness I can't quite put my finger on, almost like something just at the edge of sight that moves every time I look its way. Even the air holds a heaviness that isn't humidity.

Whatever it is, the birds don't seem to mind. There's a ton of them here, chirping and squawking up a storm. I stalk around the circle, searching for any sign of bears—or anything else.

May hoped we'd see it again today. I roll my eyes. Kids.

Even now, she dances around in the lush glade, oblivious to the weird creeping feeling crawling across my skin. This isn't natural, and trees this big would have to be old. Really old. Some of them are wide enough to be two of me, and trying to see the tops requires craning my neck back way too far. No way would they just sprout up naturally in such a perfect formation either.

May sets about finding a four-leaf clover in the carpet of them growing around us. At least she's entertained. After my dream last night, I assumed Riven would be here waiting for me. What other circle of trees could he possibly have meant? This is it. I know it as well as I know myself.

But an hour later, I've reached my conclusion.

I'm broken. I really did make him up in order to cope with the accident.

That's it. It has to be.

In the shade of the biggest tree, May stretches out beside me on the ground, giving a wide yawn. "Dad's really going to sell the cabin?"

I wince, my lips pressing in a hard line. She wasn't supposed to know. I thought she didn't.

"Where'd you hear that?" I ask, keeping my tone as cool and calm as possible. Maybe she guessed. Maybe she doesn't know.

May glances away then back to me. "I heard Mom and Dad talking."

Shoot. My head thumps back against the tree. Little eavesdropper.

"Is it true?"

"Guess so." I sigh and slide down the trunk, letting the bark scrape against me through my shirt. No good lying about it if she already knows.

She frowns. "I don't want him to."

I offer her a weak smile. "Me neither."

Just the thought of it makes my stomach turn over. She enjoys the trees, our hikes, sleeping in her little attic room. But there's no way it means half as much to her as it does to me.

"Then why's he doing it?" she asks.

"I think it's just too much work." It's a lie, but hopefully, she doesn't know that. We need the money for medical bills. They just keep coming, and money has been even tighter since Elise reduced her hours to spend more time with May. My little job barely helps.

"Only rich people have two houses, and that ain't us," Dad said to me when I asked him about it. He was right, that wasn't us, but he couldn't hide the hurt in his voice when he said it. Our cabin is his favorite place too.

"Will we be able to come back here?" May asks now. "Or to the lake? What about that path we always see the deer on?"

My heart clenches. Okay, maybe she does love it too.

"I...I don't know." Maybe, but it won't be the same.

She buries her head against her arm and mumbles something I can't make out. A minute later, she's sleeping soundly...on the ground in the woods. Every now and then, she surprises me with how much we're alike.

I fish out my cell phone and check the time. Damn. My lips press into a thin line. Later than I thought. No wonder it's gotten so warm. Honestly, it's a shock that Dad and Elise haven't blown up my phone with messages asking when we'll be home because they—

My grip tightens as I spy the little signal bars. Or lack thereof.

No service.

I push to my feet and walk to the middle of the circle, holding the phone up in the air as if those extra few inches might make all the difference and messages will chime in. Nada. My heel grinds into the grass in frustration.

No happy vibrations chirp and buzz from messages arriving. Actually, I don't hear anything at all. The birds have gone totally quiet too.

I sigh and pocket the phone just before a hand clamps over my mouth.

CHAPTER 3

A SCREAM RISES UP, but the hand over my mouth muffles everything. My heart thunders as I struggle against someone as hard as iron.

"Shh. Don't wake her."

That voice. Honeysuckle invades my nose. My body goes limp as all the fear and tension flees my form. His hands fall away, and I nearly collapse.

Riven. It's him. It has to be.

But holy fuck, that means...

Time slows. My mouth goes dry as I turn to face the man behind me. Just as quickly, it speeds up again. Blood rushes under my skin. My pulse flutters like a hummingbird.

He's real. Oh my God, he's real! I blink. I pinch myself.

Until now, I couldn't fully believe it. But he's here. He touched me. Held me. And shit, is that armor? The memories I have of our first meeting are vague at best, but I have to believe I would have remembered the bronzy gold metal armor that adorns his tall, lean form like some fantastical knight. Pieces are strapped to his arms. A breastplate bearing a tree covers his chest. His shoulders have spikes like thorns, and the metal greaves on his boots...well, that's kinda hot for some reason. Actually, all of it is. But it's so *not* normal.

"What *are* you?" I hiss in a whisper. The very last thing I need is to explain this to May. A quick glance confirms she still sleeps. Thank goodness.

His grin is heart-stopping. The glimmer in his green eyes even more so. Riven could slay me in the most delicious way with just a look, and all I can do is shiver. "Your people have had many names for us," he says. "But most call us the fae, and our world, they call Faery."

Fae. A freaking fairy.

"I thought fairies were smaller." I clamp my hand over my mouth. *Oh geez, Lia. You had to say that out loud.*

A small laugh rumbles from his chest. It's soft and rich, the kind that settles around me like a warm blanket.

Heat creeps up my neck. "Kind of an important detail to leave out."

"You never asked."

No, I hadn't. Somewhere deep inside, I knew, if he was real, he wasn't human. Though now, knowing doesn't bother me the way I expected. Oh, a small part of me screeches at the top of my lungs. It holds the same primal instinct that sensed the wrongness of this whole area. The rest of me is calm though, as if I've finally found that one last, annoying puzzle piece that has slipped under the rug.

His gaze slides past me to land on my sleeping sister. "So, that's May."

I step to the side, blocking his view. I've told this man—no, this fae—so many things, but that same little voice that screeches at the wrongness of this all doesn't like his attention on her.

He shakes his head as if clearing it. Such a human gesture. "I'm glad you came."

A flush breaks out across my cheeks. "I had to know if you were real."

"You really weren't sure?"

"Fae"—I look him up and down—"aren't supposed to exist."

"We do." He steps closer, so close I have to tip my head back to see his face.

A lock of rich, brown hair with shimmers of gold slips over his shoulders, and I have to fight the urge to push it back. Keeping my eyes off the pointed ears poking through it is even harder. I'm burning up, and it's not the weather's fault. It's hard to focus with him so close. "I noticed."

His grin says more than any words he's spoken. But it vanishes as quickly as it came. "You talked about selling your...*cabin*." He stumbles over the word. "Leaving?"

"You heard that?" My brows draw together. "I didn't see you. I looked."

"I waited on the other side of the door until she fell asleep." He nods to May.

Oh no. How long had he been there? Did he see that time I adjusted my bra? Or when I tripped coming up the hill? And wait...

"Door?" My brows arc with the word.

"The door to Faery," he says, as if that's some normal thing I should know about. "You're leaving?"

Disappoint looms in his eyes with something else I can't quite understand. It's too much, too invasive.

I look away. "Yes. Dad wants to sell." A sudden thought snaps my attention back to him. "You can still visit, right? In my dreams?"

Losing the cabin is one thing. But losing him too? I'm not sure I can handle it. Not now that I know he's real. I need his visits, the comfort he offers. It's been the brightest part of the last few months.

"It's hard when you're so far. It takes so much..." Now it's his turn to glance away. "Stay. Come to Faery with me."

"I—"

"At least let me show you?" Riven stretches out his gloved hand.

It's the most natural thing in the world to take it. His hand dwarfs mine. Supple leather caresses my skin and sends a rush of tingles racing through me. Though his grip is light, the strength there is obvious. He could crush me if he wanted.

A heartbeat later, the world is different.

I gape as the trees surrounding us become stones. A forest looms beyond. Its trees stretch far above the monoliths and bear splashes of red and gold like ours in autumn. Even the air is different—cleaner, crisper. I inhale a breath, savoring the way it fills my lungs and clears my head.

"How? Where?" I twist my head this way and that.

"This is Faery. You wanted to see it, so the door let you through."

So simple. "The circle is the door?"

He nods.

Some of the trees around us are familiar, others, decidedly not so. I flex my fingers and grip Riven's hand tighter. One violet-tinted tree has a bulbous trunk like a bottle of pomegranate juice. Some are so thin they sway like reeds in the breeze—maybe they're not even trees at all. Another has limbs that dig into the ground like a clawed hand ready to rip out the soil. Flat ground prevails instead of the hilly, mountainous terrain back home.

"It's beautiful." And horrifying. Even so, I can't stop staring.

"It's dying."

I flinch. He can't be serious. "What?"

"I'll explain. Come with me."

I want to go. To see this world with him, to know what's wrong, and possibly linger in his embrace. So many mornings I've awoken wondering what it would be like to curl up next to him, to feel his strong body next to mine, to kiss him, to—

I shake myself. "I can't leave May."

Riven glances beyond me, the direction where May lies slumbering, but all I can see are the massive stones and odd trees.

"It'll be safer for her, for all humans, if you come," he says.

My brows pinch together. Words lose themselves on the tip of my tongue.

"The forest grows weak. Unseelie"—the word chimes from his lips like brittle glass—"threaten our land, our people."

"Unseelie?" I stumble over the word, tasting the terror in the recesses of my mind.

"Dark fae. Wild. Animalistic."

My skin turns clammy as my lips part. *Like the bear?*

Riven takes my other hand in his, snapping me from my shock. "Please, Lia."

"But how can I help?" I shake my head, trying to reason out the concern in his features. As if I could help someone, much less a fae. It's ridiculous, especially since he knows what I did to May. How I keep screwing up.

"You're gifted," he says.

A bitter laugh catches in the back of my throat. I'm anything but.

"You can see me, my world. You can help my magic, heal the land, give us a chance against the dark fae. But if we weaken, if they win..." Shadows cloud his eyes. The very trees stir and shake as if in terror.

Dark fae. *Unseelie*. A threat to him and to us. They shouldn't be real, but if Riven exists, so could they. The world around me spins, closing in like a looming darkness. If not for his steady hand, I might stumble.

He shakes his head, and the look is gone. "You don't know the horrors they've wrought against humans in the past, what they could do again if they get through this door or any other."

I stare into his eyes, which almost seem to glow a soft, eerie green. It's mesmerizing. Breathtaking. His hands flex around mine. Heavy breaths rise and fall from his chest as the full silence stretches. Riven's gaze begs as much as his words from moments ago. This man, this fae, led me from my own darkness so many times. If I can help, shouldn't I try?

An answer blooms from my heart, crawling up to the tip of my tongue. *Yes, I'll go. I'll help.*

"Lia?" a soft voice calls close by, but also far away.

May. I pull away from him, and once again, I'm in the circle of trees. I twist and turn, but no matter where I look, Riven is gone. Or...on the other side of the door?

"Riven?" A tinge of panic cracks through his name.

"Who?" May looks at me funny as she rubs the sleep from her eyes.

May. That's right. How could I ever think to leave her here?

"I—" But I can't answer her question either. She wouldn't understand, and it'd be worse if she did. A kid knowing about Faery?

No way. She'd want to go. She'd beg and whine and tell our parents all about it. May wasn't one to quickly move on either. It'd be a mess. And if she did go there... Nope, no way. My little sister is not going to another world with people who aren't even human.

"Let's go. Mom and Dad will be worried." I've known Elise more than half my life, but it's still weird to call her Mom. It's not that I don't like Elise—I really do—but Mom isn't a happy word for me, not since mine left ages ago. I like her better as Elise. I do it for May though.

I shoo May toward the path and glance over my shoulder, hoping to see Riven, to explain. But he's nowhere to be seen.

May shrugs then straightens with a grin.

"Race you to the bottom!" She's past the ring of trees before I fully register what she's said.

"May! Don't run!" Shit, if she falls—

A hand wraps around my arm. The scream building in my throat evaporates into a burst of air as I whirl around and smack right into Riven's chest. A very hard chest, particularly since it's covered in armor.

"Stay."

My pulse hammers against my throat. I pull back, gasping for air. He lets me, but he doesn't release my arm. His world looms behind him, a perfect oval that blurs into mine. He stands in the threshold of the door.

"We need you. I need you."

My chest clenches so tight it's hard to breathe. "I want—"

"Lia!" May calls.

I twist toward her voice. She's out of sight down the hill. A cold sweat breaks out across my skin. What happened to her? Is she okay? She can't get hurt on my watch again.

"Please."

Riven's plea stabs between my ribs. "I want to. I do, but—"

But I'm just me. I don't help. I screw everything up.

"Lia!" May calls again.

His eyes widen, pleading.

I stumble back, my hand slipping from his. Riven's arm is still outstretched, that palm empty and waiting.

Pain washes across his face. His shoulders hunch.

That look alone is like a punch to my gut. I should go with him. But May...

"I—I'm sorry." Everything is a blur of tears as I turn away and race down the hill after my sister.

I wake in a cold sweat.

Leaving Riven at the door was a mistake. I knew it the moment I got a few steps away from him and looked back, only for him to have vanished completely. Again.

Everyone noticed my unease after we returned. Dad and Elise kept asking what was wrong, but I never had a good answer for them. I couldn't possibly say, "You see, Dad, I've been seeing this guy in my dreams some nights. Actually, he's not a guy, he's a fairy, and he wants me to run away with him, I think." That'd go over so well. A small, humorless laugh slips from my lips into the darkness of my room.

I flop back onto the pillow and press my eyes shut. Elise, once again, offered to make me an appointment with a therapist. Only if I wanted to, *of course*. Which I didn't.

Damp hair clings to my face. I push it away. It's always a little warm on the second floor this time of year—southern heat, old cabin, and all. The fan humming on the side table takes care of that though. This sweat, this mess of emotions rolling around in me so fiercely that I got all tangled up in the sheets, that's all me.

It wasn't because of a dream this time though. I'd expected one—prayed for it, actually. Then I could explain to Riven why I left him standing there and how much I really do want to help. I suck in a deep, steadying breath.

Figures he wouldn't visit me tonight. Not after how I left things.

The soft mattress tugs me back to sleep, cradling my body just so. Tomorrow, I have to go back first thing and try to find him.

I'm about to drift off when I finally realize what's been bothering me since I woke. It's quiet. My fan hums, but beyond that, there are no bugs, no owls—none of the things I usually hear at night.

A warning bell sounds in the recesses of my mind, and I bolt upright.

It's the same feeling I had at the circle of trees.

The covers flutter away as I jump out of bed and run to the window. Tree branches sway in the breeze. Moonlight highlights the dark landscape in shades of gray and muted colors. No sign of Riven or anyone else.

Not outside then.

Inside? I flush and shudder at the same time.

Yes, I want to see him and explain things. So much. But here at our cabin? At night? My nails dig into my palms. Dad would kill me if he found out—doesn't matter that I'm old enough not to need his permission to see anyone I want. Even if I was fifty, he'd still find a way to scold me for sneaking someone into the house at night.

I creep around the house on bare feet, stealing like a thief through the night as I check the door locks, the windows, look inside closets, in the cabinets, anywhere a body can fit.

Nothing. Not a damn thing out of place either.

I run my hand through my hair, fighting against the ever-present tangles. Far away, an owl hoots. The bugs strike up their midnight symphony once again.

Overreacting, Lia. Just overreacting. Who wouldn't after learning Fae are real?

I sigh and climb the stairs toward the bedrooms on light feet, dodging the spots that always squeak. No sense in waking Dad and Elise now when everything is back to normal.

At the top of the stairs, I halt. Something's still off. The wrongness of it echoes in my bones, tugging at me like a caught thread.

I peek back in my room, half expecting to find Riven lying on my bed, a grin on his face.

Alas... My shoulders drop as I take in the space. My bed is empty. As always.

There're only two rooms I haven't checked: the suite Dad and Elise share and May's room.

May.

My blood runs cold. She was at the door with me. She saw the bear, the Unseelie? I lunge to her door and throw it open.

Empty.

Her bed is empty.

All the world goes still and stops as I stare at the rumpled pink sheets.

"May!" The scream cracks as bad as my heart. My knees crash to the ground next to her bed as I look under it. Nothing. Nor behind the door.

I suck in one short breath after another.

Empty. It's just—She's just—

"What's going on?" Elise stands wide-eyed in the doorway.

Her pale blue nightgown is a hazy blur through the tears streaming down my face. "I can't find May."

Elise goes rigid before springing to the bed. She shoves me out of the way as she searches all the places I've already looked while calling for her daughter.

From the corner of my eye, I catch Dad bolt toward the stairs in nothing but his boxer shorts, calling for his youngest child. But I've already looked there. And here. Everywhere except my parent's room, which they were just in. Elise flees from the room, back to her own, where various objects thump onto the floor as she roots around, still calling for May.

Nausea bubbles up in my throat, threatening to choke me.

A stiff breeze blows my hair around my face, snapping me out of the shock threatening to overwhelm me. The window near the bed is open. Thick curtains ruffle in the breeze.

I lurch to the window. My fingers dig into the frame as I poke my head out the open bottom pane, fearing what I might see below.

Nothing.

Thank you, Jesus.

Elise runs down the stairs as I pull my head back in.

"Anything?" Dad's voice floats up from the stairwell.

"No." Her reply is a half-sob.

"The doors are still locked. What about the windows?"

Elise's response is a cry of frustration.

Another gust of wind slips through the window, carrying with it a whisper of sound. It may be nothing, but I hear the voice that's whispered to me so often lately. "Come."

The lump in my throat plummets to my gut as a flash of pink snags my attention. May's teddy bear pokes out from under the edge of the bed, flopped onto its stomach. It's her constant companion. She would never leave it behind.

"Was that window open?" Elise charges toward me, frantically pushing me out of the way to look herself.

"It was when I opened the door."

"May!" Elise doesn't bother to acknowledge my response.

Dawning terror grips me in a vice.

He couldn't have. It's not possible.

Riven was there for me when I was at my lowest. He listened as I spilled all my hurt, my pain. He told me the accident wasn't my fault, that I was valued, important. He wouldn't—

"I'm calling the police," Dad says from the doorway.

A sick certainty settles into my heart. It had been quiet when I woke, as it is every time Riven is around, as if all life fled in the presence of fae. Riven or... *The Unseelie?*

A shudder wracks my form.

Dark fae. A threat to humans. He warned me, but I never thought he meant so soon.

Elise pulls her head in, tears streaming down her face, and rushes back out of the room.

"Yes, John Ashmore, 545 Bent Pine." Dad snaps into the phone, demanding the police get here as soon as possible.

I have to find her.

It's my fault she was there. That they... they must have followed her scent like Riven said he did mine the first time he found me alone in that circle of trees.

My fault. Mine. Again.

My hands fist in my hair, tugging at the roots.

She can't get hurt because of me again. No. Never.

I bolt to my room and grab the first thing in the top of my drawer, my favorite yoga pants and an athletic tank. After the quickest change in my life, I shove my cellphone in the pocket of my pants.

Dad paces near the top of the stairs, still on his phone. He reaches out for me as I hurry past.

"I'm going to find May," I snap, brushing off his arm before I slide past him and down the stairs.

"Amelia," he calls.

But I can't stop, not now. I have to find May.

"Amelia!"

I grit my teeth at the panic in his voice, but I have to go.

Now.

Can't stop.

The door rattles on its hinges as I throw it open and sprint down the steps and into the woods.

CHAPTER 4

MY LUNGS BURN BY the time I reach the circle of trees at the top of the hill. The whole run I've begged for Riven to be there—waiting for me. But another part, the part I refuse to acknowledge, is afraid to find him. Afraid to see my sister clutched in his arms.

A bear lounges in the clearing instead. I skid to a stop.

Everything in me locks up at the sight of the predator standing in the clearing staring back at me. Its too-intelligent eyes gleam in the night. I hadn't made any attempt to be quiet on my way here. No doubt it heard me coming from far away. My heart thunders, adrenaline mixing with fear.

The bear assesses me as I gaze at it, wide-eyed and uncertain. A thick, furless scar mars the side of its face. It's the same bear from the other day, I'm almost certain.

Wild. Animalistic.

"Riven!" My voice cracks as I call his name. *Please, oh please.*

The bear's form wavers. For a moment, it's the shadowed outline of a man crouched on the ground instead of a bear. Not Riven. Someone else.

Unseelie?

"I know what you are!" I shout, flinging out my hand and pointing at it. Either I'm right or an idiot. Doesn't matter. "Give my sister back. Right now!"

Its intelligent eyes take me in for a moment longer before it shakes its big head from side to side.

Okay, that's an answer, right?

I steel my nerves and step toward the bear. He blinks at me and makes a deep grumbling noise in his throat. My body locks up midstride. Not a growl—it didn't sound threatening—but I have no idea what it means. The bear turns his bulky form around and lumbers toward the tree line. Instead of walking into the forest, he disappears.

Goosebumps race across my skin.

Fairy. Definitely a freaking fairy.

But a good fairy or a bad fairy?

"Riven!" I stomp through the grass, my hands in fists at my sides. "Shit. This.... Shit!" Can I go to Faery without him? How do I get there? God, am I seriously considering this right now? I run my hands down my face.

If May's there, I have to go after her.

Before, I took his hand, and we were simply somewhere else. *You wanted to see it, so it brought you through.* His words echo in my mind.

Could it really be so easy?

"Take me there."

All at once, the world shifts.

With Riven, it was seamless. Alone, the world tilts and spins. Trees dive into the ground as monolithic boulders spring up. I lose my balance and fall as a scream rips from me. My head is still spinning when the world stops shifting, and once more, I'm in Faery.

Night cloaks the forest. Of all the wondrous trees I saw during the day, the only ones I can seem to focus on now look like giant clawed hands with their spindly roots digging into the ground. Colorful leaves, muted by the glow of the moon above, litter the forest floor as if it's early autumn. The air holds a crispness that conjures visions of apple pie and Halloween. If I didn't know better, I'd say I stepped through time instead of into a different world.

Both? Surely not.

"May? Riven?" I scrabble on the ground, trying to see everywhere at once. God only knows what waits for me among those horror-movie trees. And where the hell did that bear go?

A light breeze is the only response. Well, that and some decidedly odd nocturnal noises that better just be normal-sized, totally non-venomous bugs.

Mistake, mistake, mistake, my inner voice yells. But I have to find May. I can't leave her.

"May?" I pace around the circle, looking back over my shoulder every few seconds, expecting something or someone to appear. A half-moon, a little too blue, and with all the wrong craters hangs overhead.

Shit. I stomp through the crisp leaves. Staying here is out of the question. I came to Faery, for fuck's sake, but it's not like there's a sign: Find your sister here!

"Ma—" I screech, stumbling back.

Between the stones, tall figures appear wearing similar armor to what Riven wore the day before, though less ornate. More practical, to be honest. With the browns, greens, and tans of their pants and tunics, they blend with the forest around them. Even the metal of the breastplates and arm coverings looks more matte. How long have they been out there? This whole damn time?

"W-who?" I raise my arms in front of me. A poor defense but all I've got.

"A human," one gasps. From the sound of his voice, you'd think I was a unicorn.

"It is."

It? I'm an 'it' now? My teeth grind together before I can shove my irritation anyway. "Where's my sister?"

Blank stares greet me.

"Little girl? Blond. Always happy. Was wearing..." Shit. I have no idea. "Pajamas?"

There are half a dozen of them. They look between one another as if they can't understand a word I'm saying, but they spoke my language a moment ago.

I raise my hands. "I come in peace?"

Total lie. I loosen my stance and shift my weight to the balls of my feet. If they've hurt May, I'm about to kick some ass. Or at least I'll go down swinging.

One fae man steps forward. Dark brown hair wraps around elongated, pointed ears like Riven's, but a golden earring dangles from one ear and this male's hair ends at the nape of his neck. His skin is tanned or tawny—it's hard to tell in the moonlight. A golden tree is emblazoned on his chest, different than the green of the others. Their leader?

"We should take her to the king," he says.

Oh, hell no. I back away, my hands out in front of me. "Not a chance. I have to find May and take her home. Or Riven. Maybe he took her." Still can't rule him out, though just the thought of it makes the back of my throat burn. "Do you know him?"

More silent looks, but this time it's not confusion. They know that name. The fae glance at golden tree guy, who says, "He didn't take her."

My lips thin. The certainty in his voice offends me. "How do you know?"

The man holds my gaze, not even blinking. "He's been with the high court all night."

The high what? My nails dig into my palm. I could just scream. "Have you seen a little girl? Tell me!"

"Seen. No." Golden Tree steps closer. "But we scented one."

May. Oh, God. Tension flees my muscles, and I nearly sink to the ground. It has to be May. I knew it. I knew... "Who took her?"

The fae look at one another again. "Unseelie."

The word chimes through the air in dissident notes. Shivers race across my skin. Bad, bad, bad. "I have to find them. Right now."

Golden Tree shakes his head as he advances. "I'm taking you to the king."

"Hell no!" I stiffen.

He halts.

"I'm not going anywhere with you." I look around the group with my teeth bared in a snarl. "Not a damn one of you."

"You are if you want your May. The king can help," one says.

A rebuttal is about to spill from my lips when gold tree guy says, "You called for Riven. He's our king."

The world sways. All I can do is blink. He's a...

He talked about his people, but holy shit, I never thought he meant that way. He never said...

I shake my head. There's so much he never said. He only told me he was fae today. Or yesterday, whatever. And I never asked. My heel grinds into the dirt. Idiot. Idiot. Idiot. Why did I always talk about myself so much? But I know the answer to that. I needed someone I could talk to, and he was my person. He listened. He understood.

How selfish I'd been, using him to vent and heal but rarely asking about him. And yet he still came. He still wanted me with him.

I swallow my regrets and look back at the fae who'd spoken.

"How do I know you'll take me to him?" If they really wanted to do me harm, they probably would have already, but still.

"Fae cannot lie."

My brows rise. I'm supposed to believe that?

I jump as a horse trots into the circle with us as if from nowhere.

"You don't believe me, do you?" He grabs the horse's reins, and it nuzzles his shoulder. Point to golden tree guy. He extends his hand. "We don't have time for this. Come with me."

My teeth grind together. *That* sounds familiar. When I don't move, he signals the others. I brace and shift my weight to the balls of my feet, expecting them to come for me. Instead, they jog off into the forest.

Golden Tree flicks his fingers for me to come, annoyance clear on his face in the way his features shift and scrunch.

Shit. Fine. Every minute we waste here is one more away from May. If Riven is what this fae says, he can help, surely.

Reluctantly, I take his hand and let him help me into the saddle. I haven't been on a horse in years, but it definitely wasn't this comfortable. The saddle is firm but soft all at once, cradling me. In one easy move, he's up and sitting behind the saddle. Somehow, we fit, though being this close and wedged between his strong thighs feels all kinds of wrong.

He's been nice enough so far, handsome too, but I can almost see Riven scowling in my head. It shouldn't matter. I'm not his. He's not mine. Shit, he's not even human.

"Hang on, Lia." Golden Tree's words still ring in the air when the horse bolts.

I screech as we plunge into the forest, barely dodging trees, vines, and all manner of plant life. My eyes slam shut on instinct. It's all I can do to suck in one breath after another as my nails dig into the strange leather.

No normal horse should be able to run through the wilderness like this at night. Not safely.

"Look."

The horse slows, and I dare to crack open my eyes. The forest has thinned dramatically, and through the sparse, thin trees, lights sparkle like a sheet of stars. My eyes adjust, and I gape at the structure before me. A castle stretches up, many stories high, into the night. But it's not simply stone or wood. Plants grow and creep along the surface, and trees spring up from within. It's like the legendary Hanging Gardens of Babylon on steroids.

"Virideria," he says. "Seat of the King of the Forest and his court."

"King of the Forest," I whisper. Awe and wonder consume me. Riven once told me that he lived in the forest, but I always pictured a little, rustic cabin, simple but comfortable. This—Virideria—is beyond anything I imagined.

I crane my neck up as we approach, taking in the upper levels and the massive trees that seem to rise up from within. Either they have very complicated roofs or they don't mind the rain. Given the plant life, I guess the latter.

I'm ogling the immense stone archway we're approaching when Golden Tree's words from earlier smack me like a brick to the face. "How did you know my name?"

"I guessed." He says without the slightest delay or flinch. "Riven told Ambrose about you, and I overheard him."

My cheeks flush. Riven talked to others about me, and I haven't told a damn soul about him. "Um, who's Ambrose?"

We draw near to the castle, close enough for me to see fae guards standing near the archway and the flickering lights—torches?—beyond.

"The Captain of the Guard."

"You were eavesdropping on them?"

He moves in his seat but doesn't answer. Maybe he really can't lie.

The winded horse slows to a trot, a little foam gathering at its mouth. We pass the guards, who give my companion a brief nod, as if this is a normal occurrence. Ahead lies a tunnel of rock and roots lit by hovering balls of light. Not torches. Nor light bulbs. This is something else.

One guard whips around as we pass. I turn to find his attention on me. He's saying something to the other guards, getting their attention. Walls mixed of hard-packed dirt, stone, and thick tree roots, some of which loop out at odd angles, wrap around us.

"Are we in trouble?" I squeak, facing forward as they fade from view.

"No."

"Am I?" Claustrophobia pushes down on my shoulders.

"No."

Right, we're just headed into this dark, earthen place. If there's a dungeon, we're near it. Panic wraps its hand around my chest, squeezing tight.

We pass by a few offshoots, never slowing. He knows exactly where he's going. Unfortunately, the way ahead is blocked by a curtain of leafy vines.

"Um..." I start.

"Galen."

"What?"

He's not slowing. Oh God. I brace my arms in front of my face and give a little screech, but the plants part as we reach them. The scent of new leaves and blooming flowers hits me in the face like a blast of spring. A moment later, the horse leaps into an open courtyard where more guards wait.

"That's my name," Golden Tree says.

Oh. *Oh.* I really should have asked. I roll my shoulders, a little of the tightness slipping away, but this place is far from normal.

"My apologies if I scared you." He drops from the horse and offers me help down. "I took the more private route. Didn't want anyone slowing us down."

"Um..." Breath catches behind my pressed lips. *Polite. Be Polite.* "Thank you."

The urge to run is heightened as ever as he helps me slide to the ground. My teeth dig into my lip, nearly drawing blood. If only the pain could wake me from this nightmare.

The elongated courtyard sports a number of guards dressed like Galen's companions. Green trees, one and all—except for near the dramatic door at the far end. Two golden trees stand on either side of the arched, two-story monstrosity. The plant life is just as dramatic. Trees that look like giant weeping willows drape their branches toward the plush carpet of grass. Stones pockmark it, forming a loose pathway. Water trickles somewhere nearby, though I can't make it out.

If May weren't missing, I might find it beautiful, but all I can see is wrongness, a threat, shadows waiting to eat me up.

Whispers pick up around us. The word 'human' tickles my ears and raises the fine hairs along my neck. The men and women here could be human if not for the pointed ears and the hint of otherness—magic?—that radiates from them. Varied human-like skin and hair tones show a world as diverse as my own. But I'm far from comfortable in their presence.

"This way, please." Galen ignores the other guards and leads me through the weaving path of stones to the giant doors.

"Riven's in there?" It comes out an accidental whisper. My stomach tosses and turns like a flag in a storm, and it's all I can do to put one foot in front of the other.

You've got this, Lia. You're May's only hope.

A near-hysterical giggle wells up in me. I barely choke it down.

"He should be." Galen glances over at me, where I rub the material of my shirt between my fingers. "They're—" He cuts himself off. "I have orders to follow." He dips a small bow as we come to a stop in front of the double doors carved with varied designs of animals and plants.

None of it makes me comfortable. Something is wrong.

"I—" *Don't leave. Stay with me. You're not as scary as the rest.*

Before I can settle on what to say, the guards are pulling open the massive doors by the thick ropes where door handles might go.

My heart leaps into my throat as a wave of conversation and laughter washes over me. And then it plummets, falling fast and hard to settle like a boulder in my stomach, as a mass of colorful fae turn toward the open doors.

CHAPTER 5

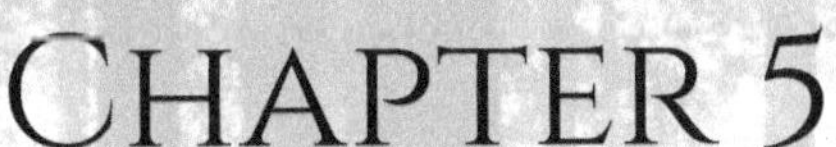

MY BACK STIFFENS AS their gazes crawl over me like spiders. Roving. Intrusive. Prying.

Pointed ears twitch. Heads cock to the side. Some begin to shove at one another and whisper.

I stare back at the riot of colors before me, trying to muster every speck of strength in my spirit. These fae wear outfits as grand and colorful as a garden in summer. Some have layers of billowing fabric, others, little at all, yet they all make it appear fashionable and high class, like a red-carpet awards party. Hell, someone could tell me I'd just stepped into a fairyland-themed Met Gala, and I'd believe it.

Galen walks me a few feet into the room because I can't make my body obey anything. His firm hand at my back and another on my arm guide the way. My fingers clutch at the armor he wears, as if I could squeeze hard enough to make him stop.

He does, but then, worse, he steps back, leaving me an odd and unusual statue among strangers.

My heel slides back and forth across the stone as I tug at my shirt. I'm the ugly duckling in a sea of swans, and they know it. A tingling sensation starts in my cheeks, and I know I'm moments away from losing my dinner in front of all these fae.

Expressions of confusion turn to wonder.

Yes, let's stare at the poorly dressed human. A hysterical laugh shakes my shoulders as I choke it down. Conversation rises in a wave of whispers and exclamations rolling back through the room—no doubt spreading word of my arrival.

"I leave you now," Galen says behind me.

Those words snap something in me. I can move again, and I do, twisting around toward him in a move so quick I almost fall. "No."

His eyes widen, and for the briefest moment, his expression freezes before he says, "You'll be fine."

He offers a small smile through the crack in the doors. They're closing. Shit. How'd he get so far away? I step toward them, but it's too late. His form vanishes behind the carved wood that seals me in with a weighty thump.

Chills skitter down my spine, and it takes everything I have to turn, inch by precious inch, toward the fae at my back.

They beckon me forward, waving like I'm some celebrity.

Rising up from their midst are tall tree trunks, spaced evenly in rows like pillars in a cathedral. They soar into the air, reaching toward a ceiling that isn't stone or plaster but rather the branches of those trees, fanning over the room in a canopy of dark green. Balls of light the size of my fist float through the air of their own accord, illuminating the space in brilliant light that shimmers off the silks, sparkling lace, and gemstones adorning many of the assembled fae.

Movement above and beyond the fae draws my attention like a magnet. An escape from this terrible awkwardness.

Breath catches in my throat. Relief and panic war for ownership over the flush that rushes across my chest and up my neck.

Perched upon a throne of green stone, *he* sits. One strong leg is thrown over one side, an arm lays casually across its back, and another holds a glass, which he slowly raises to his lips to take a sip.

Riven.

On a throne.

I blink, but he's still there.

And is that a golden crown woven through his hair?

His gaze locks with mine, and I swear his eyes widen. But he's too far away to know for sure.

A tall fae blocks my view. I try to step around him, to move past, but a woman takes my hand and tugs me with her. I jerk my arm, but she holds tight, her grip almost painful. Music joins the din of conversation, and I'm pulled into a dance. My sneakers skid and knock into one another as I move like an awkward marionette.

She releases me, and another fae, wearing a ballgown shaped like a rose blossom, takes her place and twirls me around. It takes everything I have to stay upright, to keep my wits as the world spins. A yelp rips from my lips as I stumble over something or someone. A man wearing barely anything at all catches me in his arms. There's no time to be embarrassed by his lack of clothing or the way I'm pressed against him. I can hardly tell I'm right side up before he dips me back over one arm and the end of my ponytail brushes the ground.

"Plea—" I begin, but then I'm upright once more.

Another fae grabs me about the waist and lifts me to the beat of the song. The throne peeks above the dancers perched on a raised dais, and breath catches in my throat.

Riven has vanished.

No. The man sets me lightly on my feet. Another woman advances.

"No!" I push past her grasping arms. Laughter and music—an orchestral song unlike any I've heard—swarm my senses as I dodge advances and slip between fae toward the throne.

A fae man in flowing robes of gold snatches me from between two others. I'm in his arms, twirling again, stumbling across the glimmering stone floor.

"Let me go. Let me go!"

I pull away. Too hard. I'm falling. Two others catch my arms. They're dressed alike in sheer green with flowering vines laced through blond hair. Twins? There's a pull and tug as they war for possession before I jerk away.

My breath comes in short gasps. Sweat slides down my back. Fae advance. I shove them away and slip past. It's rude. I don't care. So are they.

This is a nightmare. I can't escape.

An arm wraps around my waist, and I screech. They pull me in. I slam my fist against a hard chest.

"Lia."

My head snaps up, and I'm staring into the grinning face of the Forest King.

"Riven," his name cracks from my lips, half a sob.

His form wavers behind a haze of unbidden tears, but that's definitely a twisting crown of gold and emeralds on his head. Riven. A king. *The* king. My body goes limp as I give in to his embrace, letting him cradle me against the silky, soft material of his clothes.

"You came," he says. Long fingers slide through my hair and cup my head.

I'm all too eager to bury my face, forget these fae, forget every single moment since I woke up. One giant never-ending nightmare.

But I can't. Not yet. Not until I find May. I suck in a breath full of honeysuckle and pull back.

"May is missing. Kidnapped." I drop my voice and lean in. "She's here. The...er, fae near the door, they smelled a child. It has to be her."

His face grows solemn. "Yes, she's here."

How could he know? Unless...

I shove at him but end up stumbling back myself. "How could you!"

The other fae have stepped away, leaving us the center of an empty ring. They're looking at us. Whispering. Nudging one another.

I don't care. "Y-you stole my sister!"

"Have I?" He questioned innocently, raising his brows and cocking his head to the side. His empty hands are lifted, palms up, in the air between us. This man before me is nothing like the one I know, yet there's no question who he is.

My lips thin. "Yes, you—"

"I did not steal May."

"You're lying."

Gasps fill the air. The music has gone quiet, everyone listening in.

He shakes his head, almost sadly. "The fae cannot lie."

The same thing Galen said. Beyond Riven, I can just make out the bob of heads, others agreeing with him.

My hands ball into fists. "Then how do you know she's here?"

Riven's stance relaxes. That grin is back, taunting me. He looks every bit the king staring down a worthless subject, and I hate it.

"My wards alerted us that a human came through." He gestures around us. "My captain of the guard confirmed the scent matches the area where you and May were near the door yesterday, so it must be your sister."

I narrow my eyes at him, trying find a lie, but the words ring of truth. As they should if he truly cannot lie.

"And he found this." Riven pulls a tiny, torn scrap of fabric from inside his coat.

I lurch forward and yank it from his hand. My heart threatens to crush into powder at the familiar pattern of little blue bunnies—May's favorite pajamas.

Truth hits me like a hammer. Till now, a piece of me was so sure this was a bad dream and that any moment I'd wake up, safe in my own bed and May asleep in hers. But this... My worst nightmares aren't this terrible.

I can't even look at him. All I see are the bunnies. "Who—"

"The Unseelie."

The fae hiss like a pack of feral cats. The sound is so sharp and grating I can't help but look to them all and then up at Riven. He sneers, his face set in hard lines. Slightly pointed teeth peek from between his lips. In all our times together, I've never seen him like this.

"Help me find her. Please. You said they're dangerous, a threat. She's just a little girl. We have to get her back!" And I can't do it alone. Not in this strange world. The air seems too thin, and I can't get enough of it. It was my fault May nearly died. I won't lose her again. I can't.

His sneer fades into a grin. His whole form seems to soften and shift. I hadn't realized how strung up like a stiff statue he'd been only moments ago until now.

"And I need your help, my dear Lia." He paces, circling around me like a lion ready to pounce.

"What do you want?" But I know. He asked, after all. A knot forms in my throat that I can barely swallow. "I'm already here."

Riven halts. "Let's make a bargain, you and I," he says as if I haven't spoken. "I will ask a boon of you, and in return, I will make sure that you are able to return your sister safely to your home."

My lips thin. Not enough. "You'll help me find her. You and your people. Immediately."

Riven's mouth quirks up in a half-grin as he steps closer. Almost too close. "An exacting bargainer. I think I like you even more. Agreed. I will locate your sister and assist you in returning her safely to her home. Assuming that you uphold your end of the bargain, of course."

He holds out his hand. It glimmers with emeralds set in golden rings, a perfect match for the golden threads accenting his attire that shimmer in the light.

Seconds stretch painfully before I place my hand in his. "What can a human offer a fae?"

Money? I hadn't brought any of that. Everything I have is probably worth less than the clothes he wears, and considering the wealth that oozes through the room in glittering jewelry and fine silks, that can't be it.

Riven drops my hand and grabs my chin, sharp nails grazing my skin. I stumble forward, nearly falling into his chest. His body brushes mine as he leans in. The scent of honeysuckle teases my senses. I've wanted to touch him, dreamed of it, but right now I'd give anything to shove him away.

His lips brush my ear and he whispers so only I can hear.

"You."

The lone word echoes through me like a gong. Me. He wants me. The stroke of his hand along my waist is intimate, possessive in a way few have ever dared.

"I want you, Lia," he echoes, a sinful reminder that cannot be misconstrued.

I shove him away with all the strength I can muster.

The room lets out a collective gasp before murmuring among themselves again.

Riven cocks his head to the side, eying me up and down. "Little is more valuable than a human. Your bright, fiery spirit."

When I don't answer, he begins to prowl again, a beast within my cage of fae onlookers.

"I had thought," he continues, "that after our time together, all we'd shared, you might be more amiable to this exchange."

The words cut me as little else has. I spilled my heart out to him. When I needed him, he listened, he comforted me, as best he could without touching me anyway. He was my long-distance friend that I only sometimes got to speak with, and I treasured each moment. Yes, I'd longed for more.

But this...it isn't the easy companionship or friendly courtship I've longed for. This is something else entirely. *He* is something else. This man, this king, is not the Riven I've shared my nights and my heart with. Every step he takes around me breaks me a little more.

"What shall it be?" he asks.

The silence is almost painful. Everyone waits on my answer. Tripping and falling down in front of the entire cram-packed lecture hall on my first day at college was less embarrassing and uncomfortable than this fiasco. Sweat blooms on my skin. My clothes are too hot, too constricting. I'd jump out of my skin if I could.

"What am I"—the words crack into the silence, loud despite my whisper—"to be to you?"

He waits until I meet his gaze. Mirth dances within his emerald eyes, and it takes everything I have not to look away. "I'd have you as my consort."

My mouth forms a silent O. Suddenly, the stone beneath my feet is very interesting. In all the times I'd fantasized about him, what it'd be like to touch him, to kiss him, to maybe do something more, I never dreamed he'd done the same. Did he though? This...

Something is missing. A big something. This isn't seduction or a chase. It's a demand, a promise—a bargain fueled by desire.

Supple leather boots enter my field of vision. Close. Too close. My retreat is stopped before it can begin by a strong arm pulling me close. I push against his chest, trying to get away, panic and fear strengthening their hold around my racing heart. I can't move him an inch. Riven holds me until I succumb to the uselessness of my efforts and finally look at him again.

"Some time with me in exchange for your sister's life and safety." His voice is almost gentle, a seductive half-smile playing about his features. "Surely that's not a bad bargain? Her whole life for just a little bit of your time?"

He sounds generous when he phrases it that way. The benevolent king in front of his congregation, and even I have to admit he's convincing.

"How long?" I bite out, barely audible. "How long is a little bit of my time?"

"One year."

One year. Forever and no time at all. Much less than the fullness of my life, which he could have asked for, and which I would have given to save my sister.

I owe her that for what I almost took. Besides, she has more of a chance at life than me. I almost killed her, drove Mother away, and I'm so sure Dad and Elise are just waiting it out a little longer to tell me how disappointed they are in me for, well... everything. The accident, dropping out of school, not to mention all my other faults. Really, I'm not that important to anyone at all.

"If I refuse?" I can't, of course. Saving May alone is too impossible a task for me, and I'd definitely find a way to ruin things again. I need all the help I can get. But the way he's holding me so close, acting like an asshole version of himself, chafes my nerves. There's enough of my stubborn-ass self left that I can't just give him whatever he wants without a fight.

He ponders this a moment, elongated brows wrinkling, his ears even twitch kind of like a dog. Triumph lights in his eyes, and I know he has his answer before the words are even out. "Well then, perhaps I'd find your sister and wait on her to grow up."

Unchecked fury wells up inside me, fueled by the chorus of laughing fae. How dare he imply that he'd capture and keep my little sister? I lift one hand and rear it back to slap the grin off his face, but he catches my wrist in his and holds it firmly in the air. So fast.

My teeth grind. *Damn it.*

His face grows serious—all humor fleeing his features. Everything in me stiffens as he leans in, his lips a hair's breadth from mine. "Do we have a deal then?"

There's no way on God's green Earth I'm letting him or any other fae get near my sister ever again once I get her back. She's going home, even if I'm not, at least not right away.

One quick nod seals my fate.

The assembled fae stare in rapt attention as Riven glances around the circle. Clearly, they don't want to miss a moment of the spectacle playing out in front of them.

His voice echoes with authority and something else I can't name, as he begins his oath. "I, Rivenean Lutheon Silvanus, shall promise to find and free May and return her to her rightful human world with no mental or physical harm or alteration. I shall also promise that she shall not be sought out, spoken to, captured, or otherwise interfered with by myself or my people in the future, other than any action of her own free will. In return for this pledge, Lia shall willingly be my consort and reside with me for the next human year. Upon completion of her pledged time, she shall be free to return home without interference." He pauses and looks down at me, as if this part of his pledge was for me alone. "I shall also promise that I will guard Lia while she is here, and she will come to no harm at my hand or at the hand of any under my authority. She will bear my mark and my protection so long as she stays by my side."

The crowd goes deathly silent, but they're no longer waiting. Looks flash from one to another. Curious. Questioning. A few, maybe, angry? But why? It's all I can do not to squirm at the feel of prying eyes roving over my skin. Had they planned some torture or trickery for me that had just been cut short?

Part of me is grateful for Riven's clarity and for the protections he promised that I didn't think to ask for. The bigger part, however, still tries to process whatever unexpected thing just transpired without me truly knowing what it was.

I chew my lip, trying to reason it out, and come up with nothing.

"If Lia agrees to enter into the terms of this bargain, let it be known." His words snap my attention back to his serious, composed face, lacking in its normal cocky, amusement. Well, normal for this evening anyway. This man, the one looking at me now, waiting for my response, is the Riven I know.

Fine then.

"I agree," I say.

As the final syllable leaves my tongue, the air around me constricts, cocooning me in a thick blanket. A chill slides down my spine. Just as I begin to panic, the bubble of pressure pops like a balloon and slithers away in every direction.

Magic. My soul knows it without really knowing. The bargain must be bound by magic.

Hope replaces the chill that washes over me. Riven squeezes my hand. He's still my Riven in this moment, staring at me as if I've given him the world.

And then he changes, like taking off one mask and slipping on another. He tilts his head. Lust-filled half-mast eyes stare me down far too intently. A moment later, Riven's thumb slides across my lower lip, tracing a path that's the mirror of wicked tongue he slides across his own.

The reminder is clear: I'm the consort to the fae king. But which one—the one looking at me now or the one I treasure?

CHAPTER 6

T HE CIRCLE OF FAE surrounding us constricts. Chatter fills the air. Most of it's a language I've never heard and couldn't repeat if I tried. I've never been one to long for attention. That drama class I took one semester? The worst. Now, everyone's eyes are on me, and all I want to do is sink beneath the ground and pretend none of this exists.

Riven wraps me in his arms. His chest is solid, warm. But I can't forget the look in his eyes a moment ago or his pronouncement. The safe cage of his arms is tainted, as if thorny vines have wound themselves through my haven.

"Silence." Riven's single word carries a resonance the fae are powerless to ignore.

The quiet that slips over is so absolute I can hear my heart pounding. Hesitantly, I glance around at the colorful assortment of fae, who still look at me as if they could peel back my skin and see within my soul.

"Lady Lia is tired. You shall excuse us."

Lady Lia? My brows wrinkle.

Before I have the chance to question my title, the world around me shifts and warps. My stomach turns itself upside down and inside out. A sharp screech rings in my ears—my own.

All at once, it stops.

But I don't. My head spins, and the last remnants of dinner crawl up my throat.

Riven holds me upright against him. "I suppose it can be uncomfortable the first time."

"Wha—" It's all I can manage.

"Shifting from place to place like that," he says, as if we were just having one of our chats and that whole mess hadn't just happened.

I pull away. He lets me go.

The room we're in now is entirely different than the one moments ago. The other fae are gone, thank God. A few small flames under crystal globes like fancy oil lanterns provide the only light. Oh and, wow, yep that's moonlight lancing through the lush trees canopied above us. There's not a roof here either. What's with the lack of roofs?

Lavish furniture occupies much of the expansive space—a sitting area with chairs and a small table, an elaborate writing desk, and various other pieces for lounging and storage. Rain should be a problem for a room like this. However, the furniture shows no sign of water damage.

"Your room?" My voice is too loud in the quiet space. Which frankly, shouldn't be so quiet given there's no ceiling and the far wall is completely open to a large balcony. Probably more magic.

"It is. And yours for the duration of your stay."

My cheeks heat, and I whirl on him. "What the hell was that a minute ago? Your, your..." I can't make the word come out.

"A king?" He raises one careful brow.

I roll my eyes. Arrogant bastard.

"No! I mean, yes, there's that. But, shit, you asked me to be your *consort?*" My whole chest burns.

He nods, a slow grin spreading across his features. "And you agreed."

It takes everything I have not to slap him.

"You never, not once, all those times we talked... And then you spring this on me? Here? In front of all those people?" I'm pacing, my nails digging into my palms. At least I can speak again. Crowds always steal my words, but one on one? This I can handle.

"I did what had to be done."

I skid to a stop. "What the hell does that even mean?"

"I guaranteed your protection and agreed to save your sister. Is that not what you wanted?" His shoulders are slightly slumped. The lust-filled glint is gone from his eyes, and for the moment, he's my Riven again. Was his attitude in the throne room a mask, or is this? Maybe they both are, and he changes them to suit his needs.

"But the other part. Why do I have to be your..." Shit. My teeth dig into my bottom lip. Why is this hard? It's not like I've never dated before, not that those were shining experiences, but whatever. When he doesn't immediately respond, I continue, "You really want me? After all I've told you?"

Gosh, I can't even remember the things I've told him.

Almost killing May, that's for sure. We talked about that at length. My guilt, the uneasy feeling I've had around my parents since, the pain that stabs through me every time I look at her.

Riven cups my cheek, forcing me to look at him. His green eyes are solemn. "Yes."

My heart skips a beat. I want to be pissed, to yell at him some more. But the anger of moments ago is washed away by that word, that vow all its own. How long I've wanted someone to want me, even with all my broken parts.

Forever. All my damn life.

It'd be so easy. To lean in and kiss those lips I've fantasized about more than any woman should, especially since I didn't know he was real until...today? Yesterday?

May. Her name hits me like falling into an icy bath.

I pull away and nearly collapse on a nearby sofa. So soft. The plush, dark green fabric pulls me in, and I let it, pressed down by the weight of my thoughts. "How are we going to find May?"

"You're worried for her."

"Of course I am," I snap and gesture wildly with my hands. "I should be out there looking for her now. She's alone. She could be scared or hurt or..." I choke on my words. A few seconds and all my worries are back, drowning me. "And you! You could have been out there looking for her! You know what she means to me."

Riven looks away, and his lips dip into a frown. "I...I'm where I have to be. My presence would not go unnoticed."

"What the hell does that even mean?"

He ignores my question and wanders to a nearby table laden with various crystal pitchers and glasses that would probably cost a fortune in the human world. Red liquid tumbles from the pitcher into a glass.

"Drink this," he says, handing the glass to me.

I eye the drink skeptically. If I take a sip, will I be like Persephone, doomed to live forever in the underworld?

You promised a year, Lia, the last rational part of my brain reminds me.

"It's just wine to calm your nerves," Riven says like he can read my thoughts. "It's likely stronger than whatever drink you are used to, but it shouldn't have any ill effects."

Fine. Whatever. I'll have to eat something while I'm here. He watches as I lift the cup to my lips. I nearly sigh as the liquid slips over my tongue. Fruity. Rich and light at the same time. Divine. So many times better than the cheap boxed wine I'd had at parties in college or the bottles from the local liquor store that Elise sometimes opened at holidays.

Riven sits next to me, a respectful distance between us. Even Grandma would be proud. "My guards are searching for your sister now, following the captors. They have been since she came through." His voice is considerate, comforting, and soft like a breeze through the leaves. "They won't hurt her. Humans are too rare and valuable for that."

"She's just a young girl. What if..." I can't name the worries choking off my words. Speaking them would make it too real. "What if all this breaks her mind?"

He shakes his head, that beautiful golden hair swaying with him. "She's too young for her gift to have matured. Likely they put her to sleep before they even took her and have kept her that way. They wouldn't want to damage her."

"What gift?" I take another sip, savoring the flavors on my tongue that ease the tension radiating through my body.

"The ability to see the fae runs in your blood. It's rare. It was more common in ages past when the trait was recognized and intentionally bred into family lines. However, most humans seem to have forgotten the gift, or so we believe."

The wine sours on my tongue. Intentional breeding. Now that's some straight sci-fi stuff. Though, in a way, it makes sense that humans did that, at least many years ago, when only the strong and fit could easily survive. Despite the thread of logic, I can't help but shift in my seat. Many of the fae had looked at me as if I were the fairytale creature, not them. Given their earlier reactions and Riven's statement on the gift, humans must be rare here indeed. At least now I know what he really meant by being gifted.

I wring the glass in my hands. Riven is quiet, but I can't mistake the feel of his eyes on me or the slow trace of his fingertips across the back of the sofa near my shoulder. "I want to be out there, with your guards."

He stills and stiffens. "It's not safe."

My head snaps in his direction. The wine sloshes precariously near the rim of the glass. "More reason we have to find her. Now!"

He touches the back of my hand with his.

I flinch.

Riven retreats. It's a dance of touches and silent words.

"We will," he says, and his hand settles on my leg.

This time, I don't pull away.

"It's easier to search with you here. Once they've located her whereabouts, we'll go."

"You make it sound so easy." Frustrated, I get up and walk out onto the balcony.

Trees arc overhead, rising up from walls that arc a mix of plant and stone, just like the rest of the castle I've seen so far. I lean against the cool railing that hits just below my breasts. We're higher than I thought. It's a lucky thing heights don't bother me...too much. The balcony looks out over the sprawling complex, trees and plant life springing up among stonework. Little lights filter up from below like huge fireflies floating idly in a field. I blink, but the image stays the same. A vast forest, or at least what appears to be a forest, stretches out toward the horizon.

I close my eyes and take a deep breath. The clean, floral scents fill my nose and calm my senses. I've always loved the night, especially in recent months.

A faint rustling sounds behind me. Moments later, Riven is at my side, arms propped on the railing, looking out over the scene below. The breeze blows his long hair. Moonlight paints his skin in even paler hues.

He truly looks like a Forest King here, one assessing his domain and finding it perfect.

"She will be safe." The certainty in his voice wraps me in a blanket of comfort and calm. He can't lie, right? If he believes it, then it has to be true.

She'll be all right. She has to be.

CHAPTER 7

MAYBE THE WINE IS starting to do its work, but I finally build myself up to asking about one part of our bargain that keeps swimming up to the surface of my mind. I raise my wine glass to him in a mock toast.

"In our bargain, you mentioned that I would bear your mark. What does that mean exactly?" *Please don't say you're going to bite my neck like a vampire.* Vampires don't do it for me. Blood? Big no go.

He looks at me calmly, almost like a normal man having a conversation over a cup of coffee on a weekend morning. For a brief moment, I delude myself into believing that vision.

"A mark is both a magical and physical representation of a fae mating bond," he rattles off as if reading from a textbook. "When two partners willingly consummate their partnership, the mark appears on their bodies as a physical symbol, a tattoo, you might call it. It has its own magical presence as well, which can be felt by anyone with even limited magical ability. It will remain as long as the two continue to be intimate together and will fade over time without it."

Certain key words stick out in my wine-fogged mind: Consummate. Tattoo. Willing.

Riven slides closer and brushes some stray hairs out of my face. His touch is feather-light, almost gentle. I nearly spill my remaining wine as I back away and knock into the railing.

A mischievous grin spreads across his inhuman features. He whispers, "More simply put, once we're together, everyone will know that you are mine."

I groan. "Just when I'm starting to think you're a nice guy, you go off and say something like that. Seriously, ugh!" I slam the glass down on the railing a little too hard. It clinks but doesn't break. "And you just had to go and announce that in front of"—I gesture to a host of invisible fae around me—"everyone?"

His eyes twinkle. "You'd rather have every one of them seeking your hand?"

My eyes nearly roll out of my head. Yeah right. I tug at my worn shirt. Like any of those glamorous fae would want a little human like me.

Long fingers graze my shoulder and trail down my arm, causing me to shiver despite the warmth of the night. "You should get some rest."

Rest, right. It's gotta be super late, but with May still out there... I bite my lip and look back out over the forest.

Riven's hand twines with mine and gives it a squeeze. "We'll get her back as soon as my guards locate the ones who took her. You'll want to be there, I assume?"

My attention snaps to him. "Of course."

He leads me back inside, the wine forgotten on the railing. We pass through a curtain of honeysuckle vines dripping with blooms and enter another room lit by the same little flames under crystal. A large bed in the center of the back wall snags my attention. Layers of pillows, sheets, and furs dominate its surface.

Warmth creeps up my neck. A bedroom. Of course, he said sleep, but...

"There's only one bed," I practically vomit the words.

A small chuckle slips into the silence as Riven squeezes my hand. "You did agree to be my consort."

Holy shit. I rip my hand away.

"I d-did, but..." Now? Right now?

"We have a bargain that—"

"We do," I snap. "And I'll keep my word." Anything for May. "It's just..." I squirm under his gaze. "I can't... How can I do *that* with my sister missing? Even if she's asleep or whatever, she's missing, and I can't, not with her in danger."

It's not like I hadn't fantasized about him, but he can't be serious. No way. I'm not a first-date hook-up kind of girl. Not my style. Not even for May. And this is sure one heck of a terrible date.

His fingers drum against his crossed arms. "You're asking—"

"I'm asking you to be a gentleman, a proper king worthy of respect."

He flinches. Riven's mouth works in his jaw before he drops his arms with a sigh.

"We'll take it slowly, get to know each other...in person. Here," I say, anything to fill the silence.

"As you request." A stiff nod accompanies his answer. "Though I must say, it will be difficult. Do you know how much I've longed for you to be here with me?"

The heat in my chest slides lower.

"You have?" I say, like the dumbstruck idiot I am.

I don't retreat as he closes the distance between us. Instead, I stare at him in return, even as he rakes me with a gaze that could strip the clothes right off me. The warmth of his body spreads through the space between us.

"For months I wished to touch you again." The back of his hand grazes my cheek, sending a shiver up my spine. "To see you here. To have more than fleeting moments in your dreams." A smile creeps to his lips. "You're so much feistier in person, even that first night when you called me... What was it?"

"The devil?" I swallow the tightness in my throat.

"Ah, yes, the devil."

I could have sworn he was then, come to claim me for almost killing my sister. It should have been me who was hurt. I'd prayed to switch places with her, and in that moment, I thought someone had answered them.

"A kiss then. Can you give me that?" he asks.

My tongue flicks out to lick my lips. "Yes."

I want this too. I have wanted it for months.

Without a word, he pulls me tight against him, honeysuckle and crisp leaves in my nose, his warm breath on my face, the press of his fine silken shirt against my arms where they remain trapped between us.

"Riv—" I start.

His mouth crashes down on mine, hot, hungry, and devouring. Every nerve ending springs to life, filling me with a delicious buzz that isn't just the wine. I dig my fingers into his shirt, leaning into the hot press of his lips and the arms that hold me like a treasure.

His tongue urges my lips open and sweeps inside, tasting, savoring. A fae king demanding his due and taking all that I give to him. One deft hand tugs up the back of my shirt while the other caresses my skin.

The slow slide of his fingers up my spine has me groaning against his lips.

All too soon, he breaks away. The touch of his skin against my own and half-mast eyes threatening to eat me up do things I'm not prepared for. I breathe heavily, head still swimming, when he tugs at my shirt.

Without thinking, I lift my arms. The fabric is gone, lost somewhere within the room.

Riven goes motionless as I stare back at him in just my sports bra and yoga tights. They leave little to the imagination. If he's breathing, I can't tell, but every bit of his focus is glued to the figure he's revealed.

A smug smile tugs at my lips. Point for me.

Finally, he speaks, the words almost a growl, "Will you be removing the rest?"

"Just a kiss, remember?" I wag a finger at him. "We agreed." Though my words are airy, flimsy at best.

His eyes flicker, glowing unnaturally bright before returning to normal. "Did we?"

I nod, unable to hold back the grin spreading across my face.

"Well, you'll at least want to change for bed."

"And where will I be sleeping?"

"Here. With me."

My mouth forms a silent O. Okay, totally saw that coming, but hearing it confirmed, I can't help but squirm where I stand.

Riven steps over to a nearby dresser and jerks open the top drawer. "I had some things brought up for you."

"When?" The word slips out as a whisper.

But Riven ignores it as he grabs a second item. He holds each up in turn—two short and silky nightgowns trimmed with lace, one green, one blue. They're like something straight out of the high-end lingerie stores I can never afford.

My toes curled in my shoes. "Surely there's something more... just more."

Amusement twinkles in his eyes. "You could sleep naked."

I suck in a breath, my throat suddenly dry. "I'll take the blue one."

He chuckles as I snatch the nightgown, avoiding his gaze. He says, "There's a washroom across the sitting room."

Thankfully fae plumbing works like the human sort, maybe even better, with the constant floral scents and a little stream trickling through rocks in the room to cover any sounds. It's one of those things I never thought about until now, but damn, I'm so glad this castle isn't like the one from history books with chamber pots or whatever the hell people used before plumbing.

With a huff, I re-enter the bedroom.

Riven lays stretched out on top of the bed, dressed in only loose, light-colored pants that hang low on his waist. Almost too low. It's an invitation to look, and boy, do I. With his sculpted chest, defined abs, and fine dusting of hair that disappears down below the edge of his waistband, who wouldn't? Every inch of him screams lean muscle and golden skin. A few wicked scars mar his chest and arms in pearlescent patterns. They only add to his wild beauty.

"I'm glad you enjoy the view." His voice rolls over me, snapping my attention to the wicked smile aimed my way.

My nose reaches toward the trees above as I avert my gaze and stroll to the far side of the bed. I won't admit it, nope, nope, nope.

"One more kiss?" he asks, as I crawl under the soft furs, my back to him. Long fingers trail down my bare shoulder. Hair tickles my skin as he scoots closer. His strong arm snakes around my body, pulling my back against a chest firm as granite. Soft kisses grace my neck, my shoulder.

"Riven..." My breath comes short and fast. It's too hot. Too much.

A deep chuckle rumbles through his chest before he releases me and scoots away. "Goodnight, little consort."

CHAPTER 8

S UNLIGHT BATHES THE ROOM in a cascade of light. Blinking the bright glow out of my sleep-blurred eyes, I gaze at the vines of honeysuckle climbing the walls and draping the window. An immaculate wooden table is set in front of it, two chairs angled to take advantage of the view.

I jolt upright. This is not my room.

Memories of the day before crash into me. May. Racing through the trees. Galen. The fae party. And...

The warm weight on the bed beside me shifts and groans.

I whip my head around. Riven gazes at me, long hair a mess, a sleepy smile on his face.

"Good morning, Lia," he purrs. "I trust you slept well."

Holy shit!

I leap from the bed. Belatedly, I remembered the short night-gown and reach back, tugging a heavy fur about me as best I can. Like hell I'm going to stand there half-naked in front of some...some...

My skin prickles at Riven's soft laughter as I jerk and fumble with the heavy fur. My scathing look only increases his humor.

"So eager to get away from me?" he asks with a mock pout. A night of sleep has refreshed his roguish demeanor from the party or whatever it was. Pity. His expression shifts as he pats the sheets. "Care to come back to bed?"

Not when he's back to his asshole version. Why can't he just be the gentle companion from my dreams?

"We had a deal, remember?" I remind him with a scowl, wagging my finger for emphasis. "You're supposed to be finding my sister." He wants a bargain? I'll hold him to every word.

Riven groans and stretches his arms wide over his head before sliding out of bed. I purposefully look away. The last thing I need is another view of his semi-naked, glorious self to weaken my resolve. Clothing rustles as he dresses. God, it's so hard not to look.

I bite my lip. Hard. A little peek can't hurt.

"I'll have food sent up for you," he says.

I jump at his words, like a child caught stealing cookies. I hadn't even turned my head yet, dang it.

"And there are clothes for you in the walk-in wardrobe."

My brows rise. At that, I do turn my head. A small sigh slips from my lips. Of course, he's already almost dressed. "A walk-in wardrobe?" Like a closet?

Riven gestures to a curtain of vine across the room that I hadn't noticed the night before. With half the room alive and lush with greenery, there might be even more *doors* I missed.

"My guards should have located where they've taken May by now, so we can go as soon as you're ready."

A tingle rushes under my skin. I shove the furs away and search for my clothes. "We can leave now. Let's go!"

"Calm down. I don't know, exactly. I need an update." He threads his fingers through his long hair, brushing it back from his face. "They should have by now though. They've had enough time. And you should ready yourself and eat. It may be a long ride."

Food, right, whatever. Not important. Not with May out there. I scoop up my clothes from where I left them on a low table last night.

Riven stops at the curtain to the main room and glances back over one shoulder. "You'll want to wear new clothes."

Um, no. Why can't I wear my own things? I sniff at the fabric. Seriously, they aren't that dirty.

He must notice my scowl because he continues quickly, "Those odd pants you wore leave too little to the imagination." His gaze slides down my leg like a caress.

A prude or possessive? "Some of the fae last night were wearing much less."

Pointed ears twitch in return. "See if you don't find something you like."

He vanishes into the other room without waiting for a reply.

Okay, I'd been pissed about the clothes, but damn, this wardrobe is *not* what I expected. My mind conjured up light, frilly dresses in pale greens and pinks—and there are some of those—but several of the items are much more practical. And, oh my God, the feel of them! Cashmere? But maybe even softer somehow and much sturdier. The impossibility of it catches at my mind like thread on a nail in the flimsy way I just know these clothes would never unravel. Even the underclothes fit like a dream, just the right support, no digging in. Almost all the garments are varying shades of green, brown, and gold, but there are a few other colors dotted among them.

I've never been a thief. Stealing grates against my sense of morality way too much, but some of these are going to have to come home with me. After we find May, and—

A shiver chases away my moment of joy. May.

I shake my head and pull myself away from the clothes, the basics I need in tow. This isn't the moment to waste time on fashion.

I wash and dress as fast as I can in clothes that fit eerily well. I'm shoving a delicious pastry in my mouth when the large wooden doors of the main room groan open.

Riven strides in, hair pulled back in a severe ponytail. Last night, he had appeared a prince of pleasures, but today's attire paints him as a warlord. Fine metal and leather armor with golden leaf accents, fitted, unadorned boots, a riding cape—all he's missing is some fearsome helm with antlers, and he could be a druid knight from a storybook. He surely hadn't been wearing *that* when he'd left, and wherever he changed is beyond me.

The flakey dough catches in my throat and I swallow it down, hastily wiping crumbles on my pants.

A grin twitches on his perfect lips. Riven takes his time inspecting me like I'm a model about to traipse down the catwalk and I can't have a hair out of place.

Too bad for him. My face is still puffy from the tears that accompanied me into sleep as I thought of May, Dad, and Elise in the quiet of night. I washed my face, but I have literally no make-up on, not even the moisturizer I don every morning like a religious ritual. I cross my arms and stare him down in return.

"Perfection," he proclaims, and damn it if a flush doesn't bloom up my neck.

"You just happen to have a bunch of clothes in my size?" My chest burns so hot I might break out in a sweat.

"I hoped you'd come someday, and when you did, I planned to spoil you." His gaze coasts down my form then back up. "Human women like clothes, do they not?"

I rub the back of my neck. He might not know much about humans, but he got that bit right. Well, about some of us. Fashion isn't my obsession, but I'm not about to balk at comfortable, pretty things either. "It's just..."

"You don't like them?"

"Oh no, I do! I'm just...not used to presents." To say the least. A whole dang wardrobe when I hadn't even come here yet is overkill.

"Fae like to give gifts," he says like that's the most obvious thing in the world. "Shall we go?" He holds a hand out to me.

"Abso-freaking-lutely."

He tilts his head to the side.

"Means yes."

"Interesting." His ears twitch.

"First, though, I need you to take me back to the door."

Riven goes utterly still, frozen as surely as if he'd turned to stone.

"Just for a minute," I blurt. Dad and Elise have to be a mess. Not only is May missing, but I ran out on them too.

"Lia." His tone is as sharp as the fangs peeking between his lips. "Your sister—"

I hold up my hands. "I want to go to her. Right now. As soon as possible. But our parents will be worried. I want to tell them—"

"Out of the question."

I stiffen.

"You can't leave Faery. You bargained it."

Irritating man. "I won't." I pull the cell phone from my pocket. "I just want to leave this at the door."

He rears back like I'm holding a snake. "That's..."

"A cell phone." His blank stare tells me he has no idea what that is, so I continue, "It's how humans communicate."

He frowns, his fist opening and closing as he holds himself still.

"It doesn't work here," I ramble on quickly. For whatever reason, he's pissed as hell. "I just want to leave them a message on it. So they know we're okay if they find it." Well, sort of okay.

I'd swear the temperature drops as he stares me down.

"It would mean a lot to me," I push.

"You cannot leave the doorway." He holds out his hand again as if to say he agrees.

"Fine." *Bastard.* I'll take it.

His fingers twine through mine, sending a jolt of...something, straight to my heart. "Hang on."

No sooner are the words out of his mouth than the world shifts and warps around us. I bite my lip, holding in the screech crawling up my throat. A moment later, the magic spits us out, and we're standing in the circle of stones.

Riven grips my hand tighter as the stones fade and the tree circle appears. I glance at the phone in my hand. Nothing. Still no freaking signal. My chest tightens, and I take a deep breath.

Somehow, I hoped it would work today. Figures. Nothing's going my way.

I try to send a text to them again. It fails.

I tuck the phone down in the grass with a prayer for no rain. Riven clutches my hand in an almost painful death grip the whole time. Really, what's so dangerous about a door? If they come here, if they find it somehow, at least they'll be able to see what I tried to tell them: "We're alive. I'm bringing May home. Don't worry."

That last bit, I delete. It's foolish to tell them not to when I know they will.

"Okay, we can—" I start.

The words hang incomplete in the air when the world shifts around us again, and we're standing in a grassy field under the blazing sun.

"A little warning next time?" I stomp my foot in emphasis. Impatient man. I want to get to May as much as anyone, but he's wasting no time at all.

"My apologies," he says with a slight dip of his head.

The ground under us is stone, engraved with odd grooves and swirls that we might be standing in the center of. A few feet beyond lies short grass, as perfect and manicured as lawns in rich neighborhoods. Well, except for the places where the horses have kicked up little clumps here and there. A number of fae wait with them, tightening packs on their back and giving them treats.

I twist around, and the castle looms a little way behind us. It was impressive at night, a twinkling tower. In the daylight, it looms like an ancient ruin, many stories high with trees of all sorts sprouting up within and on its walls. If I didn't know better, I'd think it abandoned to time long ago, but unlike the ruins of our world, the plant life hasn't taken over as if to return the construct to nature. Instead, the two live together in a weird harmony, as if nature embraces and strengthens it. I shudder at the oddness, the strange beauty that could never exist in my world.

Only then do I realize my nails are digging into Riven's hand where I clench it in a death grip. It *has* to hurt, but he doesn't say anything, just lets me get my bearings.

I return my attention to the fae. They've stopped what they were doing and stare our way. Waiting for us. I suck in a breath of crisp, fresh air and release his hand. Or I try to, but Riven keeps a light grip and tugs me with him toward the waiting fae and all too earth-like horses. With all the other oddities, unicorns would make more sense.

"These are the members of my elite guard." Riven brings us to a halt and gestures to the assembled. "May I introduce you all to Lady Lia."

Bows greet me in return, and I stiffen. There's that title again. The urge to hide behind Riven or run back to the castle has never been so great. *Lady...* As if I were a high-born, proper lady being presented to a queen in ages long past.

I nearly snort. It's too grand for someone like me.

"Ambrose." Riven slips his hand from mine and joins the man. It's all I can do to keep my attention from wandering to the various outbuildings dotting the landscape or the forest looming beyond the grassy field.

Something about the fae Riven speaks with tickles a memory. Tall, almost Riven's height, with shorter, dark brown hair and a jagged scar running along one cheek. The armor that he wears is a little nicer than the other fae around us. They're all gold trees today.

Those eyes. That scar.

"You were the bear!" I clap a hand over my mouth.

Conversation halts.

Ambrose slides his brown gaze over to me and winks. "Bright girl." He swats Riven firmly on the shoulder. "I like her already."

I grin at him. It couldn't hurt to have a bear on your side, especially one who treats a king like an equal. Though dang, it would have been so helpful if he'd just talked to me then instead of stalking away.

Riven beckons me over. "This is Ambrose," he says. "The captain of my military and head of my elite guard."

How does one introduce themselves to a fae? Having no idea, I decided to stick with the human approach and hold out my hand. "Nice to meet you. I'm Lia."

Ambrose takes it and gives me one firm shake. "Well met. I can already see you'll be a boon to us here."

A what? My brows wrinkle, but I shake the question away in favor of a better one nagging at me.

"Can you become a bear like Ambrose?" I ask Riven.

"Unfortunately, that skill still eludes me."

A deep jovial laugh rumbles from Ambrose. "He's always been jealous of me for that little trick. We don't all have the same skills, you see. Some are common. Others rare."

Huh, like humans, I guess. Some of us are good at sports. Others music or art. And a few get all the gifts. Too bad I'm not one of those.

"You were saying that the Unseelie who took Lia's sister are hiding out in the eastern wood?" Riven asks.

May. I bounce on my toes, eager for news.

"They've set up a makeshift camp for now," Ambrose says. "Don't know how long they'll stay there, but I have a scout watching their position in case they move on."

"And my sister?" I ask.

"Safe from what we can tell. They appear to have put her into a magical slumber." He lays a hand on my arm as if to offer comfort.

Riven's mouth draws into a line. Possessive much?

Ambrose whistles, and a black mare with a white, diamond-shaped patch on her forehead trots over, escorted by another fae.

I nearly sigh in relief at the familiar face. "Galen."

Galen gives a shy smile in return. "Good morning."

His horse is stunning—bright coat, clear eyes, strong—a piece of home in this strange land.

"Can I touch her?" I ask.

"Go ahead," he says.

I tentatively reach out a hand toward her nose, praying she won't try to bite me. Warm. Coarse yet soft. She even smells right.

"She's just like the horses back home," I say while stroking her nose.

"She is," Riven replies. "Some creatures from your world made it into ours long ago and have thrived here ever since."

The horse enjoys Riven's attention, letting out a soft whinny of appreciation. A big checkmark in his favor.

Galen hands Riven the reins. My chest constricts as he walks off toward another group of fae.

"Some of our creatures thrived here but not the opposite?" I ask.

A grim cast colors Riven's features before he speaks. "No. Separated from the magic of our world, we...fade."

Well... I swallow the sudden lump in my throat. Whatever fading entails, it can't be anything good, at least not for them. No wonder you don't see fae running amok in the human world.

"Do you know how to ride?" Riven asks, pulling me away from my thoughts.

"It's been a while, but I can figure it out." I went through a horse phase when I was twelve. Dad took me riding several times that summer at a nearby ranch. I'm not an expert, not by any means, but I at least know the basics. "But why don't we just teleport there?"

His head cocks to the side. "Teleport?"

Oh hell. Though these fae know my language, some things don't translate. "You know, we were in your room, and now we're here?"

"Ah, shifting."

"Sure, whatever. Why don't we do that?"

"The longer the distance, the more magic it requires. So many of us over such a distance would be felt by the Unseelie."

"Felt?"

He nods. "We all feel it, the use of magic."

Well that's weird and inconvenient.

"We can't risk them feeling our approach. They could flee, be on alert, or..."

A chill races down my spine even as he takes my hand and gives it a squeeze. They could hurt May. "I get it."

Riven tips my face up to his, trailing a soft caress down my cheek. "We'll save her. She'll be with you soon."

CHPATER 9

I T TAKES ALL MY concentration to remember how to ride. The
reins dig into my palms. My stiff body aches despite the incredible fae clothes and boots that hug my feet and calves like a
second skin. No one talks as we venture through the forest at a
fast trot. These fae are professionals, their features set, intent on
their task. And I... well, I don't trust myself not to beg for someone
to let me off this horse, however sweet she is.

But I can't do that. I won't delay our rescue of May.

The forest here is very different from the ones back home. Even
though I spend a lot of time outside, I've never seen half of this
plant life before. Tree branches arch and hang down, making them
look like giant spiders. Others sport impossible colors such as navy
bark. The deeper we go, the more odd sights, sounds, and smells
war for my attention. A whiff of something like lemon cake sends
my mouth watering, yet we've passed no towns or structures. It's at
once enchantingly unique and horrifyingly different. Any minute
now, one of the trees is going to come alive and speak with us, and
then I'll know for sure I've stepped off the deep end.

Several trees are already dropping leaves, more evidence of the
early autumn season settling over this world. Though the crunch
and thump of horse hooves along the worn trails isn't as loud as it
should be. More magic at work, no doubt.

I give silent thanks when Ambrose calls the party to a halt.
My back aches, my tailbone is definitely bruised, and my legs are
starting to chafe.

Riven helps me down—thank goodness because, even with his help, I literally fall into his arms. Standing on my feet again, a whole new set of aches make themselves known, though none as distracting as his closeness.

"What's wrong?" Riven brushes away a few stray hairs that have come loose from my braid.

I hold on to him, not trusting myself to stand on my own. Something that might be genuine concern creases his face.

"My body isn't used to this." I gesture to the horse. "It's been a long time since I've ridden."

Understanding lights his features.

"I'd forgotten how much more delicate human bodies are than ours," he says, almost to himself. He jerks a riding glove off with his teeth, similar to the ones I've borrowed, and wraps his palm around my wrist.

A shiver races up my arm at the skin-to-skin contact. A moment later, my whole body tickles, like being lightly caressed by feather, even under my clothes. I sigh as a delicious warmth follows in its wake. My aches fade away, leaving me comforted and sated, like being wrapped in a warm blanket. Or cuddled close in a delicious make-out session.

My cheeks heat, and I shut down those thoughts.

"How are you now?" he asks.

"Much better." I let him go and step away. "Thank you."

"You're welcome, of course. I promised to keep you safe, and I will." He flashes a lopsided smile. Here, among this group of his elite guard, he's the Riven I know. Calm, kind, enchanting. Not the asshole from last night that I hope to never see again. "It seems I'm out of practice with humans."

Speaking of humans. "May," I whisper. "Is she close?"

"Not yet. But fae, horses, even charming little humans"—he grazes my arm—"need moments of rest to keep going."

It makes sense. Not that I have to like it. "What will we do once we find them, these Unseelie?"

His features sharpen. His ears twitch.

And I know, I *know* what he plans. A cold sweat breaks out across my skin.

Riven reaches for me, but I flinch away. He and his men carry weapons—swords, a few bows. I should have known. Somewhere in me maybe I did, but didn't acknowledge it until that moment.

"The Unseelie have become uncivilized. The Wild Tribes, we often call them now, for that's what they are. Disorganized. Animalistic. Reckless." Each word off his tongue is harsher than the last. "The things they've done..." There's a chill in his voice that's almost tangible. "You have no idea, Lia. Far worse than stealing a human girl. They deserve their fate."

Whatever they've done, it doesn't make the truth any easier to swallow. I hug my arms around myself and give a little nod. Stealing May is horrible, and I don't know all they've done but—

Riven pulls me into his arms. "If there were another way..." He shakes his head. "I must protect my people and your sister."

That's right. He's doing this for May. Still...

I sag against him. "How did they even find her?"

"Perhaps they saw her in the woods? Or"—he trails a hand along my shoulder, down my arm—"they may have followed your scent as I did when I took you home that first time I met you."

Back when I thought he was the devil. How ironic there were other monsters lurking about that I didn't know existed.

He lands a kiss on the top of my head. "I'll remember to ease your pain along the way this time," he whispers. "You'll be safe. May will be safe."

I can only hope he's right.

Sunset paints the sky in pink, fading to dark blue, by the time we stop again. Riven had held true to his word and used his magic to periodically ease away my soreness and pain when it returned.

The bright moon, bluer than the one at home, edges its way above the treetops.

My stomach growls, but I ignore it. I have bigger problems than my seemingly endless appetite.

May is out there. She's been gone almost an entire day.

I bite my bottom lip and rub the reins between my fingers. Dad and Elise must be a mess. An absolute disaster. Especially if they haven't found my phone.

My fault. Again. The bad fae must have followed our scent. It should have been me.

Memories of the car crash suck me back in time. The crunch of metal. May's scream. The eerie silence that followed. The blood... It should have been me then too. I rub at my face, forcing away the tears trying to break free.

I can't cry. Not here. Not in front of these fae.

Night has always been my favorite. Long before I looked forward to Riven's occasional visits in my dreams, I would sit on our back porch and enjoy the peace and beauty it offered, especially in the woods. There's nothing like the hum of crickets and hoots of owls.

They're pleasant here too, but there are other sounds, different tones, that I can't place. Almost like Faery itself can't help but remind me that this isn't home.

I slide down from my saddle with Riven's assistance. My legs are wobbly, but his magic has cured the lingering pain.

"It's not far now," he whispers, and my heart gives a leap. "You'll stay here with Ambrose and a few of the guard." I open my mouth to protest, but he places a finger across my lips, silencing me. "It'll be easier for me to ensure May's safety if I'm not worried about yours."

"She's *my* sister." I narrow my eyes at him. "And you just want me to stay here and what, knit?" My voice rises an octave on the last word.

"Yes, if that keeps you safe, I do."

I change tactics. "Take me with you. I'll stay out of the way, I promise, just let me be there."

"No. Trust me in this."

"Why?"

I gasp as he grasps my waist.

"Because I made a bargain with you, to return your sister, and I will not break it." His eyes are intent, burning into mine.

"Fine," I bite out.

Riven releases me and walks over to a group of fae, seemingly unbothered by the death gaze I aim his way. They converse in low tones too quiet for me to hear.

Should have known. Even he thinks I'm a problem. No good for anything but sitting around like a dog waiting for her master to return. I snort air through my nose. He brings me all this way and expects me to just sit here? If I wanted to sit and wait, I'd have done it back in Viri—whatever-it's-called.

My horse whinnies as Ambrose strides over with a golden apple of sorts in his outstretched hand. She snaps up the treat the moment he's within reach.

"Stella here did well today." He pats her neck.

"Stella," I repeat the name, committing it to memory.

"Her previous rider met an unfortunate end. She hasn't been content with anyone else. At least, not until today."

She nudges me with her, nose.

I give her a rub. "I'm glad we got along."

Ambrose's lips quirk up as he scratches at his beard. "She'll be yours, I think, while you're here."

Mine? I stiffen, only to receive another nudge. "O-okay."

A horse of my own, how odd. I give her another scratch before glancing back over my shoulder. My eyes lock on the vacant space where Riven and his company of men were only moments ago.

"He'll be fine," Ambrose says

"I'm not..." But it's a lie. I *am* worried about him.

It was buried so far below my worry for May it hadn't occurred to me, but I am. He and his men are going after the Unseelie, who he himself called animalistic, to save *my* sister. For me. If anything were to happen to him, to any of them, it'd be yet another mark on my heart. I sway on my feet.

Ambrose steadies me. "He'll do all he can to bring your sister back safely too."

My lips press in a tight line. Ambrose's optimism can't wash away my uncertainty, in their safety or May's. I rub the fabric of my skirt between my fingers, already impatient. This is going to be a long wait, no matter how short it actually is or isn't.

"Come with me," Ambrose says. His words are polite enough, but the command in them is obvious. No one argues with the captain of the guard.

The remaining fae are hard at work assembling tents from impossibly small packs. Ambrose leads me to one nearby. It's massive, elaborate, and dare I say, comfortable looking, with various pillows and such inside. No clue where those came from. The sturdy sides and high ceiling make it look more like a prop from a movie than something my family would use. A dozen people could stand around inside with ease.

"We're camping?" I balk.

Ambrose shrugs. "Might need to rest before we shift back to Virideria. Stay inside until Riven returns."

"What—" I protest.

Ambrose cuts me off. "It'll be safe for you here. We aim to protect our lady."

Lady. The title rubs against me and kills the retort dangling unspoken in my gaping mouth.

"Rest." Ambrose claps a firm hand on my shoulder. "He'll be back soon."

I don't have the chance to argue before he retreats, leaving me in the care of two fae who watch the entrance of the tent like I'm some sort of ancient royal too important to be disturbed.

It'd be so easy to sit like a good little human on my feathered pillow and wait until Riven gets back. It's what they want me to do.

I pace back and forth near the entrance. Sit and wait? Yeah right. It's only been a few minutes and already my anxiety tingles across my skin like a rash.

One of the fae guards looks through the entrance—again, as if I could have disappeared in a puff of smoke. My sister is out there, in the hands of their enemy, and yet they're worried about me?

I stalk to the entrance and yank the flap closed. If they're going to cage me and keep me from helping May, the least they can do is stop staring.

No sooner does it flutter shut than noise outside snares my attention. A loud bird call squawks from the trees opposite of the direction Riven went...I think. The fines hairs on the back of my neck rise.

Fae speak in low tones, moving swiftly toward the sound. The ones outside my tent move a few feet away to speak to another guard.

A sudden stiff gust of air slips through the tent sending goosebumps rising across my skin. If I'm going to leave without being seen, now is the time.

I can do it. I need to do it.

For May.

How could I ever forgive myself if something happened to her while I sat here like a good little human? I couldn't. And that decides it for me.

I peek out between the tent flaps again. My guards are still distracted. Another loud bird squawk demands their attention. A quick glance around proves this is my opening. My chance.

Riven, I'm sorry.

CHAPTER 10

I BOLT INTO THE woods heading in the direction Riven and his guard gestured toward when we stopped. The opposite of whatever caught the guard's attention—thank goodness. Fae would be faster than me, quieter, more apt to these conditions, but just sitting around and waiting to see whether or not Riven could indeed keep his bargain and rescue May is out of the question.

My feet slip out from under me. They fly up into the air as my upper body slams into the ground. Pain flares in my back. I roll down a shallow embankment and something sharp scrapes my arm. My head's still spinning when I finally stop.

I groan, pushing myself up on the ground. Leaves cling to me. My faery outfit is smeared with dirt. I grit my teeth against the aches and shove myself to my feet.

Shit. The forest looks almost the same in every direction. Dark, skeletal limbs baring pointed leaves reach for me from all sides. Dubious dark heaps that could be shrubs, boulders, or something far worse, rise from the ground. The dense foliage overhead only lets a few strands of moonlight through, making it hard to see anything too clearly.

A sudden squawk, quieter than the ones near camp but nonetheless jarring, sends me leaping backward against the trunk of a large tree. The bark bites into my back as I glance around.

The squawk comes again, accompanied by a dark flutter in the tree limbs in front of me. I gasp, my hands clawing at the trunk, willing myself to fade from view. A bird steps into a stream of moonlight, which illuminates its gray head, dark wings, and lighter stomach. This fae bird dwarfs the size of the hawks in the woods back home. An eagle, maybe, but the coloring is wrong.

It tilts its head. Dark, glassy eyes assess me. The branch bows and creaks as its wings stretch wide before it flutters off to a bulbous tree on the right. Another squawk echoes into the too quiet night.

"I don't have time for this," I mumble before shoving off the tree and heading in the opposite direction.

A gasp rips from my throat as the bird lands right in front of me, flaring its wings.

My heart thunders. What the heck?

It flies off to the right and waits.

"Do you want me to follow you?" I whisper.

It squawks.

Is that a yes? "I'm looking for a human, like me. Can you help?"

And now you're talking to birds. Good job, Lia.

The bird flutters two trees to the right and ruffles its wings. Definitely a sign.

I can't believe I'm doing this, but I shake my head. "When in Faery."

I hurry after the bird. Branches and shrubs fight back against my clothing as I run through the forest, following this ridiculous bird. More moonlight spills through where the forest thins ahead. The bird halts near the edge of the clearing, waiting at head height until I catch up.

Breath catches in my throat. Human-like forms huddle together. A few stand a little further out—guarding those on the ground? Fae?

My brows wrinkle. Even from here, they don't look like Riven or his people. One has unnaturally long arms. Claws, like long knives, glint in the moonlight on the hand of another. Antlers adorn the head of a third.

An icy stillness settles into my bones.

These are the Unseelie. The Wild Tribes. Animalistic—I never thought he meant the way they looked.

The bird, some kind of fae eagle I've decided, shuffles down the branch until its wings almost caress my face and the branch creaks under its weight. It, too, stares at the strange company in front of us.

Something moves in the grass to the right of the cluster of fae.

I stiffen, a gasp lodged in my throat. Long, thick, and dark, it resembles a giant anaconda slithering through the tall grasses.

The Unseelie fae see it too. Raised voices and shouts clamor in the night as the sentries flock toward it, spears and swords at the ready. On the ground, more figures rise in a hurry, grabbing up arms and forming a new perimeter.

More slithering creatures snake through the brush.

No. I lean a little closer, despite the little voice shouting in the back of my head to run away and never look back. They're not creatures. Vines. Pointed thorns poke out haphazardly as they ripple across the ground like waves on the sea. My stomach roils at the horrifying sight.

Blades stab and hack toward the invading greenery. An animalistic cry splits the night as one form topples over.

It does not rise again.

I shudder. The eagle fluffs its wing, caressing my shoulder with the edge of its feathers. Its head tilts to the side, watching me instead of the battle. The wingtip flicks out again, and its head jerks back toward the original circle.

What the hell, bird? It blinks then glances back at the figures in the field.

My legs threaten to give out below me as I choke on a scream. There, lying on the ground in a pool of moonlight, is a small figure with shimmering blond hair.

May.

I don't think, don't look, just bolt toward the prone figure on the ground. I stumbled over hidden rocks and fallen branches. My ankle flares with pain as it rolls to the side in a small hole.

Doesn't matter. No time.

I ignore the stabs of pain, hobbling as fast as I can toward her still form.

A vine wiggles in front of me to encircle the camp. I leap it. I land hard on my good ankle, and my knee dips to hit the ground. My fingernails dig into the hard dirt as I swallow the pain and push myself up.

So close, so close. The small blue bunnies on her pajamas are almost visible.

A scream rips from my throat as a monstrous fae steps out in front of me. A barbed club, bigger around than my waist, is raised in one meaty, blueish hand. Horns curl out of the side of its head like a big-horned sheep. A patchwork of hides and cloth cover its bulging body.

"Human." The gravelly voice rumbles over me, sending bile rising up my throat.

It lumbers toward me, each step shaking the ground under my feet. I stumble away from it, away from May.

No.

The club swings out between us, arching through the night and buffeting me with a puff of air smelling of decay. I gag and retreat until my heel knocks into something. It throws me off balance and onto my backside. A sharp shot of pain jabs up my spine.

The fae closes the distance between us in quick steps, reaching out its thick hand.

No. Please don't. I close my eyes against the inevitable, shielding my face with my arms.

A grunt sounds. Something wet splashes onto my arms. A heavy thump follows. My nose burns from the rusty, metallic scent that fills the air.

I peek around my arms. The knot in my throat drops into my gut.

Riven stands before me. Long claws extend from his hands, painted with crimson that drips onto the ground. Behind him, the fae clutches its neck.

Blood spurts between thick fingers. Its club lays forgotten at its feet.

Riven's jaw twitches, all hard angles and sharp gritted teeth. Green eyes glow with a surreal light. His hand rears back before slicing across the fae's face. I gasp and raise my arms, catching another splatter of blood across my skin, my hair, my clothes.

Lifeless eyes, or what was left of them, stare at nothing from where the head lolls upon the ground.

"Lia." Riven's urgent voice calls to me. He kneels on the ground, cupping my cheek with a hand sticky with blood but no longer bearing claws. "Are you hurt?"

I barely hear him. My eyes are locked on the monstrous corpse and the blood painting the grass black in the darkness. Shouts and screams reach my ears. The clang of metal. Grunts of pain. Guttural war cries.

Riven tilts my face away from the dead fae to stare at him instead. The harsh lines have softened, the glow of his eyes muted. "Talk to me."

Magic tingles under my skin, easing the burning pain in my ankle, my stinging back, and bruised knee.

"May. Where's May?" I pull my head away, leaning around him in search of my sister.

A warrior, the one with antlers, charges our way, a sword raised above his head.

"Riven!" I call.

He leaps up at my cry. Drawing his sword, he steps between me and the advancing enemy.

A petite fae with blond hair and wearing Riven's colors crashes into the antlered fae. Her sword cuts deep into its side. The enemy cries out, body hunched in pain. The cry is cut short as Riven attacks from the opposite side, severing the creature's head as the blond dips low to avoid the swing of his blade.

I gag as the head and body fall in opposite directions. One more headless corpse on the bloody field.

Worse is the sight beyond.

The bare spot of grass where May's body had lain.

I'm up and running before Riven has the chance to wipe the blood from his sword. His hand latches onto my arm as I sprint past. My feet slip on the bloody ground as he drags me to a halt.

"Stop," he says. "Stay with me."

"May! Where is she?" I claw at his chest. My heart threatens to leap from my ribs. Tears run unchecked down my face.

Riven's head whips to the side, his eyes widening as they settle on the empty ground.

"Sylvie," he snaps to the blond.

"On it." She's off in a flash, running like a sprinter in the direction from which she came, her long hair trailing behind her.

"We'll find her." His grip on my arm tightens, almost painfully, as his head whips side to side, scanning our surroundings. "She has to be here."

The sounds of battle dwindle around us.

"May!" I call for her, but she doesn't answer.

Riven sheathes his sword and tugs me closer, holding me against his chest.

"Stop. Let me—" No matter how I squirm, I can't free myself.

Darkness rises up at the edge of the tree line. I gasp as the thick vines intertwine themselves, forming an impenetrable, thorny barrier around the clearing. Riven's jaw is set, his eyes far away in concentration.

He's doing this. I freeze as the revelation settles in.

"Riven!" Ambrose's bellow jerks him back to the moment. The vines fall still and lock into place.

In unison, we turn toward his voice across the clearing. He and three others stand staring down a fae with a long tail. One who holds a small figure in blue.

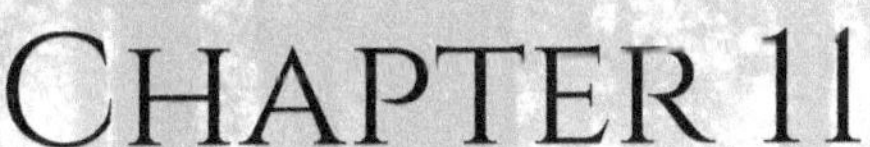

CHAPTER 11

M Y BREATH HITCHES AS the air around us pulls and warps. A moment later, we stand next to Ambrose, staring down the fae who holds my sister. One arm is curled under May's shoulders. Pointed claws extending from the other are aimed at her throat.

No. Oh, God, no.

Two sets of ears twitch atop the fae's head: the long, pointed ones all the fae have and a second set of cat-like ears. Golden eyes gleam in an angular, balanced face. Light pink hair cascades down her back.

"You've made a mistake dealing falsely with us, Forest King." Her voice is a hiss, accompanied by a show of pointed canines.

"Give her back, please! She's just a child!" I reach for May, who hangs limply in her arms.

"Give us the girl, and you go in peace," Riven echoes.

"Peace?" she huffs, her tail flicking behind her.

"Please, she's just—"

"If you want the little human"—she slides her gaze between Riven and me—"return to this place in seven days with something of equal value. If not, the girl stays with us."

Within the blink of an eye, she's gone, disappeared into thin air with my sister.

My heart crushes to powder as my knees give out. I sink to the ground. An enraged male bellow fills the air, echoing into the night.

That creature, that fae, has my sister.

I slip away, everything going dark and numb as the horror of it drowns me. Dimly I'm aware of angry words and rushing feet. But that activity is worlds away, far away from the black hole sucking me down.

A question. My name? Something on my arms, my cheek. A blurry face in front of me.

"—back to me."

The blurriness clears. A figure takes form. Riven.

"Please." His eyes are wide, panicked. His chest rises and falls with heavy, quick breaths.

"You promised." My accusation is a cracking rasp.

"I'll get her back. I'll find a way," he says. Blood splatter mars his face, hair, and clothing, painting him the wild warlord I thought he resembled before this trek. Magic hums under my skin, searching for wounds that can't be repaired.

Even magic can't heal a broken heart.

"Why are you here, Lia? I told you to stay away." Riven smooths the hair back from my face, running his other hand up and down my arm in what may have been a show of comfort.

"She's my sister. I had to save her. Those vines, they could have crushed her, and those creatures—"

"The vines were mine. I almost had them all trapped when you ran into the clearing."

What? I gaped at him. The darkness creeps in at the edges of my vision again. He almost had them all. Did he...? Did I...?

No... No, no, no.

"I had to stop to save you. I couldn't risk them harming you or taking you as well." He wipes at my face, clearing away rogue tears and something sticky I refuse to consider.

My chest burns. I can't get enough air. "It's my fault. I got in the way."

Riven presses my face between his hands, forcing me to meet his burning gaze. "It's my fault. I underestimated them. And you. We will get her back."

He releases me, but I don't move. Instead, questions spill from my mouth like a waterfall. "Where did she go? Why did they take her? What do they want?"

"I don't know where they went, but my guards are searching."

"You can't feel it? The magic?"

He winces.

I look around, frantically searching the clearing for my sister though knowing I won't find her. The vines ringing the clearing are gone though. Instead, thick piles of leaves circle the area.

"Lia."

I'm panting for breath. Sweating like I've run a marathon. He holds me, an anchor in this storm, just like the night I almost killed May.

"We. Will. Save. Her." His eyes are wild, fierce.

Tears threaten to spill again, but I hold them back, nodding as I bite my bottom lip. He's here. Riven is here. We have a promise, a bargain. He'll save her.

"Can you stand?" He helps me to my feet.

Dark crimson splatter covers my arms and clothes. I sway, reconciling it with the metallic scent that hangs in the air.

"I'll be right back," he says. "Stay here this time. Please."

I wipe my hands and arms on my clothes, trying ineffectually to remove the evidence of my error.

May is gone. People died.

Because of me. All because I messed up. Again.

Why? Why, oh why, do I only cause problems?

Riven talks with Ambrose and a cluster of other fae guards. They arrived at some point during the battle. Did they come after me, or did Riven summon them? Doesn't matter now. An injured fae groans. Riven lays his hands on him, likely pouring out the same healing magic he'd used on me.

May. I'm so sorry. Tears roll down my cheeks. She was so close.

I watch Riven through the blur of my tears, trying to focus on anything at all to take my mind off May. The carefree, cocky fae male from last night is long gone. He's the Riven I've come to care for...almost. Instead of the calm confidence he always has with me, his shoulders slump, as if weighed down by a heavy burden. His jaw works his mouth as if, like the rest of him, it can't be still. Most disconcertingly, long claws keep extending from one hand and retracting while he speaks with his guard.

It's still so strange to see him before me. When he appeared in my dreams, he was more shadow than man, a ghost of a form I could only somewhat see and never touch. His voice...that was the same. The one that listened and comforted when I needed him most. Though even that has a slight edge to it now that I don't remember.

I jump as a large bird, the same one from before, settles on the ground near my feet. It stares at me, head tilting side to side.

"What are you?" I ask.

This bird sticks near me like the forest animals to Snow White, but I'm no princess. The tips of its broad wings brush against my stained pants. The urge to pet it overwhelms the rational part of my head screaming that wild animals are dangerous, especially ones in Faery. I stretch out my hand, aiming to rub its feathered head.

"Stop!" Riven's voice rings through the space between us.

I halt, my fingertips inches away. The bird gives a loud caw before shifting its focus to the fae king frozen a few feet from us.

Ambrose swears and grits his teeth. Galen is wide-eyed beside him.

What on earth... Do they think it's going to eat me?

A snarl rips from Riven's fang-bared mouth as he flicks his hand toward the bird.

A snap sounds, followed by a pained screech.

I stare in horror as a vine wraps around the bird, threatening to crush it under the thorny green length. Already blood mars one wing.

"No!" I'm up and running toward Riven before I think.

Another snap. Another frantic squawk.

"Please." I launch myself at his chest and scramble for his arms. My fist slams against his armor. "Riven, please."

His arm jerks to the side as the sounds behind me quiet into an eerie, full silence.

The knot in my throat threatens to choke me. My body goes limp. I can't bring myself to turn and look. Riven cradles me to his chest.

"Why?" The word is as much a sob as a question. How could he be so cruel? The other fae I almost understood, especially since they'd had my sister, but a bird?

"It was an enemy. A threat. If it realized what you are, what you mean to—" Riven's words cut off as his arms tense around me. In one movement, he lifts my feet off the ground and spins me around, putting himself between me and whatever had been at my back.

The fae around us step back, all except for Ambrose, who shifts ever so slightly in front of Riven. Riven gazes down at me even more wild and frantic than before. His mouth is slightly agape.

I blink away my tears. "What—"

"Well, that was rude." The deep, melodious voice floats over us.

Nearby, fae reach for weapons and backs straighten.

"At least I was trying to help the poor girl." The male voice is calm.

Even so, the reactions of those around me say much. He must be monstrous, even worse than those they fought here in the clearing.

"And such a pretty little human she is." Laughter flutters through the air.

My body stiffens. Me. Oh God, he's talking about me. I cling to Riven with a desperation I never expected.

A resigned sigh slips over me. I'm awash in honeysuckle as Riven places a gentle kiss on my head. His arms loosen around me.

No. Please, don't let me go, my body cries out as the safety of his arms retreats.

Riven tugs me to his side, one strong arm around my waist. His shoulders are squared, back straight, amused mask back in place as a grin pulls at his lips.

"Sigurd." His voice fills the name with casual indifference, as if he hadn't just been stunned into silence at the male's sudden appearance.

Ambrose steps back to flank my other side, providing a view of the fae standing next to the ruined corpse of the eagle.

My mind had constructed him into a monster of a man, or rather, fae. Excessively tall, bulging muscles, sadistic, wild eyes, and a maniacal grin. I'd even given him horns.

He's none of those things.

Tall but not excessively. The way his clothing drapes about him speaks to strength, but it's lean, agile muscle, not the body-builder bulk I'd envisioned. Dark hair crowns his head in a slightly messy wave, curling about his ears. The cut is much shorter than Riven's and many of the other fae, though he and Riven look similar in age.

If Riven's eyes are emeralds, Sigurd's are sapphires, shining out of his pale visage with an inhuman glow. Those sapphire eyes snap to mine. The glow flares before dimming out.

A grin spreads across his handsome face. "There we are."

It takes everything I have not to hug my arms about myself and hide from his piercing gaze.

"What do you want? Showing yourself in my territory like this," Riven demands.

Sigurd's lips twitch as he brushes invisible lint off the dark material of his overcoat. Black? Navy? It's impossible to tell in this light. "I was curious what the Unseelie were up to."

An involuntary shudder rattles through me at the mention of those monsters.

Riven's fingers tighten on my hip in response.

"Then there's no need for you to still be here." The amusement fades from Riven's countenance, his words turning sharp.

"You don't want my help? Though it would be easier to offer if my eagle had not been treated so poorly." He gestures to the body of the bird on the ground, the one I still refuse to look at too closely.

"You have others." The dismissal is too casual for the brutal death. "Besides, what did you expect when you used it to spy on us? Especially in my territory. Leave us. You're not welcome here."

"Still? After all this time?" He *tsks*. "I do have others but not here. It may take some time for them to arrive with my guards. If you accept my offer, that is."

"No."

"Really? What would Evelyn think if she knew you'd let a poor human get taken by the Unseelie?"

Riven hisses. The fae guards around us tense. Even Ambrose adjusts his stance and reaches for his sword.

Something foul slithers in my gut at the female name. I lean away, suddenly uncomfortable pressed against Riven's side. He's not mine, not really, no matter what we bargained. Even so, the thought of him with someone else makes my blood simmer.

"You don't get to speak of her," Riven all but snarls.

Sigurd's lips pull into a frown. My stomach twists. Whoever she is, Riven cares about her. Sigurd as well.

"Perhaps the human should decide." His gaze slides to me, the grin returning. "Lia, wasn't it?"

"How do you know—" The words spill out before I can check myself.

"Leave her out of this." Riven tugs at my waist, urging me behind him.

But I root my feet to the ground, holding firm. I won't be sidelined. Not again.

Sigurd waltzes in our direction, closing the distance between us as swords slide free and fae close ranks around us. Eyes roll in his perfect face. "Call off your guard. We don't have time for this."

No one moves.

Sigurd shifts his attention to me again. "She's important to you. Your sister? Do you want my help or not?"

This fae, this stranger, would help May? "Yes."

"Lia—" Riven begins.

But I cut him off with a sharp look. "We have to get her back. You promised."

He winces at *that* word.

"If he can help..." I gesture to the newcomer. With what just happened, we need all the help we can get.

"He doesn't trust me. None of them do." Sigurd's words capture my attention again. "But even you"—he looks to Riven—"know how I feel about the Unseelie taking humans." Sigurd's countenance flattens out. Something dark, maybe a memory, flashes across his features.

"What do you propose?" Riven's words hold less venom than before.

"I'll bring some of my guards to help search for the little girl."

I practically bounce for joy.

"And I'll help restore your wards. I mean, they are rather pitiful if my eagle can stand next to your human without notice. And for the Unseelie to just wander so deep into your territory." He *tsks* again. "It's an embarrassment, really." He waves his hand through the air as if his words are light, airy, frivolous. The absolute opposite of the slap in the face he clearly intends.

Riven's whole body goes rigid at my side. I rub my hand along his arm. No more fighting. Not now.

"But I digress," Sigurd says. "Where should we meet?"

"The border." Riven swallows. Some of the tension flees his form. "We'll focus on the wards first. Then Arbrean."

"Ah, close to our mutual borders and the Shadowlands. I should have expected as much." Sigurd looks off into the distance as if seeing something that I can't. "Until then."

CHAPTER 12

S IGURD DISAPPEARS, VANISHES AS completely as the feline fae who took May. I can't help but search for him, even though I know he's gone. Hands slip from pommels. Shoulders roll. Sighs fill the air as the members of Riven's guard relax.

"Will he come back? Tonight, I mean," I ask.

"No." Riven releases me and scrubs a hand down his once-more-weary face. "My wards must really be weakening for him to shift all the way here."

"Who is he?"

"King of Air," Ambrose answers.

My brows rise at the title.

"He controls the territory next to mine. The Shadowlands, the home of the Unseelie, border us both."

"He just disappeared. Like the cat woman who stole my sister." I frown at the unintended reference.

"I should have noticed, and yet..." Riven shakes his head.

"Wards?" I ask. They keep talking about them like I should know, but I don't. Honestly, all these fae terms are starting to chafe.

"Magical barriers," Riven says. "I have them around my land. All fae rulers do."

A near-hysterical laugh slips from my lips. All fae rulers. Implying many. Of course, just what I need, a bunch of arrogant fae monarchs.

"They should keep fae of other courts out, the weak ones anyway, and slow down the stronger ones."

"Or at least let us know they're here." Ambrose scratches at his beard.

"The magic has faded too much." Riven paces. "I should have..." He runs his hands down his face again.

"That's why the Unseelie didn't shift away with my sister from the start?" I ask.

"Only the strongest fae can shift," Ambrose says, watching Riven wrestle with his internal struggle. "Unseelie are weak after... It's a long story. They shouldn't have been able to. We didn't think they could."

Nausea churns in my gut again. Had all the strong fae come out to play this evening? "So, the woman who took my sister..."

"Is much stronger than she should be, especially for an Unseelie," Riven says. "I haven't seen an Unseelie who could do that since the war."

Ambrose traces the scar on his face. "Aye, if one can grow strong enough to shift and do it within wards, then we may have bigger problems than we know. None of our reports indicated the Wild Tribes growing so strong."

My nails bite into my palm. This conversation isn't helping. Not at all. "Where do we start?"

Both men look in my direction.

I gape back at them. "May. Where do we look to find her?"

"We'll comb the forest, but we don't know where she went," Ambrose says. "We should be able to feel it. But I don't."

The stiff set of Riven's jaw is silent confirmation that he doesn't either.

"What does that mean?" I ask.

"Nothing good," Riven answers. "And if we can't find her, we'll need something to trade for her in seven days."

Fury boils up within me, overflowing as I stomp my foot against the ground. "We are not waiting around for seven days!"

"No, we're not. But we need to prepare for that possibility just in case."

"Trade me," I say.

Both men look at me like I've grown a second head.

"Out of the question," Riven replies at once.

Ambrose nods in agreement.

"She's my sis—" I start.

Riven places a finger across my lips, silencing my retort. "We know, and we'll get her back. But losing you in the process is not an option."

I bite my lip to keep from shouting in his face.

"Do you think we can trust Sigurd?" Ambrose glances in the direction of where the King of Air had stood.

"No. But he has spies, likely more than one, watching me if he already knows so much about Lia, much less the Wild Tribes."

Spies. The word has me squirming in my boots. First strong Unseelie, then another king, and now spies. I huff air through my nose. What's next?

Ambrose rubs the scruff on his chin. "I thought so too."

"I've assumed it for a while, but he's not bothering to hide it now." Riven runs his hand through his hair, which came loose from its tie at some point. The movement, along with the sweat and blood, has it sticking out like a wild mane around his head.

Riven whistles, a long shrill sound that has the members of the fae guard rushing over. He shouts assignments in pairs and trios, ordering his guard to scour the woods for any sign of May or the Unseelie, return the extra horses and equipment to the city, and other tasks. I tune him out until a particular command snags my attention.

"—return with us."

"What?" I interrupt. "We can't just leave. Not without May."

"We can, and we will. It's too dangerous right now with how little we know. We'll return at the first sign of something promising. You're covered in filth, we only have a day's worth of food, and May will be much better served by more of my guard looking for her and not just this handful. Not to mention, it will give us time to find something to trade for her if it comes to that."

I wince as he details each item in exasperation. Freaking fae making it seem so simple and orderly when all the world is one big disaster.

"Do you still want to stay?" he asks.

A retort hangs on the tip of my tongue, sour and bitter. Gosh, I'd love nothing more than to scream at him, but everyone is watching me, waiting. Every minute I spend arguing is one less that they're searching for May.

Not to mention that his comments made me painfully aware of the gunk still coating my body. Even now, something sticky is drying to the side of my neck. The wretched metallic scent I'd somehow managed to block out is back now too, and with a vengeance.

"Let's go." Riven senses my defeat. He holds out his own grime-coated hand.

The moment we touch, the world warps and bends. When he did it before, the sensation faded quickly before planting us in our destination. Now, the magic takes its time. The world skews wildly around us, sending my stomach on a rollercoaster ride. My hand clenches his in a death grip. I never want to find out what happens if we separate.

The moonlit forest fades into darkness black as a tomb. Colors and shapes return slowly, bit by bit in wavering forms, until a room—Riven's—coalesces around us. The wavering stops as the room solidifies.

A captured breath escapes from my lungs in a whoosh. The scent of budding leaves and honeysuckle, which cling to the room like spilled perfume, refills them. Riven releases me to yank on a long rope hanging from a bell on the wall. A tickling wind chime fills the room, the only sound other than my heavy breathing. Riven pokes his head out the door and speaks to a guard standing watch.

Everything is a blur of loss and pain, so much like that night after the crash.

"When Karin or one of her women arrives, have her bring food for Lia and me." Riven's gaze flits back over one shoulder before returning to the guards. "And call for Solona."

I flinch. Karin sounded like a maid, but that likely means Solona isn't. So many women's names keep coming up, and I know nothing about any of them. Even now, Evelyn's name still clangs through the back of my mind, taunting and teasing every insecurity I've ever had. Who is she? What is she to him? I hug my arms around my chest, as if I need one more thing to hurt over.

Ridiculous. I give myself a shake. He's not mine, he's not...

But then, I guess I always thought of him that way before yesterday. He was mine, my secret companion I never had the courage to tell anyone about. Not that they'd have believed me anyway. Dad would have given me a side-eye look at best, and Elise would totally have insisted on more therapy. My friends... Well, they hadn't really been there for me when I needed them either. Funny enough, the only one who might have believed me is May.

It's hard to reconcile the man of my dreams with the fae king before me. Not just that he's real but all that realness entails. Responsibilities, relationships, lovers...

My teeth bite into my lip, almost drawing blood.

This isn't like you, Lia. Jealousy isn't normally my thing, but tonight I can't shake it. It's just one more wave in a sea of churning feelings. *Think about something else, anything else.*

As always, my thoughts float back to my sister, however painful it may be.

Riven stalks toward me, and I can't handle the silence anymore.

"If you can teleport, then why didn't we just drop down next to my sister, grab her, then come back?" I ask.

"Telep—"

"Shift. Whatever you call it."

"All magic can be felt. Our best chance was to travel the normal way and sneak up on them." His hands are in his hair again as he paces in front of a sofa. At one point, he started to sit but halted halfway, maybe remembering the grime and blood clinging to him too.

"You couldn't feel that Unseelie, the one with my sister."

His grimace deepens. I've wrenched the knife, but I don't regret it a bit.

"And what about in the clearing, huh?" I spit the accusation. "Even I saw her on the ground. You couldn't just shift in and get her then?"

He freezes, head snapping toward me. The distance between us closes in three quick strides until he looks down at me from inches away. "A mistake. One I bitterly regret."

I search for a retort, anything to fling at him to calm the fire of guilt and pain raging within me. My hand clenches and unclenches at my side as I came up empty.

"Why did you want his help?" His tone is deathly calm, almost icy.

I shrug. "Because we might need it."

Riven looks past me at the night still darkening the sky outside the balcony. "What is he playing at?"

The question was a whisper through a clenched jaw and not directed to me, but I answer anyway. "Maybe he does want to help."

"Unlikely."

His attention shifts back to me, and his eyes soften. The muscles in his face relax. Riven's hand caresses my face, scrubbing at something on my cheek. That simple touch stirs up so much. Everything fades until only he and I are left.

"When I saw that Unseelie coming for you..." He shakes his head. "If I'd lost you..."

His face dips closer to mine, cocking slightly to the side. My heart kicks into high gear. All my focus drips to his slightly parted mouth, my tongue moistening my lips in anticipation. He's warm, solid, strong, real—everything I need.

A loud knock sounds at the door, causing us to jump apart far too soon.

The door swings inward, held open by one of the guards, as a woman strides in. Her brown hair, pulled back behind her head, highlights pale, pointed ears. Golden eyes shine out of a middle-aged face. A tray is balanced in her hands with two steaming cups.

"Karin, thank you for coming so quickly," Riven says.

"I came prepared. My girls will bring food along shortly, but for now—" She halts, her gaze sweeping me head to toe and then moving over to Riven. "Oh, my word. What happened?"

He runs his hand through his hair again and looks away.

"Poor dear." Karin basically drops the tray on a table and rushes in my direction. "And you just let her linger in this mess." She shakes her head in dismay. "Let's get you cleaned up."

I'm too exhausted—mentally, physically, and emotionally—to argue as she drags me to the washroom.

CHAPTER 13

A SERIES OF PLANT-COATED archways curve down from the ceiling to waist high on one side of the washroom, letting in the cool night air. The view beyond is starlight and treetops. Calm. Peaceful. The opposite of me.

A splash catches my attention. A torrent of lightly steaming water flows like a small waterfall into the stone bathtub below it. Karin moves around the room on autopilot, lighting more little lanterns, grabbing towels and a basket of small vials, and who knows what else. The water has me transfixed. I long to dive in and scrub my skin until it's red and raw.

"Shall I wash your hair for you?" she asks.

Heat floods my cheeks.

"I, uh...I think I can handle it myself," I say gently, trying not to offend her. For all I know, that's common here, but it sure as heck isn't where I'm from. At the salon? Sure. Naked, in a tub? Nope. "I'd like to be alone. If that's all right."

Karin nods, replacing a vial she'd pulled from the basket. "There's a robe on the shelf." She points to the dark wood piece near a matching bench. "I'll lay out some clean clothes for you in the other room."

"Thank you. Really." I lay on the sugar, as Grandma used to say. "I appreciate it."

"It's no problem at all." Her sweet smile and gentle pat on my arm as she departs mirror the kindness of her words.

Alone in the steaming water, I hug my knees to my chest, trying to hold in the sobs that threaten to overtake me. Without distractions, all my thoughts return to May. Have they kept her asleep? Is she hurt? Not knowing eats away at me. Those worries terrify me more than the dark stains on my clothes, even more than the blood matted in my braid.

I choke down a sniffle and eye the vials sparkling in the lamplight.

Nothing a good hot shower can't fix, Elise likes to say. I doubt she's right in this case, but it can't hurt.

The door creaks open behind me. Karin returning?

"I'm all right," I say, not bothering to turn.

Something ruffles then hits the ground.

"What—" My words die as I turn to find Riven standing shirtless and barefoot within the room. Already his hands work on the buttons and ties of his pants.

I cough, nearly choking on air. My arms squeeze tight over my chest as I slide down in the water. Its heat is nothing compared to that sinking down into my gut and between my legs.

"Y-you can't," I protest when I finally find my voice.

"There's space for two, and I'm filthier than you." The hint of a grin pulls at one corner of his mouth.

I turn, sloshing water near the sides of the tub as his thumbs hook into the waistband of his pants. "Surely there is somewhere else you can bathe."

"Of course, but I'd rather be here."

Skin enters my periphery, and I turn further away.

Naked. Naked. Naked. The word flashes like a neon sign in my head, consuming my every thought.

Water sloshes and the level in the tub rises to my shoulders.

"Oh, my God." Fire races up my back as I visualize him behind me, reclining in the water in all of his glory. "You just, you—"

His low chuckle does things to me that I can't even fathom. "Let me wash your back. Your hair."

I gasp as one finger traces a path along my shoulder and curls down my back into the water. "I can wash myself. Get out."

"Pity." He grabs my braid. "It's hard to clean hair when it gets like this. I would know."

The water nearly touches my nose as I hunch further over. "I'm quite capable."

"Oh, I have no doubt of that." He sighs and drops my hair back into the water. "You want me to leave?"

The way he phrases it...it feels like a trick, a test of some sort, but I can't puzzle it out. Maybe he truly isn't used to people who can lie.

"I want..." Damn him, I really don't want to be alone, not trapped here with my misery. "You can stay but—"

A gasp leaps from my lips as his arm hooks around my middle.

"Riven!" Impossibly, more heat settles between my legs, which I keep firmly closed.

His lips settle on my shoulder, planting little kisses down an arm that can't be entirely clean yet. "So shy."

Ridiculous man. Great distraction but— "Isn't there someone else you should be flirting with? Solona? Evelyn?"

He stiffens and not in a good way. Silence hangs thick and heavy in the air.

"You're mistaken." The chill in his voice cools even the bathwater. "Solona is my advisor, almost like a mother to me." His voice dips low, almost a whisper. "And Evelyn...she was my mother."

Shit. I haven't just stepped in it—I've jumped in headfirst.

His mother. She *was* his mother. I don't have to ask to know she's dead. I couldn't have screwed that up harder if I'd tried. Now would be a great time to vanish through the floor.

I half turn in the tub, just enough to see the pain etched on Riven's face. My chest constricts. I know the impact of an absent mother on a person's life, that emptiness the rest of life struggles to fill. For the first time, I pity him, though I don't know how long it's been or how exactly that loss affects him.

"I'm so sorry." I turn further, stretching until my fingertips trace wet lines in the dirt and blood on his face. "I had no idea."

"I know. It was a long time ago." But shadows still linger in his eyes, even as his hand traces a pattern on my side in return. His arm unwinds from around me.

Unwilling to glimpse *that* view as he rises from the water, I spin around.

I hug my knees, regret sloshing within me worse than the water in the tub. I'd scolded him, but I hadn't meant to hurt him in the process, especially not over his mother. Had she been kind? Beloved? Everything pointed to that, which only made the pain sharper. I remember little of my mother, not enough to know whether she had been loving toward me before she left us, but the leaving tells me all I need to know. Dad refused to talk about it for a long time, and when he finally did, he simply said she wasn't ready to be a wife and mother. She'd wanted her freedom. She'd taken it and never looked back.

I inhale a sharp breath as Riven returns to the tub.

The steaming water embraces me as he settles in once more. His return brings a flush that burns away my painful memories. He tugs my hair. A moment later, the ribbon securing my braid hangs over the edge of the tub, sopping wet. Citrus perfumes the air as he rubs soap into the mangled mess.

"Lean back," he says.

"This is a bad idea."

"Just a bath. I'll keep my hands...well, not to myself." A deep rumble of laughter rolls through the air.

Such a bad idea.

I sink further beneath the water and tip my head back to the fae behind me.

He lathers in the suds, inching up the length of my hair. "Further."

I bite my lip, giving in to the hand that tilts my shoulders back until they touch the water, and my head floats just above the surface. Hooded eyes flick to my arms, covering my breasts, barely exposed above the water's surface. Riven's hands fall still in my hair.

"Aren't you supposed to be washing something?" I tease.

The water ripples with laughter, but he resumes his activity. Long fingers massage my scalp as he works the mess free.

I dip my head, rinsing out the suds.

"Let me return the favor." My words are slow, thick, like cool syrup. I turn toward him in the tub and pull my wet locks over my shoulders, shielding my chest as best I can. Too bad it likes to float.

My breath catches in my throat at the greedy gaze he aims my way.

When he finally turns, giving me his scarred back, I can breathe again. Unable to help myself, I trace a curved scar down one shoulder with one finger.

Oh, to know the stories his body tells.

"The soap?" My voice wobbles.

He leans out of the tub, giving a generous view of his firm, shapely ass, to grab the vial. Riven's head floats on the water above my lap as I massage in the soap, scrubbing his hair clean as he did for me.

His eyes close under my ministrations, leaving his face peaceful in a way I've never seen.

I ease my hands under his neck, around his shoulders, and over the top of his chest, soothing away the day's worries and clouding the water with soap and other things I try to forget. Even my own anxiety has eased in the cooling water.

"I wish I knew your thoughts," he says.

When did he open his eyes?

"Do you?" I raise my eyebrows at him, refusing to relinquish even a hint via my words, though my hands as they trail down his chest tell their own tale.

"Would you like to know mine?"

"Yes."

Riven flips over onto his knees. Water splashes in a torrent over the side. Just as quickly, he pulls me to him. My chest crashes against his, wet, slick, and warm. My knees press against the stony bottom as I hover over his lap. An unmistakable hardness brushes my stomach.

"Riven," I gasp.

"Please." Those long fingers slide down my back to cup my bottom.

"It's not... We can't... I..." Broken thoughts spill from my lips as I squirm against him.

The movement earns me a low groan of pleasure and a look that nearly has me saying yes. It's not that I don't want him. Hell, I've never wanted anyone like this. But with all that happened today...

Riven's arms loosen and fall away. A gentle push sends us sliding to opposite sides of the tub.

All at once, I'm cold. I miss his warmth, his touch.

He could be a god, the way he looks reclined in the tub. Lantern light glimmers off his wet hair and skin. Even the way his head lolls back against the rim as he stares up toward the ceiling—or lack thereof—is a graceful work of art. I, on the other hand, probably look like a drowned rat.

An apology forms on the tip of my tongue, but I swallow it down. I have nothing to apologize for. He'd get what he wanted. Sooner or later.

What's a few minutes of pleasure with someone you're attracted to? My fingertips dig into my arms. *He did save your life today.* It's an inner war, one I've fought more in the last two days than in many months.

But May is still out there.

Riven groans and climbs from the tub, giving me a view that dries my throat.

Dear God. I blink, trying to erase the image without success.

He pulls a robe around himself before saying, "They should have brought food by now, and I'm sure you're hungry."

Riven holds out a hand to me, offering aid from the tub.

But standing up now would give him the same view he'd given me. My eyes flick to the pile of robes and towels then back again.

A tight grin tugs at the corner of his lips. "It was worth a try."

I can't help but roll my eyes. Ridiculous man.

He grabs a clean, dry robe of deep green and holds it open for me. Like a gentleman, he averts his gaze. "I won't watch, though I'll admit wanting to."

I slip from the tub into the waiting embrace of the robe. It wicks away the water like nothing I've ever used and cocoons me in soft warmth. You'd think the things are heated, but I don't see a fire.

Riven pulls me into a firm hug, only the robes between us.

"Just a moment," he says when I squirm against him. The softness in his voice, the need, affects something in me.

And if I'm honest with myself, I need this too, especially after the horrible events of the evening. Lingering in his arms, the place I longed to be for so long, does more to cleanse me than water ever could.

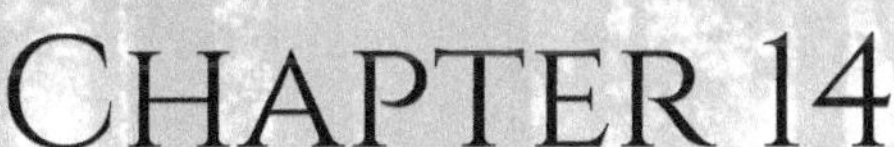

CHAPTER 14

E VENTUALLY, WHEN I'VE SOAKED up enough of Riven's comforting strength, we make our way into the main room. His presence is more soothing than a spa day, and that's saying a lot.

But my peace is short-lived.

My legs lock up when a woman rises from the sofa in the center of the room.

She might as well have walked straight out of a storybook. Black hair haloes a regal head. A long, blue dress hugs her lean form. Its color is a perfect complement to her dark hands clasped in front of her. The delicate pose evokes the image of a fairytale princess.

Or a fae queen...

My heart constricts before blazing with jealousy.

"Ah, thank you for coming so late," Riven says.

Her eyebrows rise as she looks between the two of us, a hint of mirth playing about her features. She waves one manicured hand through the air. "That's no trouble, though you may want to introduce us before the dear girl gets the wrong idea."

My back straightens as she strides my way. My nails dig into the edge of my sleeve. It's not fear of the woman herself. She seems the type that wouldn't hurt a fly. But rather, I fear her connection to the man I'd just shared a bath with. And what does she imagine we'd done in there? Heat blazes across my cheeks.

Riven wraps an arm around me, pulling me close. "Lia, this is Solona, my advisor and Minister of Economy. Solona, this is Lia."

Solona holds out a slim hand to me in an oddly human gesture. "It's nice to meet you at last."

I take it. Her other hand wraps around our joined ones, accompanied by a motherly smile that softens her features. His advisor. That's right. Like a mother to him, he said. Not a lover.

"Though I should admonish him for his indiscretion and parading you about, in a robe no less," she chides him as if he's a child.

Yeah, about that... My eyes lock on the various articles of clothing that someone, likely Karin, laid out across a nearby chaise lounge. "Please excuse me. I'm going to change."

Hiding in the bedroom and never coming out sounds like a great idea. Weariness begs me to slide under the sheets, tuck my knees against my chest, and fade into blissful sleep. But Riven won't be waiting for me there anymore. He's here. And sleeping my time away won't ease my failures, not this time.

Muffled voices from the other room win the battle for my attention. I smooth a hand down the simple, navy dress and return to the sitting room.

"—when I go there tomorrow," Riven is saying.

"Don't you mean when *we* go there tomorrow?" I interject, walking up behind Riven where he sits on one of the couches with his arms on his knees.

Sugar and spice tease my senses. Platters of food dot the coffee table across from him. The colorful array of food has my mouth watering in an instant.

A quick grimace crosses his features. "It's not safe. If anything were to happen to you..."

I cross my arms. "You're not leaving me behind again. How'd that work out for you last time?"

He frowns. "Not well. But if you'd only listened—"

"This is my sister we're talking about! She's out there alone and in the hands of... What did you call them, Unseelie? The Wild Tribes?"

"The Wild Tribes *are* Unseelie."

I roll my eyes. Not important. "Give me one good reason why I can't come with you."

He doesn't blink before the response spills from his mouth. "Because Sigurd, or someone else, could shift you away. Or you could be injured. Or who knows what else."

"Well, we already did the injured thing, and Sigurd had the chance to shift me away and didn't. Actually, he helped me."

Every inch of him goes deathly still. Even Solona straightens at my words.

"What do you mean?" His voice is low, dangerous.

I drop my arms. The sudden pressure in the room urges me down onto the chair across from Solona. "His eagle led me to the clearing where the Unseelie were."

Riven groans and holds his head in his hands.

Solona's hand trails to her cheek, a finger running along her jaw as her brows furrow. "Perhaps he genuinely wants to help us?"

Ever so slowly, he raises his head, a scowl etched across his face. "Or he was trying to get Lia captured or worse."

That grim proclamation has me stirring in my seat. "Why? He doesn't know me."

"You need to tell her, Rivenean." Solona casts him a meaningful look before rising to her feet. "I will see you tomorrow. Good night, Lia." She nods in my direction before making her way around the sofa and out of the room without a backward glance.

Riven plucks a piece of fruit from the table. It crunches like a ripe apple, despite its purple appearance. The juice glistens on his lips, but he refuses to meet my steady stare until the doors close behind Solona with a woody thump.

I expect him to explain, but instead, he attends the fruit, taking another juicy bite.

Ugh, that fruit, whatever it is, looks good. The man eating it isn't bad either. My stomach rumbles, though hunger isn't the only thing twisting in my belly. "Tell me what?"

"Come sit with me, eat something"—he gestures to the table, fruit still in his hand—"and I'll tell you." His eyes are still downcast, staring at nothing across the room. All the heat and fire is gone from his voice.

What happened to the arrogant king I met last night? I snag a fruit twin to Riven's and sit on the cushion next to him with my bare feet curled up on the cushion. Sticky sweetness with a hint of spice dances across my tongue. I wiggle the orb with its missing bite in the air between us.

"Our world is entangled with yours and has become dependent on it," Riven begins as if settling in for a long tale. "Long, long ago, they were separate, and each existed on its own. But one day that changed, and the doors, like the one you came through, opened up, linking our worlds together. Over time, our world became dependent on yours, and similarly, our people became dependent on humans to sustain our magic."

Does he know his description makes the fae sound like leeches? I take another bite and listen as he continues.

"Human spirits are different than ours and enliven our magic. Without the presence of humans, our magic grows stale and weakens over time. Having a human with the gift reside with us increases our magic."

A gifted human. Like me.

"If just my presence here helps, then there was no need for a certain... element of our bargain," I state frankly.

"It's not enough just to want you?"

I swallow, hard. It's so tempting to throw the fruit at his smirking face.

"Anyhow, the closer the bond between fae and human, the stronger the effect. If you accept my mark, it will further strengthen my magic and, since I lead my people, all of them as well."

I flush and look away. But a different thought nags at the back of my mind. "Is that why they want May? Because she's a human and will help their magic?"

"Perhaps. Though she's so young, her presence will not improve their magic much, but they may not know that."

"They'd risk going to the human world"—*what did he call it?*—"fading, to get her?"

His gaze darts away then back to me. "Those who are desperate will do anything. And the Unseelie... Yes, for a human, they would risk that and much more."

"You risked yourself then. For me?" That very first night, the first time he met me, he'd taken me home from the circle of stones, tucked me safely away on the porch of our cabin.

Some emotion I can't name races across his features. "You wouldn't come with me, and leaving you there felt..." He seems to taste words on his tongue, searching for the right one. For truth? "Wrong," he says at length.

His vulnerability draws me like a magnet. I scoot closer until my leg barely touches his.

Riven brushes a strand of hair behind my ear, causing a little shiver to race across my skin. "Do you remember what I told you when you stepped into Faery with me?"

I give myself a little shake, trying to clear my racing thoughts. Faery. He had said something, words that caused me to ache amidst so much beauty. "It's dying? But it's so beautiful here."

A sad smile pulls at his lips. "I'm glad you like it. But yes, Lia, the Court of the Forest is dying. Our magic has been fading. Dangerously so." He sets the fruit aside and wipes his hand on a fine cloth napkin. What a proper gentleman. "The last of our humans passed recently. They were old, their lives run through. Their spark gave us little power, yet they were beloved all the same. It's been many years since a young human has come here—their gift bright and bold. And...I've never marked one."

A bite of fruit lodges in my throat before I choke it down. Never marked a human. Of all the things I expected, a fae virginity discussion was not it.

"The Unseelie, Sigurd...none of them should be able to get here without me noticing. I should be able to protect my people. But with our magic fading, I haven't been able to. It's taken all I have and it's not enough. I didn't have the slightest hope"—he takes my hand in his—"until recently."

The sorrow in his eyes twists my heart, the dull ache sliding through me in a slow wave. "Because I'm here."

"That's why I can't let anything happen to you. If we lose you, if *I* lose you, so soon..." He shakes his head, giving my hand a squeeze. "Our fate would be bleak. But with you here, even for a little while, we have a chance."

The sweet fruit turns sour in my mouth, and I jerk away. "I get it. You want me for the magic."

Should have known. Why would someone who knew all my broken parts want me?

The fruit core clunks to the table. I shove to my feet. That's why he'd been so adamant in pursuing me. All those times he begged me to come, said I could save his people... It was all for the sake of his magic, not really for me.

"Yes." The word carves a groove in my heart.

My shoulders hunch around the blow as I turn away from him.

A calloused hand wraps around my wrist. His light tug asks me to stay. A plea but not a demand. "At first, when I met you all those months ago, that was all I wanted. You were lovely, gifted, but hurting. I could take you away from that pain and bring you here to help us. It seemed perfect at the time, if you'd wanted to come. But then I truly got to know you, and the magic is not all I want anymore."

I suck in a breath. *He can't lie. He can't lie.* I want to believe it. So, so much. My head whips around, meeting the sad green eyes staring up at me.

"Give me a chance?" he asks. "Give us all a chance? Not just because we made a bargain, but because you give us life. In more ways than one."

CHAPTER 15

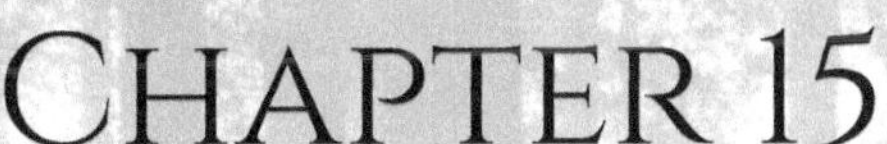

R UMPLED SHEETS ARE ALL that share the bed with me when I
wake. Bright morning light slants across the room. Blue sky
and puffy clouds linger beyond the foliage. The faint scent of
honeysuckle still clings to the bedding, mixing with the leafy smell
that permeates Riven's rooms. He hadn't touched me after our
talk, nor asked for a kiss, but I'd shared his bed without argument,
and somehow, his presence had lulled me into a mostly peaceful
sleep.

I stretch, reveling in the beauty around me until reality catches
me in a stranglehold.

May is still out there. Held hostage by the Unseelie because I'd
been so foolish as to interrupt her rescue and not skilled enough
to save her myself.

Of course I hadn't. What was I even thinking? The truth—I
wasn't thinking at all. I had to save her. Had to prove I could do it
and could erase my mistake of endangering her once again.

Still, I failed. Every. Damn. Time.

The weight of my failures drags like an anchor behind me as I
dress for the day.

No sooner have I slid into the blue dress from the night before
than the main door opens, and two fae walk in. Karin, I almost
expect, but the blond woman who enters with her is a surprise, as
is the matching tray of food she carries, so at odds with the guard
uniform cloaking her body.

"Good morning," I call.

Both of their countenances brighten at my words. That face. It hits me all at once. "You were at the battle. I saw you cut down an Unseelie."

Her eyes widen, softening the masculine tint to her features. "You remember."

Wearing guard clothes and with no real chest to speak of, she had blended right in with the men, unlike the other women in the guard who had a more feminine shape.

"That battle would be a hard thing to forget." I try my best to smile. Fail.

"I'm Sylvie." She sets her tray on the coffee table next to Karin's. "Riven asked me to keep you company since he's busy."

Busy. I twist my hands behind me. No wonder he was gone this morning. Curiosity gnaws at me, but I hold my tongue.

Karin steps back and glances between the two of us. "Do you need anything else?"

"Would you like to eat with us? You could share mine." I wave a hand at the tray she's set down before me.

Karin's smile falters, and her shoulders straighten. I flick my gaze to Sylvie, but she's still smiling, expression unchanged.

"I've already eaten, my lady." Karin twists one hand in her dress.

My lady. I nearly snort, but she's so serious it would be inappropriate.

"Come sit and chat with us then," Sylvie offers, still smiling. "Lia would like you to stay if you have time."

Karin hesitates then replies, "All right. If it's not a bother, I'll stay."

Thank you, Sylvie. If I made some error—probably—she smoothed it out.

The conversation is light and trivial, likely just to keep my mind occupied and lift my spirits. It's everything I need. A few times, the companionship and friendly meal remind me so much of home that tears sting the corners of my eyes and the food loses its flavor. But then, Sylvie says something funny, and my worry for May, Dad, and Elise slips ever so slightly back into the depths of my heart and mind. By the time our plates are almost empty, Sylvie has both Karin and me laughing about a mishap one of the guards had on his horse a few days ago.

"I'm going to the stables if you'd like to join me," Sylvie offers.

Oh? I stiffen. "I thought we'd be leaving today? To fix the wards and search for my sister."

"We are but not until this evening."

I bite my lip, holding in my frustration. Just sitting around here isn't helping.

Karin busies herself stacking plates and trays. "I have things to attend to. I'll take these to the kitchens on my way."

I reach to help, but she waves me off with a click of her tongue.

"Many members of the guard have already been dispatched to search for your sister." Sylvie reads me like a book. "We've been busier than we've been in years planning, moving supplies, relocating horses." She shakes her head. "Preparing to work with another court is...new."

Breathe, Lia. They're trying. I nod to her, acknowledging the words meant to comfort and soothe. Wasn't her fault they didn't help much.

The stables are well kept and large, with space enough for many horses under the pointed wooden roofs. Open, grassy fields for the horses to run in surround the buildings outside the castle proper.

We find Galen brushing down a horse. His words to the mare are a language I don't recognize. He slips her a treat. The barest hint of a smile tries to stretch my lips. Guard and stable master or just an animal lover?

Sylvie offers our help with the horses. My eyes widen as Galen leads Stella over for us to brush.

"How'd she get back so soon?" A thread of panic rushes through me. I swear, if I missed a whole day somewhere—

"Ambrose ordered the best shifters to bring them back here late last night," Sylvie responds. "It takes significant effort, moving something so large, but it saved much time." As if on cue, she yawns, hiding the involuntary action and twist of a half-smile with her hand.

"Will she be coming with us to..." I trail off, searching for the name.

"Arbrean," Galen finishes for me. "No, she'll stay here. They have their own stables, and we'll use those horses first before we consider moving our own there. It's far and would take more magic than we can spare right now."

"Ah, and you both just like horses?" I raise my eyebrows.

He shifts from foot to foot and looks away. Sylvie stifles a giggle, shifting behind Stella's head as Galen looks back in our direction.

"One of our responsibilities as Riven's elite guard is seeing to our own horses." It's impossible to miss the hint of pride in his words. "We look after Riven's as well, and now yours."

Mine. My cheeks heat. As if I'm someone important. Though after what Riven said last night, I suppose maybe I am.

Stella flicks her tail merrily as I slide the brush down her side.

"And I might just like the horses," Galen adds.

Sylvie mimics his words just out of his sight. It's impossible to miss the happy smile on her face as she mouths them, one she's donned since the stables came into view.

"Do you like being members of Riven's guard?" Riven's face flashes through my mind, not the arrogant Forest King from the throne room, but the soft male I'd known long before I came here.

"Oh yes, it's a huge honor, especially since we've made it into his elite guard now," Sylvie interjects before walking around to Stella's other side.

Galen follows her with his eyes, his lips quirking up in one corner.

As we work, Sylvie's gaze periodically slides over to Galen when he isn't looking. A secret truth lingers unspoken in the air that I likely wasn't meant to notice—a hint of shared longing that they both pretend to be oblivious to.

The sun hangs high in the sky when Sylvie and I walk back toward the palace city of Virideria, Galen in tow. Warm air wraps around us, a balm to the chilly ache still hollowing me out inside.

"We can eat in the main hall if you'd like," Galen says. "It's usually busy at this hour, but there's a lot of space, so we should be able to find a table."

His words call to mind the night I arrived, only two nights ago, but it could have been a month for all that had happened. My entrance into the swarm of fae was uncomfortable at the very best. Even now, quizzical glances aim my way by any fae we pass.

"Or," Galen starts again, maybe sensing the weight of my silence, "there's a nice courtyard not too far from the kitchens. It's usually quiet."

"The courtyard sounds great." Whatever being Riven's consort entails, other than the obvious, I'm not ready to face it today.

Sylvie takes me to wash up while Galen gathers lunch for all of us. The courtyard is as quiet and serene as Galen described. Distant noise from the nearby rooms and halls drifts in the background, but it's so much better than the constant din of activity and conversation inside.

The space itself holds a riot of plant life, interwoven with stone pathways, little benches, and sitting areas. A few fountains gurgle. The whole area reminds me of a botanical garden. In a castle literally teeming with life, this place still impresses.

For a moment, I can almost forget where I am.

Almost.

"I haven't seen many children around here," I say. Their absence might have gone unnoticed if not for the constant simmer of worry that's taken up residence within me. My mind paints May everywhere: trailing her hands in the water of the fountain, chasing the iridescent creature resembling a large butterfly, sniffing the bright pink blossoms the size of a dinner plate. Each one is a beautiful, torturous reminder of her absence.

"Children are very rare for fae," Sylvie says. "Couples often try for years without much success, so every child is highly valued and protected."

A familiar voice interrupts our discussion. "There you are."

Solona strides out of the shadowed walkway surrounding the courtyard. She's wearing a long dress of dark green that swishes upon the stones of the pathway. A gold headband binds her mahogany hair.

"Minister Solona," both Sylvie and Galen say, almost in unison. They rise to their feet and dip a small bow in her direction.

"It's good to see you both," she says.

Without thinking, I follow suit.

Solona clicks her tongue. "Now, now, our Lady of the Forest should not bow."

My cheeks heat as I raise my head, swallowing down the tightness in my throat. Okay, no bowing.

"That's right, chin up," she says. "Now, I have a gift for you, one that should help."

She clasps a small box of polished dark wood inlaid with intricate, pale designs that shimmer in the sunlight.

Solona holds the box out in my direction. "Please take it."

CHAPTER 16

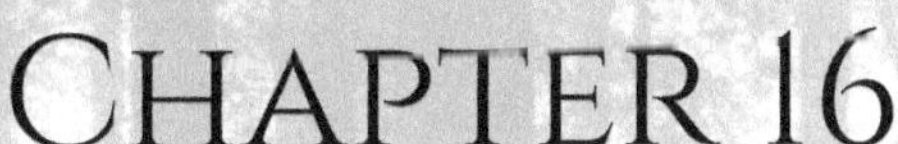

T HE SMOOTH WOOD IS cool against my skin. Sylvie and Galen scoot closer, one hovering over either shoulder as I tilt it this way and that. Galen's body, tall like most of the fae, casts a shadow over one corner. Sylvie inches herself higher, possibly rising on her toes. Though a fae, she's only about an inch or so taller than my average human height.

"Thank you," I say. "It's beautiful, but what does it do?"

Solona chuckles. "The gift is within the box, not the box itself. Open it."

Of course. I stifle a groan of embarrassment. But this is Faery, so who knows what's valuable and what's not.

My thumb finds the seam of the lid, sliding it up to reveal a golden bracelet sparkling with small green stones of mixed shades—emeralds, possibly, and some darker stones. My breath catches. Jewelry like this would be worth hundreds, if not thousands, back home.

"It's"—*stunning, breathtaking*— "too much."

"Nonsense," Solona replies, waving her hand in the air. "Plus, when you wear this, no one can shift you away."

My brows rise as I peer at her over the box lid.

"I've been looking for it all morning. With this, you can join Riven without being in quite so much danger of being stolen away."

My reservations about accepting the gift evaporate into the early afternoon air. I can go with him and search for May. Surely he can't object now.

"That's brilliant." Sylvie echoes my thoughts. "I didn't know such a thing existed."

"Neither did I." Galen scratches his chin in a way that reminds me of Ambrose.

"It's the only one of its kind, at least that we have. And it only works on humans. But in this case—"

"It's perfect," I blurt. "Thank you so much, really."

"May I?" Solona nods toward the box. In a moment, she has the bracelet clasped around my wrist. Its stones glitter in the light. "You'll have to take it off for Riven to take you to Arbrean, but make sure you put it right back on." She pats my wrist in emphasis.

Joy bubbles up, stretching my hesitant smile into a broad one. "I will, this is—"

Voices from the walkway surrounding the courtyard interrupt my thoughts.

"A ball!" a woman screeches in delight.

My head whips to the left, catching sight of two elaborately dressed fae women strolling arm in arm. Even their hair, one brown and one blond, is curled and pinned atop their heads in intricate up-dos, strung through with leaves and flowers. Their high giggles set my nerves on edge.

"And with the Court of Air, can you believe it?" the brunette squeals.

My smile dies. Teeth grind together in my mouth as my vision paints red.

"A ball. That's what Riven's been occupied with today?" I can't mute the venom in my voice or the way it grows shrill. Fingernails bite painfully into my palms as I clench my fists. The beautiful bracelet is forgotten in an instant. "My sister's out there, and he's—"

"Hush," Solona says.

My teeth rattle as I snap them closed, staring daggers at her for her command. Sylvie and Galen scoot closer, Sylvie blocking the women from my view.

"Don't say another word and come with me." Solona reaches between them and grabs my fisted hand. She pulls me through the courtyard before I can form the biting retort inching its way to the surface.

A ball. A freaking ball! Anger burns so hot through my veins I might catch on fire. Not like they didn't just have one, what, two days ago?

My two guards follow as we practically jog from the courtyard, the remnants of lunch forgotten. After two turns and a trot down a short hallway, Solona throws open a door and pulls me inside. Galen closes it behind him, securing us all in a cramped room resembling a large supply closet. A scoff catches in my throat. Even the graceful fae have rooms for storing all the stuff they can't find a place for. One high window on the far side provides the only light filtering into the dim and dusty space.

I cross my arms as she releases me. What possible explanation can she have for that nonsense in the courtyard? Treating me like a queen one moment and a scolded child the next.

She glances at the door then me. "There are bigger concerns than just your missing sister."

Her words hit me like a punch to the stomach, followed by a slap to the face. Even Galen winces. I can't do anything but gape.

"What did Riven tell you last night?" She pins me with her fierce gaze.

My fists clench and unclench as I try to reign in the fury about to spew forth like a volcano.

"The magic is fading because there haven't been many humans around. He's grown weak. You all have."

Not that you'd know it from her grip. My arm still stings.

"Anything else?" she asks.

"My being here helps." A different sort of fire sparks to life when I consider his words about never having marked a human, but I'm so not bringing that up right now. "Yeah, that was the gist of it."

"That boy." Her eyes flare with a golden glow. Sylvie and Galen share a look as Solona shakes her head and the glow fades.

"That's not true?" I ask.

"Of course it is. We cannot lie, but it's deeper than that. Our waning magic has made his position weak. He has no heir, Lia. There is no direct line of succession. Some of the nobility are honest and good, but others scheme, hoping to inherit the magic if Riven were to fall. His bravado has been his strength in a time of great weakness, but even that will run out." Her tone is dire, sharp, as she relates the details of their predicament. "This ball you sneer at is an opportunity for him to solidify his position and could help us improve relations with the Court of the Air. They were our strongest ally once, but relations have been poor at best throughout Riven's reign."

I bite my lip, some of my anger dying away. So much is going on that I don't know about or understand.

Solona lays a hand on my arm. "Riven will do everything he can to find your sister. He is worried for her and did not expect his rescue to fail, but you have to understand how many burdens are on his plate. He is responsible for all of us, and the safety of the Court of the Forest balances on a knife's edge. Your stay here can change everything for us, help save us all, and we'll do what we can to repay that favor. But you must be patient."

It's the third time in fewer days that I've heard how dire their situation is, yet all I can think about is May and my need to protect her and get her home safely. A deep, steadying breath fills my lungs as I meet Solona's stern gaze.

"I understand. I do, and I'll do whatever I can to help." I glance at Sylvie and Galen with their equally serious expressions. "For Riven and for all of you."

Solona's features soften back to their normal, pleasant expression. The stiff set of her jaw relaxes as her lips turn up into a soft smile. Just as quickly, the tension between us fades into the dark recesses of the room.

"The ball was just announced, but already the people are ripe with excitement." Her smile brightens further, dark eyes turning wistful. "It's been sixty years since Riven's father died and relations between our courts broke down."

"So long, I had no id—" A chill runs down my spine. I step back as shock radiates through me. My heel catches on a box, and I wobble toward the pile behind me.

"Lia!" Sylvie catches me in her dainty but strong arms before I can tumble backward into the mess of stuff. But my legs won't support me, and I lean heavily on her.

Sixty years. Riven's father died sixty years ago.

My lunch turns leaden in my stomach.

"What's wrong? What happened?" Galen's at my other side, looking me over frantically for injuries.

My mouth opens and closes. Words are thick on my tongue and won't come out. When they finally croak to the surface, all that comes out is, "Sixty years?"

Sylvie and Galen freeze on either side of me as they stare at one another. Solona's eyes widen. Her head bobs ever so slowly up and down. The dawning realization threatens to crush me.

My legs find their strength again. Sylvie lets me go and fiddles with the end of her ponytail. Galen shifts uncomfortably on his feet.

A question screams in my mind to be asked, but I dread it. Everything in me rallies against it, but I have to know. "How old is Riven?"

Heavy silence hangs between us all.

Answer me. Someone.

Sylvie's face is etched with pity. Galen fidgets and looks away. I find Solona, who looks at me as if watching a young child who is trying to learn their alphabet and getting half of the letters wrong.

"Eighty-two. Still very young for a king," she adds, as if somehow that helps.

Maybe it does. If you're a fae.

All I can see is the ground beneath my feet. Eighty-two. So old. Obviously not in fae years, but it is for humans. For many of us, it's a lifetime. And Solona called him young.

I want to laugh, to cry. Hysteria burns up my throat and sends my legs shaking again.

"We age like humans in the beginning," Sylvie begins. She's trying to help, to explain the concepts my mind struggles to absorb. "But once we reach maturity, and our magic blooms, the aging process slows rapidly for us. The stronger our magic, the slower we age."

The extra information doesn't help the confusing thoughts running through my head. I kissed someone more than three times my own age. Lusted after him. Shared a bed and tub with him. A male who I would have sworn just a minute ago was in his late twenties, early thirties at the most.

A gentle hand rests on my shoulder. I force myself to look up at Solona.

Pity shines in her eyes now too. "I'm sorry I upset you. It was not my intention."

A small laugh slips out. "It's...a surprise."

Understatement of the year.

What can I possibly say when I see him again? *I promised to be your consort, but damn, you're freaking old, and that would have been so helpful to know before we made that little bargain.*

Hell, here I've been making out with a guy old enough to be my grandfather. Another humorless laugh bursts free.

Great. Just great.

CHAPTER 17

S HIFTING, I LEARN, IS not a simple thing. While one can poten-
tially shift anywhere, shifting to a random location is very
taxing. Further, the greater the distance, the more energy it takes.
Honing oneself to a particular location reduces the effort, as does
the use of enchanted spaces called honing points. Sylvie tries ex-
plaining how exactly they hone themselves and the complicated,
many months, process of creating a honing point, but my head
starts to throb after just a few minutes. The intricacies of fae magic
are better left to my imagination—for now.

One point is clear, not every fae can shift, even with the use
of honing points. And then there are the wards, a whole different
mess of fae magic.

Though Riven's wards have weakened significantly with their
failing magic, they're still enough to prevent some fae from other
courts from shifting through them and make it much more taxing
for the strongest of them like Sigurd. So, members of the Court
of Air will meet us at the border and travel the traditional way to
Arbrean. Walking through, apparently, is easy now that the wards
are weak.

Between Riven and Sigurd's borders lays a narrow strip of land
that still belongs to the Wild Tribes of the Unseelie. Though *belongs* might not be the best word where that land is concerned.
Based on Riven's description, it's more of a neutral zone than
anything else. The bulk of Wild Tribe land lies further east of the
territories of Forest and Air.

Much of his personal guard, key staff members and advisors, and some of the nobility who had been in the throne room that first day—my absolute *favorite* people—will join us in Arbrean. Best to greet visitors with a large host.

"What's wrong?" Riven's soft caress stirs up butterflies within me. The good kind and the awkward ones that can't seem to figure out which way to go with their injured wings.

I haven't told him what I learned this afternoon, not about the magic or that disastrous revelation in the closet. I'm not really sure what to make of any of it.

I stare at his smooth skin, the delicate point of his ears through his thick hair, and the strong planes of his face. He doesn't look old. Not at all. But fae can't lie. If they could, they certainly would have lied to me earlier today, to calm my near hysteria if nothing else.

Ambrose pokes his head into the bedroom where we stand. "I'm shifting Karin to Arbrean."

The sudden comment causes me to jolt and stiffen.

Riven drops his hand from my cheek.

Perfect timing, Ambrose. A soft sigh slips from my lips as I relax. At least his interruption gives me more time to think.

"Where do you want to meet before we go to the border?" Ambrose continues.

"The honing point in the outer yard of Arbrean. Make sure the horses and supplies are ready to go."

"They will be. See you soon." Ambrose winks at me before retreating from the room.

Karin has already gathered a trunk of clothing and supplies they'd be taking there for Riven and me.

"Shouldn't we go as well?" I'm eager to avoid the conversation we started only moments ago.

"Repairing the wards will take some time, even with Sigurd's help. I thought we might have a moment alone together." His voice turns silken and seductive.

Heat blazes to my cheeks. I wring my hands together in front of me, fingers slipping over the green stones around my wrist.

Riven's brows draw together as he reaches out to finger the bracelet.

"Solona gave it to me. It's to prevent anyone from shifting me away so that I can come with you to the border."

He drops his hand. "So she was able to find it after all. That's quite the treasure. But taking you to the border—" His words break off at my scowl.

"Don't leave me behind again. I know you're worried, that the territory needs me, Solona made that crystal clear, but please..."

His chest heaves in a sigh. "You can come to the border."

My heart leaps. Finally!

"But," he adds in a hurry, "if things go wrong or Sigurd does even the slightest thing suspicious..."

One sign of trouble, and he'll send me back to safety.

Fine. Baby steps. I'll take it.

His fingers trail fire in their wake as they drift up my arm. His head dips toward mine, sending my heart thundering despite the thick cord of unease, marked with the number eighty-two, coiled around it.

I step back.

"Lia?" His brows wrinkle as his head cocks to the side.

I can't meet this gaze. Instead, my attention flitters around the room, searching desperately for an excuse, an escape.

"Something happened," he says. This time, he pulls away from me. A flash of pain mars his features before he turns his back to me.

Shoot. This isn't what I wanted. "I..."

Where do I even start?

I cross the space between us and wrap my hands around the rich green cloth of his sleeve. "I learned something today. And I just need a little time to digest it."

The corner of his mouth quirks up. "That sounds mysterious."

I try to smile but fail. "Fae age differently than humans."

The smirk vanishes.

"And you're...much older than me." I cringe as the words spill out, but I strengthen my grip, rubbing my thumb across the fabric.

"Ah." The muscles in his arm relax under my touch. "Is that so abhorrent to you?"

No? Maybe? I don't know. I search for the right thing to say and come up empty.

"I just...need some time." I can't even look at him as I say it, can't bear to see the disappointment and hurt there.

Silence stretches until I just can't take it anymore. Hesitantly, I peek at his expression. His jaw shifts to the side. His lips are pulled thin as he stares at nothing across the room.

I nearly groan. It's worse than I thought.

He sighs and pulls away. "Let's go to Arbrean."

The words strike like a dagger, even if they aren't meant to. Why does it hurt so much? Why?

I undo the clasp of the bracelet and hold the coiled length in one hand. The other, I stretch out to take the open hand Riven offers, though he still won't quite look at me. No sooner do our hands touch than the world around us bends and warps. My hand digs into his as the magic wraps us in a thick blanket of air.

The old room melts away, and a new one builds back in its place.

This sitting room is similar to the one I've grown used to but slightly smaller with different trees comprising its walls and canopy. A large balcony wraps around the room on two sides, with a broad tree as the corner post. Even here, touches of autumn highlight the green leaves with splotches of crimson and orange.

"Oh, you're here already." Karin stands off to one side of the room, unpacking items from a trunk. She brushes a stray hair back from her face and reaches in for another bundle.

"We are, but we'll both be heading to the border in just a few minutes," Riven responds. He drops my hand as if it burns, then says to me, "Take some time to change and refresh yourself. We'll leave as soon as you're ready."

He strides off into an adjoining room without another glance. I watch him go. The knot in my chest twists tighter with every step he takes away from me.

I've hurt the feelings of a fae king.

"I picked out something I thought you might like." Karin carries a bundle my way. A touch of color dusts her cheeks. "If you don't mind, that is."

The outfit Karin selected is a dress of dark green, accented with golden thread. Riven's colors. The bodice and sleeves hug tight to my body, supported underneath by a soft, snug layer resembling a sports bra. The skirt of the dress is cut in a high scallop at the front, revealing the fitted pants underneath. Knee-high boots with little accents of gold complete the look.

Karin clasps her hands in front of her when I emerge. "Well?"

I twirl. The back of the dress flutters out behind me.

"I love it." Understatement. It's abso-freaking-lutely awesome. Give me some pointed ears and I might just fit in. Her taste is spot on. I couldn't have picked out something better myself.

"Excellent, I've packed some other things for you as well." She tips her head toward a bag sitting in a nearby chair.

"Is he…" I angle my head to see around her, gazing in the direction of the assumed door to the bedroom.

She glances away, unease crinkling through the lines of her face. "I'm not sure."

My hands part the curtain of vine like a rock on the crest of a waterfall as I push the strands open and step into the adjoining space. Late afternoon light cascades across the room, highlighting the golden strands of Riven's hair where it's pulled back behind his head. Weapons are laid out across the bed, waiting to be strapped to his body. He's hunched forward on his knees as if the weight of the world rests on his back.

From what Solona said, it might.

His head lifts at my arrival, away from the arm guard he's just finished affixing to his outfit. Once again, he's dressed as the ferocious druidic warrior, ready for battle. Will it come to that?

I swallow the lump forming in my throat.

Yes, if he finds May, as I dearly hope, then battle will be inevitable.

"I'm ready whenever you are." I stretch out the edge of my skirts in a mock curtsey.

Despite my playful act, he frowns. "I'll be out in a few minutes."

I fiddle with the bracelet in my hand, the backpack slung over one shoulder, when Riven finally appears in the sitting room, wearing his full armor and weaponry. Karin's already left, off to deal with other chores as men and women of the court arrive and ball preparations begin.

"Let's go." The command is simple and cold, full of the strange tension that's formed between us.

Moments later, he shifts us outside amidst a throng of people and horses.

But the change of scenery isn't the only difference. The sad warrior is gone. The Riven who stands before me now is the one from the throne room. A wicked grin spreads across his face, his eyes twinkle with confidence and mischief, and his shoulders are squared and strong.

If I hadn't been with him moments ago, I'd have assumed he'd switched places with an arrogant, evil twin. And screw that guy. The few times we'd been together, he'd been such an ass.

"Ambrose, are we ready to move?" His voice thunders with authority and practiced ease.

Ambrose's broad grin mirrors Riven's as he joins us. Real or fake? Around them, the guard perk up, some marked in the gold colors of the elite and others marked in common green, confidence marking their own features.

Riven moves on from Ambrose, talking to another set of fae in the yard.

Pride glows in Ambrose's eyes as he watches his guard organize the final preparations. How long has he been their captain? A few rare strands of silver in his hair capture the sunlight, shimmering in its glow. A dash of fine lines accents his features. He's still strong and obviously more than capable of his role, but he must be well over a hundred years old. A relic.

"I hope you're not thinking I'm more ruggedly handsome than our young king." Ambrose turns to me and winks, chuckling all the while.

My cheeks flame as I drop my gaze to the ground. Shit, I guess I did look like I was checking him out. And I was, but not like that.

"That's not... I'm sorry." Gosh, no good way to recover on this one.

Blessedly, he wanders off to join Riven, leaving me to stew in my own embarrassment.

Forest circles the outer yard on the two sides not bordered by the palace-like city resembling a small Virideria. However, the trees here are not as dense and consist mostly of varieties of pine. Well, the ones I can distinguish. The air here holds a crispness that reminds me of the mountains, and sure enough, tall hills stick up on the horizon, their crests touched by low-hanging, gray clouds.

"I'll take that if you want." Galen's voice stirs me from my thoughts. His arm waits in the air between us as he motions for my pack.

"Oh, sure, thank you." The strap slides from my shoulder.

"It's no problem." He flings the pack over his shoulder with ease, sending the golden earring—a leaf—dangling from one ear swaying. "Ambrose said we're to...what's the phrase?" He taps a finger to his chin as his lips pull tight to one side.

"Stick to you like glue," Sylvie finishes for him, coming to stand beside her companion.

These two really know how to lift my spirits. Thank goodness for that. I look between them with a smile. For the first time since we shifted here, I don't feel like a flaming torch stuck into the ground.

A sharp whistle cuts through the cacophony of activity and sound. Fae rush around, spurred into action by the signal, leaving us an island of stillness. My toes bounce in my boots, ready to join the fray.

"Time to go," Galen says with a tight smile.

Riven and Ambrose join us. Together, we form a tight-knit group of five. Much as I hate Riven's kingly attitude, I don't balk when he takes my hand and gives it a little squeeze. It's probably meant to be reassuring, but having Ambrose on my other side, bracing me between, is much more comforting.

A moment later, the world bends and warps as we shift from the outer yard of Arbrean.

CHAPTER 18

THE WORLD THAT TAKES shape around us is nothing like the one we've left. Behind me, it is—yellowing grasses, colorful trees, life everywhere.

But I barely notice that, not with the host of fae standing just beyond a visible line on the ground. They're dressed in predominately grays and blues. Their neat rows, carriages, and men and women on horseback are formidable, but it's the land causing gooseflesh to break out over my skin.

Cracked earth, sparsely populated with dried grasses and shrubs, is dotted with twisted, mostly-dead trees whose barren branches hang toward the ground like boney claws. If someone told me the life had been literally sucked from them, I'd believe it. The hills beyond are no different, sporting little life but plentiful tales of misery. A winter without its biting cold came to this land and never left.

"I-it's dead," I say.

"The Shadow Lands. Home of the Unseelie." Ambrose doesn't take his eyes off the fae contingent.

"That's what happens when the magic of a land fades." Riven gives my hand a tight squeeze.

Blood ices in my veins. That could happen here. If their magic continues to fade, they could end up like the Unseelie, living in a barren wasteland.

A shiver wracks my body, and I fight the urge to hug myself.

Sigurd breaks away from his people and steps across the line onto Forest lands. Unlike Riven, he has not dressed for battle but rather wears a tailored navy coat over a silver-gray shirt and dark pants. Not a weapon can be seen on him. He's dressed to conquer the dance floor, not a host of Unseelie.

Electricity zips through the air. I twist to find more of Riven's people behind us, a host as formidable as the one we've come to greet.

Riven breaks from us without a word and strides to meet Sigurd between their respective peoples.

I fumbled with the bracelet, trying to re-clasp it to my wrist as the collective audience holds its breath. My heart thunders so loudly it'll be a miracle if no one hears it.

Silence stretches as they stare each other down, so thick I can almost feel it.

Finally, Riven breaks it.

"Welcome, Sigurd, King of Air. You and your company are welcome in my territory and in my city of Arbrean, where we will hold a ball in three days' time to commemorate this event." The words are stiff, too formal for the man I know.

Sigurd flashes a blinding grin before his features settle back into their continual smirk.

"A promise of peace while we are here? No violence toward each other until the human is recovered?" Sigurd extends his hand to Riven, an oddly human action.

Riven takes it, and though I can't quite see, I'd wager he shows an arrogant smirk of his own. "Agreed."

"It's a promise then."

Magic rolls off the two in a shimmering wave, passing through the assembled so that even I feel its pulse. Silence reigns once more, cut only by the distant sound of birds behind me. However, movement resumes as fae shift on their feet and loosen the tightness of their shoulders.

Danger has passed. For the moment.

"Some of my guards will escort your guests to the city," Riven says.

"And some of mine will aid your search while *I* fix your wards." Sigurd gestures to his right with a grand flourish.

An insult, though Riven doesn't flinch, still playing the arrogant king for his guests.

Sigurd's gesture draws my attention to the intricate pattern carved into the earth in groves and mounds not far from where we stand. Similar to the honing circles I'd seen but different. The nuances of it are indecipherable from here, but it has to be something similar—a source or tool of magic, something to do with the wards.

"Oh yes, I have something else as well." Sigurd glances past Riven and stares at me among the crowd.

My back stiffens. Nothing good can come from that. Ambrose tightens his grip on my hand, one he's not released since we arrived.

Sigurd swirls his finger through the air.

I gasp as an object lifts from one of the carriages at his back and floats to him on a phantom breeze. A rock settles in my gut as recognition sets in. A large, white rose on a leafy stem.

Tension crackles between the opposing parties, even thicker than before. A sizzle and hum—magic?—tingles across my skin.

"A gift for the lady." He snags the flower from the air.

Shit. Everyone stares at me. No one moves.

Riven is stiff as a statue, his gaze averted.

Thanks for the help.

Finally, Riven turns to me.

What should I do? I try to ask without words.

Just when I think he might reject the gift on my behalf, he steps aside with a casual shrug of indifference. Though it's impossible to miss the twitch in his jaw as Sigurd steps past him.

The King of Air grins like a champion. Pure mirth twinkles in his crystal blue eyes as he approaches, and it takes everything I have not to look away.

"Captain." Sigurd nods to Ambrose before taking my free hand in his.

My stomach knots. The urge to pull away is almost too much to bear. Without Ambrose at my side, I surely would have, but his grip is absolute. Sigurd raises my hand to his lips, placing a gentlemanly kiss on its back. However, the smoldering look in his eyes is anything but chaste.

He says so much without speaking, and I can't help the flush racing across my face.

Sigurd releases my hand and holds out the flower as an offering. But an offering of what? Rejecting it and increasing the bad blood between these two courts is out of the question. I won't have that on my conscience too.

"Thank you." It's all I can do to hide the quiver of my voice before taking the gift.

"Oh, it's my pleasure."

His wicked grin has Ambrose's grip tightening almost painfully on my hand.

A moment later, Sigurd returns to Riven, stretching his hands over his head like an athlete preparing for his race. "So, when shall we start?"

Work on the wards starts immediately.

The swirls and mounds I'd noticed on the ground at the border were a honing point. Even with the honing point's assistance and the skill of two fae kings, the process is a long one.

I watch them work at the first honing point for a while. Riven and Sigurd sit a few feet apart on the oddly patterned ground in a sort of trance as the magic flows from them into the border wards. A ring of guards, or rather two rings since neither king trusts the other, surrounds them on all sides, lest the Unseelie come back. Their mutual dislike and wariness of the wild, dark fae seems to be the only thing they can agree on.

Sitting and waiting around sucks. It sucks so damn much. Enough that I literally have to find something to do—anything—to keep my mind off May, off the awkwardness with Riven, and the disastrous gift from Sigurd.

A whole, ridiculous tent city has sprung up in minutes like a fancy renaissance fair. The fae lack no luxury, even at the edge of the Court of the Forest. I'll give it to them—they travel in style, at least when two kings are involved. But the rose Sigurd gave me taunts me every moment I spend inside my tent, and someone is bound to notice if I throw it away. Sitting inside like the good little human they all want me to be is out of the question, but I'm not about to run off and ruin things again.

Instead, I find a better use for my time.

"Like this?" I ask.

"Almost." Galen adjusts my stance, pursing his lips and squinting at me as if I'm some work of art he's in the process of crafting. "There. Much better."

"Now, watch my movements and block my punch," Sylvie says.

I stare her down like a hawk, waiting for the slightest movement. Her right leg slides back ever so slightly to brace herself. I raise my right arm in return, just in time to halt the punch flying my way. Skin smacks before she pulls the punch. A full force one would have knocked me to the ground. Maybe broken something. Fae are hella strong. Who knew they'd been *gentle* with me this whole time?

"Excellent. Now you're getting it," Galen says.

My one success of the morning? Convincing Sylvie and Galen to teach me how to fight.

We started with self-defense. Galen decided I needed to learn how to block a punch before learning to throw one. Had I known even a little bit of this two days ago, I might have been able to save May. It's a stretch, but the thought of being better prepared to save and protect her keeps my thoughts from crushing me with despair.

"Reset and go again," Galen says. He's proclaimed himself my instructor.

The scent of wet pine fills my lungs as I inhale and adjust my stance. Three successful blocks later, Ambrose strides from the dense fog clinging to the forest around us.

"They're still not done?" I ask, our lesson put on hold.

"No." He rubs at the stubble on his jaw. "Should be soon though."

This is our third shift to a new location to repair the wards. Each time they finish at a honing spot, the tents come down, they shift everyone and everything, they start at the next spot, and the tent city comes back to life. Rinse and repeat until done. Horribly boring and infuriating with my sister still missing.

The only thing keeping me sane is Ambrose's confidence that the repaired wards will keep the Unseelie trapped within their territory and help locate May faster.

We'd come to this spot late in the night. Riven and Sigurd rested for just a few hours before trudging through the woods to the nearby focus point to apply their magic. Sylvie shared a tent with me instead of Riven, a blessing I am grateful for. The age difference still sits oddly with me, and the thought of wounding him further over that knowledge makes me ill.

Though, it'd be a lie to say I don't miss him or the comfortable way we were before.

"Let me take you back to Arbrean," Ambrose says. "If we find any trace of your sister, I'll come get you."

This again.

I nearly groan in frustration as I roll my shoulders. "I want to help." Who knows my sister better than me? No one. "We're already out here."

He shakes his head. We've had this conversation already, several times in fact, and even I have to admit he's being patient. But damn, he wouldn't have to be if he'd just let me look for her. I pace and redo my ponytail, just to have something to keep hands busy.

"You've got spirit, as much as any of my guard," he says. "But they're trained to know the forest and read its clues. You're not."

Sylvie plops down on the ground in front of me. "He is right, you know."

My lips thin, and I turn away. All ganging up on me. How sweet.

"And if I'm not here watching you, then I can search for your sister as well," Ambrose says.

His words knock the wind out of me. I twist back to look at Sylvie and Galen, who both give silent nods. Guilt churns in my stomach, a sick twisting mass of knots that refuses to loosen. How could I be so shortsighted? Possibly their best tracker, and he's stuck here watching after me.

"I-I didn't know." I should have but... "You should have told me."

"Aye." He nods and looks at the ground before gazing back at me. "Perhaps. But you were so determined last time. Didn't want you running off on your own again. I thought if we gave in a bit..." He shrugs.

I stare awkwardly at the ground. How many times can I mess up? At this point, it'd be easier to list the things I haven't screwed up, though right now, I'm not even sure what those are.

Make the fae aware of May? Check.

Let her get kidnapped? Check.

Fail to save her? Check.

Delay her rescue? Check again.

And that doesn't even cover mine and Riven's relationship or any of my previous life failures before the past.

God. I groan. It hasn't even been a week.

Ambrose clamps a hand on my shoulder. "Don't feel too bad. We're very grateful you're here. More than you know."

Still. "I need you to do me a favor."

He releases me to rub the scrub the scruff on his face. "Am I going to like this favor?"

"Maybe. Hopefully." I wring my hands in front me. "If I'm getting in the way or making things more difficult, I need you to tell me.

Especially if it's delaying us in finding May, I—" The words catch in my throat.

"That, I can do."

"Good." I give a sharp nod. "Take me back. Sooner the better if it helps May."

"We'll take you," Galen offers. "We're to stick with you anyway, whether out here or back in the city."

At least I won't be alone in my misery.

"Leaving so soon?" That voice steals every thought from my head.

I turn to find Sigurd striding from the foggy woods, his characteristic grin in place. The fog parts for him like the Red Sea for Moses.

Worse, he's alone.

"Too bad, I've enjoyed the view around camp." His smirk deepens.

Heat crawls up my neck, accompanied by icy dread climbing up my back.

Riven. Where is Riven?

CHAPTER 19

MY HEART RACES AS I search the tree line for Riven.

He's not there. He should be.

Where—

I jump as a strong arm encircles my waist.

"She's not yours to toy with," Riven says.

The heat of his body seeps into my back, easing away the chill of moments ago. Thank goodness. I relax into him, preferring his safety to the quandary approaching us.

"Unfortunately." Sigurd brushes off his shoulder. "Doesn't seem like she's yours either though."

Because I don't bear Riven's mark. The ground below my feet has never been so interesting.

"It's disappointing." Sigurd continues. "But her absence will give me more motivation to fix these wards so I can visit your city."

Riven's chest rumbles with a growl. His arms tighten around me. "Leave her alone, Sigurd."

"Humans should be free to make their own choices, wouldn't you say?" His tone shifts, turning just as hard and biting as Riven's. "To choose who they want to spend time with. And who they don't."

"Exactly," Riven snaps. "You should be familiar with being told to stay away."

Ambrose swears. Magic sizzles in the air.

Shit. I can't let things fall apart now, not because of me.

"It's all right. I'm fine." I run my hand along Riven's arm in smooth, slow strokes, trying to calm him down. His jaw is set, teeth slightly bared. "I'm yours, remember?" It's so easy to say, so right, despite the last two days. "There's no need to worry. I'm going back to Arbrean."

Riven's face smooths out. He releases me as his mask of cocky arrogance snaps back into place. "You heard her."

Sigurd's grin fades. His thinned lips twitch, followed by his pointed ears. A more annoyed fae there has never been.

The other fae around us, who stopped to watch the verbal sparring match, start to leave.

It's over. Finally, I can breathe again.

All of a sudden, Riven tilts my face to his and claims my mouth in a quick, unexpected kiss.

My body stiffens. My eyes fly wide.

He breaks away before the shock of his kiss has the chance to sink in. He strokes my cheek, my arm. It's not the comforting touch I'm used to.

This is possessive, a show, just like that damn ball the first night I came to Faery.

"I'll see you again soon," he promises, a little too loudly.

He stole that kiss, and I don't even have to ask why. My attention is glued to the other king, the annoyed and disappointed one a few feet away from us, as I undo the bracelet about my wrist.

"Get me out of here," I mumble, my jaw stiff and set.

Galen and Sylvie hold out their hands to me, and I take them. After one backward glance over my shoulder to Riven, who's not even looking my way, we're gone.

Solona talks me into spending the afternoon with her in the library. For one, it's an excellent distraction from...well, everything. More importantly, though, if Ambrose and the others can't find

May, we need to have something of value ready to trade for her on the seventh day, a deadline that grows closer with every passing minute.

"What are we looking for exactly?" I pull another heavy tome off the shelf.

"Something of value. Beyond jewels or food or weaponry. Humans can restore their magic, even just a little bit. They'll expect something equally effective."

My stomach bottoms out.

So pretty much a miracle. Or the holy grail. Or something equally impossible to find in a handful of days.

I drop the large book, three times the size of ones in my local bookstore back home, on the table with a huff. It thumps open to a random page, sending the scent of old paper wafting into the air. Just like all the others. The books aren't written in English or any language I've ever seen.

Some have been spelled to allow humans to read them but only a few. The magic terrified me the first time. My mind processed the shapes into words, making sense of what I could not and should not understand. It happened so suddenly and unexpectedly that I'd dropped the book onto my boot, earning a bruise in the process.

Whatever spell they crafted is imperfect, causing a slight headache to throb behind my eyes after a few pages. Better than nothing though.

I frown at the tome. This one, sadly, hasn't been spelled. Lazy librarian. Guess they didn't see the point when there weren't many humans around to read them anyway.

"I've got another one," I say. "Same color and symbols on the binding that you told me to look for."

Books of spells, she'd said. No wonder it's not human-friendly.

Solona looks up from the book laid open in front of her and purses her lips. "Add it to the pile. I'll get to it eventually."

Alone in my room—well, Riven's room—later that night, the weight of the situation threatens to crush me. I hug my knees to my chest, pulling the covers over my head as tears leak down my face.

No news from Ambrose means no May.

No success in the library means nothing to trade for her once the clock runs out.

And Riven's still working on the wards, leaving me alone in the still, silence of his—*our*—room.

I miss him, much more than I expected to. Yes, we'd kissed a few times, shared a bed…

My thoughts halt completely as scenes from the other space we've shared flash through my head. I enjoyed it, my bath with him. I wanted him, and a part of me, which I try so hard to ignore, wants him now.

You're lusting over an old man who isn't even human.

The logical half of me knows that. The passionate side doesn't care.

My fingers trace my lips, wiping away the tears resting there while I remember the feel of his skin on mine. Somehow, despite the horrors of the past few days, things aren't so bad when he's with me. The impossible challenges ahead seem doable. Not to mention he knows me in a way no one else does. He understands my pain. I don't have to hide it from him.

And I need that, someone who truly knows me and still wants me anyway. I've needed it so much longer than I ever realized.

Come back to me. Soon.

Sylvie arrives over breakfast and offers to continue my training with Galen. First though, we decide to try out the new running pants and shoes Karin scrounged up for me somewhere in Arbrean.

Fresh air in my lungs, that sweet ache in my legs, adrenaline pumping through my veins... Wow, I've missed it.

During the days after the accident, after I'd stayed with my family as long as I could stand without breaking down in full-body sobs, I'd lace up my running shoes and set out on the trails. Cold as hell, windy, a light drizzle? Didn't matter. The rhythmic motion and pushing myself to the limit let everything slip far, far away. It was the only escape I had during the day when I couldn't drift off into a peaceful slumber with the hopes of seeing Riven, if only for a minute or two.

It has the same effect today, pushing my worries and confusion from the night before to the recesses of my mind. The company doesn't hurt either.

"Slowpokes," Sylvie taunts as she zips past Galen and me.

He grins and shakes his head, keeping pace at my side.

They're much faster despite my penchant for running. Most fae are—seems they're better at just about everything, actually. However, at least one of them has slowed their pace to run beside me all morning, the other often running ahead to push themselves and then doubling back to trade places with the other.

It's a race I'll never win, but I try anyway.

"Watch this," Galen taunts when Sylvie laps back to us. He takes off at a sprint as she slows up near me.

Their relationship could be more. I see the spark of it, the occasional tension of something more than friendship. Galen's oblivious to it, or tries very hard to ignore it, but it's clear as day in Sylvie's actions. At least to me.

Sweat runs down my back, my chest, my legs, basically everywhere, by the time we stop. I laugh—maybe the first true one I've uttered since May was kidnapped—between heavy gasps as Galen suggests we head to the sparring ring, as if our run was just the warm-up and not the workout itself.

"Give me...just a few... minutes." I nearly collapse on the bottom row of a set of benches outside the sparring ring where several fae are training. "So..." I say once I've finally caught my breath. "How did you two meet?"

I shove sweat-slicked hair behind my ear as I glance between them. Honestly, I've been dying to know, but the last two days were too...everything. Bringing up such lighthearted topics felt wrong. The ache in my chest is proof it still does, but I need the distraction, anything not to slip into the dark pit of my worries for May.

Sylvie stretches out on the bench. "We met while training after we became members of Riven's guard."

The whole story spills out in gushes as she rambles about their early days of training. Galen nods along politely, adding a detail here and there.

I steadfastly refuse to ask their ages—not going there again—but I gather they're younger than Riven.

A hint springs up when Sylvie says, "Galen's older and has been with the guard longer, but I'm more talented, so we were promoted to elite around the same time."

Galen shrugs, unbothered by the statement. "It's true."

They'd been bitter rivals at first, but that rivalry drove them to exceed and earn their promotion. Then it softened into strong friendship and comradery. The hint of a smile creeps to my lips as I spy Galen's stolen glances at Sylvie as she wraps up her tale.

No sooner has she kicked up her feet, signaling the end of her tale, than Galen starts pointing out the moves performed by the sparring fae. Their strengths, their weaknesses, and how I can apply them to my own fighting. He's taking this instructor bit seriously, and I sure as heck am determined to be a good student.

"Entrancing, isn't it?" someone says behind me.

I jump in my seat at the unexpected question, my attention snapping toward the voice and away from the action in the ring. Ambrose strides toward us, extra stubble shading his jaw.

I leap to my feet. "Oh, please tell me you found her."

My hope crashes and burns at the look on his face, falling further with the somber shake of his head. He taps a thick piece of paper on one palm.

My legs give out. I collapse back onto the bench.

No.

"That letter. It feels wrong." Sylvie's voice holds a note of something I've never heard from her. Fear.

"It's from the Unseelie," Ambrose says.

A deathly chill strips the heat from my body.

"One of them delivered it to us, via an arrow through Argus's thigh. A poisoned arrow."

Galen swears. Sylvie goes pale and looks like she might be sick.

"Is there an antidote?" My voice shakes.

Ambrose looks away, his jaw hard. "Took him too fast. His magic couldn't hold off the poison."

Bile burns my throat. A fae died searching for May. One of their friends, their comrades. And they still have her, my sister. I clasp a hand over my mouth, holding in the scream begging to rip from my throat.

Galen recovers first. "What does it say?"

"They've changed the meeting point. They now want to meet at Keles, at sunset on the seventh day."

"Keles." Sylvie's voice is a breathless whisper. "The Shadow Lands."

Tears blur my vision. Every moment the news gets worse and worse.

Ambrose swallows visibly. "It's near the border, but it likely means they've slipped out of our territory. Probably felt the wards going up and ran." He sits down heavily on the bench near us. "I'm sorry, Lia. We'll keep searching, but we need to have a backup plan, something to offer them, just in case."

Sylvie wraps her arms around me as I nod to Ambrose, unable to form words around the lump lodged in my throat.

Everything keeps getting worse.

Sometime later, we try to train, but I can't pay attention. My thoughts keep straying to May and the Unseelie, earning me a few bruises and a hurt tailbone. I thought a bath would help, but it only serves to remind me of the one I shared with Riven two days ago.

Not the kind of distraction I need.

He still hasn't returned, and no one really seems to know when he will. Before the ball, but that's so vague its laughable.

More fruitless searching through the library fills my afternoon, with one break where Karin has me fitted for a ballgown I have no desire to wear. I select books off the shelves as Solona pores through them, assisted for a time by Sylvie and Galen, who probably need the distraction as much as I do. More spell books, legends about old relics that could be helpful—if anyone actually knew where they were.

Weariness urges me to sleep, but the thoughts running through my head won't let me fade into the soothing darkness I crave. I've worried so much for my sister, but what about Dad and Elise? Guilt crushes me every time I think of them. They've almost lost May once. Now she is gone again, and me with her.

Did they find my phone with my message? Or worse, are they already planning a double funeral?

I grip the sheets in my fist and let out a cry of frustration. God, what have I done? I have to go back, to check and see. I mentioned it, sort of, but no one will take me back to Virideria, and especially not to the door, without Riven. Even tried reminding them that I'm Riven's consort, their Lady of the Forest. Hell, if that gave me any kind of real power, I was sure going to use it.

They almost budged at that.

Almost.

Apparently any request from me is still second to orders from their king. Freaking figures.

I tug the sheets over my head and pray for sleep.

It almost works...until there's a crash in the other room.

CHAPTER 20

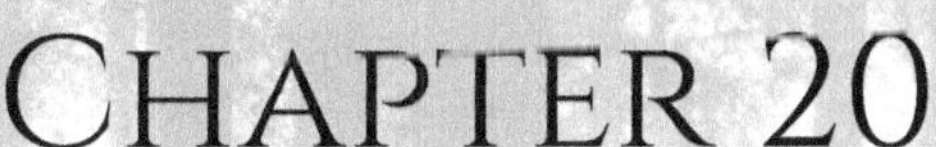

I SIT BOLT UPRIGHT in the bed. Darkness reigns, both within and without. Noise echoes into the room again, shuffling followed by the hard thud of something large knocking into the furniture.

My adrenaline kicks up, heart pounding.

Oh, to have a knife, a sword, a skillet—anything to protect myself. I've got nothing, just my poor self-defense skills.

I creep on silent, bare feet to the wall separating the bedroom from the sitting room beyond. A chill skitters up my spine when I hear a loud grunt, followed by something, or rather someone, knocking into more furniture.

How did they get past the guards? They were always watching this hallway, checking to make sure no one disturbed their king's rooms. Riven promised me I'd be under his protection, and maybe I'm naïve, but I believe it. He's been true to his word thus far...though he's not here.

Steeling my nerves, I step into the threshold and shove back the curtain of vines. A table is knocked over, another askew. A shadow in the form of a man sits on the couch.

A scream lodges in my throat as I brace to bolt back into the bedroom.

A disoriented groan stops me. "Lia."

My breath catches. I know that voice.

Riven.

I race across the room and hop onto the sofa next to him.

"What's wrong? Are you all right?" I run my hands along his arms, his chest, his face. He's clothed. There's nothing wet like blood. No obvious injuries.

Riven grabs me about my waist and pulls me onto his lap.

A gasp wrenches from my lips as I straddle his hips, my shins pressed into the cloth of the couch.

"Much better now," he whispers against my neck, placing kisses after his words.

Each touch sends a shiver rolling across my skin. His hands hold my waist, keeping me firmly atop him. My heart hammers. The sensation of his hands on me through my silken nightgown, his kisses, his scent in my nose—it's more intoxicating than the strongest drink.

I push on his chest. "This is no time for jokes. You really scared me, bumping around in here in the dark. When did you even get back?"

He lets out a deep sigh and collapses into the cushions.

Though I can barely see him, the feel of his gaze raking my body is unmistakable. I adjust the top of my nightgown which had gone askew. Fae vision is so much better than a human's. He can probably see just fine. The bottom hem has ridden up dangerously high, but there's no helping that, not in this position.

"Just now," he says. "I shifted straight here."

"Where from?" I poke him. "Are the wards complete?"

"So many questions tonight." His chest rumbles with laughter. Daring hands rub my sides, pressing the silk of the nightgown against my skin. "Yes, they're finally done."

A thumb trails along the underside of my breast.

I slide my hand along his arm, gently pushing it down and denying him the touch.

Riven sighs. "We worked constantly since you left, eager to get this chore done. And when Ambrose told me of the letter, I was even more desperate to get back."

The letter. My heart clenches, but I push through the pain. "And Sigurd?"

A faint growl rumbles in his chest. "Here. Somewhere. Or he will be soon. He *requested* my guard shift him and his attendants to the city to rest since they cannot shift here with the wards renewed. But I'd rather not hear his name on your lips. Not tonight."

He drops his hands from my body, the tiredness in his voice unmistakable. I cup his face in my hands, and it goes limp, falling to the side.

"You're exhausted." I'm not faking the concern in my voice. "You pushed yourself so hard you could barely stand when you got here. That's how the table got knocked over."

I feel the smile I can't see.

"My clever one. Exhausted, yes, and my magic burned through. It takes a lot of energy to shift. Even more to reinforce the wards."

He's used up too much magic too quickly and hasn't slept. No wonder he was so clumsy, even when he can probably see just fine. Leeches, I'd considered the fae when I'd first learned of human's effect on their magic. And maybe they are, but as a human, I can help replenish Riven's magic. It's worth a try anyway.

My lips seek his. Gentle. A caress. One after another, I grace him with kisses on his lips, his cheek, his brow.

Deft fingers grip my hip and exposed thigh. I find his lips again.

This kiss isn't gentle. His enthusiasm makes me tremble, especially when his tongue urges my lips apart to dance with mine. The hand on my hip slides back to grab my backside through my nightgown.

A deep groan rumbles into my mouth.

The silk nightgown is an unnecessary barrier between Riven's hands and my skin. I want it gone, but I don't dare. Already, warmth gathers between my legs, dampening my underwear in the area pressed against his waistband. Everything is warm and blissful.

I'm falling, sinking into this sea of wonder too quickly.

I pull myself back, breaking our kiss and letting my hands rest against his chest.

"We should get you to the bed—to get some sleep," I add hastily. "Do you have the energy to make it there?"

Riven stands.

I gasp. My legs lock around him to avoid falling. Such strength, when moments ago he could barely hold his head up. I wrap my arms around his neck and snuggle into his warmth.

"You would tease me so?" he taunts.

My effect on him is quick and effective, much more so than I intended. I'd only hoped to get him someplace more comfortable, but now...

Fur tickles my skin as Riven lays me upon the bed with utmost care.

Then he's following me down, covering my body with his.

"You need rest." I shove his chest, but it's a poor effort.

I want him. I can't lie about that, not to myself. When he's close like this, his honeysuckle scent swarming my senses, it's easy to forget my worries. I could melt into him, give into the pleasure I yearn for. It'd be so sweet, freeing, perfect.

But in the back of my mind, there's a voice that won't be quiet. Its whispers are impossible to ignore. *Remember how old he is? Or May, your sister who's still out there?*

He groans and rolls onto the bed next to me. "I know, I know. But stay with me?"

"Yes." No matter what the voices say, I have no intention of leaving him.

A grimace creases his face as he pushes himself up and discards pieces of clothing one at a time. When only his pants are left, I turn away as his slow fingers undo ties and buckles. The slip and slide of fabric taunts my ears. Riven gives another groan before sliding under the covers.

Only a layer of fur and fabric separate our bodies as he presses up against me, where I still sit on top of the bed.

The glide of his fingers across my side has me turning back to him. His sleepy face and wild hair spread across the pillow dries my mouth. Hell, he should not be that attractive when he's so dead tired and exhausted. I'd be a hot mess, yet he's even more handsome now somehow.

"Lay with me," he asks, barely a whisper.

There's a rawness, a vulnerability, that I haven't seen in days.

I snuggle against him on top of the bed. This close, I can't help but trail my fingers over his shoulder and down his chest. Invisible sparks float between us where we touch. A pleasant buzz fills my head.

The age difference doesn't dampen the way I feel for him. He doesn't look old, feel old.

And so, I conclude, he isn't. Fae ages are just different. The number doesn't matter, just the man before me.

His half-mast eyes lure me in until I close the breath of space between us and press my lips against his again. His spark of energy has burned through, yet he still kisses me back with reverence. A soft, gentle match to my own efforts.

Sleepy eyes stare at me across the pillow after I pull back. Our breaths mingle in the narrow space between us. I want him. In every way.

"I'd give so much for the look I see on your face to be true," he whispers, caressing my face.

"Rive—"

He cuts me off with a finger to my lips. I have to restrain myself not to lick it.

"You know I want you, but when I finally put my mark on you, I intend to do it properly, when I can take you in all the ways I've imagined. Not when I'm like this." He gestures limply to his body.

"Oh." Disappointment colors my response, yet it does nothing to calm my racing heart or to halt the moisture building between my legs. "Is there anything I can do to help? With your magic?"

"Stay close to me. Skin to skin might work even better. We could try it." Mischief dances in his eyes.

Excellent idea. I lick my lips. Before I can think better of it, my nightgown is up and over my head, leaving me in only my underwear. Cool night air tickles my stomach, my breasts. But the chill vanishes as soon as I catch sight of Riven's eyes on me, locked to the areas I've just exposed so brazenly.

Dark laughter floats from his parted lips. "You would choose to tease me when I have the strength to do little about it."

"Who says I'm teasing?" I join him under the covers, leaving just a few inches of space between our naked bodies. Well, his naked body and my barely clothed one.

This close, I can't keep my hands to myself. He's just too damn inviting. I trail them down his chest to the ridges of his stomach. The muscles tense and tighten. A faint growl rumbles from his throat.

"Roll over," he grates.

I give a mock pout but do as he asks. Strong arms encircle me. Delicious warmth seeps into my back where it's pressed against his solid chest.

"My delightful little human." His palm splays across my stomach. Breath tickles my neck. "Does this mean you're no longer bothered by my age?"

His thumb grazes the sensitive skin under my breasts.

I squirm against him, savoring the touch and feel the unmistakable nudge of something both soft and hard against my upper thigh.

"Yes," I whisper.

"Good." The hand teasing my breasts slides down to rub lazy circles around my belly button.

I gasp as his pinky finger slips under the edge of my panties before retreating again. Another circle has his hand sliding lower, a second finger venturing under. On the third slow rotation, his hand halts below the fabric. "Do you want me to stop?"

No. Never. "Please don't."

I relax my hips and part my legs ever so slightly in invitation.

When he doesn't move, I rub against the bulge behind me. A knot of desire tightens the friction between us. I nearly whimper when his fingers finally advance to find the wetness between my legs.

His hand halts. His body goes rigid.

"Riven?"

"You really do want me." He's almost breathless with wonder.

I angle my head just enough to see his wide-eyed, awed look in the moonlight filtering into the room.

"Yes." I gasp.

He grazes the sensitive nub between my legs as a deft finger slips inside.

A second joins the first. All my focus narrows to the feel of him inside me. So much so that I don't notice his other hand until it palms one breast, squeezing and kneading my puckered nipple.

I rock against his fingers, desperate to feel him move inside me, to touch my sensitive bud again. The movement grinds my backside against him, eliciting a hiss and groan of pleasure.

Riven nips my earlobe, those sharp teeth mixing a twinge of pain with pleasure. His thumb presses down with a thrust of his fingers, eliciting a gasping squeal.

"You like this." He rubs his thumb again.

I bite my lip, barely holding in a moan.

"How I wish I could take you like I want. Right now. Deep and hard." He thrusts his fingers for emphasis, twisting the knots in my stomach tighter.

I'm greedy and I know it, but he's underestimated just how much I want him too. Riven growls deep in his throat as I find the hard length of him. Just the thought of him buried deep inside me has me whimpering.

I want him. So badly. So much more than ever before.

One stroke of my hand, and he's bucking against me.

"Lia," he moans against my neck as I tease the moist slit of his cock.

I time my strokes to his, giving all that I get to the strong male at my back. Each flick and twist of him against me builds toward the precipice of bliss, so close to falling into that wondrous oblivion. My breast aches as he continues to tease it with maddening skill.

"Come for me," he groans. "Let me feel your pleasure."

With two quick flicks of his thumb, I burst. A scream of pleasure breaks from me as the orgasm shudders through my body.

Amazing. Glorious. Perfect.

My legs clamp around his hand, still working my tender flesh and ringing out the last of my pleasure. Half the city may have heard my cry, and I don't care. With him, nothing matters.

My head falls back against his shoulder. As if by instinct, I still caress his hard length.

I shudder and shiver against Riven's chest when he stills. His arms tighten just before his cock pulses and jerks in my hand. He all but roars into the night.

This powerful, beautiful man, and he's coming apart, wracked by pleasure—from me.

I work his silken length, savoring the feel of him until he softens.

The tip of his tongue flicks out to lick at my neck. "Beautiful, Lia."

He retreats from between my legs, leaving me bereft and somehow still aching for more. No amount of him will ever be enough, not if it's anything like tonight. And holy God, that glorious length of him wasn't even inside me. If he was...

I shiver.

I twist for a better view and snuggle against the fae king, who just worked my body to perfection. A small shudder wracks his body as his eyes close. A content smile plays about his features.

"Riven?" I brush golden hair back from his face.

One green eye cracks open, glowing faintly in the night. A smirk tugs at his features. "Sleep well tonight, little consort, because once I'm rested, I won't be able to leave you alone."

CHAPTER 21

T HE NEXT MORNING, I gently untangle myself from a still sleeping Riven. Despite my movements, his chest still rises and falls with smooth, even breaths. In sleep, he looks even younger than normal, so much more than his actual age.

My cheeks flush as my gaze lingers on the solid muscle of his chest, just visible over the edge of the furs. Now that's a sight I could get used to. That warmth spreads down my chest, through my stomach, and lower as I recall the way his hands moved on me and his breath against my skin.

With a shake and a shudder, I will away the naughty thoughts urging me to crawl back in bed and wake him up. He needs rest, and once he wakes...

I cover my face with my hands. What have I gotten myself into?

I mean, I promised to be his consort, but I never planned to be the one begging for more.

A stab of guilt, sharp as ever, jabs into me. Here I've been enjoying a night of pleasure when May is still in the clutches of an enemy. I only hope they've kept her asleep and that, once she returns home, all of this might seem like a bad dream. That's the best-case scenario, and I have to hold onto it. Otherwise, I might shatter.

Just a few more days, May. You'll be home safe. I promise.

I wash and dress quickly in what's become my workout attire. I need to clear my head and drag it out of the gutter. Anything. Scouring records for some way to free May is going to be impossible if I can't stop thinking about all the things I want Riven to do to me. Solona even has scholars bringing over extra books from the capital, which she thinks might be helpful. Likely they already help her comb through them. I can't slack off when they're working harder than ever.

And May... May! She's been gone for days, and I'm no closer to getting her back.

Walking through the halls of the castle city always jars my nerves. Fae stop to gape or drop short bows in my direction. Murmured conversations tickle my ears after I pass. My skin crawls from so many eyes on me. At least the guards escorting me outside keep the others a safe distance away. Having a title has some perks, such as no one trying to accost me like that first night.

As I near the swooping archway, composed more of vine and roots than stone, I practically jog for it, eager to be outside. Cool air rushes around me as I squint into the morning sunlight. Gooseflesh breaks out over my skin. Crisp air fills my lungs, reminding me of early October back home.

A commotion catches my attention before my eyes fully adjust to the bright light.

Fae encircle the training ring. Shouts and cheers ring through the air, though their tall forms completely block the view beyond. One in particular, I recognize, as she bounces on her toes, trying to see over the male partially blocking her view.

I wave my guards away and hustle across the grassy field to Sylvie, who stands on the packed dirt ring just outside the railing.

"What's going—" Breath catches in my throat when I glimpse the duel they watch.

Sigurd stands shirtless, a faint sheen of sweat glistening on creamy skin. A thick, wooden staff is angled toward the opponent he's staring down. The other male, slightly taller, with darkly tanned skin and long hair, sucks in a labored breath. Trails of sweat run down his muscular chest and arms.

"Oh, Lia, they're—" she starts.

But I don't hear the rest of her words.

Not when Sigurd's eyes flick to me and a wicked grin spreads across his features. With a huff of laughter, he charges his opponent faster than a gust of air. Their staves meet in a crash and groan of wood.

Riven could barely stand the night before, so drained by reparation of the wards, and still, he slumbers. Yet this king looks like he's rested for days, unphased by the exertion of such a task. True, he didn't shift himself back here, but that activity alone shouldn't make such a big difference.

Another shiver wracks my body. Sigurd has more strength, magical and otherwise, than I thought. Much more.

Sylvie's hand on my arm jerks me back to the moment.

"Let's go," she says. "It's probably best not to ogle these showoffs."

At some point, Galen had appeared at her side and now nods along with her words. His jaw is stiff, as if something bothers him, but I can't say what.

We retreat to the well-worn jogging paths from the day before. But after only two laps, Galen skids to a stop in front of me, nearly sending me careening into his back as my shoes slide against the dirt, scrambling for purchase.

"Hey, wha—" I step to his side, even as he stretches an arm in front of me, urging me back.

Sigurd waits where the path turns through the edge of a clearing, still shirtless and smirking. He brushes a lock of dark, sweat-dampened hair behind one pointed ear as he stares us down.

Sylvie comes to a stop on my other side, bracketing me between them.

"Did you enjoy the duel?" he asks. The question could have been directed at any of us, yet his blue eyes focus only on me, twisting a cord of nerves within my stomach.

"I..." Suddenly it's hard to speak, to find the right words. "I only saw a moment of it."

"A pity." He shrugs. "Come. Walk with me." Sigurd holds out a hand in my direction.

Both Galen and Sylvie stand utterly still in my periphery, giving nothing away.

"Why?" *Danger, danger, danger* flashes inside my head. Whatever he wants, it can't be good. I fight the urge to step back, to turn and run.

"As a favor for someone who helped repair the wards here and whose guard helps to search for your little sister." He looks down at his hand as if picking at his nails, but I'd wager they're clean as ever. "Surely a conversation isn't too much to ask for?"

I swallow. When he phrases it like that, no, he's not asking for too much.

But with him standing there so casually, sunlight glinting off the sheen of sweat on his bare chest, stepping even a foot closer to him feels impossible.

My gaze flicks between my guards again, begging them to intervene.

They don't. Maybe they can't, not when facing a fae king.

"Sit with me then?" He nods his head toward an elaborate wooden bench only a few feet away. Its back railing blooms with orange flowers. "Your guards can stay near if it gives you comfort."

I swallow. "It would."

This time, Galen gives a brief nod. I fumble with the bracelet around my wrist, the beautiful emeralds from Solona. Sigurd can't shift me away—if he even can with the wards up—

and he and Riven made a pact of nonviolence until May is found. I should be safe.

And yet...

Sigurd, ever the gentleman, motions for me to sit first before he occupies the other end of the bench. One booted foot crosses over his knee as he reclines in all his half-naked glory. And he is glorious. There's no denying that, no matter how his presence sets me on edge.

"I heard that you made a bargain with him," he says. "Why?"

There's no need to ask who *him* is.

I draw a sharp breath, my attention snapping to his face. Spies. He definitely has spies in Riven's court if he knows so much. And if he's aware of the bargain, then he should know why I made it. That was part of what we agreed on, after all.

"My sister," I say, quieter than I'd planned. Just talking about it cuts at my heart. "I promised to stay with Riven if he helped me find my sister and return her home."

"Just stay with him?" he cocks an eyebrow.

My cheeks flame. "And to be his consort."

"Interesting." His fingers trail along the back of the bench, brushing over the open petals of a flower just smaller than his palm. Sigurd's gaze rakes my body, sending a shiver down my spine. "Though it doesn't appear you've upheld your end yet."

"How—" But the question sticks before I finish it. Riven said marks are a magical and physical representation of a bond. Whatever magical signal one holds, I clearly don't bear it.

"Do you find your Forest King lacking?"

"No." I purse my lips. Asshole.

"Hmm." He drums on the wooden bench. "If you did, a human such as yourself would have options. Other *choices*. Though that bargain is a bit of a complication."

I squirm at the implication of his words. "Why tell me that?"

"I may have a soft spot for human women." He shrugs. His words send an unwelcome tingle of warmth coiling low in my body.

"And you, you don't bear a mark?" I ask to move the conversation away from me.

Sigurd smirks. "Does it look like I do?"

I look away to keep my eyes from trailing across his exposed skin again—that chiseled six-pack, the muscles disappearing down below his waistband to regions I dare not think about. "I wouldn't know."

"Each fae's mark is different, but they all appear in the same place." He pauses. "Look at me, Lia."

Reluctantly, I tear my gaze back to him. He rubs a spot just above the waistline of his pants. *The* place I've tried hardest not to look. "If I shared my mark," he continues, "you'd see it here."

My mouth goes dry. He couldn't be more direct if he'd held up a blinking sign that said single.

"I'd think fae would trip over themselves to get into the bed of a king." My teeth rattle as I snap my mouth closed. Why, oh why, did I say that aloud?

He chuckles. "Perhaps. But staying away from unnecessary entanglements was one of the first lessons I learned—that any decent king learns. Besides, why would I want a fae when a human is so much more... helpful?"

His eyes practically glitter on the word.

I shove to my feet and move away, unable to sit still next to the predator at my side. Sylvie steps in my direction, but Galen holds her back. I flash them a tight smile. My discomfort isn't reason to cause a bigger scene than necessary.

"Humans are rare in your territory too then?" I don't turn to look at him but gasp as he circles around to stand before me, his movement stirring a gust of wind that ruffles my ponytail. I hadn't heard him move.

"Not nearly so much as here."

On instinct, I retreat a step, but his words raise more questions than answers. Humans are more plentiful in his territory, wherever it is, yet he'd chosen not to mark one, despite the magical boost it would provide him and his people. My brows wrinkle in confusion as I stare down the enigma before me.

His smile falters. Something flashes across his face, too quick to interpret, but it wipes away his playful amusement, leaving a somber note in its wake.

"I loved one once, long ago," he says, maybe in answer to the question on my face.

I rock back on my heels. Of all the things I expected him to say, that hadn't been anywhere in my imaginings.

"Others have...not compared."

"What happened to them?"

His lips tug downward. The blue of his eyes reflects deep sorrow. Just when I expect him to respond, the look vanishes, and his characteristic smirk slides back into place.

"I have a feeling someone comes for you," he says instead and grabs my wrist.

"What—"

He tugs me along.

"Wait."

Galen and Sylvie rush over, almost faster than my eyes can follow.

"Lia, are you—" Sylvie starts.

I shrug best I can at her question while Sigurd leads me through the field, back toward the doors of Arbrean, which I'd exited that morning. He draws us to a halt and releases my arm moments before Riven steps through the doors.

Riven's attention snaps to where the four of us stand in a tight clump near the edge of the stone pathway. All the gentle softness that had graced his face in sleep is gone. Magic crackles in the air as his gaze lands on the shirtless fae king standing at my side.

I step away, increasing the space between us, but that only thins Riven's lips further.

Shit. We'd finally gotten back to a good place—better than—and now this.

"Thank you for keeping me company," Sigurd says to me, ignoring his angry counterpart. "We're still to have a ball this evening, are we not?" This question he poses to Riven.

Riven smooths out his features and inclines his head. However, I don't miss the way his fists clench and unclench at his side.

"Excellent." Sigurd stretches his arms over his head, the picture of a relaxed guest. "Well, I do think some rest and relaxation is in order before then." He snatches my hand before I can react and places a courtly kiss upon it. "Until then."

CHAPTER 22

TENSION STILL RADIATES FROM Riven when I emerge, cleaned and changed, from the washroom. Lunch is spread across a table on the balcony, tempting me with sweet baked goods and savory roasted vegetables, but even those delights haven't softened the mood of the male waiting for me at the table.

The situation from his perspective has to look bad—I mean, shit, me standing next to his shirtless rival? Who wouldn't take that the wrong way? Galen and Sylvie rose to my defense, which calmed Riven a little, though not as much as I'd hoped. It was as if all the closeness and connection we'd developed the night before had been washed away in a moment.

In my head, I pictured this day going differently. My thighs squeeze together. Much differently.

"Will you eat with me?" Riven gestures to the table. At least his voice is pleasant, even if the hard set of his jaw still lingers.

We eat in silence, though every time I gather the courage to look up, I find his gaze rapt on me and something other than worry or anger stirring the emotion in his green eyes.

Finally, he sets down his polished utensils. "About the ball..."

My own fork stills. Not the topic I expected, but a dying woman will take any water she's offered. "It's all right. Solona explained the situation."

One brow arcs up. "Did she?"

"She said it's an opportunity to show strength to your court and improve relations with the Court of Air." Still doesn't make me happy about it. It's the very last thing I want with May missing and the Unseelie causing trouble, but the logical side gets it. There's strategy at play, and he does, in fact, have more to worry about than just my sister. But damn if I didn't wish it was different.

He nods. "It's tonight. I'd like you to accompany me."

I spear a piece of fruit and bring it to my lips. Cool sweetness coats my mouth. Let him stew a bit with my silence.

"I need you to be there," Riven continues.

"Oh, I know," I say around a bite of food. "Karin already had me fitted for a gown."

"Good." He grabs his fork again but releases it in the same motion, his mouth working in his jaw. "About this morning..."

Here we go. I barely stop the eye roll. "Nothing happened. We were running and he—"

Riven raises his hand. "I know. I overreacted. But seeing him with you this morning after last night..."

He runs a hand through his loose hair.

The mention of last night has me reaching for my glass of water.

"Why do you dislike him so much?"

Every time his name comes up, he frowns, growls, bares his pointed teeth, or all of the above. Much as Riven might dislike him, Sigurd has been kind to me. He showed me to May, offered to help find her, and helped fix the wards. And he gave me a flower. I don't know why that lingers with me even though I left the darn thing in my tent.

By all accounts, he's acted like a friend, even if he occasionally sets my teeth on edge and flirts way too much.

Riven's frown deepens, and he pushes away the rest of lunch.

Okay, definitely missing something.

"We are not on the best of terms," he says.

Yeah, I gathered that. "But you're not at war?"

"No. Almost once, but no, it hasn't come to that yet." He shakes his head. "A war between courts would be catastrophic for both of our people, and we cannot afford that right now, not with other threats at our borders." He scrubs a hand over his face. When it comes away, he's not even looking at me. Instead, he stares at something on the far wall—a scene from the past that's invisible to me. "The Wild Tribes, the Unseelie, have become more aggressive over the years. Growing in number and audacity. The Seelie Courts warred against them years ago when I was still very young."

I swallow another piece of food before setting my own utensils down. Lunch is a thing of the past. "Will you tell me about it? The war and whatever happened back then?"

Riven nods. His attention drifts back to me. "Come sit with me."

He motions to the interior sitting area. When we're seated on the comfy furniture inside, he resumes his tale.

"It was a hard-fought war, over many, many years, but eventually we decimated their forces and pushed them back, deep into their Shadow Lands. I was young then, barely into my power, but I fought in my father's army anyway. I was proud to lead our people into war. It was hard though, worse than I could have imagined, to see my people fall around me, despite my best efforts to fell the enemy first. Perhaps we should have taken it even further than we did then. But the victory we had was hard-won as it was, and we were tired of war and death. Their leaders were dead, their armies dead or scattered. Pursuing a broken, retreating people even further seemed unnecessary."

His words are solemn, pained. It's easy to see that he suffered loss in that war, and it still cuts him deep.

War isn't something I can even begin to relate to. I've read about it many times. Heck, that was mostly what they'd taught us about in my many years of history class. I've seen it in movies, in video games, and in nightly news reports. But nothing comes close to personal experience. It doesn't even touch it. Pain, though—that, I know.

I offer the only comfort I can think of and set my hand on top of his.

His head jerks toward me as if he's forgotten I'm there. I squeeze his hand, giving him a small smile, no matter how I hurt inside thinking of May trapped with a brutal enemy. After a moment, he returns it, moving his hand to lace his fingers through mine.

My heart aches for him. For May. For my family. I want to do more. To wrap my arms around him and hold him against me. To run my hands through his hair and soothe away his worries. I might just need that too.

This story isn't done though, the look on his face says that clear enough, so I hold myself back, content to feel the warmth of his hand in mine.

Riven sucks in a breath before he continues. "My father died in that war."

I squeeze his hand tighter.

"Sigurd was our ally. Our people fought together, side by side, as he and my father fought side by side. The war changed all of that. In one of the final battles, Sigurd and my father led the front together. My father fell. I was too far away in the battle to see it happen, but I felt his power falter and then go out, like a piece of myself suddenly fading into nothingness. All the people of the forest felt the loss of our king. And then the power settled on me, a crushing weight that pushed me into the ground along with my grief until it settled under my skin. Those who survived the battle said that Sigurd could have saved him." His hand tightens on mine, almost painfully before going slack. "He didn't though. My father died there, and Sigurd survived. Injured but barely."

I inch closer to Riven on the sofa, my free hand coming over to clasp our joined ones, trying to offer further comfort.

"I'm so sorry." The words are insufficient but all I have.

His tight-lipped smile doesn't meet his eyes. "He and my father had been close friends once, before I was born. Sigurd coveted my mother, but she chose my father instead. It drove a rift between them, but they remained tentative allies despite that."

Evelyn. His mother who had also passed, though I don't know when or how. I can't add to Riven's sorrow by asking about that now. Though I wonder about it and about Sigurd, who must be much older than Riven, despite the fact that they appear similar in age. He, too, carries a burden of loss.

Riven looks away again, seeing memories across the room that I can only guess at. "I think Sigurd always hoped my mother would change her mind and pick him instead. She would never have left my father though. Her heart was irrevocably his. Getting my father out of the way was the only way to make it possible." He shakes his head at the memory. "Sigurd came to visit my mother at the end of the war. I was there when she asked him if he could have saved my father. He didn't respond. Couldn't lie to tell her no."

Riven leans back on the couch and closes his eyes.

"She screamed at him. Hit him. Called him names I still don't understand. He took it all without lifting a hand or letting his magic stir. It may be the only noble thing he's ever done. When her anger had burned through her, I pulled her off of him and held her as she cried. She told him she never wanted to see him again. The look in his eyes... I'll never forget it, but he honored her wishes and stayed away until after her death."

"You still hate him," I whisper. It's not even a question. It's as real and true as his hand in mine.

"Yes." The last letter hangs in the air of the quiet room.

Riven opens his eyes and turns his head to look at me, a sad smile on his face. "But I need him. A war would weaken us both too much and make us vulnerable to the Wild Tribes or even other courts, if they were so inclined."

I shiver. This world is so much bigger and more complicated than I ever guessed when I first arrived. If it's the same size as my world...

No, I can't even go there. It's too much to consider.

The sad smile still clinging to his face, his vulnerability, his honesty, his openness—it's enough to wreck me.

This is Riven. My Riven. It's no mask or show of power but his true self.

I want to cheer him up. Need to. And frankly, sometimes you have to laugh just so you won't cry, and the tears are trying so hard to win, burning at the corners of my eyes.

So, I paste a goofy smile on my face and tilt my head to the side. "We could just kidnap him and ransom him to the Unseelie for May."

A huff of laughter burst from his lips. "I like your thoughts. Unfortunately, I doubt we could pull it off, and that would definitely pit his army against us."

His countenance brightens ever so slightly, but the shadows in his eyes linger.

Before I can think of anything comforting or clever to say, Riven gets to his feet.

"There's much to do before the ball, and I'm sure you want to spend some time in the library," he says, his gaze somber but resolved. "Solona's probably waiting for you. I'll be back later."

That's right. There's work to do.

I watch him leave, his back straight and strong, despite the pain I know he's feeling. If he can be strong for his people, for those he loves, I can too.

CHAPTER 23

LAYERS OF FABRIC HANG over Karin's arms as she carries the gown into the room. Green and gold. Riven's colors. She holds it up for me to examine.

The fine lace that glimmers in the light takes my breath away. The delicate pattern consists of mostly deep, forest green leaves with shimmering gold ones falling down the bodice and skirt to pool in a pile along the bottom hem like a mound of shining coins. Dark green material, the same shade as the lace, lines the interior of the fitted bodice in strategic places to fully cover anything I don't want to show.

"It's beautiful," I say. Fit for a princess or a beauty queen, not for me. Or rather... A shiver rolls across my skin. A fae queen.

Karin smiles. "It will look lovely on you. Especially once I do your hair and make-up."

Make-up. Pretty sure she doesn't mean L'Oréal either. Normally, I wear at least a little something. Tinted moisturizer to smooth out my skin, maybe a little concealer for bad days, a touch of eyeliner to bring out the golden flecks in my brown eyes. With everything going on, make-up has been pretty low on my priority list. Like, the very bottom of it. I haven't seen any, haven't asked, and in a lot of ways, I don't miss it. But if she's offering, sure, why not?

Karin turns me in front of a mirror once she's finished.

I gape at the woman staring back.

It's not me, even though this woman mirrors my every move. Small golden leaves that sparkle in the light are interwoven through my hair, forming an almost faux crown. A few delicate wisps of hair escape here and there, draping down like artful, twisting vines.

Karin giggles as she packs away the little jars of make-up.

My face has never been so perfect and contoured. Gold dust around my eyes and the freshly crushed raspberry of my lips highlight all my best features. Between the gown, the make-up, and the fading light of sunset on the balcony, I practically glow, inside and out.

"Ready for the finishing touch?" she gestures to the gown.

I nearly laugh. Finishing touch, my ass. That gown is a work of art all its own.

Karin laces up the back, securing it tightly around me. The last thing I need is it slipping off in front of everyone. Now, that would be something the fae would never forget, and they'd probably enjoy it way too much.

Once, I read that make-up is a woman's body armor. It would have to be mine tonight. I've no illusions that this fae ball will be any more pleasant than the first I stumbled into. Quite possibly, it'll be worse, given there's another fae court in attendance as well.

I need all the armor I can get. How many times have I almost cracked? Almost broken down in sobs because my sister is captive and it's all my fault?

So many. Too many to count.

And it can't happen tonight, not in front of all these fae. I won't let them see me break.

Riven strolls in from the adjoining bedroom.

Everything stills as we stare at each other across the room.

He's resplendent, literally almost glowing with power. His outfit oozes decadence and wealth. Finely cut brown pants; a silken white shirt; a fitted overcoat in deep green, decorated with golden thread; tall, dark brown boots that hug his calves to utter perfection. He's left his hair loose, flowing down behind his head and shoulders. Atop his head sits a crown of golden leaves twisted together and spotted with emeralds.

This is the King of the Forest. Undampened, in all his fearsome glory. Had I not known him, I'd be tempted to fall to my knees in a mix of fear and awe.

"Perfection." His word of praise holds an air of awe.

It takes a moment to realize that he's addressed that comment to me and had not been answering my own thoughts on his attire. I run my hands along the lace as he continues to sweep me with his gaze.

I have no words to adequately describe him. It'd take too many. Instead, I settle on, "Thank you."

This fae king is regal as a lion and just as much the predator. I'm his prey; there's no mistaking that. If he had a tail, it'd be flicking back and forth, an indication he's ready to pounce. The amused, playful mask of the fae king is back in place tonight. He may need it just as much as I need my armor of make-up.

As he stalks closer, it's all I can do not to retreat. But it's not fear causing my heart to race. Quite the opposite.

"May I have a few minutes alone with Lia?" He croons, gently fingering one of the golden leaves in my hair.

I shift on my feet. Butterflies flutter in my stomach.

Riven's so close. The sweet hint of honeysuckle invades my nose, blending with the distinctly odd feeling of magic rolling off him.

Karin fixes him with a hard stare. "Do not mess up my masterpiece."

Riven chuckles at her words as he wraps a tendril of my hair around his fingers, bringing it to his lips.

"Will you be there?" I ask her as she gathers her things to leave. Anything to distract him. Not to mention it'd be nice to have another familiar face around.

"No," she replies a bit too quickly. "I don't think I would enjoy it, but I'll see you tomorrow."

When the door clicks shut behind her, I gather my courage and turn to face Riven. He lets go of my hair and settles his hand on my shoulder.

"You look..." I start.

Riven raises his eyebrows, expectant. "Like the most handsome male you've ever seen?"

Always so humble. I can't stop the eye roll. He *is* the most handsome man I've ever seen, but that's not what I'd planned to say. "Different. I... I think I can almost see the magic coming off of you."

"Today, it's necessary."

It *is* magic. My mouth forms a silent O. A show of power. Clearer and more definite than any military might. Intended to intimidate Sigurd and remind him who rules here. All those things he doesn't say, but he doesn't need to.

"Is it so repulsive to you?" he asks.

Is it? It makes him even more otherworldly. No one could ever confuse him with a human when magic literally seeps off him like thin, wavering steam that glitters in the light. Not that you really could before, but it's even less of a possibility now.

Something in me, something in my very DNA, wants to quake in terror at the sight of him.

It's so wrong, so other. And yet, it's him.

"No, it's not repulsive," I reply. Truth. His power is somewhat terrifying, otherworldly for sure, but not repulsive.

Riven pulls me to him, and I go, almost tripping over the hem of the gown. He holds me close, but not enough to upset Karin's careful work. A little thrill zips through my blood when he places a kiss atop my head.

"Be confident," he says. "Do not let any of them intimidate you."

Easier said than done, but I nod all the same.

"It will help me if you look happy to be here." His voice softens. "If, say, you look at me like you did last night."

Heat creeps down my body in a slow wave to settle in my stomach...and lower. I bite my lip and turn away. "Is that really necessary?"

"It would make a statement. To Sigurd and to my court."

The reference to his court brings to mind his talk of spies from a few days ago. Is he any closer to discovering who it is? So many people grasping for power, within his own people and without. No wonder he's determined to put on a show.

"Consider it. And be wary of Sigurd. He likes to play games," he adds. "But either way, I have something for you."

I turn back in time to see him fish in his coat pocket and pull out something that shimmers in the light.

Riven holds a necklace up between us by either end of a golden strand. A large emerald hangs in the center. My eyes widen at the glittering gem. Holy shit. That stone alone could have paid my college tuition.

"May I?" he asks.

A squeak that may have been a yes slips out.

The heavy stone settles around my neck as he clasps it in place. It complements the bracelet Solona gave me, which I still wear at all times.

I catch a glimpse of myself in a tall mirror.

This is the finishing touch, the missing piece I didn't know was missing but completes the startling transformation I've undergone.

Riven's satisfied smile in my periphery doesn't hurt either.

"Now." He extends an arm to me. "Is my lady ready for the ball?"

CHAPTER 24

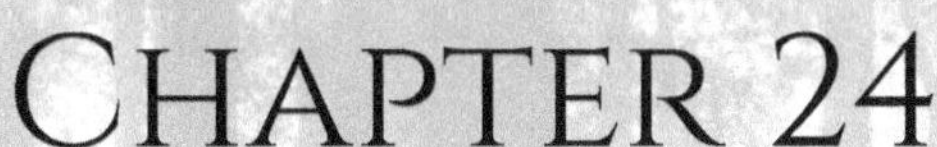

THE THRONE ROOM IN Arbrean resembles the one in Virideria in size. However, more stone than plant life comprises its structure. Trees still interweave with the walls, and the roof opens to the sky, broken only by the spiderweb pattern of limbs and leaves. But the ground is smooth, white stone, unbroken by plant or stream. Two sets of double wooden doors, smaller than the ones at the entrance but no less grand, adorn either side of the room. A wide, white marble throne, big enough that one man can have his legs stretched wide and still not taken up its width, sits on a dais near the back as the focal point of the space.

Riven sits on that throne, a wine glass in one hand, the other curled around my waist. His cocky, amused, and playful demeanor is firmly back in place. It's the mask he shows his court, who he believes a nest of spies, and the one he'll show to Sigurd when he walks through those doors with his entourage any minute now. I hated it the first time I was here—when the man I'd come to care for had vanished to be replaced by a twisted version of himself.

Though I can't help but wonder if it's really an act or just another side of himself that he brings out to suit his needs. I hold in a sigh and pray for the former.

I lean against the crook of his shoulder. One arm reaches across my body to toy with his shirt so I appeared draped about him. To all the court in their riot of colorful outfits, I'm the besotted, silly human, enraptured with their leader who's claimed me in word, if not yet in body.

And damn if they don't believe it. Their smiles, whispers, and giggles are proof enough. It's weird, to be such an object of fascination, but I'm thankful to be safely at Riven's side rather than down in the midst of numerous fae who would literally trip over themselves for the honor of touching my hand or snagging a strand of my hair. Their desperation for humanity and whatever it can offer them is...a lot.

For the moment, they're appeased.

Their king has conquered and won—claimed a human to ensure their magic will slowly return as I reside with them. It should be hard to act this way, to make the courts of Forest and Air think I've fallen head over heels for Riven, thus strengthening his reign.

But it's not all an act.

Though I surely can't call it love, I care for Riven and his people. Maybe not these idiots staring at us, but at least the few I've spent time with.

Riven's hand rubs a lazy pattern on my hip through the fine lace of my gown. Between our planned ruse, his hands on my body, and myself all over him, it's entirely too easy to forget where we are. I don't have to fake the gentle sigh that escapes my lips or the heat rising to my cheeks. Pretending not to care for the male next to me would be exceedingly more difficult.

The doors creak open in a groan of wood. A hush falls over the room as conversations halt midsentence.

I refocus my gaze toward the doors on the opposite side of the room, all the while trying to school my face to remain casual, concerned only with the fae whose lap I'm practically sitting in. I tighten my fingers on Riven's shirt as the knot in my stomach pulls taut.

Two sets of Riven's elite guard, dressed in their customary attire emblazoned with Riven's golden tree, step over the threshold and pull the doors wide.

A set of six guards march in first, dressed in attire resembling Riven's guard but mostly whites and light grays. It looks lighter in weight too, almost airy. Pretty poor defense in a fight, but maybe magic helps with that too. On each one's chest is a crest belonging to Sigurd. A white bird—no, an eagle—on a field of blue.

I examine each of them in turn. No obvious weapons, though they undoubtedly have an arsenal of magic at their disposal. Although their uniforms are the same, each guard varies in appearance, their hair and skin a combination of human-like tones. An even mix of men and women.

My brows arch higher. Point for Sigurd.

Members of Riven's elite guard are scattered all around the sides of the room. I briefly catch Sylvie's gaze. She gives me a small dip of her head in return, something that would be unnoticed by anyone unless you were looking for it.

I am, and it gives me comfort. Some of the knots in my stomach manage to loosen. A little bit.

The six guards separate, three lining up along each wall of fae standing on either side of the space. Fae lights float through the air, casting shadows on the doorway and the space on the other side, cloaking it in darkness. The center pathway from the door to the throne is open, inviting someone to walk down it.

Sigurd accepts that invitation and strides in from the shadows, a trail of brightly attired courtiers following him.

His attire today is much the same as it had been when we'd met him at the border. Simple, yet elegant. No crown adorns his head, yet there's no mistaking the air of power and authority that hangs around him like an outfit all its own.

Riven's fingertips continue to tease the material of the gown along my side. The playful amusement on his face never wavers as we watch our guest approach.

How easy he makes all this look.

Sigurd's gaze roves over me as he crosses to the throne. It's deeper, more intrusive, than any of the other fae. It's so, so hard not to seem bothered by the fae king dissecting me with his eyes. Hushed silence fills the room, waiting, as he comes to stand in front of Riven. Magic hums in the air, thicker than normal, like high humidity that isn't damp.

"Welcome, Sigurd, King of Air," Riven announces, not rising or changing his posture.

I stifled the urge to sigh in relief when Sigurd's eyes stop their close inspection and find a new target.

"I trust you've settled in well to my city," Riven continues, ever casual, ever confident, despite the formal event and the tension zipping in the air.

A deep chuckle rumbles in response. "Of course. This city has quite beautiful scenery." His head twists around as he takes in the attending fae. "It's been quite a long time since we gathered like this."

"Perhaps too long," Riven agrees. "As such, I thought we should celebrate our joint efforts and allow our people the chance to get reacquainted. We have prepared a feast for you all, and there will, of course, be entertainment and dancing." The last he adds as if that is obvious and expected. To these people, it may very well be.

Riven sets his wine glass on the arm of the throne and rises.

The colorful mass of fae fills the room like sardines in a can. Several crane their necks over and around one another, trying for the best view of the two kings. Or me. Maybe both. Too many of them stare at me, and all I want to do is flee.

Riven claps twice. The sound echoes through the space, much louder than it should. Guards flanking the wooden doors throw them open to the massive courtyard that lies beyond.

Now it's my turn. Riven told me what to expect, the order of things. My part is so simple, but it takes ten times the effort it should. I link my arm through his extended elbow and embrace the protection and comfort he offers. My skin tingles where we touch, a reminder of the position we were just in and all the wicked, delicious things that transpired last night.

It's only a few steps from the raised dais to the floor, but it takes all my concentration not to trip over the golden hem of the gown and tumble. That'd be just like me too. It'd probably go down in fae history. Clumsy human trips on her own gown and breaks her arm—the highlight of the reunion ball between the courts of Forest and Air.

Safe on level ground, Riven's grin broadens as he addresses Sigurd once more. "You shall have the place next to mine at the high table this evening."

"I would expect nothing less," Sigurd replies. The cunning mind behind his disarming face peeks out through his trickster smile and twinkling, deep blue eyes. His serpentine gaze rests on me again, sending a shiver down my spine as he looks me up and down. "I assume your lovely companion will be joining us."

As if he doesn't already know that.

Then, Sigurd stretches out a hand to me in a courtesy greeting.

Do I take it? I flick my gaze to Riven, the question in my eyes, but his focus is still on the fae in front of us, his arrogant mask firmly in place for all his court to see.

My jaw clenches.

Reluctantly, I stretch out my free hand and placed it atop Sigurd's. His fingers wrap around mine as his head dips to place another kiss. But his lips are not all that touch my skin. The unmistakable swipe of the tip of a tongue flits across my hand between barely parted lips.

Oh, my God. The muscles in my arm lock up.

I jerk back, but he holds firm, concealing my disgust with his stiff grip.

He did not. He...

Sigurd drops my hand. His grin twitches into a momentary smirk. "I've brought a gift for your lady."

Another one. A wave of unease washes through me. A muscle ticks in Riven's jaw. His wide smile falters for the briefest moment. Shit. If they come to blows here in the throne room, it'll be the end of everything. Their tenuous peace, the search for May—

I cannot let that happen, no matter what.

Sigurd pretends not to notice as he reaches into his pocket and pulls forth a small silver ring affixed with a blue stone. A sapphire, it has to be, cut in a pear shape.

"Human women like jewelry, do they not?" He addresses the question to me, holding up the ring between his thumb and pointer finger. "Consider it a token of my regard. I do hope it fits."

I stare at his grinning face. Confusion and apprehension freeze my actions and choke off my words. Fae murmur around us, leaning around one another for a better view of the scene playing out before them. Which is worse—taking it or refusing?

I wait for Riven to intervene, to choose for me, but just like at the border, he doesn't.

Of course not. When I actually want him to act, he doesn't.

Improve relations with the Court of Air. Solona's words echo through my mind over the din of conversation around us. My actions will make a difference for both courts.

And for May.

For her, I steel my courage and don a courteous smile.

"Thank you for your generosity." I extend my hand to him again, accepting the ring.

Sigurd inclines his head as he slides his gift onto my ring finger.

It fits.

Too well.

My hand shakes when he releases it, though maybe less than the smile wobbling on my face.

His gift looks for all the world like a human engagement ring.

CHAPTER 25

T HE COURTYARD IS DECKED out with trappings of both the magical and tangible variety. Fae balls of light float aimlessly
through the air, casting a soft glow on the whole area. They bright-
en up the darkness of the evening as if the stars themselves have
floated down from the heavens to join us. Fountains gurgle. Tables
both large and small are arranged around the area for seating.
Others are laden with platters of food. If I didn't know better, I'd
say it was a celebrity wedding reception.

Or one for royalty.

I swallow the knot in my throat, all too aware of the ring on my
finger. Riven doesn't say a word, not a damn thing, as he leads the
procession out here with me on his arm. Actually, he hasn't really
looked at me at all, which says as much about his fury as words
ever could.

My stiff smile twitches as I side-eye him—hard. Did he honestly
expect me to rebuke a gift from his guest? That wouldn't have gone
well.

Dancers weave through the crowd in scant costumes. They
move to the hypnotic rhythm played by a small group of musicians.
Though they number only seven, their song has the resonance of
a full count orchestra. Something about it stirs my soul, inspiring
awe and reverence. Even the air itself is perfumed by flowers at
the peak of bloom.

Despite the dread wrapped like a noose around my neck all
afternoon and the guilt over May that could drag me down into
an open grave, I want nothing more than to wander through the

crowd and lose myself to the sights, sounds, and spectacle of it all. Maybe there's magic at work in that too, something to encourage everyone to relax, enjoy themselves, and forget for a time that they're not exactly friends.

Our table is near the middle back of the courtyard in a place of honor, widely ringed by open space for both visibility and respect. Fanciful carpets coat the ground. The table itself is draped with green silks and golden flower petals.

I relax considerably once we're seated. Riven keeps up slow but steady conversation with Sigurd, and I don't have to do a darn thing but eat. Which might be easier if the food wasn't so strange.

"Hah, make sure you don't touch that one." Ambrose laughs as two small, red vegetables, resembling stuffed baby peppers, are ladled onto my plate. "Too many of those will set your mouth on fire."

I grimace at the new addition. He might be serious.

Nothing ever seems to dampen Ambrose's jovial spirit. Even the grim events of yesterday hadn't kept him down long. I poke at the food with my fork, rolling two purple beans back and forth. Wasting food sucks, but the magic clinging to my skin makes even the most appetizing selections taste like sand.

"Strange how active the Unseelie have been lately." Sigurd's words catch my attention where none of the earlier conversation has.

"It is," Riven agrees. "They've gotten much bolder in their attempts to regain power, and something must be working. I didn't know they still possessed the skills to shift, much less in my own territory."

Sigurd makes a sound that could almost be a snort. "Even I didn't know your wards were so weak that you would have missed such a significant trespass."

"I was"—Riven twirls his hand through the air—"distracted."

Sigurd's next words are muffled as Ambrose lets out a loud guffaw to my left, completely engrossed in conversation with another advisor.

"We may need to do something about the Wild Tribes soon." Riven shrugs, as if that's a small problem as opposed to the realm-threatening one he describes. Whatever magic holds their words to truth clearly doesn't do the same to their actions, and Riven takes it to its full advantage.

"We?" Sigurd questions. He's blocked from view, but I can envision the raised eyebrows and mock surprise.

Riven laughs. "Unless you've decided to join the Unseelie."

"No one changes that much."

Both grow silent. Riven takes a sip of wine, leaning back in his chair.

Sigurd enters the corner of my vision, precisely spearing a piece of food and bringing it to his mouth. His table manners, unsurprisingly, are impeccable. He glances over at me as he swallows. I've stopped playing with mine, making it all too obvious I've been listening in. Not that they're speaking anymore.

Riven beams with pride as he turns to me. His hand strokes the top of my thigh under the table.

I bite my bottom lip, pretending to be embarrassed. It's not hard. Every touch stirs up the butterflies in my stomach and has me aching with memories of the night before.

Sigurd coughs and takes a sip of his wine. "I have some men in the Shadow Lands."

Riven twists back to him so fast his hand bumps the table, sending dishes clattering.

Fae can't lie. Why share such valuable information? I edge to the side of my seat, straining to listen in to their conversation.

"The Wild Tribes, as you like to call them, have been organizing and gathering together. The Unseelie who took the girl is one of their leaders. Katiya, I believe they call her. My guards have been able to find out little else thus far, but I expect they will be able to learn more with time."

An olive branch? Goosebumps race up my arms. If he's truly trying to atone for his past sins and forge a better relationship, it could mean so much to all the fae.

"My guards have had similar findings," Riven replies. "Someone organizing the tribes, bringing them together."

A pair of performers step into the open space before our table and bow deeply. Riven gives them leave to proceed. Conversation dwindles as various fae perform acts of agility, skill, speed, and other talents.

Riven explains each act to me. Respect glitters in his eyes. Praise rings in his voice. He's proud of his people. He loves them.

An unexpected warmth settles in my chest. It's not lust or desire, though I've felt those often enough recently. It's not even the wine I've been slowly sipping.

Something else. Something that scares me as much as it excites me.

I jump in my seat as someone touches my shoulder. Solona's pleasant face smiles down at me, where she stands just behind me. The long sleeve of her golden gown cascades down the back of my chair.

"Shall we take a walk, dear?" Her tone reminds me so much of Elise. Soft, comforting.

"Yes, I'd…" I'd love to. That's what I want to say. Sitting here with a fake smile plastered across my face is agonizing. But it wouldn't fit the ruse I play. My gaze turns to focus on Riven.

Pretend like you're in love. Like you don't want to leave him, I coach myself as I school my features.

"You should go with Solona." Riven breaks off the conversation with a fae male who'd stepped up to the table. "I'll come for you shortly."

"Two lovely ladies taking a stroll. That sounds quite enticing." Sigurd's rumbling laughter chases his words.

It's all I can do not to cringe.

Solona's pleasant smile thins infinitesimally, so slight I almost miss it. "This stroll is ladies only. You'll excuse us for needing some time in each other's confidence."

"A pity. You wouldn't rather catch up with an old friend?" He leans back in the chair, rocking on its legs, that terrible smirk back on his face.

"I'm certain we'll have time for pleasantries later," Solona says before turning her back on him.

She leads me away from the crowd, my arm looped through hers, until we reach the edge of the courtyard. My lungs filled with mossy, floral air as I breathe deeply, willing my body to relax.

"Sigurd called you a friend," I whisper. "Is that true?"

Solona pats my arm. "An old friend, he said. And yes, once we were, long ago when our two courts were allies and mingled like this often." She turns us around, her golden hem swishing on the stonework. She sighs. Her gaze both takes in the sights before us and is far away all at once. "We had parties like this often when I was younger. I looked forward to them."

"Before Sigurd let Riven's father die in battle?" I whisper, conscious of fae hearing which is, sadly, much stronger than my own.

A pained expression crosses her face. "Yes, just so. Riven told you about that, did he?"

I nod. "He said Sigurd could have saved him but chose not to."

"That's what we were told. I still wonder if we were too harsh and acted too quickly, cutting ties with the Court of Air the way we did." Her gaze wanders back to where the kings occupy the main table.

Riven still wears the mask of the cocky, amused fae king, that side of him that's so different than the one I know. He looks for all the world as if there are no problems weighing on his shoulders, as if his reign is strong, secure, his lands blossoming in prosperity, but that's far from the current situation.

Her eyes follow my gaze, looking from me toward her king. Her voice drops low, conspiratorial, as she leans her tall form over to whisper to me, "That's not him. Not his true form."

"I know." I do. He plays a game, the same way I'd been trying to play one all evening.

"Good." She parts my arm again. "Don't forget it. No matter what you see. He tries so hard to act like Theon, to project the unfailing confidence he had even unto the end."

"Theon?" The unknown name has my brows wrinkling.

"Lutheon Silvanus, his father."

"Oh." My shoulders droop.

"He was beloved, respected. His reign a time of prosperity for the Court of the Forest."

I study her expression, the softness in her dark eyes.

Riven's isn't so far. She doesn't need to say it. This mask he wears, it's all an attempt to act like his father, to be someone he's simply not.

"Enough about that. More importantly, I wanted to tell you I found something that might help our cause." Her hands clasp over mine.

I straighten, pulled up by the hope in her voice. "What?"

"Spells to heal their land. They're old, complicated, but it might be enough to sway them."

"That's..." I'm speechless with relief.

Her smile is tight. "There's no guarantee it'll work, but I thought it may lift your spirits."

Guarantee or not, it's something.

Solona pulls me along, walking slowly back toward the assembly. "I have appreciated your company in the library." Her voice returns to its regular pitch. The time for secrets is over. "Perhaps you'd continue to help me, even when our current quest is done? I've been looking into ways to improve the economies of the smaller cities, and I could use your assistance. If you're willing, of course."

A laugh catches in my throat. Before the accident, I'd been studying business. Focusing on growth and development strategies proved impossible after that. I dropped out, walked away from that dream. Well, took a mental health break was what I told everyone, but really, how could I go back? Still, there's a kernel of my heart that leaps at the thought of stretching those mental muscles again. I'd been good, promising, one professor said.

Deep within me, that girl is still there. Somewhere. Maybe. "I think I would enjoy that."

We walk and talk of her plans until Riven pulls me away and onto the dance floor.

Fae music is hypnotic. It's easy to forget that mass of fae around me and the way they warred for my attention at the first ball I'd stumbled into.

They don't dare now.

Lingering glances, whispers, sure, but no one would dare to steal their king's partner.

That alone gives a lift to my chin and confidence to my step.

I'm Riven's consort. Lady of the Forest.

With the music taking hold of my spirit and Riven leading me across the floor, it doesn't even matter that I'm a terrible dancer and don't know a single fae dance.

The last stanzas of a song weave through the night.

I giggle as Riven twirls me around in a circle, the hem of the long gown fluttering. This night has turned out so much better than I expected. His strong arm snakes around my waist, halting my turn and pulling me against him. His head dips. The world fades away, and all I know his him—his warmth, his scent.

My heart flutters, ready to be lost in his kiss, when something catches my attention out of the corner of my eye.

I turn as fae couples lurch out of the way.

Sigurd strides through the crowd like a shadow on a sunny day, seeping away the warmth of the moment.

A growl rumbles from Riven's chest.

Sigurd saunters in our direction, smirking all the while. The nearby fae practically trip over themselves to get out of his way.

"May I have the next dance?" His half-smile and mischievous, sapphire eyes are in sharp contrast to the courtesy of his out-stretched hand.

Riven grins a wolf's smile. "Sorry, but I prefer to dance with women."

Sigurd's lips twitch. "As do I."

I hang on to Riven for dear life as the two kings stare each other down.

Please no. My thoughts plead as I try to keep my features neutral. *No.*

"Well, what friend would deny such a request?" Riven's smile is too broad, the words so sweet they hurt my teeth.

A chill leeches into my skin as he releases me from his protective embrace. I scramble for a hold of his coat, but he steps away.

No. I wobble on my feet. This can't be happening.

Riven claps a hand on Sigurd's shoulder as he passes by. His broad smile never breaks, but the words he grates out between his white teeth are so low I almost miss them. "If you do anything to her..."

Sigurd shrugs him off. "It's only a dance."

The nearby fae are as frozen and wide-eyed as me when Sigurd steps into Riven's place.

The King of Air extends his hand with a dip of his head, but this time it's empty, waiting for the gift of my company. "Lia."

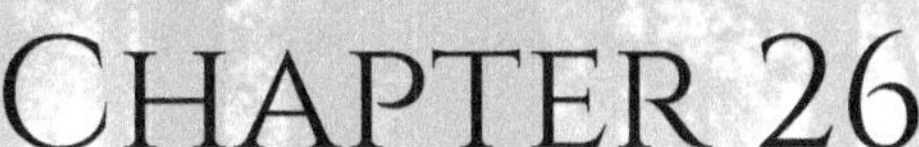
CHAPTER 26

R IVEN'S RETREATING BACK VANISHES into the crowd. My teeth grind. All the warm, pleasant feelings that gave my feet wings moments ago are gone.

Fine. If he's going to leave me with his hated adversary, then I'll dance with him, and dammit, I'll do my best to enjoy it. My heel grinds against the stone floor. Let him watch me linger in Sigurd's arms.

I paste a tight smile on my face as I turn back to Sigurd and notch my chin just a bit higher.

"Sigurd." I take his hand with a small bob of my head.

His eyes widen for the briefest moment.

I don't cringe as his hand comes to rest on my hip, nor do I flinch when he draws me close. My own hand rests on his shoulder like we're two kids at a middle school dance.

Leave room for Jesus, Dad had said back then.

This might be the first time I've actually tried to apply that saying.

A new melody carries into the night, and Sigurd pulls us into the crowd of dancers. It should be hard to dance with him, but it's not. His lead is as easy to follow as Riven's, even with his intense gaze studying my every breath.

If I hadn't heard stories of his past, I might actually find him charming. He's handsome enough, dare I say, sexy. The kind of guy I'd totally have tried to flirt with if I met him in a bar somewhere. His appearance is disarming. It's likely meant to be.

But I know what's he's done. Beneath his fair façade is a cunning, fierce, and possibly two-faced king who has led his people since before my father was born.

"You're not what you pretend to be." The words are quiet, just audible above the music.

It takes a moment to register he's spoken.

"What do you mean?" I stare at him.

"You're pretending to be a simple, lovesick human. That's not you though. You're too clever, too fiery, determined. And something else... Uncertain? Fearful? You don't fully trust your Forest King." He spins me in a circle before tugging me closer, far closer than I'd like. "I saw it in the woods, I saw it this morning, and I can see it in your eyes now. You may fool much of the court, but someone completely devoted to him wouldn't stare me down so boldly."

Now I do look away. Away from his eyes that see too much. Away from his grin that says he knows he's right.

The music continues to play.

We dance, but each step, each breath, is a challenge as I fight against the fear taking hold.

"I've been thinking about your bargain and your little sister," he continues.

Pain lances through my chest like a sharp, pointy dagger. She's still out there, with the Unseelie, and yet here I am, dancing at a ball.

My steps falter. I stare at the floor, hiding tears that threaten to fall.

It's too much. In minutes, he's broken down my walls and brought out all the worry I've tried to so hard block out.

Sigurd brings us to a stop. Other couples flow around us as if we're a rock in a stream.

I blink away the tears and hazard a glance at my companion. His countenance is serious, assessing. Instead of resuming the dance, he takes my hand and leads through the throng of fae.

They don't dare stop us.

Maybe they would if I asked, a favor for their lady, but my throat's so tight I can't manage anything. On the far edge of the dance floor, the music doesn't beg me to dance the way it did only moments ago.

"One might think a generous king would have offered to save her regardless of your choices." Sigurd glances back at the crowd and then me.

This dagger, too, finds my heart, slicing deep.

"What if I were to be the one to find and return your sister?" His fingers curl around a loose tendril of hair near my face. One manicured nail grazes my cheek, and I shudder. "What would you offer me?"

I pull away, adding much needed space between him and my pounding heart.

"I have nothing left to give," I say. Riven already has my time, my promise, and though I try to deny it, a piece of my heart.

"We'll see." Sigurd's response sends goosebumps rising along my bare arms.

He circles around me, his smile feral.

I hate the crowds, the eyes on me, but what I wouldn't do for them now. It's dark here. Shadowed. The twinkling fae lights haven't floated to this section of the expansive courtyard. There's too much space. We're too far. I retreat until my back bumps against a stone wall.

"What if there was a way to break your bargain?" he asks.

My pulse hammers against my ribs. "Is there?"

"Nothing is impossible, but you wouldn't do it, would you?" His voice grows sharper. An eerie blue glow alights in his eyes. "Do you love him? Is that it?"

He's too close.

If I could crawl up the wall, I would. I look around, desperate to find Riven, Ambrose, anyone who might come to my assistance.

"No." He leans into my line of sight. "No, you don't. At least, not yet. You haven't even let him mark you, though I'm sure he's tried." His tongue clicks in his mouth as his head swivels.

One hand plants against the wall near my head, and I gasp.

"But you love your sister." He leans in closer, until the scent of pine swarms my sense. "It's that love that makes your human spirit burn so brightly, so resiliently."

Sigurd grabs my waist. The touch burns, and not in the delicious way that Riven's does.

My mouth dries. I need out. Now.

A slap or punch might not do it. A kick between the legs?

A vine whips out from the wall with an audible crack.

Sigurd releases me and stumbles back a step, but his features are even, collected, almost as if he expected that.

Hands are on me, turning me, and then I'm buried in Riven's chest, his scent enveloping me like a shield.

"What happened here?" The anger in his voice is palpable.

Is he asking me or Sigurd?

"We danced. We talked. Nothing more," Sigurd says, not even the slightest off-note in his voice.

Riven pulls me back to look at me, holding my face in his hands, likely mussing my make-up.

"I'm fine." The lie comes so easily.

The wavy aura around Riven flares. The crack of a vine snaps in the air behind me.

I capture his face in my hands and turn it away from Sigurd. I can't let the goodwill they've built come crashing down. Not over me. I won't destroy something else. I won't delay May's rescue.

Never again.

"I'm fine," I repeat, more strongly.

Rustling, like a snake slithering through tall grass, echoes around us as the vines dissolve into leaves that flutter to the ground.

I breathe an inward sign of relief.

Ambrose and Galen hurry toward us. Looking past them, most of the crowd is oblivious to the altercation. Another good sign.

"Everything all right here?" Ambrose asks. His deep timbre demands attention.

"It is now," Riven bites out.

"Of course," Sigurd replies simultaneously.

Galen pales, shifting on his feet, not meeting anyone's gaze. I don't blame him. This is awkward at best.

"Well," Sigurd says with exaggeration. "If we're all fine here, then I'll return to the party. Good night." He gives a little mocking bow before turning and walking off.

Riven lets him go, but I don't miss the hard set of his jaw or the way his eyes stare daggers at Sigurd's back as he swaggers off into the crowd.

We don't return to the party.

Thank God.

My gown, which I'd thought so fantastical at the beginning of the evening, clings to my curves. The lace itches. The make-up, which had once been heavenly, is thick and pasty.

I want out of it, all of it.

Riven's stiff posture says more than words could. Fitting, since he doesn't utter a single one as we walk through the halls back to our room. Palpable anger rolls off him for the second time today.

Great, just great.

It's not directed at me, but I had a part in it. I knew it'd be hard for him to face his hated counterpart and carry on with another court here. And seeing Sigurd with me twice in one day...

I shake my head.

Silence threatens to smother me once the doors to his room close behind us. A few flickering lanterns join the dim moonlight illuminating the space. Pine wafts in on the night breeze, ruffling the curtains of vine at the edge of the balcony.

Riven stomps off into the bedroom without a word.

A heavy sigh is all I can manage as I stare at the threshold, waiting for a man who doesn't return.

Good job, Lia. Just great.

Instead, I decide to wash my face. That ritual always clears my senses and calms me. Besides, my pores need to breathe again.

A full pitcher of water waits by a bowl in front of the mirror across the room, the same one where Karin worked her practical magic hours earlier. I fill it, listening to the soothing sound of water as it trickles into the porcelain.

My chest feels lighter with Riven's necklace unclasped and set off to the side.

One swipe of a damp cloth after another, I wash away the emotions of the day.

The heartache from Riven's story.

My interactions with Sigurd.

My worry for May, lost somewhere out there, and our family who undoubtedly still searches for us back home.

I still, a gasp caught in my throat, when I catch sight of Riven in the mirror. He was so quiet I didn't hear him return. He watches me, clad only in loose pants that hang low on his waist.

Talk about a distraction.

Heat prickles my skin as he draws close. Without a word, he plucks one of the golden leaves from my hair. Another follows. Slowly, carefully, like a child plucking wildflowers, he removes each one and untangles the pins to let my hair fall free.

"I can smell him on you," he says.

I wince and hug myself. No need to ask who *he* is. I turn to face him as the last of my hair falls free.

I've never seen him look so weary. Even when he'd returned from resetting the wards, barely conscious and unable to stand, he had more spunk than he does now.

Riven scrubs a hand down his face. "You looked pleased to be dancing with him. You smiled even."

I frown. Possessive much?

"You left me with him. I was just making the best of a bad situation. Besides," I poke him in the chest with my index finger, "wasn't I supposed to be the happy, enamored human?"

"With me." His eyes cloud. "What did he say to you?"

What did he say? So much of it is already a blur. "He said...that I'm not what I pretend to be. He talked about my bargain, which he'd already known about this morning."

My throat grows thick as I contemplate telling him the rest. He wouldn't like it. Not at all. Especially the parts about breaking a bargain and whether I love him or not.

I care about Riven, more than I probably should, more than I thought possible only a few days ago, but love?

I can almost see the wheels churning in his head before he says, "Why did you stop dancing before the song ended? Why did he pull you away?"

"Why did you leave him with me at all?" I retort.

He glances away. "A confident king wouldn't mind if his lady dances with another."

My eyes roll before I can stop them. This again. Trying to be someone he's not. But at least he answered my question. "I got a little overwhelmed thinking of May and my family when he brought up the bargain, and I lost the beat of the dance."

Riven's lips flatten into a thin line. "He was all over you when I shifted next to you."

"It was nothing. Really." Totally uncomfortable and awful, actually, but no doubt that's what Sigurd planned.

"You're still wearing his ring."

Shit. I rip the gift off and toss it on the table behind me without a backward glance. From his point of view...

"Are you jealous?" I blurt.

He opens his mouth. Closes it. A muscle ticks in his jaw as he looks away.

I blink.

Oh my God. He really can't deny it. Can't lie.

"I have no interest in Sigurd." I close the distance between us. My lusty smile is back. Unlike in the throne room and at the party, this one isn't fake. "In fact, the only male I'm interested in is right here."

The muscular planes of his chest are hard as granite but smooth as silk. Other than his scars. I trace one down the side of his chest, along his arm...

"Humans can lie." Heat already simmers under half-drooped lids.

"Yes, I can lie, but I've always been bad at it."

His bicep tenses under my touch.

"You've called me out on that before, remember?" At first, I had trouble being honest with him in dreams. It took days, weeks for me to be fully honest, for him to pry out the brokenness I tried so hard to hide. I'm still not sure why he kept trying in those beautiful stolen minutes, but I'm so thankful he did. I'm not sure I could have made it through otherwise. "I think you know I'm not lying."

He pulls me tight to him as his only response.

"Should I prove it to you?" I arch one careful brow.

A wide, feral grin stretches across his face. "I think I might enjoy that."

CHAPTER 27

R IVEN'S LIPS CRASH INTO mine, demanding their due. I meet him with the same fury, eager to give just as much.

Earlier in the day, I was unable to comfort him when he confronted the memories of his past. I failed after all the times he'd listened to me and convinced me things would be okay.

I plan to make up for that now. To erase any doubts he has about my interactions with Sigurd.

I say everything with my kiss that I have no words for.

I'm here. I care for you. I want you and no one else.

Something shifts in me, clicking into place.

You're my missing piece.

It's a lightbulb going off within me, a realization I tell myself as much as him. My head swims, and without his arms around me, I might collapse. He holds me steady. His answers to the questions of my kiss don't have words either, but they say so much.

I'll be your rock. I care for you. You're mine.

The gown is stifling, constricting, too much. I need it gone.

I whimper against his lips, trying to pull at the laces behind me. It's no use. This lost in him, in us, I can't think, can only feel and react and follow where my heart leads.

I pull back, gasping for breath, for a moment of sanity. He lets me go...with his hands. His gaze, however, is still glued to me, watching me with that cat-like grin. I could melt. Slide right out of my gown and into a puddle on the floor, but the damn thing won't budge.

I turn around, giving him a view of the back of the laces. "A little help?"

"Certainly." A click sounds as his nails lengthen into pointed claws.

I suck in a breath. My back stiffens as I recall the last time I'd seen those wicked claws used.

Riven rakes the claws down the back of my gown so fast I don't have time to flinch. The distinctive sound of ripping material reaches my ears as the ties split down the middle. Severed lace floats to the floor. The gown sags around me. My back is undamaged, not even grazed.

That is *not* what I had in mind when I asked him to help with the ties. Effective, yes, the precision impressive, but my gown...

I frown at it.

Riven waves his hand in the air, and the claws disappear as if they'd never been. "If you liked it, I'll have it repaired."

I sigh. Impatient, fae male.

With my back to him, I shove the gown down my body, letting it slide along my curves. I wiggle in what I hope are sexy swishes until it finally pools on the ground at my feet. Night air caresses my bare skin, sending goosebumps along sensitive flesh. It's a sharp contrast to the volcano threatening to burn me up inside. My underwear follows in a repeat show.

I glance back over my shoulder at Riven. He reclines, half sitting, on the back of the sofa, arms crossed. The telltale tenting of his loose pants is impossible to miss.

His arms come loose as I prowl the short distance to him. He grips my waist, drawing me close. Heat from his chest melts against my palm. I slide my fingers through his hair. A near growl rumbles when I accidentally graze one sensitive ear. He jerks my hips into his, melding us together.

"You'll refrain from that unless you want me to take you right here and now." His deep laugh reverberates through my body.

So tempting, even if just to call his bluff.

My nipples graze his chest in the most delicious way and send a surge of liquid fire building between my legs. Riven's lips trail kisses down my neck then my chest. His hands pave the way as he feels then tastes.

"How I've waited to sample these," he whispers against my skin. His teeth graze one sensitive peak. He teases the other with a calloused hand, just as wicked and delightful.

My eyes roll back in my head.

All too soon, he releases my breast with a last flick of his tongue and continues trailing kisses down my stomach.

Lower.

"You want this? Me?" His voice is a hoarse rasp. A plea melted with the question.

"Yes. Yes, please," I whimper.

Gently, intently, he pushes my legs apart.

Breathless, I stare down at him in rapture. A king on his knees.

His half-mast eyes and lusty smile cause my legs to wobble as I spread for him. He reaches around my thighs to palm my backside as his head dips....

Oh, holy fuck!

The first flick of his tongue sends a shudder up my body. The second floods me with heat. By the third, rational thought flees.

He devours me. Relentless.

Whimpers and moans escape my lips. I'm lost to the feel of him tasting me, teasing me with each lap of his tongue.

"Rivenean." His name is a prayer on my lips. An oath.

My hands tangle in his hair to steady myself, not caring that I brush against the sensitive tips of his ears.

He growls against me, fingers digging into my backside as he pulls me closer.

The tip of his tongue invades my tight channel.

The world fades until all I know is his hot mouth against me. The knot deep in my core tightens, drawing me to the edge of release. Lightning races under my skin as his lips close around the sensitive nub between my legs.

I explode. A torrent of emotion races through me as I rock against the man between my legs, still lavishing me through the waves of my orgasm. My eyes water. I pant his name, barely able to stand.

My legs shake as he releases me to wipe my wetness from his face.

"I've wanted to do that since the first time you tried to touch me in your dreams." His tongue flicks over his lips, tracing away the last of what his hand failed to remove. "I'd wanted to touch you for so long. Craved it. And when you finally wanted the same, when you trusted me enough to spill your heart to me and sought me for comfort... Lia, I can't tell you what it meant to me. What it still means."

I've wanted him too. So long. At first, I just imagined curling up against him—comfort, safety. Then one day, it was a kiss, the touch of his hand against my skin. I craved it. Needed this man who saw me, healed me when no one else did.

An echo of release shudders down my spine.

"Maybe I can return the favor?" I lick my own lips.

In a heartbeat, I close the space between us and trail my fingers down his chest. I halt at the waistband of his pants.

"Lia," he groans. His hands weave themselves into my hair and around my back.

His eyes are pools of hunger. One look, and I shiver in pleasure and anticipation. I give him my best wolfish grin as I hook two fingers in the waistband of his pants and pull.

He springs free before me, flush and stiff in readiness.

Holy hell, even in my wildest imaginings, I never envisioned this.

But I see it now. I want it. Need it.

I caress the velvety length in a firm but gentle embrace. Riven groans in pleasure, but he grabs my arm, stilling my movements.

"Need you," he purrs between gritted teeth. "Inside you."

My mouth forms the 'oh' that echoes in my thoughts. Impossibly, more heat pools in my stomach, travels lower.

I'm ready for him. I ache for him.

In a quick move, he rights his pants, hiding himself from sight again before he lifts me into his arms. One arm under my knees and the other wrapped securely around my chest, he bridal carries me into the bedroom.

I curl my arms around his neck, reveling in the silken fall of his hair over my arms and the honeysuckle scent that bathes my soul.

Without a word, he deposits me atop his bed and steps back.

His eyes trail across me, slowly, deliberately, taking in every curve and dip. Between his ministrations and inspection, it's the perfect storm of sensation and emotion. The furs tickle my sensitive skin, but I ignore them, preferring instead to focus on the fae male in front of me.

Cloth rips in his urgency to shed the pants I tried to divest him of.

My stomach does somersaults as Riven climbs atop me on the bed, gently spreading my thighs to fit himself between. I'm covered in his heat, his smell, him.

His gaze levels with mine, all serious and somber, despite his heart racing against my own. "I want to be with you. I want you to bear my mark, but I will do whatever you wish in this."

My eyes widen. His mark. Of course.

He told me what such a marking entailed. And despite the tingle of apprehension, I want his mark. It would give him strength, magic. Not just him, all of them. More power they can use to recover May. But even if not for my sister, I want it for Riven and his people.

That and... "I want you. I want to be yours. I want your mark."

He stills against me, his weight pressing me into the furs at my back. "You mean it?"

"Every word."

His mouth is on mine then, and my hesitation flees, overwhelmed by desire, by certainty. It's me and him, this moment—touching, tasting, coming alive at every point of contact.

One hand traces the muscles of his back. The other tangles in his hair.

Riven adjusts his weight, rising up on his arms over me. Cool air rushes between us, tickling my heated skin.

"Oh." I gasp at the firm pressure against my opening.

"You take me willingly?" he asks through gritted teeth, his voice thick.

He waits, frozen in the moment, staring at me with rapt anticipation. If I tell him no, he'll leave me alone. I know it with a soul-deep certainty. His pause and question are a hint, but his eyes hold the truth of it. I'd promised to be his in our bargain already, but even if I hadn't, I know my answer.

"Yes."

As the last syllable leaves my lips, I feel him begin to push inside. Pain, a tingle of fear.

I gasp and grip Riven's shoulders as he slowly slides into me, giving me time to adjust to his impressive size. So much bigger than I imagined. So much...more. Small stabs of pain wash through me as he penetrates deeper, not letting up in his conquest. He wants everything, won't take anything less, and damn, I want him to have it all.

I whimper at the fullness of him within me, but not in pain.

It's desire. I need him to move, to slide within me, but he goes utterly still.

Riven cups my face and runs his thumb over my lips. "All mine, Lia," he says. "Mine entire."

Warmth floods my chest.

Finally, *finally*, he begins a slow, gentle thrust. With each movement, torrents of pleasure ripple through me. My body relaxes, opening to him, inviting him in.

He takes his glorious time, making sure I feel every inch of him. His brow creases, in concentration or control?

I can't hold still. My hips roll against his. My hands touch every inch of skin I can find. A sheen of sweat breaks out on my skin. Everything is Riven, and I'll never have enough.

There're no awkward movements, no discomfort. He fits me perfectly in every way. Moans echo through the room, and only distantly do I realize they're from me. His lips capture mine, swallowing the sound as he claims all of me.

The most delicious pleasure builds deep in my core. I have no desire to fight it. Instead, I yearn for it, reach for it, joining Riven in a dance of trusting and stretching to a delirious rhythm. I drift into a fog of pleasure, rising higher and higher, back to that magical place. I'm lightheaded, standing on the edge of something brilliant.

He releases my mouth in a grunt of pleasure.

"Riven!" I call his name, sucking in desperate, gasping breaths.

He dips his head to nuzzle my neck but doesn't let up in his conquest. It's slick, powerful, all consuming, and so easy. Easy and breathing.

"Come for me." His hoarse whisper courses through me.

My vision swims as I follow his command and hurtle over the edge. My legs are locked around him, holding on as he meets me in my pleasure with a moan of his own.

Riven rests his forehead on mine, his heavy breaths mingling with my own as we ride the waves of pleasure down together, locked around one another.

Something cool circles in my gut and settles in a tingly ripple on the skin just above my left hip. Riven pulls out and sits back on the bed between my legs.

All at once, I'm bereft.

I want him back, now, right now. No amount of time with him will ever be enough.

His gaze rakes over my body laid out before him. Admiration shines in his features as he rubs his thumb over the spot that tingled moments ago.

"Beautiful. You wear it so well." He meets my questioning gaze with a lusty grin.

"What do you mean?" I raise myself half up for a better view, halting at the sight. In the dim light, I can just make out a silver dollar sized white flower, similar to a rose, painted on my skin like a tattoo.

It *is* beautiful. A few faint green leaves accent the delicate petals.

His mark.

"It's"—wild, stunning, strange—"lovely."

Much better than a vampire bite or some of the other more creative things I'd originally imagined. A matching one marks Riven in the same spot, the mirror of my own.

"I didn't mean only the mark, Lia." He eyes me up and down.

I grin, still reveling in the sweet ache of satisfaction from having him inside me. "You're not bad yourself."

"Beautiful and so fiercely courageous." He grins and returns to recline at my side. Riven pulls me onto his chest, one leg tangled with his and my head on his shoulder. The quick thump of his heartbeat hammers under my palm.

"Do you believe that you're the only fae I want now?" I toy with a lock of his hair.

His thumb rubs circles over my mark, sending out delicious waves of warmth that have me craving him all over again.

"I do." His head dips to mine, confirming his words with his lips.

"Should we get cleaned up before bed?" I ask, still staring into eyes I could drown in.

"Oh, I don't intend to sleep yet." Riven flips us over in one smooth movement, his body half covering mine and pressing me into the sheets. "In fact, I might keep you up quite late."

I grin.

Wicked, wicked fae.

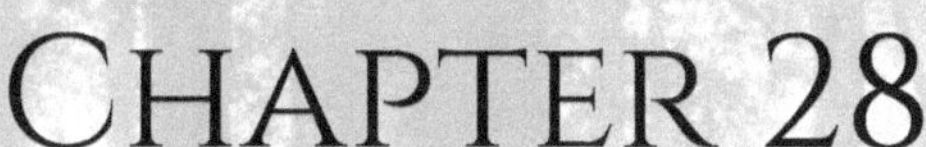

CHAPTER 28

I STRETCH LIKE A content kitten. Morning light spills across the bed, revealing the empty space beside me. My toes curl into the sheets as short snapshots of the night before play like a video through my head. The things he did...we did... I will never regret a moment of it. Being with Riven is all consuming. Delightful. And though he kept me up late, as promised, I've never slept so well and woken so utterly relaxed and refreshed.

A sheepish smile touches my lips. If only he were still in bed. What I wouldn't give to snuggle back down under the sheets and...

Ugh, stop it, Lia.

This is bad. Falling for him, having these kinds of feelings. It can't happen, not yet, not with May still missing.

Every blissful, happy thought turns oily and wrong at the reminder of her absence.

I slide from the bed and search for my nightgown. Except I hadn't worn one. My cheeks burn. A coil of desire tightens in my stomach. I literally hadn't worn anything to bed, not after Riven cut the clothes from my body with his claws.

Claws. Not human, Lia. Don't forget it.

The chest of drawers nearby contains several sets of clothing brought from Virideria. I pull out a dark green nightgown and slip it over my head before padding out into the main sitting room.

Riven sits at a desk to one side of the room, studying a large book laid open on the table before him. His hair is pulled back this morning, and he wears some loose pants similar to the ones I tried to divest him of last night.

With his super-human hearing, he's probably heard me by now, but he doesn't turn as I cross the room, coming up behind him. He turns the page. I peer over his shoulder on my tiptoes, hands propped on the back of his chair.

Fae words are scrawled across the page in neat lines.

"I can't read it," I say as my feet come to rest back on my heels. Not a bespelled book then. Bummer.

Riven doesn't respond at first, completely engrossed in whatever it says. Eventually, he raises his head and looks back over one shoulder at me, a pleasant half-smile brightening his features.

"Good morning." He waves a hand and beckons me to stand next to him at the desk.

I comply.

The large book, almost two feet across, occupies a sizeable portion of the desk. Its edges are worn and frayed, showing its heavy use. A faint odd scent, like an antique store, wafts from its pages. Despite the apparent age, the pages retain their clarity and sturdiness. Time hasn't taken its toll on them as it has the binding.

"What's it about?"

"It's a former king's account of the events of his reign."

The book is thick. Either the king was verbose, or his reign had been very long.

"That sounds...interesting?" I reply, searching for the right word. Reading about history first thing in the morning sounds incredibly boring, even to someone like me who geeks out to the history channel on occasion.

Riven chuckles. "Most of it's actually rather dull."

He pushes his chair back from the desk but doesn't move to rise. Sitting there, shirtless, with his legs apart, the invitation to come and sit in his lap is as clear as if he'd spoken it. The mischief dancing in his eyes makes the offer extra appealing.

I lick my lips. Tempting, so tempting, but that would likely lead to other things, which would draw me deeper into the black hole that is Riven.

Not what I need when we should be searching for my sister.

I hop onto the edge of the desk instead. But sitting like this, with my bare feet dangling in the air, I can't ignore exactly how short this nightgown is or the way the wood grain tugs it up further.

Ugh. Maybe not the better choice after all.

"So." I search for something, anything, to break up the sexual tension. "If the book is so dull, what were you reading about so intently?"

Riven sighs and adjusts his posture, crossing one ankle over his knee.

"He describes an object that was created as a gift to a group of humans with which they had close relations. However, after some time, relations broke down between that clan of humans and the fae. A human witch sought revenge via our own gift." Pointed fangs peek out of a soft snarl. "She used it against us and then hid it here in Faery."

Interesting. Except witches aren't real. Although, fae aren't supposed to be either.

"Humans don't have magic." I say. "At least none I've ever heard of."

"Really?" Riven replies with a small frown. "That's a pity. Many of our records describe some of the gifted having magic. It's not as powerful as our own, but it would be a shame if it has died out completely."

No kidding. Magic would be so helpful, not to mention fun. But that can wait. "What's the object? Why did the fae give it to humans?"

"It's an enchanted stone. When more humans visited this land, we often gave them gifts. A fair return for their presence here and their ability to enliven our magic and our land. This encouraged humans to visit, of course, and kept the relations between our people strong."

"You don't give humans gifts anymore?" I raise my eyebrows at him, half teasing, but also somewhat serious.

Riven grins. "Have you not received any gifts?"

My cheeks flush. The necklace he gave me last night, the bracelet from Solona, even the ring from Sigurd... I guess I hadn't realized they were mine to keep.

"If we have more visitors, we'll certainly give them gifts as well. You're the first to come to my territory in quite a while." He'd said that before, not long after I came here. Relations with humans must have broken down very badly indeed.

"Why do so few humans come here now, if there were once many more?"

"The particular stone I mentioned was a door key. A show of good faith to the humans to allow them to open and close doors into Faery. Rather a foolish gift, really, and it came back to hurt us. The witch closed several doors within this territory and then hid the stone here. Right under our noses but inaccessible due to her curse." Riven shakes his head with a sigh.

A thought strikes me like lightning, and I practically jump from the table. "If we find the stone, could we trade it for May?"

Hope explodes within me like fireworks on the Fourth of July.

The humor dims from Riven's eyes. "We could."

But? A coil of fear twists in me as I wait for him to continue.

"But the stone could help my people for generations to come. If we could open more doors, allow more humans to come here..."

I slam my hand onto the desk as all my pent up hurt and worry breaks free. The force of it rings up my arm. "So more humans can get stolen away by the Unseelie? More little girls you promised to save?"

He flinches as if struck.

Good. Feel my pain. Anger burns hotter than a volcano in my heart, and it exploded from nowhere just as violently.

"We have to save May. You promised." My voice cracks on the last word. It rings in the air, filling the silence. "I thought magic bound our bargain? Besides, I'm upholding my end."

He flinches again.

A low blow, but for my sister, it's worth it.

"I will save your sister, Lia. But giving them the key... If you want more humans to get stolen away, that's the best way for it to happen."

My fists clench at my side. His logic does nothing to soothe the fire in me.

Riven runs his hand down his face. "I should have saved her that night. We were so close." He shakes his head. "The key will be a last resort, a last offer. Let's see if we can find something else to offer before then."

"Two days, Riven. We only have two days left."

He takes my clenched hands in his, staring into my eyes. "Trust me. I know."

"And if we don't find anything?"

"There are other ways to get what we want." He glances away.

Violent ones, no doubt. Too risky. A trade would be so much easier. Safer. For May and all of them.

I suck in a deep breath. Arguing isn't going us any closer to a solution. "So this stone, key, whatever. Where is it?"

Riven releases my hands. "Nearby. A hedge maze outside the ruins of an old retreat."

"A maze? You can't just...magic it out?"

"Unfortunately not. The magic the witch used only allows humans to enter and not all of them." His lips thin. "My magic can't touch it."

"Let me guess. You'd like me to find this stone for you?"

Riven nods slowly, his eyes boring into mine. "But it may not be easy. Not all humans can enter it. Even then, there are records of others trying and failing, and once they leave the maze, they cannot enter it again."

So, I'd only have one shot at best. Lovely. Still, better one than none. "If I find it, I want to be able to trade it for May. If it comes to that."

He stands. Long, calloused fingers tug my chin up to look him in the face. "And if it doesn't, you'll use it to help my people? Assuming you can get it?"

If. Way to be ominous. "Yes."

"I'll be satisfied with that for now."

Riven leans in and claims my mouth with his. This kiss is deep, passionate. When he pulls back just a few moments later, I breathe heavily, aching for more. The remnants of my anger fuel a different sort of fire.

"We'll leave today and travel there." His eyes sparkle with mirth. From our kiss or hope of the key, I can only guess. Maybe both.

"Is that okay?" I am still trying to calm my racing heart. "With *guests* here?" I choose the word carefully.

Riven shrugs. "It gives us both an excuse to get away from Sigurd, and I'll leave enough of my guard here that he won't be tempted to try anything foolish."

CHAPTER 29

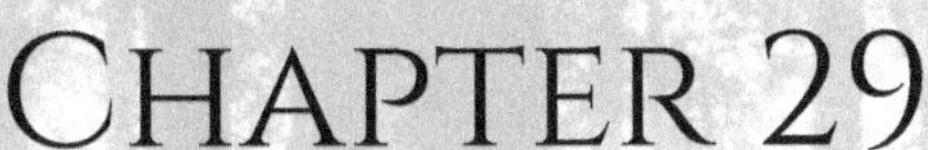

I RUB AT MY aching head as I scan another page of the fae book. "What are we looking for again?"

"Namenshia," Solona says.

It's one of the ingredients needed to work a complicated spell that might be able to heal some of the Unseelie lands. But offering to perform the spell in exchange for May won't work if we can't find all the ingredients. Old spells like this, according to Solona, take more than just a fae's inherent magic. It needs tangible elements too.

What I wouldn't give to be able to use Google search right now. For all the luxuries of fae life, the lack of internet really sucks.

"Maybe it's an error?" Sylvie says. She and Galen joined us in the library this morning in lieu of training.

"I don't—" Solona breaks off, her eyes widening.

"So this is where the lovely ladies spend their time." Sigurd leans against the door frame.

I stiffen. How long has he been standing there?

Sylvie and Galen jump to their feet, sending chairs clattering across the floor as they step between Sigurd and me. His smile falters. No doubt he senses Riven's mark on my body. My friends haven't commented on it...yet. But they've been in high spirits this morning.

The frown tugging at Sigurd's lips vanishes in a flash of teeth that even back out into his characteristic grin.

"Ah, the faithful guards," he drawls at my companions. "But there's no need to worry. Riven and I promised no violence while the little girl is missing. And I see that dutiful Lia still wears her bracelet." His eyes dip to my hands, sprawled frozen across an open book, and back up again.

Next to me, Solona stiffens.

Sigurd cocks his head to the side, stepping into the room. The door behind him swings shut on a phantom breeze. "Though you seem to have lost the ring I gave you."

"Enough. Why are you here?" Solona asks, steel in her voice.

"Curiosity?" He shrugs. "My court leaves tomorrow, yet you're all cooped up in here, out of sight. Such a curious thing." His fingers trail along the bindings of a row of books as he stalks in our direction.

Sylvie and Galen shift their positions, keeping between the King of Air and myself.

"Let me guess," Sigurd says. "You're looking for a way to deceive the Unseelie. Or possibly something to trade for the girl?"

My hands curl. Nails scrape along the page of the book.

He smirks at my reaction. His hand stills on the row of books. Shit.

"I could offer my assistance," he continues.

This again.

"You already offered your assistance to search for her, but how has that turned out?" Bitterness laces my voice. I've chosen Riven. Doesn't he realize that?

His lips twitch. "So feisty. Though I gather Riven's men haven't had any more luck than my own. And where is the King of the Forest? Not out searching for your sister?"

The verbal jab hits like a punch. His men are searching. Even Ambrose returned to the forest this morning. But Riven himself...

"I said, enough," Solona repeats, stepping in front of me.

Her words jolt me from my spiraling thoughts.

"Well, if you don't want my help..." he trails off.

I lean around her, catching the end of Sigurd's shrug as he steps away from the bookshelves.

"Though, Lia," Sigurd's eyes snap back to mine. "Wear the ring. At least while I'm here. It wouldn't do for a Lady of the Forest to offend her neighbors." He looks pleased. Far too pleased for a guest that's just been jilted.

There was that title. Lady.

He says it like I'm some kind of European noble. It's too important, too significant, for our relationship. Riven and I aren't married or anything.

Sigurd turns, ignoring the daggers we all stare at his back, and strides toward the exit of the library. Before he reaches it, the door opens wide, and Riven fills its frame.

"What's going on here?" Riven looks from Sigurd to the rest of us and back again.

Tension hangs heavy in the air between them, thicker than the magic at the ball.

"I'm just on my way out," Sigurd replies, tone nonchalant. He pats Riven on the shoulder and slides around him out the door.

Riven watches him go before fully stepping inside and closing the door behind him.

All stiffness of his form vanishes with the click of the lock.

"Any luck?" he asks no one in particular.

So, we're just going to ignore Sigurd's words.

"Not yet," I answer.

"Then we leave shortly, as planned," he says. Solona, Ambrose, and other close companions had already been filled in on the morning's discovery and our forming plan.

"I don't like this, Rivenean." Solona stares him down. "We don't know if she can do it, and she'll only have one chance."

Talking about me like I'm not even here. Great. Not to mention that she hadn't been that surprised by the story of the key. My lips draw thin as I suck on my teeth. She'd known about it and never mentioned it as a possibility for retrieving May.

"We should wait," she continues. "Let her get settled, more accustomed to this world. It can only help."

"May cannot wait." I slam my hand on the desk.

"Lia..." she starts.

The back of my neck burns. "I know. You don't think I can do it—"

"That's not—"

"But I can. I will."

Solona sighs and shakes her head. "Even if you can, the stone is too valuable."

Her comment hits me like a slap to the face. Doesn't matter that she's probably right, but I can't—

"If Lia can get the stone," Riven says, stepping into the conversation. "And we have no other options, I will let Lia choose whether to trade it."

His comment sucks the air from the room.

Sylvie and Galen stare between us all, wide-eyed. Solona's lips thin.

At length, Solona says, "If the rest of the court finds out..."

"They don't need to know." He stares at them each in turn. It's an order as much as a statement. His attention slides to me. "It's my fault May is in the hands of the Unseelie, and we'll get her back. I believe that, as I believe Lia can help us with the stone."

Solona lets out a weary sigh. "I really hope you know what you're doing. I'll keep searching here. Perhaps we can work out this spell or another to offer the Unseelie in exchange."

They ignore Sigurd's words, but I can't. "Sigurd mentioned something about tricking the Unseelie. Could we?"

Heads turn in my direction.

"Would it be possible to offer them the key without really offering it?" I continue. "Maybe we could create a duplicate and give that to them instead."

Anything is better than all-out war or losing May. And this way, the forest fae wouldn't lose their key either. If I can get it.

Solona's brows wrinkle. "We cannot duplicate that kind of magic, but perhaps we can think of something."

Riven nods. "But first, we'll need the real key."

Galen, Sylvie, and I wait at the honing point just outside the city as the remainder of the guard joining us file out into the space.

One tree resembling a poplar, my favorite, keeps drawing my attention. I could have sworn it was entirely yellow the last time we were here, but now it sports several green leaves toward the bottom. It stands out from the others with their mix of red, orange, green, and even some purple leaves. You really can't beat the beauty of a bright yellow poplar at the height of its leaves changing.

"Sylvie, are the seasons in Faery like the ones in the human world? Spring, summer, autumn, winter." I list them for emphasis.

She nods, blond hair shining in the sun. "I've never visited your human world, but I believe they do work the same way."

"It's just... I could have sworn that tree was yellow before, but now it has green leaves again, like it's moving backward from autumn to summer instead of forward."

She looks at me for a moment then cocks her head to the side, a hint of amusement playing about her features. "It's summer everywhere right now."

What? My nose twitches. Okay, maybe the seasons aren't the same after all.

"Our land is affected by more than just the changing of seasons," she continues. "The king's magic affects it also. Because our king chose you, a human"—she eyes the area where Riven's mark hides under my clothes—"you have been able to revitalize his magic and thus start to heal the magic of our territory as well."

"I know that part but the trees..."

She smiles.

My whole face practically lights on fire as realization sets it. The seasons aren't moving backward, but the land is healing back to what it should be, to proper summer. Every fae knows exactly how I help their king's magic, and it's clear as day in the land around them.

I bury my face in my hands. Talk about too much information...

Sylvie grips my arm. "You shouldn't be embarrassed. It's the way of things, and we're glad you're here."

I glance around, making sure no one else is close before dropping my voice to a whisper. "If I help so much, then why hasn't he marked a human before now?"

Sylvie drops her hand and looks down. She's quiet for a moment before she glances back at me and whispers, "It's not my place to question the actions of my king."

I bite my lip, sorry I've asked—until she continues.

"However, I've read about kings in the past who marked many humans, rarely keeping one for long before moving on to the next, all in the search for more power. They say even Sigurd's father was that way."

My stomach roils. Though Sigurd infuriates me, I can't help but pity him. That one fact about his father tells me a great deal and none of it is good. A fae king moving from one human to the next in a string of lovers, just with the goal of obtaining power... Talk about twisted.

The disgust must show on my face because Sylvie continues quickly, "I don't like the thought of that either. Most of us don't, and wouldn't, use humans that way. I think that a strong bond with one human would be better than short, weak bonds with many humans. I believe Riven feels the same way also."

Her words don't answer my question, but they comfort me all the same.

"Thank you." Warmth blooms in my heart, gratitude for her presence and her honesty.

We break apart as Riven strides our way with the last of the guard members who will join us in retrieving the key. The mask of the Forest King is back in place today, broad grin, confident stride, commanding voice. Though, mask or no, the excitement shining from his face is real.

"Ready?" He unfurls his hand toward me in a graceful swoop.

I've already unclasped the bracelet and let it slip from my wrist into my palm. "Yes, though didn't you say this requires a lot of magic? *Someone*"—best not to say who—"might feel it?"

My fingers twine through his.

Riven draws me close. A feral grin breaks across his features before he leans in and covers his mouth as if whispering a secret. "We don't have a choice. There's not enough time to travel there and back without it. We'll just have to make it quick."

A gasp lodges in my throat as the trees begin to twist and warp. The city of Arbrean disappears. Dense forest rises up in its place.

I shiver as the magic rolls off my body and the world stops spinning.

Riven gives my hand another squeeze before relinquishing it. "It should be just this way."

CHAPTER 30

No one needs to tell me we've arrived. Looming among the trees is a crumbling mansion. Unlike Virideria and Arbrean, plant life consumes what little remains of rock and wood. Tree roots and vines choke the decaying ruins. High grasses and moss cling to the exposed surfaces. If there was a roof, it's long gone, and many of the walls have cracked or fallen.

For as broken and neglected the old mansion looks, the hedges beyond are precisely the opposite. If someone said they'd been trimmed and pruned that day, I'd believe it. Fog hangs low and thick, obscuring much of the view, other than the one opening in the hedge—the presumed entrance to the maze.

I shiver and hug myself.

"Tranquil Grove," Riven says at my side. "A retreat for the nobility in ages past."

Humorless laughter bubbles out. There's nothing tranquil about this place. Not anymore.

"Maybe..." An odd quaver warbles his voice as he reaches for my hand again. "Maybe it is too soon. We can try another time."

"No." I wrench my hand away. May needs me. I have to try. "I can do this." If only I had the confidence of my words.

One firm nod from Riven seals the decision. "Guards, spread out." His voice rings with all the authority and surety it lacked a moment ago. "Watch the perimeter."

"Watch for what?" I ask as members of his elite guard spread out into the fog-laden land.

"Everything. Anything. We cannot be too careful."

I swallow and shift on my feet. All these fae, and I'm the one who has to do something important where none of them can. I sigh, staring at the yellowing grasses.

That bodes well.

Not.

Riven clasps my shoulders. "You're strong. Brave. You can do this." A squeeze. "I believe in you."

I can only blink in return.

"I know you, Lia. I've seen the way you give all of yourself for those you love. If I could do this for you, I would, but only you can go in there." He points to the gap where the overgrown cobblestone path disappears into the hedges.

That's right. A deep, steadying breath fills my lungs. Leave it to Riven to pull me up from the darkness trying to drag me away.

"I can do this." This time, I believe it.

He releases me and pulls a sheathed dagger from his side. "No humans have come to harm from what we've discovered, but just in case."

The blade is heavier in my hands than it looks, but it's a comfort all the same. "Can't be too careful."

"Never. May I?"

I hand the blade back, and he secures it to a belt at my waist. When he's done, he slips his hand in mine. "I'll go with you. As far as I can."

A good thing too because every step I take toward that shrouded hedge only increases the voice in the back of my head yelling at me to turn and run. As far as he can, turns out to be about two feet from the entrance. Riven grits his teeth and smashes his fist against the invisible barrier to no avail.

"It's okay." I swallow my nerves and force a tentative smile. "We knew I had to go alone, right?"

"Lia... I..."

I take a step. Other than a slight drop in temperature, nothing changes. I turn to the man at my back, kept from me by the witch's magic.

"You do..." He trails off, staring at me in wide-eyed wonder.

He really didn't think I could go through? I tilt my head to the side.

Riven shakes his head and the look is gone. "You can do this."

"Yes." I suck in a breath and bounce on my toes. Somehow, I think I can. He starts to say more, but I shake my head. "It's okay. I'll see you at the exit."

Wherever the hell that is.

Before I can lose my nerve, I turn and enter the maze without a backward glance. One second more and I'd have run the other way.

It doesn't take long to get lost. There are no markers, no signs. The perfectly manicured hedge walls reach over my head and disappear into the heavy fog above. The packed dirt of the floor is the same every path I turn down.

The worst of it, though, is the eerie quiet. No birds. No bugs. I call for Riven, and no one answers, as if I've stepped into a different world. I start to turn back, to try and find my way back to the entrance and come up with a different plan, when whispers tickle my ears, the words just out of reach.

Goosebumps shiver across my skin.

"Hello?" I call, turning in a tight circle. Straining. Searching.

More whispers answer. "...stone. You..."

I run in their direction, heedless of anything, as I turn one corner after another, chasing the phantom words.

"...seek it..."

"...so long..."

"...trust..."

I turn another corner.

A ghost looms between the hedges.

I scream. My boots skid on the dirt as my body locks up, nearly tumbling me forward onto the ground.

Her angular, refined face stares at me, surrounded by a halo of dark hair that drifts down around her pale shoulders as if she's underwater. Faint bits of blue and black accent her long dress.

Like a faded photograph, she lacks color. The dark green hedges visible through her translucent form have more vibrance than she does.

"It's been so long, sister."

I gasp as the words echo in my head, spoken...but not. "May?"

Her head tilts to the side.

No. I step back, my brows winkling. It can't be. They're nothing alike, not in appearance or voice. She even feels different. There's something though, an echo of recognition deep within me. This woman...

All at once, the pieces click into place. "You're the witch!"

She folds and unfolds her hands in front of her. "They called me that. Yes."

My pulse hammers in my throat.

"But how? You're..." Super old. Dead. Not here.

She drifts nearer. "You seek the stone," she says, ignoring me.

"Yes."

Her head bobs as if in a nod. And then she turns, drifting down the path away from me.

"Wait!" I sprint after her.

She turns the corner. I follow.

My steps falter as we enter a wide circle with many paths leading off from it. Along one wall, the only one that's not an opening, is a marble statue resembling the witch.

"You may ask one question," her words ring through the clearing, coming from everywhere and nowhere at once.

One. I notch my chin higher. There's only one that matters. "How do I find the stone?"

"That is your choice."

My... I gape. "Wait, that doesn't make sense."

She turns and drifts away, heading for her statue.

"Wait!" Shit. No. That can't be my only clue. I race toward her.

Her form begins to merge into the marble.

"Why did you curse the stone?" I blurt.

Her fading form halts, and so do I.

"You closed their doors and hid the stone to hurt them," I shout. "Why?"

She turns and floats a few steps toward me. It takes everything I have to stand my ground. Tendrils of cold ghost along my skin before she says, "No one has asked me that."

"I'm asking. Tell me...sister."

Her form rises and falls as if in a sigh. "I loved a fae. A king."

I barely stifle my gasp.

"My family rejoiced when he took me as his consort. He gave me gifts, paraded me in front of his court. He even built this maze for me here at my favorite home."

A love story. My chest grows tight. She loved him. Then how...

"But he never loved me." The hard, bitter edge that slips into her voice cuts at me. "He used me for his pleasure, his magic. I was nothing to him but a means to power." Her eyes darken, going fully black as night. "He marked other fae. Took them in our bed. I could not let my sisters suffer the same fate."

If Riven did the same to me... Bile burns my throat. "So, you stole the stone."

Light flares from her form as she drifts higher. "It belonged to my coven. I used it, as was my right. It was ours!"

I raise my hands. "Yes, it was yours."

She lowers, appeased. "I had to protect them, my sisters, until the fae could love again."

My brows wrinkle.

"Until they became worthy of love." Her words are a whisper. The translucent form wavers, almost completely disappearing. "Stay true, sister."

Her words still ring in the quiet space when she fully fades into the statue like a mist settling across the grass.

I wait, each heartbeat the only sound in the clearing, but she doesn't return.

A woman scorned. For her vengeance, she doomed a whole people to wither and die. It's a horrible, selfish act, but... I hug myself. Part of me understands too. If only she could have doomed that terrible king and not them all. I chew on my bottom lip. But maybe...

I twist around, looking down the various identical paths. If I can find the stone, not only can I save May, maybe I can fix this too. Goosebumps race over my skin. Right now, I'm the only one who can. Me, the screw-up who hurts everyone she loves. A humorless laugh carries through the clearing. No pressure.

"Human girl."

I turn with a squeak.

The Unseelie fae who took May, Katiya I think they called her, stands at the entrance to one pathway. Her tail flicks behind her like a cat ready to pounce.

"Searching for the child?" Her ears twitch.

I pull the dagger Riven gave me and angle it at the woman. "Where is she? Where's May?"

"What would you give me to save her for you?" a velvet voice asks from behind me.

I twist around to see Sigurd leaning on the hedge at the end of another pathway. His characteristic smirk is present, as is the simple yet elegant attire he wore at the ball.

"How?" I all but scream. "How are you here?"

Riven tried and failed, yet here these two stand. Adrenaline surges through my veins as I twist between them, pointing my blade at each in turn.

"What would you give, human girl?" Katiya slinks closer.

Each breath is shorter than the last. My heart thunders.

"Come with me, Lia." Sigurd advances, a hand outstretched. "Let me help you."

The dagger shakes in my hand.

How, how, how...

"Lia." Riven's calm voice washes over me.

Tears slip down my cheeks as I turn and run toward his open arms.

"Thank, God, you're—" I skid to a stop where he lingers in the threshold of one pathway. The heel of my palm wipes away the tears as I take in the man waiting before me. Too calm. Not the cocky fae king, nor the protective man who would have bounded into the clearing to keep me from harm. "You're not—"

"Lia?"

This new voice cracks my heart in two.

I almost can't bear to look. Tears blur her form when I finally turn around. She's still wearing her blue bunny pajamas and rubbing at her eyes as if she's just woken from a long slumber.

"May!" Finally! I race for her, ignoring the fae kings and the Unseelie woman who glare my way.

I trip over something and go down hard on one knee. The impact echoes up my body.

"May!" I reach for her, but she just tilts her head and blinks at me.

No... The dagger falls from my limp fingers. My hope gutters to ash.

May would come to me. My sister wouldn't be this calm, not in a strange place, not with these people.

"There you are! My girls."

I don't turn at Dad's voice. I can't handle another familiar face. A shudder wracks my form as my eyes squeeze closed. Tears flow unchecked, and I don't bother to wipe them away. Sobs wrack my body.

"We've missed you so much," Elise says. "Please, just come home."

"Let me help you, Lia," Sigurd says.

"Come back to me, please," Riven begs.

I can't get enough air. My fingertips dig into the hard-packed dirt.

"You're just going to hurt them all? Again? Can't you see they need you?"

This voice does snag my attention.

I twist my head to the side and see the mirror image of myself standing at the end of a pathway. Except this Lia isn't sobbing into the dirt.

She rolls her eyes in disgust. "So like you to fail."

I shove to my feet, staring down my doppelganger. Are my eyes really so cold? My smile so vicious?

"Look at you." She smirks. "Pathetic."

The others call for me, but I tune them out.

"I'm not pathetic." I wipe at my face.

"Aren't you? You got your sister captured. You fled from your parents and left them to worry. You turn your back on every fae you come across."

"No, I—"

"You play Sigurd and Riven against one another, each hoping to win your affections." She stalks my way. "And poor Katiya. You let her people get cut down, and now you want to deceive her?"

"That's not true. I didn't... I don't—" Guilt chokes off my words. But she's—I'm—right.

"Sitting here sobbing like a child. So typical."

Nausea churns within me. The world sways. It takes all my focus to grab the dagger from the ground again. The handle in my grip is solid and strong. Something real and true in this maze of terrors.

"God, Lia, you can't help anyone. You're such a baby."

They all want me to come to them. All except one.

I stalk toward my mirror self.

She rolls her eyes again. "Turning your back on all of them, huh? So like you. If you hadn't been so selfish, maybe you'd have kept your eyes on the road instead of yelling at May, huh?"

I stumble and hunch forward, the breath knocked from me. That horrible memory swells to the surface, nearly dragging me under.

"You're the reason she almost died. You're why she'll bear those scars for the rest of her life. You're why she got captured."

It takes everything I have to stare myself in the face. "Yes, I am."

I brush past her and race for the pathway she exited.

"Stop! Lia!" voices cry behind me.

But I don't. I can't. Not anymore.

"Stop!" An unearthly voice scratches at my eardrums like nails on a chalkboard.

Leaves rustle. Then all is quiet. I look over my shoulder and hedges have closed behind me. My sister, my family, Riven, Sigurd, Katiya...they're all gone.

A cool breeze blows past my face, taking my fear and heartache with it.

I can breathe again. My heartrate slows.

Win or lose, there's only one way forward now. I square my shoulders and press on.

Around another turn, the path dead-ends into a square court-yard with a pedestal in the middle. Atop it sits a stone the size of a chicken egg, slightly oval, completely smooth, and brownish-gold in appearance.

My mouth goes slack. The stone hums a foreign tune, sending out little waves that ripple through the air. It draws me forward like a magnet, begging me to take it.

Twigs snap and leaves rustle as the path closes behind me.

Lightning courses under my skin, sizzling with excitement, po-tential, anticipation. This is it. It has to be.

Hesitantly, I take the stone. An unnatural chill radiates from its surface, crawling across my skin. It literally sings as I hold it. The chiming melody is strange, a tune so foreign I can't begin to describe it. Dissonant notes war for dominance yet weave a strange harmony that's both perfectly in balance and skewing wildly all at once.

No human musician could make it. No fae could stand it.

A wave of air rolls out from the pedestal, knocking me back. I scramble to hold on to the stone. Limbs crack. Leaves rustle. The hedges around me shake and waver as their leaves leach of color.

I twist around, fear seizing me by the throat and squeezing tight.

There's no way out.

CHAPTER 31

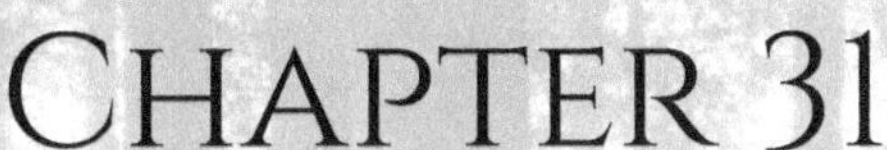

S HIT.

I'm trapped in this collapsing maze with no exit in sight.

"Lia!" The fearful cry cuts through the hedges.

Riven. My heart cries out, but only a breathy whimper escapes my lips.

It's him. Really him. I know it in my bones. I swallow the trembling fear threatening to crush me and cry out, "I'm here!"

The ground shakes. The hedges buck and bend like palms in a hurricane. Dried leaves take flight and pelt me, cutting like little blades.

"Riven!"

"I'm coming!" But his voice is far. Another leaf slices at my cheek. He won't make it, not at this rate. "Be still!"

"I—" A scream chokes off my words as brown limbs split from the earth like skeletal hands.

No. Oh, no. I clutch the stone to my chest and hunch against the invaders, still trying to keep my feet. The tree limbs arc above me, weaving together. Green leaves sprout from all directions, sheltering me, blocking the debris tossed by the crumbling hedges.

Things crash and crack outside my cage. The earth heaves, and I fall, only to land on cushiony moss. A vine of honeysuckle springs to bloom, dousing me with its calming scent.

Riven.

He's doing this. Sheltering me. Protecting me.

Wind howls against my shelter, whistling worse than the tornado that ripped by outside our house when I was a girl. The shaking that grips my body is just as bad as then. Maybe worse.

Then all at once, everything is still. Quiet as the grave.

"Riven?"

My shelter crumbles. I brace for the worst, my arms curled over my head, when colorful flower petals rain down on me.

"Lia." Riven kneels on the ground in front of me in a puddle of petals.

I'm its epicenter and beyond—

Breath catches in my throat. Nothing. Short grass dominates the barren landscape as if the maze never was. One blink. Two. He's still there.

Riven. My Riven. Not some witch's illusion. Thin scratches mar his face like he crashed through the dying hedges to get to me. Maybe he did. He hasn't even bothered to wipe at the little trails of crimson dripping down his skin.

I fling myself into his arms with a sob. One arm catches around his neck. The other still clutches the stone against my chest.

All the world is safe and good again as he cradles me to his chest.

"It's you. It's really you," I sob.

"Yes." The warmth of his breath caresses my cheek.

Magic tingles under my skin. It eases my wounds, soothes my soul. His fingers twine through my hair and massage my scalp. Ever so gently, he tilts my face up to his. "What happened?"

"I—" Words are hard to find. "You were there. But not. And May and—" I leave out the rest. Can't manage to tell him about his enemies, *our* enemies. "I saw the witch."

His eyes widen. "The—"

"Yes," I stumble on. "And she..." I shake my head. "It doesn't matter. I made a choice, I ran and—" I unfurl my hand between us, revealing the stone.

His gaze locks on the simple object, and he goes utterly still. Doesn't breathe. Doesn't blink. All at once, movement returns.

His breaths come fast and hard. His body shakes as he sputters in disbelief. "That's—"

"I think so."

Riven takes my face between his palms. "Lia, my beautiful Lia."

The look on his face holds utter adoration. Awe. Wonder. And something else... something that sends every butterfly in my stomach fluttering in a wild display.

His lips crash into mine. Strong arms pull me tight to him. The kiss is deep, passionate, and I accept it without question.

Then we're falling.

I squeal as we spill into the flower petals. Half of me is on the ground, the other half is sprawled across his chest. Everything is right, and warm, and beautiful.

I have the stone. We can trade it for May.

A loud cough has us pulling apart, but I can't stop the delirious giggles or the smile stretching across my face. Sylvie, Galen, and other members of the elite guard circle us, staring down with a mix of wide smiles and sheepish grins.

Hesitantly, I hold up the stone.

Eyes widen. Whoops and cheers split the air. Riven helps me to stand.

It's a victory—for me, for them.

"That's really it?" Sylvie asks, her mouth agape.

"I think so." The maze is gone, so if it's not, we're really screwed. It's definitely not a normal stone, but is it the key? "What do you think?"

I hand the stone to Riven.

Immediately, he grimaces, holding the stone away from him.

All my joy flees in a moment of terror. "What is it?"

"It feels... wrong," he replies at length. His lips curl back to bare his pointed teeth as he snarls at the stone.

It didn't feel wrong to me. In fact, it's as right as anything here. A trap?

"Take the stone, Lia," Riven orders, not unkindly.

I pluck it from his palm. No sooner has it left his hand than he's wiping his palm on his pants as if removing something unsavory.

The stone, still cool, sings for me again. It *wants* me to hold it. *Needs* me to.

"It feels the same as it did before," I say, though he hasn't asked. "Can't you hear its song?"

"Song..." He looks from me to his men, who shake their heads.

My brows draw together. None of them can hear it?

But I can. The dissident notes have softened, blending into an even more perfect harmony than before.

"There's one way to find out for sure." Riven wraps his hands around mine, avoiding contact with the stone.

I take a deep breath and nod. Test it. Of course. "Which door?"

"The one you came through. It's only partially opened. Fae with weak magic, like the Unseelie, can use it, but I cannot go far outside its bounds without feeling the fade of my magic."

"The stronger your magic, the more the door holds you in?"

"Just so. But if it's fully opened, it should lessen that effect." Riven turns to his guard. "If you don't have the strength to make it to Virideria, then go back to Arbrean. Otherwise, come with us. Do not speak a word of what's transpired here."

The shift takes longer this time, the pull of the magic wearing down even Riven's magical energy, but soon, the all too familiar stone circle appears in front of us.

The call of the stone clangs louder near the door, a constant murmur of song buzzing about my head like a swarm of bees. The key *wants* the door open. Its song tells me in words I don't quite understand, but I know, if I want it to, the door will swing wide—or shut.

An almost eerie calm surrounds me, comforting and coaxing all at once. I lift my chin, as sure as about this as anything I've ever done. Half the guard reappear with us, Sylvie and Galen included.

But it's Riven I look to. "I can do it."

He nods, willing me to try it.

I enter the edge of the stone circle, the threshold of the door. The music grows louder, a speaker turned to high.

Open.

Golden light spills out from the stone, and I gasp and clutch the stone tighter. If the fae react, I can't hear them. The song consumes all sound around me. The light grows until I clench my eyes at its brightness, the strength of it painful even behind closed lids.

I should be afraid. A little part of me somewhere knows that, but all is still and warm and wonderful within the stone's glow, as if I've searched for this place my whole life.

In an instant, the light and music are gone.

A gasp breaks from me as the world returns. I peek, unsure of what I'll see, but the circle of stones remains. Behind me, cries of joy erupt. I swing around to come face to face with Riven.

His eyes twinkle. His grin is wide and feral. A second later, he lifts me in the air.

"Lia! You've done it!" Riven yells as he spins me in a circle.

I squeal in surprise, gripping the silent key in my hand. Dizziness overwhelms me when he finally sets me on my feet, and I grab onto him to steady myself. Laughter and joy envelopes us on all sides. It's contagious. My chest shakes in a burst of hysterical happiness.

Riven beams with unabashed pride. Even his posture is more carefree, as if a crushing weight has been lifted from his shoulders. This isn't the fae king, this is Riven. My Riven. Happy. Free. Joy practically radiates from him, from all of them.

It's that blissful moment, that pinnacle of victory, when a tendril of shadowy apprehension manages to snake its way around my throat. Darkness creeps into the edge of my vision, turning my grin fragile as a teacup in an instant.

If I trade the stone for May, it can't help them. Not anymore.

I'd be just like the witch, using the stone for my own purposes and leaving them to fade and suffer. My chest constricts, painful and awful.

But I can't leave my sister to the Unseelie. No matter what, I have to save her.

Riven throws back his head, laughing at something a guard said. My heart lurches, a sharp stab of reality bringing with it the pain of awareness. Each laugh, each smile, spills a little more of my joy until everything aches. With pain comes awareness, like a fog lifting from my mind. This fae, this king, has become someone dear. His smile is one I cherish, one I want to preserve forever, despite our differences and difficulties.

Give away his hope? Hurt him? How could I?

I can't. Because somewhere along the way, I've fallen in love with him.

Over a day has passed, and the stone's music has not returned.

"Are you sure we shouldn't be worried?" I ask.

"All magic has its limits. Likely it just needs to recharge," Riven says again, for maybe the third time. He's not worried, not in the slightest.

But I am.

A frown tugs on my lips as I stare at the stone within the crystal box where we placed it for safekeeping. Only Riven can open it, or me since I wear his mark, giving me a similar magical signature despite my lack of any actual magic. A near-identical twin of the stone sits outside the box on a small, silken pillow.

Riven instructed his best artisans to craft the duplicate, confident we can pass that one off to the Unseelie and keep the real one for ourselves.

Could such a simple trick really work?

My stomach knots. I don't like it, especially not since my sister's life depends on it.

"Besides." Riven paces the room, that confident, joyful glow still clinging to him like a second skin. He waves a hand as if this is something trivial and not the life-or-death situation it is. "We'll offer food and supplies first. Then the spell Solona found. If that doesn't work—only if—we offer the stone."

He means to be reassuring, and maybe it works for him, but not for me.

"The duplicate?"

"Yes." One careful, confident nod.

"And if they realize it's not the real one?" I raise my brows for emphasis.

"They won't." He halts his pacing a breath away. "How would they?"

I crane my neck up over my shoulder, taking in the planes of his strong jaw. "You said yourself the real one feels odd. Would they not expect that?"

Riven wraps his arms around me from behind, his chin coming to rest on the top of my head. The move forces my attention back to the object in question. "I made you a bargain, didn't I? We'll save May, even if it costs us the stone."

I lean back into his chest, savoring the feel of his body against mine, his honeysuckle scent in my nose. Strong. Confident. As sure as any king could be.

"Try not to worry so much." His fingers graze my cheek, stirring up a little shiver. "We still have several hours until we're to meet the Unseelie."

Hours that drag like years. I sigh. *Soon, May. I promise. You'll be home soon.*

"You sent those dreams to my father again, right?" I ask. "So he'll know where to find May once we rescue her?" The idea had struck me when I'd widened the door to Earth. If Riven could appear to me in dreams, it reasoned he could send them to my father as well. He could find the door. Take May home. Somewhere safe. Far, far away from here.

Far from me. It hurts just thinking about it, but it's what's best—for her.

"Yes. Last night and the night before, like you asked." Riven yawns then kisses the top of my head. "Though hopefully he is less stubborn than you and listens to them." He chuckles.

I roll my eyes. Never going to let that go, is he?

He releases me and walks back to his desk, where a mountain of paper waits for his attention. He ignored much of his duties to summon the magic necessary to send dreams to my father two nights in a row.

"What happened with Solona this morning?" I ask after plopping down onto a cushioned settee of forest green velvet.

Using so much magic had drained him, and I'd left long before he awakened, only to return to them arguing about something in a language I didn't know. He was the confident king addressing his advisor, not the man who yearned to fill the footsteps of his father. The edge to his voice, the wildness in his eyes, was something I'd only seen on the battlefield. Whatever they discussed, it was deep—personal.

Solona stormed out with a huff shortly after and didn't return. Riven was ruffled, pacing back and forth and running his hand through his hair until the shorter hairs around his face stuck out in a wild array.

The jovial expression he wore moments ago vanishes at my question. A muscle works in his jaw. "We disagreed about my handling of a certain situation."

Thick, full silence hangs in the air, but he makes no move to end it.

Despite his reluctance, I push on. "Do you disagree often?"

"No." He snorts air through his nose. "Very rarely, if at all."

"Do you want to talk to me about it? Maybe I could provide a different perspective?"

Riven gives a huff of laughter, and I squirm in the seat, smoothing out my clothes. It wasn't a funny question to me.

"No, I think it's best if I don't," he says.

The rejection stings. "Fine."

I sigh. It's not his fault my nerves are so on edge today.

It takes more effort than it should to push to my feet. "I'm going to the library."

"Again?"

I shrug. "It can't hurt."

At the very least, it'll keep my mind occupied for a few more hours.

CHAPTER 32

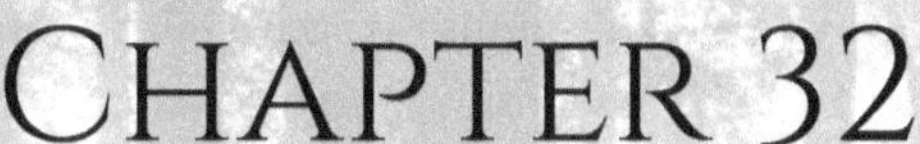

T HE LIBRARY IS QUIET today, devoid of Solona and the other fae she recruited to help her search the old tomes. Too bad. Having others around to distract me would have been helpful, but at least my two friends keep me company.

"To think people actually read these books for fun." Galen pages through yet another tome.

"A lot of people read for fun. Maybe not that one, but other books," I reply.

"Don't let it get to you, Lia. Galen has never been the best of students," Sylvie says with a wink across the table.

Galen scowls at her. "I learned what was important."

"Important to *you*, perhaps."

"How is any of this history supposed to help on a battlefield?"

"Knowledge is power, all of it."

I fail to stifle the giggle that slips out amidst their banter. They're like this all the time, getting into little arguments and calling each other out. You might think they were siblings if you didn't know better.

Both of them cut their attention to me. Sylvie gives me a half-smile. Galen rolls his eyes.

"There has to be a more interesting source of information," Galen protests, leaning back in his chair and kicking his heels up on the corner of the tabletop.

I eye him dubiously. "What would you find interesting?"

Galen shrugs, looking a little sheepish. "What are my options?"

Sylvie walks to the nearest bookshelf and reads off book titles from their spines. *"Herbal Sleep Aids. Imbuing Magic to Seeds. Cadmum Care."*

I have no idea what a Cadmum is, but Galen's scowl deepens with each title. Seems we've found the agricultural section.

"Oh, this must be misplaced." Sylvie slides a book off the shelf.

"What's that one about?" I ask.

"The Defeat of King Awern."

"Now, that sounds like a good book," Galen says with a toothy grin.

"Who was King Awern?"

Sylvie brings the book over to the table and sets it in front of Galen. Gold lettering glitters against the blue blinding. "Awern was the last king of the Unseelie."

"The one Riven's father fought?" I lean forward for a closer look.

"No, that war wasn't fought against an Unseelie king, just many Unseelie who'd banded together," Sylvie explains. "The last Unseelie king, Awern, was killed many, many years ago."

"Oh." I try to process that information. "I thought all fae territories had a king or queen. Isn't the magic of the land tied to them?"

"Awern did not have an heir or apparently any close relatives the magic deemed acceptable." Galen flips idly through the pages of the book without so much as looking up. "The magic did not choose a new monarch. Vanished, some say. Lays dormant, waiting for a suitable heir, perhaps." He shrugs. "No one knows really."

"It's a good thing too." Sylvie leans on the edge of the table. "They cause us enough trouble without having a king to lead them." She shudders. "Just think what they'd be like if they did."

Galen lets the book fall closed with a weighty thud. "I don't know. It might be good if the magic finally settled on a new monarch."

Sylvie looks at as if he's sprouted a second head, and I'd wager my wide-eyed stare isn't too different.

"Think about it," Galen continues. "The Seelie monarchs would have a cause to rally behind, a reason to work together and stop bickering with each other."

"Or they'd still fight each other *and* the Unseelie, and then we'd all be truly doomed."

One already has my sister. How much worse would they be with a real leader? Goosebumps race across my skin.

"Give them some credit, Sylvie. Do you really think they'd continue their petty squabbles if there was a real threat?"

Each volley between them rises in volume till they're almost shouting. It's not like Galen to argue a point, any point, so fiercely. This is something he cares about, has thought about more than once.

"Some of their differences are more than petty," she snaps back.

Nausea churns in my gut again at the thought of the Unseelie. In only a few hours, we're supposed to meet them and retrieve my sister. But there are still so many variables. The trade, the spell, if they'll even keep their word and do a deal with us. If war breaks out...

They both fall silent as I rise to my feet.

"Lia, are you..." Galen starts, but I cut him off.

"I'm sorry. I just need a few minutes." My anxiety has risen tenfold today. I thought I'd be more at ease since the deadline is almost upon us, but it's worse than I ever imagined. I need a whole bottle of liquor. A Xanax. Anything.

"Do you want us to come with you?" Sylvie asks.

"No. Thank you. I just need a few minutes alone."

Sylvie shoots Galen a silent look of frustration as I stride past them out of the library.

My feet carry me to an interior courtyard nearby. The secluded, empty space beckons me like a moth to flame, offering peace and quiet, a respite from my worries.

Alone in the garden, I marvel at the majestic beauty of the place. No voices break the melody of nature. Sunlight slants through the trees while birds chirp merrily in their branches. Various floral and woody smells tease my senses, calming my anxiety.

I'm reclined on a bench, soaking in the sun, when the worst fae possible interrupts my stolen moment of peace.

"I see you wore my ring."

Sigurd. The metal ring around my finger is suddenly chilling. I had put it back on this morning. We have enough trouble with the Unseelie. Adding to Riven's problems or hampering May's rescue by angering Sigurd is at the bottom of my wish list.

He steps out from between two trees, dressed in his usual gray and blue. How long has he been there?

"What do you want?" I try to keep the bite out of my voice. Fail.

He brushes invisible dirt off his shoulder. "The chance to see you one more time before I leave."

His court left yesterday, returning to the border. He, however, had not.

Sigurd saunters over to my bench all casual, as if he were a friend. But he's far from it, and I'm up and backing away before he's halfway to me. He takes my seat and reclines with one ankle crossed over his knee before patting the open space beside him. "Come and have a seat. I wish to talk."

Right, and a shark only hopes to swallow a whole school of fish. I'm very much the fish. Our last conversation alone didn't turn out well at all, and though the bench is big enough for two or three, it still puts me way too close to him.

"I promise I won't bite." His smile is predatory. It implies biting and so many wicked things I don't care to share with him.

It takes everything I have to tear my gaze from him and glance toward the library. Not far. I could run. But he'd catch me. I have no doubt of that. I could scream.

May. My throat tightens.

The sapphire he gifted me gleams in the light, reminding me why I wore it. My emeralds sparkle on the other arm, a guarantee of protection.

I won't cause any more problems. I can't.

Reluctantly, I take the seat next to him, putting as much space between our bodies as possible. This flirty king might as well be a pit viper, and he deserves the same attention and caution as one.

"Such an interesting thing, that door key that you retrieved," he says.

I gasp, taken off guard so fast that all my careful thoughts flee in an instant. Only those closest to Riven know the true purpose of our little excursion or what we found out there. He even warded the doors to his room, preventing his own people from seeing or sensing our discovery—for now.

Sigurd doesn't bother to ask, to pry out information. He *knows* what we found. He knows. And he doesn't mind telling me. Snow could drop from the summer sky, and it'd still be warmer than the chill spreading across my skin.

"An object created by the fae for humans and then bespelled by those same greedy humans so that only they could use it." Sigurd clicks his tongue in his mouth and pauses. Smiling. Waiting.

A crafty hunter, baiting his prey. He wants me to ask about the stone. If this is a game, I'm losing terribly, and I can't afford that, not now.

I tilt my head, my brows scrunching together as I blink at him in feigned innocence.

After a time, he gives up with a shrug. "Anyhow, not just any human could enter the maze and take it. It'd have been recovered much sooner if that were the case. In fact, a human must meet three criteria to even attempt it."

More bait. I met the criteria, whatever they were. I stare at him and wait, my hands folded in my lap. It's the only thing keeping them from shaking.

A small thrill of victory zips through my veins when his smile falters.

"Three things, Lia. Do you know what they are?" He raises his hand in front of me, three fingers up in emphasis.

"I suppose you're going to tell me?" I had to be human, that much Riven had said.

"One." He curls in one finger. "The human must bear the mark of a fae of the forest."

Check. My cheeks burn.

"Two." Sigurd's words draw me back as he lowers a second finger. "The human must come to Faery of their own free will."

The words slide through me, slick as an oil spill and just as messy. Riven had asked me to come to Faery with him. The night we met. Later in my dreams. Even after, once we met again in the forest. I swallow a lump in my throat. I'd refused. He could have taken me through, but he didn't. He asked. Over and over he asked.

And eventually, I came.

"Three." Sigurd makes a fist, and he might as well be grinding my bones in his palm for how I ache. "The human must love a fae."

"But I don't love..." The denial tumbles out, but I taste it for the lie it is. I do love Riven. Deep within, I know that, even if I haven't told him yet, even if I haven't fully come to grips with it myself.

"Do you not?" He raises his eyebrows, his smirk growing as they arch high. "Perhaps you lie to even yourself."

I open my mouth to yell at him. Close it so hard my teeth grind.

It's all I can do to force myself to look at Sigurd. His dark hair blows onto his face in the gentle breeze, but he doesn't even move to push it away, pleased with himself as he is.

"Thank you for telling me all this, really." False honey coats my words, and I lay it on thick, giving all I can muster. "I appreciate the honesty." Okay maybe, that's not entirely true, but I can lie. "But how do you know these things? Why tell me all this?"

His countenance darkens. "Such a legend, what fool king wouldn't know it? And you, you'll just use that key to open the doors for him?" He leans forward, an eerie glow leaking from his eyes. "Or do you plan to trade it to the Unseelie?"

I barely hold back my flinch. Close, too close.

"If you reopen the doors, more humans will inevitably come here. You may not be the only young human in the Court of the Forest then. Do you still think Riven will want you? When he has other humans to choose from whose human spark has not started to fade?"

The words cut deep, slicing at the insecurity I'd managed to push aside. Riven made it clear he wants me and me alone. Broken bits and all. But when Sigurd throws the future out there like that...

My stomach turns. If more humans mean more power, why would he want only me? But then—

"Fade?" The word jumps out at me like a flashing sign, clanging a warning bell in my head. "Wait, what do you mean?" Riven said the fae would fade and die in my world but humans in theirs... My hands clasp over my mouth, holding in the scream threatening to break free.

No.

Sigurd leans closer, his arm curling around my side of the bench. "You see, Faery has this effect on humans." His conspiratorial whisper wraps around me like his arm. "Spending time here, giving your human light to help the fae, it eats away at your humanity, lessens your effect on us, even"—he drops his voice to a whisper—"makes it harder to remember." He taps a finger on the side of his head. "I wonder how much you'll remember by the time you're free of that pesky bargain?"

His words are knives, cutting deep, bleeding me out, flowing with the tears that blur my vision. Have I forgotten anything? Would I even know if I have?

"Does Riven know about this?"

He'd said he was unfamiliar with humans. Maybe he truly didn't know. I hold that hope as tightly as I can. I can't even bear to look Sigurd in the face. The bench. The cobbled stone walkway. Anything else.

"Yes." The word is a hiss, a victory.

I choke back another sob. He knew. He knew, and he never mentioned it.

"Why?" I croak out.

Sigurd shrugs. "Who can say what Riven plans?"

"Could I really forget everything in just a few months?"

He looks me over, one finger tapping on the side of his cheek. "Every human is different."

Not really an answer.

I need to talk to Riven, to hear his side of the story. I clutch the armrest of the bench and push myself to my feet.

"Have a seat, Lia. That's not all we have to talk about." He pats the space I just vacated like a friend inviting company. The smile on his otherwise stunning face is heartbreakingly cruel.

The first night I'd met Riven, I wondered if he was the devil come to claim me.

This man, this fae, is far worse.

"Don't you want to hear the rest?" His tone is light, almost playful, like a child sharing juicy secrets.

He likes to play games. Riven's words echo through my head bringing with them edged clarity. He's playing one now, baiting me to get me away from Riven.

Of course. Of course it would be to his advantage if Riven doesn't have me by his side, feeding his magic and, by proxy, feeding the magic of everyone here.

A fire ignites in my chest, burning away the fear and insecurity of moments before.

Taking a page from Sigurd's book, I brush invisible dirt off my pants and glance at him over one shoulder. "I think we're done here."

I whip my head around and stride in the opposite direction, not waiting to see his reaction to my curt dismissal. A cold sweat breaks out on my neck. I've just turned my back on one of the most powerful fae in Faery. Undoubtedly a bad idea, but it's too late now.

A firm hand latches on to my arm and stops me in my tracks. The breath I've been holding leaves my lungs in a whoosh.

"We're not done yet." Sigurd's eyes shine with the hardness of the stone they resemble. The casual attitude he displayed earlier is completely gone, replaced instead with something feral, dangerous.

"Oh yes, we are." I yank my arm away.

Or rather, he lets me go. I'm not fool enough to think I can overpower a fae king. My hands shake, and I clasp them together, praying he doesn't notice. It takes everything I have to stare him down.

"How dare you touch the Lady of the Forest?" I fling my title at him, wielding it like a weapon, savoring the slight snarl he gives in return.

Now he's the one toying with starting a war.

"Don't you want to hear what I learned from my spies watching the Unseelie?" he asks.

I turn and walk away.

No. We're done. I'm done. If the title I hold carries any weight, if he has any sense, he'll let me go. I hadn't used whatever power it gives me, hadn't needed it. But in this moment, I'll use whatever tools I have. I notch my chin higher like the important human I claim to be—Lady of the Forest.

"They heard the most interesting tale," Sigurd calls after me, "about a fae king who paid some of their tribesmen to perform a favor for him. He shifted the volunteers back to his land. To his capital. Only one week ago."

CHAPTER 33

I FREEZE. THE FIRE in me gutters to ash as his words sink home with deadly accuracy.

No.

Oh, God, no. No. No. No.

"I thought you might be interested." The words drip honey. Poisoned, wicked, awful sweetness that belies their intention.

The ground seems to shift under my feet. My knees wobble.

Sigurd stalks in front of me like a predator circling prey.

Tears sting the corner of my eyes. I blink, refusing to let them spill. I won't give him that, not when he's taking everything else.

"Didn't you wonder how the Unseelie got so deep in Riven's territory? How they got through one of his only doors, a warded door at that, so close to his capital? Or better yet, how they knew to take a very specific human girl?"

My knees hit the ground. The shock of the fall echoes up my body.

It should hurt. I don't feel the pain. I can't feel anything over the agony of my heart ripping in two. Not just ripping, shredding bit by bit, until nothing but ribbons of torn, bleeding flesh remain inside me.

He said his land was in trouble. Dying. The Unseelie were a threat.

Truth. But not all of it.

How had I been so stupid, so naïve?

I remember that day so clearly now, standing in that hated ballroom amid strange fae who stared at me in wonder...and greed and lust.

I didn't take your sister. No, damn it, he hadn't, but that didn't mean he didn't have her taken. He'd lied without lying. Fae can't lie with their words, but they can deceive. They can deceive so horribly.

Another memory flashes through my mind, one I didn't understand at the time.

You've made a mistake dealing falsely with us, Forest King. Katiya's words.

He stole my sister. He played it off as some random raid when, really, he'd paid Unseelie to do it and then tried to kill them all.

And I'd played right into his hands. Every step I'd taken was one that he'd planned for me to take. He led me into this world, into his bed.

I can still feel him between my legs, his hands on my body, the scent of him in my nose.

I gag, choking down the bile that climbs up my throat. My hair falls about me in a cascade as I hunch on my hands and knees. Tears run unchecked down my face now, dripping onto my hands while my fingertips dig into the paving stones below me.

Sigurd kneels on the ground next to me and pulls my hair back from my face, like a friend holding my hair back after I'd had too much to drink at a college party. But this is no party, and Sigurd is no friend.

"Poor, dear, Lia," he croons, accenting each word.

"I am not your dear," I retort around gulps of air.

"No, you wouldn't have ended up like this if you were." He tilts my face toward him, still holding my hair back. "Do you still trust him to save your sister, knowing that he had her taken in the first place?" His face has lost its harshness. Instead, he's solemn.

We have a bargain. He promised. But...

"No." The word tears from my lips as a sob.

"I could save your sister for you." His thumb wipes a streak through my falling tears. "Give me the key, and I'll give you your sister. I'll even return you to your world if you so choose."

"I made a magical bargain to stay."

"The key you found is more than it appears. Its power could break your bargain. Set you free."

A glimmer of something—hope?—sparks inside my ruined heart. "How?"

"Give me the key first."

"I don't have it."

"But I'd bet you can get it. Return here with it before sunset if you want my help." His hand caresses my face. "I need to leave. Now. But I'll send someone to bring you to me."

His spy?

"Why help me?"

Sigurd cocks his head to the side in a truly alien movement. He opens his mouth, as if to speak but halts. A half-smile paints his features. "Your guards come for you. I'll see you soon."

"Lia!"

"What's happened? Are you all right?"

Sylvie and Galen hurry toward me. Tension flees as my body goes slack in a surge of relief. But just as quickly, I tense up again. Sylvie drops to her knees and reaches toward my tear-stained face. I pull back. Tears blur my eyes again, the pain of betrayal fresh and ragged in my heart. I can't even look at them.

"Lia?" Sylvie draws back. From the corner of my eyes, I see her glance at Galen.

He shifts on his feet. "We should call for Riven."

I bite my lip at his name. The tang of blood washes over my tastebuds. No. I'm not ready to see him. After what I just learned, I might never be.

May. I have to save May. That's all that matters now.

Pull it together. I suck in a breath and fight against my tears. If they figure out what I know, I'll have much less chance of getting the key and returning here. Maybe none.

Sylvie latches onto my hip. Before I can move away, she slides her thumb into the waistband of my pants, right over Riven's mark. "Sylvie, what—"

Magic rushes over my skin.

"Lia, what's happened?" His voice, the one I once adored, pierces me like a dagger.

I choke on a sob. I can't do this.

Riven drops to the ground next to me and ushers Sylvie and Galen out of the way.

I close my eyes. Tears leak from their corners to run down my face.

"What did he do to you?" The concern in his voice drives another stake into my heart. He holds me close as he wipes away the tears with his thumbs.

Another act? Another lie?

"Who?" Sylvie's question lingers in the air.

Riven responds, "Sigurd. I feel his magic. Smell him. He was just here."

"We'll go after him." Galen's voice this time. The sound of boots retreating across the stones follows.

I didn't want to see them, or anyone, but being left alone with Riven is so much worse. His magic tingles under my skin, sweeping through my body, trying to heal whatever's wrong with me. It crushes the shards of my heart into powder. He can't heal this. No magic can.

"My Ciela, please, speak to me."

I don't know the word he used. A Faery endearment? I want to hit him, to push him away, to yell at him. But none of that will do me any good.

I gulp a steadying breath and open my eyes.

Riven's face hovers in front of me. Green eyes laced with concern and a tinge of that inhuman glow stare into mine. I long to close my eyes again, close them and never open them.

But I can't. Not until May is free.

"Lia?" His hands are still on my face, stroking it softly, each soft touch grating like sandpaper against my soul.

"I'm okay," I whisper. A lie. Such a lie. "I got overwhelmed. I need some time alone."

Riven undoes the bracelet around my wrist with such care it breaks something in me that I didn't know I had left to shatter. The bracelet finds a new home in his pocket before he scoops me off the ground and into his arms in one smooth movement, as if I weigh nothing at all.

Too much, too close. My skin crawls. I fight the urge to wiggle away.

"I'll take you to our rooms."

The air bends. The scene around us twists. A pop echoes through the air, and suddenly we're in our sitting room.

No, not ours. *His.*

He places me on the chaise lounge with delicacy so at odds with what I've just learned. My head spins with questions, with threats, with accusations.

None of it will help.

"Calm down. You're okay now," Riven croons in a soft, gentle voice he might use with a startled horse.

I am so not okay.

He crawls onto the seat next to me, brushing the hair back from my tear-stained face with a tenderness that threatens to destroy me all over again. "Please tell me what happened, Lia. What did he do to you?"

I close my eyes while I think, trying to come up with something, anything other than the truth. A good lie is always as close to the truth as possible. Hadn't he himself proven that to be true? I open my eyes again but can't meet Riven's gaze. Instead, I stare across the room.

"I wasn't feeling well. I fell. I actually think he wanted to help me, but he ran off when he heard Sylvie and Galen returning." All true.

I flick my gaze back to Riven then away. He still appears con-cerned, watching me, waiting for something more.

Horrible two-faced monster. Where is that arrogant king now? The one I loathed. Him, I might be able stand.

"I need some time alone," I say. "Peace and quiet."

Silence reigns. *Please, please just leave me alone to think.*

"We have to leave to meet the Unseelie in a few hours," he says.

"Yes, just give me space until then."

Something cracks in his green eyes. His lips pull downward. Yet he rises, giving me the space I requested. Without a word, he pulls the bracelet out of his pocket and lays it on the cushion next to me.

"If you need anything..."

"I'll ring for Karin."

He flinches. In a breath, he's gone.

Chapter 34

I MOVE THROUGH THE room like a robot, carrying out one action after another with detached, clinical precision. Tears dry on my face. The hole in my chest aches with residual pain, but I push it away.

Outfit with pockets? Check.

A touch of make-up to cover the redness of my tear-stained face? Check.

That just leaves the key. I stare at the twin stones, visual duplicates of each other, where they lay side by side, one on a pillow and one under crystal.

Can I really give away their hope? Their chance for a future?

Once, a witch loved a fae king who betrayed her. My heart aches. Tears threaten again. I'm not a witch, but I understand her pain more than I ever wanted to. How she could unleash such deadly punishment for the crime against her. She cursed the stone to protect her sisters—real or in spirit, does it matter? When she called me sister in that maze, I knew she wasn't May, but something in her called out to me. Maybe our shared humanity, maybe our shared gift, or maybe some deeper connection. Who can say? But whatever she sacrificed to spin her revenge, she'd done that for me too. A human who loved a fae and was betrayed. A sister she'd hoped to protect in her own way.

I'd do anything for May, for my sister, and I know with painful certainty what I have to do.

"Do you need anything, my lady?"

The title cuts me like a knife. How long had it been since I'd wielded it against Sigurd? Relished in that moment of power and what it meant?

"Should we call for King Riven?" the other guard in the hall asks. "Or we could escort you some—"

"That won't be necessary. Thank you." The calm evenness of my voice surprises me.

They back down, obeying their lady.

A smirk twitches on my lips, aching to break free. My title. My weapon. One Riven gave to me and oh how good it feels to use it now.

Determined steps carry me through the halls of Arbrean, back to the courtyard where Sigurd promised to send his emissary. It would have been hard to find, had it not been so close to the library where I spent much of my time. The quiet section of the castle, the fae called it. One dedicated to peace and learning. I choke back a laugh at the irony.

I send the few fae I pass away from the courtyard, away from this area. They're happy to obey me.

All too soon, I reach the flowering purple trees marking the courtyard entrance.

My throat tightens, my steps turn heavy, but I push onward. I won't back down now.

But just as I pass under the laden branches marking the threshold, something catches my eye that draws me to a halt.

No.

A mental scream of fury and frustration echoes through me.

Galen sits on the bench Sigurd and I had shared, his head in his hands.

My fingers dig into the bark of the nearby tree. So close. How do I get him to leave? The others I can order without question, but him? He'd ask questions. He'd know the order to be strange—I'd never used my title with them, never wielded it like I have today, not once.

His head turns in my direction. "Lia?"

Shit.

I smooth out my features and step from the shadow of the tree. "You're back already?" Hadn't he gone after Sigurd with Sylvie?

He nods. "Come sit with me."

My feet draw me closer against my better judgment. "Was your, um, *quest* successful?"

"In a way." His shoulders hunch as if the weight of the world rests on them.

"Sylvie? Is she all right?" My eyes widen. Despite all that's happened, the thought of her being injured—

"She's fine."

Relief floods me. "Then what's wrong? Why sit out here?"

Galen pats the bench next to him.

I purse my lips and stare at the spot, the place where my world started to crumble. Reluctantly, I join him. I need him to leave, and if playing along makes that happen sooner, then so be it.

"Why here indeed," he echoes, shaking his head. "You still don't know. Haven't realized."

Dark threads float through my head, just out of reach. My skin prickles. Galen smiles a sad smile, and I gasp, my hands flying to cover my mouth.

Galen is the spy in Riven's court.

He'd told Sigurd about my bargain, my sister, the door key...everything.

He nods in silent confirmation.

And Riven has no idea. Despite everything, my traitorous heart aches for Riven. A member of his own elite guard, one he trusted to guard even me, betrayed him.

I hoped to get Galen to leave, thought to order him to do so, and yet, he's the one I need.

But...if I go with Galen, Riven will be betrayed twice today. He deserves it if Sigurd's words prove true, but if somehow they aren't...

I shift on my seat and stare at Galen, not bothering to hide the emotions that must be apparent on my face—panic, misery, confusion.

"How are you his? Why would he help me?" I whisper. Better not to say his name, just in case someone is listening. In case the memory of this place can somehow give us away to Riven later.

"He didn't tell me why." Galen shifts in his seat, unable to meet my eyes. "As for me, I'm mixed. Forest and Air."

"Does Riven know?" That'd be a huge thing to overlook.

"He knows of my lineage but not my father's loyalties." A deep frown etches across his features as he shakes his head. "It's hard. I respect them both a great deal, but I was oath sworn to Sigurd before Riven. My father is of the Air, you see, sworn to serve Sigurd. But he fell in love with a woman of the forest. He gave up his claims in the Court of Air by appearance but never in reality. He raised me to be the same. Living in the Court of the Forest but serving the Air as well." Various emotions flicker across his face. His hands clench and unclench as he speaks. "I never expected to have to betray the King of the Forest. I don't want to. You have to believe that."

He meets my gaze at last.

And I do. The grief and heartbreak in his eyes, the way it eats at him just to share that knowledge with me... A fae of two courts torn between two kings. I understand the feeling of being pulled between two places. I understand it too well.

"I do." I cover his hand with mine, just a brief touch before retreating. "I believe you."

Galen rubs his earring between his fingers. Panic flashes in his eyes and he drops his hand.

"We need to go, and go now, if we're going to do this." The urgency in his whisper slips into me like a shard of ice. "He's fled for the border, but I can shift you to him." His gaze dips to the pockets sewn into the skirts of my dress. A blue dress in Sigurd's colors. "You brought it?"

I swallow the lump stuck in my throat.

"And you're sure?" His hand wraps around mine and squeezes tight, painfully so. The hard planes of his face beg me to change my mind, plead with me in silence. He doesn't want this, any of it.

My confidence falters, my hands shake.

Sister. The witches eerie voice echoes through me.

One last chance to back out, to forget this whole plan. I might never be sure, but for May, I have no choice. "Yes."

Galen's eyes slide closed. His hand clenches around mine.

With a sigh that holds all the world, he rises to his feet. I join him and begin unclasping Solona's bracelet from my wrist.

A figure appears in the entranceway to the courtyard. "Galen?"

His eyes widen as my heart sinks. Galen hunches in pain as he takes my hand and turns his head to glance over his shoulder at the woman staring at him in shocked confusion.

"I'm so sorry," he says.

Sylvie's attention snaps to the bracelet sliding off my wrist. Her eyes grow wide. Her mouth gapes.

My fingers go slack, the bracelet almost sliding from my grip. Her pain is palpable, a double-edged blade slicing me open all over again. Another person I've hurt. Destroyed.

Galen sends out his magic.

The air bends and warps, more jagged and skewed than when Riven shifts us. The air around us thickens like high humidity, closing us up in a cloud of magic. The courtyard fades from view as Sylvie runs toward us, and a small part of me wishes to be lost in the void forever.

But tall trees rise up to replace Sylvie's vanished form as Galen closes his eyes against her pain and panic. The scent of pine rushes in as the magic pops, leaving us standing in a forest clearing.

A slow clap echoes through the air. Chills run down my spine as I grip Galen's hand, looking for the source of the noise.

"Very good. And faster than I expected."

We whirl toward the voice as Sigurd approaches from under the canopy of trees. Sweat dampens his hair, his clothes. His chest still rises and falls with deep breaths. He really has run here.

"We were spotted. He will be here soon," Galen says.

I slip my hand from Galen's and fumble with the bracelet, hastily trying to re-secure it. He helps, holding the metal firm so I can clasp it shut. A humorless laugh claws up my throat. He helps me, after all I've done to him and everyone. All I will do.

"Smart but unnecessary." Sigurd swipes a hand across his brow, pushing away sweat-matted locks. "Now, the key?"

"I need your word." I throw all the command into my voice I can muster. "Bound in magic."

He rolls his eyes. "How has that worked out for you so far?"

The verbal jab causes me to wince, but I straighten my shoulders, staring him down.

"There's no time for that, Lia. If you want your sister, give me the key."

Sigurd's eyes practically glitter as I pull the stone from my pocket.

"Well?" he asks Galen.

Galen's jaw stiffens, but he nods with a jerk of his head. "It looks like the stone."

Sigurd's head snaps to the left, as if he's heard something, but the forest is eerily quiet. "So soon?"

I don't have time to ponder his words before his attention flicks back to me. "Give it to me now, Lia, or this offer goes away."

I search Galen's face for guidance, help, anything, but his features give nothing away. Nothing other than pain and deep sorrow. My fingers clench around the stone as I war with my decision. The fate of so many lies in my hands, in my decision. The weight of it pulls on my very soul. But for May... I can't falter. I grit my teeth and thrust it out to Sigurd.

Instead of just taking the stone, he grabs me, jerking me away from Galen and into his arms. Breathe whooshes from my lungs in a gasp. The stone is plucked away and I'm bound tight against Sigurd's chest by arms strong as steel.

"Lia!" Riven's pained roar echoes through the clearing.

No. Searing agony rips through my ruined heart. Pain at the voice I most dreaded and most longed to hear, at the raw anguish it holds. I don't want to hurt for him. How can I still ache so badly when I'm so hollow inside? The fight and struggle building up in me reverses in an instant. I bury my face in Sigurd's chest, going almost limp as his warmth and heady pine scent flood my senses. It's a vain attempt to hide from the male behind me, perhaps a subconscious attempt to wound him, but I don't have time to look too closely at that.

"Let her go!" Riven demands.

Sigurd turns me to face Riven. His arm still locks around my waist, holding my back to his chest.

I open my eyes slowly, embracing the pain that comes with it.

Ten feet separate us, but even the moon feels closer.

Riven's claws flash out, raised at the man he vowed not to harm until May is found. Can he even break that promise? His focus slides from me to the arm around my waist, the one holding the door key. Surprise registers first—his widened eyes and barely parted lips—then betrayal. His claws curl in, and sharp canines slip into view. And finally, devastation, as his gaze slides to Galen then back to me.

Claws and fangs vanish. His shoulders droop. The myriad emotions rushing across his face are as easy to read as a flashing sign.

"How does it feel to have someone you love taken from you?" Sigurd taunts as he caresses my cheek with the back of his hand.

My skin crawls at his touch, but it's his comment that causes tears to well up in my eyes.

Someone you love. He can't say it if he doesn't believe it, but...

"Give her back." Riven steps closer, but Sigurd pulls back. "Please." Riven's voice cracks over the word.

"Her and not the key?" Sigurd asks, flashing the object he holds.

Riven swallows. Not even I can guess the emotions on his face now. "Yes."

"Fool." He laughs. "But no matter. You kept the human I loved from me, just like your father. Now I've taken your human from you. At least her heart."

Sigurd shoves me—hard.

I stumble, falling to my knees as Riven leaps for me. His arms cradle my body as I crash into him in a tangle of limbs and tears.

"Galen," Sigurd calls sharply.

Magic stirs behind me, thick and heavy, before it slips away entirely.

They've gone, leaving me alone in the arms of the man I loved only hours ago. The same one who had my sister kidnapped.

CHAPTER 35

R IVEN HOLDS ME LIKE a porcelain vase. "Lia—"

"Get off me! Let me go!" I thrash against him like a hellcat.

The shell of his arms parts. I shove against his unmoving chest, aiming to knock him back, but push myself away in the process, sliding back across the grass.

"Don't touch me," I hiss.

Pain washes across his features again, twisting something inside me, despite my anger. The arrogant King of the Forest is gone. Hard lines paint the face of the male on the forest floor with me, but they're not lines of anger. This is sorrow, gouged deep as any physical wound or scar. Mere feet separate our bodies, but it may as well be a gulf.

"What did he do to you?" he asks.

A humorless laugh bubbles from me. He thinks Sigurd is to blame for this? "He told me the truth."

Riven's head draws back. His lips thin and snarl all at once. "You don't understand."

"Is it true then?" The words are a shout, a wicked weapon flung his way, and it's not enough, will never be enough. "Did you really order the Unseelie to capture May? Was it all a deception to get me here and into your bed?"

He looks like I slapped him, utterly struck by my accusation. Eyes wide. Mouth parted, showing the tips of glinting fangs. The reaction dims as quickly as it came, and if possible, his countenance darkens even more. If the King of the Forest can control its shadows, he's pulled them to him in this moment.

"Calm down. We need to talk about this." Each word is hard. Icy. Brittle.

He still hasn't answered my question. And I *need* answers. Everything depends on them.

My fingernails dig into the grass below me. The dirt. "Tell me. Yes or no, did you orchestrate my sister's kidnapping?"

Riven stares back, unmoving, unspeaking.

Whatever is left of my heart utterly shatters, a million tiny knives slicing me open within. Oh God, he can't deny it. His form blurs through my tears. He can't lie to tell me it isn't true.

I didn't think I could hurt any more.

I was wrong. So wrong.

Bile burns my throat, and I twist to the side, vomiting onto the grass.

Vaguely, I'm aware of something rustling behind me.

"Don't." I fling an arm out, warding off his assumed approach. The movement stops. I wipe at my mouth, failing to scrub away the tang of bile that clings to my taste buds.

"Please..." His voice cracks and rasps. "Let me explain."

"What else is there to say?" I twist my head around and stare at him through the strands of hair sticking to my tear-dampened face.

The fae king kneels on the ground just behind me, close enough for a whiff of his honeysuckle scent to tease my senses with flashes of memories more painful than any words.

"I will return her to you. Even without the key, I will find a way. It never should have come to this. It's my fault, and I will make it right, Lia. Believe that if nothing else." His tight fists drip blood onto the grass.

"Why? How could you—" I choke on the words, unable to continue as a sob wracks my body.

Almost killing May was horrible. It wrecked me, still tries to undo me every chance it gets.

But that was an accident. A mistake. My fault but not something I ever intended.

But this... *This* was planned. Intentional. And I played into it like the foolish little human I am.

"We were desperate. *I* was desperate." Riven's unbloodied hand scrubs down his weary face as words tumble out, one after another. "I needed to find a way to get humans here in order to save my people. I'm responsible for all of them, yet we're fading. A slow death of our magic. A failure after all these generations. My father was loved, respected, and yet I, his only heir, let his legacy fall to ruin in years." He shakes, magic wafting off him like steam. "I needed you here. I wanted you and you alone. I asked so many times. I told you we needed you." He shakes his head, and the outpouring of magic stills. "You've done so much just for your sister, but what if everyone you loved was at risk? What would you do to save them all?"

What would I give for those I love?

Anything.

I look at him then—really look—wiping away the tears that threaten to cloud my sight.

I've always perceived him as the glorious, powerful King of the Forest. Immaculately dressed, pointed ears poking through long hair, emerald eyes I could drown in, the mask of cocky arrogance he often donned in public, a poor attempt to step into the shoes of his beloved father, and the fierce, kind man I'd known in private.

All of those pieces are still there, but like a shattered vase, he's broken.

All pretense of arrogance and playfulness is gone, replaced by vulnerability, honesty, a king who's laid his soul bare and stripped away all his masks.

I sniffle.

Anything. I would do whatever I could to save them, no matter the cost to myself.

He must see the answer in my eyes because he continues, his voice low and brittle as the first crust of ice over the lake. "Our fading magic would soon have given others—other Seelie Courts, the Unseelie—an opportunity to invade us. You saw how weak our wards were. As a king, as the leader of my people, I couldn't allow that. Their wellbeing has to be my top priority. So, I sent some of my best sensors, fae with the ability to sense the gift in humans, to watch the areas around our few doors in shifts. We were constantly looking for gifted humans we might entice to come here.

"We saw many humans but precious few with the gift. The gifted we found we were unsuccessful in recruiting. Most turned and ran. Others likely thought they were hallucinating. We'd begun to consider taking humans by force, but I dreaded the idea." His chest shakes, his voice rising on every word. "I hated it!"

The words echo through the trees, calling back to us long after they leave his lips. His fist clenches at his side again. Fresh blood drips to the ground. Fire burns in his eyes before gutting to a dull green.

"But even so, I can't ignore the needs of my people. Our outlook was bleak. Then, one night, you collapsed at the door. A young, gifted human, hurting, desperate...just like me. When I saw you, I knew you were the one we were waiting on." The hard lines marring his face soften, and Riven reaches for me. His eyes widen as he catches sight of the blood coating his hand, which he hastily wipes on the grass. "I feared I'd lost my chance with you when you left your home in the woods. It took a considerable amount of magic to send you those dreams, but I needed a way to reach you, to encourage you to come back to the door, to me. Some days, I could do little else. A few minutes with you took everything I had."

My eyes water again. A different type of tears form at the softness in his voice, the utter vulnerability. "I loved those dreams. Those moments. It got me through when nothing else did."

Without them...

Some days my guilt crushed me so hard it was all I could do to wander through my waking hours like a zombie, carrying out one mundane task after another until I could fade into blessed sleep. Sink down into that comforting darkness where I simply was. And maybe, just maybe, where he waited for me, to pull me back up, piece me together, and give me the strength to keep moving forward.

"As the spark of hope you gave me got me through." A weighty silence lingers until Riven continues, "When you came to the door again, I could barely contain my excitement. I already knew you were beautiful. But your determined spirit and love for your family enraptured me more than physical beauty ever could. More than I even realized at the time. You loved so deeply, so passionately. I wanted to take you through right then, but I needed you to come of your own free will. I remembered the legends about the door key, the conditions to retrieve it, and that object could save my people for generations to come. It would make me a hero. A worthy heir in the eyes of the court, not some fool boy unfit for the title and magic that was bestowed on me before my time." He shakes his head and looks away. "I wanted that. For my people. For me. Yet you rejected me so adamantly.

"And then I heard you and your sister talk about moving away. I was desperate. I couldn't lose you. In a horrible moment, I realized what would get you to come to Faery, and I knew I had to do it to get you here." He hangs his head. "She was never supposed to be in any real danger. I didn't consider that my plan may not work. It felt perfect at the time. They'd agreed to take her and keep her in a magical slumber. I knew Ambrose and my guard had the skill to find and track them. They did. Then it was just the matter of taking them out, as I'd planned to do before I involved them in my plot."

A hard knot settles in my chest at the casual mention of death and his use of the Unseelie as unwitting sacrifices in his plan. I pull my legs toward my chest and hug them. Whatever horrible things they've done in the past, this is just as cruel. Riven was desperate, and I know what desperation can make a person do, but the Unseelie are desperate in their own way. Their land isn't dying, it's already dead.

"I'd return your sister to you," he continues. "She'd be safe. *You'd* have saved her. We'd both win."

He looks back at my face and winces. I don't bother to hide everything I'm feeling, he deserves to see the pain he's caused. A win for us both, if it had worked, but at what cost? A horrible one I was never supposed to understand.

"I knew you'd hate me if you learned the truth." A sad smile touches his lips. "I never wanted to see the look on your face I've seen today. I thought if I could just get her back, get her home safely, no one would have to know the terrible truth of what I've done. I can handle my own guilt and pain—I've lived with them most of my life—but not yours. If I could go back, I'd do things differently."

"And the Unseelie?" I snap. "What excuse do you have for your treatment of them?"

Riven's lips quiver in the beginning of a snarl, his pointed fangs, ones that have yet to retract, peeking out. "They've done far worse than steal young girls. They deserve far worse." The trees around us quake, their limbs snapping. "A quick death by my magic would have been a mercy. What they did to my mother..."

A deathly stillness falls over the forest once more.

Sigurd's words come back to taunt my awareness, an unexpected certainty suddenly sliding into place. "Your mother was human..."

Riven nods. "Captured from your world by the Unseelie and brought here."

Just like May. My eyes water. He'd subjected my sister to the same fate, the same actions he hated the Unseelie for.

"She was already an adult, and they did not keep her asleep..." His words trail off in a whisper as his eyes glow an eerie green.

My insides twist and churn, horrible possibilities teasing my thoughts.

"Sigurd saved her, but she never found the doorway back to her home. Eventually, she decided to stop searching and stay here.

She was happy, with my father and all of us, until her human life ran its course."

Maybe things did turn out all right for her... in the end.

But his words don't make the grim reality any easier to digest.

"But enough of the past. I thought my plan would work. I was terribly wrong. And when I saw you in the clearing and that Unseelie coming toward you..." He reaches for me, his hand balling into a fist as I flinch away. "Every thought I had fled. Everything. Except saving you. If they had taken you as they took my mother..."

The whole forest shakes again, timbers snapping. The ground grumbles as something—a tree—crashes.

My body tenses. A veritable storm of emotion rages around us, yet every terrible quake of the forest is nothing compared to the certainty carving itself within me.

"I'm the reason your plan failed."

The horror of it threatens to drown me. I'd interrupted May's rescue. Even then, I knew that but now... Sigurd's eagle had led me there. He must have known Riven's deal with the Unseelie, even then.

"No, Lia, don't blame yourself."

He clasps my hand, but I'm too numb to do more than look at it. It's Riven who retreats from the touch. "This is my failure. Don't take this burden on yourself. Your appearance wasn't the only reason. I'd never seen that Unseelie, Katiya. She was not with the group I'd bribed and should not have known how to find them, especially so deep in my own territory."

"Unless someone told her," I murmur.

A terrible new realization drops into my stomach like a lead ball.

Riven had played me. Terribly. But maybe someone else pulled even more strings behind the scenes, someone who wanted us torn apart.

"Sigurd knew of the deal you made with the Unseelie, yet your people didn't know?" I ask in confirmation.

"I told no one at the time. Though I told Solona yesterday."

"Could she have—"

"No. You walked in on that conversation yourself. Did her anger look false?"

The memory flashes behind my eyes. Her near snarl—so at odds with her typically calm demeanor. The glow of her eyes. No, it hadn't. In fact, it may have been even more explosive than my own. I shake my head. So that's why she'd been so upset. My shoulders hunch in. She had every right to be.

"And Galen..." He runs his hands through his hair. "I had no idea. But he didn't know about that, at least not from me. I didn't tell any of them. My actions have cost more than I ever expected. You, Galen, maybe even Solona. If I could reverse time, I would, but I cannot. I can only hope to correct my mistakes."

Riven wallows in his guilt. But pain gives me clarity, honing the edges of my mind to sharp points that pierce through the haze of sorrow.

"Sigurd's eagle led me to you and the Unseelie in that clearing. If he hadn't, or if I had only been a few minutes later, things may have turned out differently. And he said he was spying on the Unseelie. What if he worked with them also?"

Riven goes still, his eyes wide, unblinking.

"Riven?" I prod.

He blinks and turns his head to meet my stare. "It's possible. How did Sigurd get the door key?"

Now it's my turn to wince. But we're baring secrets, and I won't hide from my choices. "I gave it to him."

His gaze turns hard, steely. "You—"

I straighten my spine and lift my chin. My fingers clutch at the grass under my hands, as if somehow the very ground will give me strength. "He offered to give me May and return us to our world, and when I learned what you had done..."

The hard mask breaks.

Panic flashes across his face as he lunges across the distance between us and grabs my arm. "You can't!"

Both our gazes snap to that offending spot—to where our bodies touch.

I jerk away, leaving his arm hovering in the air. "I already did."

His hand clenches as he draws it back to his body. Riven draws in a shuddering breath. "Our bargain will exact a price if you leave before it's complete."

My heart skips a beat. "What?"

"Magical bargains cannot be broken without cost," he says, the words just above a whisper. His eyes close as he shakes his head from side to side. "Leaving Faery, or possibly even going too far outside my territory, will break it. Sigurd would know that."

Shit. No wonder Riven panicked and held me close every time we were at the door.

"The price?" I swallow the tightness in my throat.

He shakes his head. "I don't know, but it could be as severe as death."

Death. The word lingers in the air, spreading an icy chill that seeps under my skin.

How does it feel to have someone you love taken from you? Sigurd words echo in my head, taking on a whole new meaning. Maybe he hadn't been referring to emotional separation but a more permanent, lethal type.

A shudder wracks my body. Fae cruelty knows no bounds. They all trade death like playing cards.

But...I'm not the only one bargain bound.

I cut my gaze to Riven. "If you don't save May..."

He nods, his jaw stiff. "Though even if I hadn't bargained it, I'd find a way. For you and your sister."

My heart twists again, ready to spill open anew. Riven deserves my anger for what he's done, but though I hate to admit it, I understand his reasons. What wouldn't I do to save one person I love, much less all of them? How many sins would I carve into my soul? Our bargain will cost him, maybe kill him. And from his perspective, I just allied with his hated enemy and gave away something that could change the future for his people. Everything he's done will be for nothing if their magic still dies a slow death.

Yet still, he pledges to help me. The truth of it scrapes something raw inside me.

I jump as forms take shape a few feet from us. Riven leaps to his feet in one swift motion, stepping between me and the arrivals.

"What's happened?" Ambrose's gruff voice carries through the space as he trots over with hurried steps.

Tension slips from Riven's shoulders at the friendly presence. A sigh escapes my lips. Riven turns and offers a hand to help me up, but I ignore it and push myself to my feet.

"Galen?" Sylvie calls from behind Ambrose.

The knots in my stomach twist painfully tight at the urgency in her voice, the fear. In that moment, I miss Riven's comfort, his care, especially as my legs wobble beneath me.

"Gone. With Sigurd," Riven says.

Sylvie freezes, eyes wide. "He took... how?"

"Galen shifted Sigurd away."

"But..." Another denial comes to her lips. Even Ambrose pales but keeps silent.

"I don't believe it was Galen's choice to help Sigurd." I step around Riven to stand a few feet from his side. Ambrose's eyes flick to the gap between us, my face, his brows creasing, but I ignore it. "Sigurd had an oath from him and called it in."

"He told you that?" Riven asks.

"Yes."

Sylvie is utterly still. The handful of other guards behind her look equally disturbed by the news.

"But why would he call in his oath now?" Ambrose ponders, rubbing his bearded chin. "Just to drag you out here in the woods when he was just with us for days?"

I stare at the grass under my feet. The time to confess my sins has arrived. I'm not ready. I'll never be ready.

"Sigurd wanted the door key," I whisper. "He offered me May in exchange for it."

"But that's what we..." Ambrose trails off, looking between Riven and me again. His attention snags on my face, my hair.

I don't need a mirror to know my eyes are red, my checks are puffy, and I probably look a hot mess.

"I made a grave mistake," Riven answers for me.

Pain washes through me anew at the reminder of his betrayal. I bite my lip and will away the tears that threaten again. Riven turns to me, perhaps waiting for me to expound upon all the ways he deceived me, to lay his sins bare for him.

But I hold my tongue.

Riven turns back to his men. "I had May kidnapped to get Lia here."

Multiple fae gasp. Sylvie steps back, her hand over her mouth.

Ambrose's eyes fly wide. In a breath, he shifts into his bear form. The ground rumbles as his front paws land upon the dirt. A bellowing roar echoes through the trees.

"Sigurd told me." I divide my attention between Riven and his guard, addressing them both. "I was hurt. Angry. And I gave him the stone in exchange for his offer to give me May."

The fae swear at this, maybe even angrier with me than with Riven. The weight of their crushing stares holds silent accusations. Ambrose growls again and paws the ground. Riven steps between me and his captain of the guard.

In Riven's eyes, I'd betrayed him too, yet even now, he protects me. Guilt twists with my anger, the unhappy cord of emotions pulling me down.

Ambrose shifts back into his human form. "You trusted him over us?"

I wince. What could I possibly say? "I... No, I don't."

"Then why?"

On instinct, I move further behind Riven, my regrets turning to shame.

"We don't have time for this." Riven's voice cuts the heavy silence.

The sun has dipped below the tops of the trees, coloring the clear sky in shades of pink and orange. Sunset. The agreed upon time to meet the Unseelie.

"We need to go now if we're to meet the Unseelie." Riven turns to me and takes my hand, but I jerk it away. Hurt flickers across his features again.

He stole my sister. Does he really think one apology will erase that betrayal?

"We have to shift there," he says. "Now."

I stiffen.

"I'll take you." Sylvie, her eyes wet and dull, holds out a hand to me. If anyone can understand my feelings right now, she can. I nod to her.

Riven's shoulders drop at the rejection. My anger has dimmed, leaving tender, ravaged scar tissue in its wake. And though I don't want to hurt for him too, I do. My shaking hands unclasp the bracelet before taking Sylvie's hands in mine.

"You know where to go?" Riven asks her.

"Yes."

"Then let's go get May."

CHAPTER 36

G RAY AND BROWN STONES litter the ground before us, the last remnants of some old structure fallen to ruin. It would have been grand once. Towering pillars, three stories high, poke out from the tall brown grass. Other blocks, larger than a car, lay on their sides. Gnarled trees bearing a smattering of brown and orange leaves twist up amongst some of the stones and dot the flat landscape beyond the boundaries of the old structure.

A hint of soil, woody dampness, and the faint trace of smoke perfume the air, though no smoke plumes dot the ever-dimming horizon. Even the breeze refuses to blow here.

A shiver races across my skin. "Where are they?"

"I don't know." Riven edges closer to me as his guards fan out around us.

"What was this place?" I ask.

"An old meeting place, back before the Shadowed Lands were so dim," Ambrose says. The short shift to this location has calmed his fury, at least by appearances, though his jaw still has a hard set to it that stirs something in my chest. "It's equidistant from the borders of Forest and Air in the thin strip of land that runs between the two. An ideal spot for negotiations."

Maybe once it had been, but little remains of the bygone meeting place. Shadows descend as the last sliver of the sun dips below the far horizon. The light of the blueish moon barely cresting the hills adds an eerie cast to the dying land around us.

"Did we miss them?" I can't keep the shrill edge of panic from my voice. If we can't negotiate with them... If I can't save May...

"No," Riven clasps his hand around my arm, but this time, I don't pull away. Not when my eyes lock on the spot he watches with careful attention. "Here they come."

Each muscle in my body tenses as forms approach across the open expanse of land. One carries a small, limp body in their arms.

I fight against the scream threatening to escape. May. *Please be all right.*

Riven's fingers twine through mine. I clench his hand in return. My anger and hurt don't matter. He offers comfort, support, and I need it, no matter the source.

Animal-like features take shape as the Unseelie draw closer. Each one unique, different. Antlers glint pale in the moonlight. Claws extend like knives. Stocky legs like those of an elephant thump across the ground. A few almost resemble the fae near me, but in the dim light, it's easy to miss whatever unique traits they may possess.

At the front walks the cat-like Unseelie who took May. Katiya. Her light pink hair is pulled tightly behind her head in a human-like ponytail. Next to her stands an uncommonly tall fae with antlers like a moose who carries May across his bulging arms.

Still no sign of Sigurd. Will he come to make the trade as he pledged?

"Forest King," Katiya hisses. Her tail twitches behind her, like a lioness ready to pounce.

Riven's guards flank our sides and back, leaving us at the front facing the dozen Unseelie standing behind Katiya and her moose companion.

"Katiya," Riven replies, his voice even, calm...amused?

I snap my head toward him. The arrogant mask of the fae king has been donned again. His strength in a time of weakness, his own form of armor.

Katiya's eyebrows rise at the use of her name, her head tilts subtly to the side.

"Don't forget about me." Sigurd's voice rings through the falling night.

Heads turn to where he sits grinning atop a broken pillar. He definitely hadn't been there a moment ago.

"Air King," Katiya acknowledges with the same hard voice she'd used to address Riven.

Sigurd's attention floats from her to us. His lips thin.

My feet itch to move, to hide, but Riven grips my hand tighter, rooting me in place.

Katiya's focus returns to Riven.

"What have you brought to offer us for the little human?" She gestures to May, who still slumbers in her blue bunny pajamas.

His chin tips up as he projects his voice with unfailing confidence. "Food, medicine, supplies. Name the amount."

"I see none of that with you." Katiya's tail swishes behind her. "You offered the same to another band of us, and they are dead." Claws extend from her hand, glinting in the moonlight. "You will not deal falsely with us again."

"We will not. I will seal it in magic if I must." Riven steps forward. The amusement has faded from his voice, replaced with firm sincerity.

"No."

"Spells then. We have ones which could enliven some of your land." He gestures to the surrounding desolation.

Unseelie murmur and whisper words I cannot understand.

Katiya's ears twitch. "You expect us to trust your Seelie spells?"

My heart lurches. Riven opens his mouth to speak again, but Sigurd interrupts.

"May I make an offer?" He stands on the ground now, mere feet from us, forming a triangle between his body, the Unseelie, and our party.

My gaze flits around the space, searching for Galen, but he's nowhere to be found.

Katiya adjusts her stance to face Sigurd. One hand settles on her hip, claws retreating, as she cocks her head to the side.

"Why involve yourself in this anymore, Air King? You could have taken the girl yourself days ago."

My heart skips a beat, my terrible suspicions confirmed. Ambrose lets out a muffled curse behind us as Riven goes rigid at my side.

Sigurd shrugs. "An opportunity presented itself."

"What would you offer for the little human?"

He pulls the stone from his pocket, holding it up in the air with a confident smirk. "A door key. With this, you can find many more humans."

The Unseelie murmur among themselves, their excitement palpable. Even the big one next to Katiya stirs, looking at her with eager interest.

But Kayita purses her lips. Her eyes narrow.

"I would touch it. To see if you speak truth," she responds. In a moment, she stands in front of Sigurd, the shift taking but a breath.

Sigurd's smirk fades. He holds out the stone in a clenched, upturned fist before her.

Dainty fingers with pointed nails trace over the top of the stone. Her arm snaps back to her side as she hisses, "You too would try to deceive us. That is not a key."

She shifts back to her people, leaving Sigurd wide-eyed and motionless where he stands.

"Of course it is," he says.

"Foolish King. Such treasures have a feel to them. That is a clever rock."

Riven's thumb rubs my hand, catching my attention. His eyes cut to me, their intensity searing. He asks a silent question, begs it.

I rub his hand in return.

Light glitters in his eyes. Relief? Triumph? Pride?

My free hand fumbles in the pocket of my dress, wrapping around the stone residing there—the true key, twin to the duplicate I gave Sigurd.

I didn't trust it with either king. This key is my hope for saving May. The only person I trust to make that bargain is me.

Sigurd's head swivels slowly in my direction. His shards of ice for eyes settle on me, skewering me with barely concealed rage and fury. Lips pull back from sharp teeth as I slide the true stone from my pocket.

"I have the key, the true key," I say.

The hint of a smirk pulls at Katiya's typically stoic features.

I gasp when she appears in front of me, no more than a foot away.

A growl rumbles from Riven's chest, but she ignores him and reaches toward the stone in my hand. Her eyes widen as one finger trails across its surface. Her gaze snaps to mine. Her head tilts, assessing me. Two sets of ears twitch atop her head before she shifts back to her people.

"It is a key," she says.

A sharp gasp rolls through the gathered Unseelie. Whispers linger in its wake.

I pull my hand away from Riven and step forward on my own.

A deep fortifying breath fills my lungs before I project my voice with all the confidence I can muster. "Make the trade with me. My sister for the key."

Riven's people wouldn't like the trade, but it's all we have left to offer. I'll take their anger, their disappointment, if it means May is safe again. Maybe I'm no better than the witch after all, but I'm me and that will have to be enough.

She grins. "Such a bold human woman. I like you."

My heart soars, victory within reach.

"But such a key is worthless without a human to wield it."

The rising hope within me chars to ash. It flutters through my chest and settles hard as lead within my stomach.

No. We can't fail. Not now. Not this close.

Katiya traces a clawed finger up and down her cheek as she stares me down. "Will you be coming with it?"

The key and me for May. I swallow my fear. I traded myself for her once, what's one more time? "Ye—"

"No!" Riven's roar shakes the ground as he jumps in front of me. "She's bound to stay in the forest." His strong back blocks my view. Outstretched arms extend the wall between the Unseelie and me.

"Don't do this," I implore, grabbing at his back, his arm, anything I can reach. "We have to save her. You promised."

He twists his head to me, his mouth still parted in a show of pointed fangs. His jaw softens as he looks me up and down. "Going with them could break your bargain. And I will not lose you, not like that."

The reality of his words crashes into me like a brick. A chill races along my skin, sucking away what little warmth remains. This trade could kill me.

"Is that a no then?" Katiya's voice calls our attention.

Sigurd still stands off the side, watching us all with an amused expression.

"Please," I beg. "Give her to us."

Fear surges through me. Tears sting the corners of my eyes. I don't want to die. But I can't live with myself if I leave her with these monsters and save my own skin. I couldn't trade places with her after the car crash. I can now.

"I'll go," Riven says.

A look of surprise crosses Katiya's face before Riven nudges me back. I stumble, almost falling to the ground as he steps in front of me again.

"Take me instead."

I gasp.

Around me, the fae stir and whisper. Voices I recognize. Ambrose. Sylvie. Even something from Sigurd. But I don't hear their words. My heart hammers in my ears. Riven's voice echoes through my mind, the implication of them sinking in with a dawning horror that leaves me dizzy.

"I tricked your people. I killed them. Take me in exchange for the girl," he continues, his voice hard, adamant. "Surely a king is worth one human girl."

"A king would offer himself for a human girl?" Her voice holds wonder and something else I cannot name. Katiya strides in our direction with precise, determined steps. Her tail flicks behind her, stirring up a small cloud of dust from the ground.

The key tumbles into my pocket, forgotten, as I grasp at Riven's arms. "Don't. You can't."

I want May, more than anything, but his people, thousands of them—more?—depend on him. And I... Sacrificing my life is one thing, but his? Regardless of what he's done, his role in getting May into this situation, I'm not sure I can live with that choice either.

Riven ignores my pleas, my tugs on his arm, my hands that grasp at the armor on his chest. His gaze slides to me, a sad smile on his face as he answers Katiya. "For the woman I love, yes."

My hands still. Our eyes lock. The world falls away as I stare into his emerald eyes, seeing the truth of the words he's spoken.

He loves me.

My chest aches as his confession settles into my body, resonating into my bones. *He loves me. He's doing this for me.*

My heart breaks anew. Shattering to dust in a way I never expected.

He loves me. And I...

"Riven, you can't!" Ambrose's protest brings the world back. "We need you. The forest must have a ruler, and the king must be with his people."

His head turns toward his captain. Ambrose's eyes are wild, flashing with panic and confusion. As are all the fae's. Sylvie, especially, stands frozen in horror, hands cupped over her mouth.

"I must make this right," he replies, his voice calm and steady. "What I did—my choices, my trickery—was horrible. I cannot change the past, but I can start to make things right again."

From the corner of my eye, I see figures approaching. I turn to find Katiya and the other Unseelie nearing, carrying May with them.

"Take May," Riven instructs Ambrose. Calm, resigned.

Ambrose opens his mouth to protest but snaps it shut with a grimace. In a moment, he's beside us, reaching for my sister as the Unseelie pass her sleeping form into his arms.

I run my hand over her head, fine hair slipping through my fingers. A sob bursts from my lips as my vision blurs. My palm slides to her cheek, down to her chest to feel the soft rise and fall with each breath as if she's truly just asleep, curled up with me on the couch or tucked safely into her bed.

Safe, she's safe. The words ring through the back of my mind, a distant whisper reminding me that I've finally accomplished my goal.

I blink away the tears as I take her small hand in mind. My fingers gentle squeeze around hers.

Safe. Alive.

But the man next to me... I hastily wipe at my face and turn back to him.

"Riven..." What can I say? There are no words.

He takes my tear-dampened hand and squeezes it once.

A promise.

A farewell.

He drops my hand to trail after Katiya and the other Unseelie as they retreat toward their party. Sigurd has backed off, his gaze unreadable as he stares between us all from the sidelines.

"Do you think to come with us, Forest King?" Katiya tosses the words over one shoulder.

Riven halts. Ambrose straightens beside me, adjusting his grip on May. Will they let him go free? Even Sigurd visibly tenses and steps backward.

"You offered yourself for the girl, and we accepted. But we have no need of another hostage. You shall suffer, as we have."

Another large Unseelie, similar in appearance to the one who'd held May, steps to Katiya's side, a bow and arrow raised in his hand.

He takes aim at Riven. Draws back.

Terror strikes like lightning.

"No!" I cry.

Everything happens at once.

The arrow releases. Its tip disappears through Riven's chest, the green metal exploding out of his back in a spray of blood.

Ambrose bellows. Sylvie screeches.

Riven clutches his chest and falls to one knee in a grunt of pain.

Sigurd's yell of "No!" echoes my own as he shifts forward to Riven's side.

The Unseelie clasp hands in unison and shift away.

I push past Sigurd and fall to my knees beside Riven, sobbing as I behold the thick arrow protruding from his hunched chest. Riven's men appear around us. Sigurd stumbles back, wide-eyed, mouth agape, and disappears.

"Riven! You can heal. If we just pull it out and—" I choke on the gasp I suck in, unable to get enough air.

Ambrose passes off May and kneels beside Riven. He grasps his king's shoulder.

"Poison," Riven gasps a wet, thin sound.

Ambrose stills and stares at the point of the arrow. A curse and bellow fill the air. The ground shakes as his fist slams into it again and again.

Riven's bloody hand caresses my face.

"May is safe?" he wheezes.

I nod, unable to speak. His form blurs through my tears as they run unchecked down my face, mingling with his blood.

"I do...love you..."

His limp hand slips from my face as my wail splits the air.

CHAPTER 37

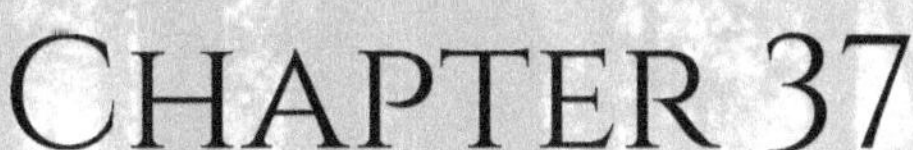

"**W**E HAVE TO GET him back. Now!" Ambrose yells. "Lia!" His fiery gaze lands on the bracelet preventing us from shifting.

In one urgent tug, I rip the stones from my wrist. The metal bites painfully into my skin before splintering apart.

The air bends and warps. Seconds tick by like hours as I hold onto the man in front of me. One, who only hours ago, had been a villain of the worst kind. Yet he'd literally given his life for my sister and me.

And he loved me. *Loves* me.

The familiar scent of new leaves hits me first. A room takes shape around us, though I don't spare even a moment to glance at it. All of my attention is glued to the ever-growing crimson stain on Riven's chest and the way his head lolls to the side. Ambrose calls for the guards before we've fully materialized. Boots thump across the floor with hurried steps.

"Get the master healer. I don't care where he is! And all of his apprentices. Call for Karin and her girls."

Their retreat sounds before the orders are even finished as they rush out.

"You, open those doors. We need to get him inside."

Two large wooden doors open. Wood splinters as they crash against walls of stone and plant life. Ambrose lifts Riven in one smooth movement, cradling him in his arms as he hustles inside. I trail after Ambrose, past the fae pressed against the doors, frozen in shock.

I recognize this room, the sitting room of Riven's chambers in Virideria.

A flash of pale blue catches my attention from the corner of my eye as a guard brushes by me to lay May's slumbering form upon a nearby couch. I trail after and drop to my knees at her side before the guard has had the chance to move away.

"Pillows," Ambrose orders. "We need to prop him up until we get the arrow out."

More guards rush in. Amidst the shouts and chaos, the only sound I can focus on is the steady *drip*, *drip*, *drip* of Riven's blood onto the stone floor until Ambrose disappears into the bedroom with his body.

"You're safe," I whisper to May's sleeping form before placing a kiss on her forehead.

And then I'm up, my body moving without thought as I push through the curtain of vine into the bedroom. Sylvie follows on my heels.

They've settled Riven on the bed on his side, pillows holding his body in place, the arrow protruding from his chest and back. The snap of wood echoes through my body as Ambrose breaks off the arrow and tosses the broken end away.

A mumbled groan cracks from Riven's lips.

Alive! Still alive. I nearly scream in relief.

"Lia." Ambrose has that look like he's called my name several times. He waves me over. "Sit here, next to him. Hold his hand."

"I—"

"Your presence helps, and he needs everything right now." He looks at me sharply. "You want him to live, don't you?"

How could he even think... But after the events of earlier today, I suppose the question makes sense. I kneel by the side of the bed, afraid any movement will cause more pain, and take one bloody hand in both of my own.

The smallest twitch of recognition greets my fingers.

"Please don't die," I whisper as tears drip down my cheeks.

In the moment I learned of his deception, a part of me wished him dead. I wanted him to suffer for his actions. But now, seeing him lying in pain, an arrow through his chest, one he'd taken for his own sins but also for me, death and suffering are far from my list of desires.

A large man I've never seen, with darkly tanned skin and a fall of midnight hair, rushes into the room. He wears robes of dark green with a sash of white and gold around his waist. The material of his robes doesn't have time to still before he leans over the bed and lays his hands upon Riven.

The air around us grows thick and heavy at the outpouring of strong magic.

"This poison..." the man's deep voice rumbles across me.

"The arrow was the same style as the one that killed Argus. Has the same feel to it too."

The healer's face draws tight. "He didn't have time to avoid it?"

"He should have, but he took the shot instead."

My chin quivers. He'd taken the arrow for May, for me, even though he could have dodged it.

"The poison took Argus in moments," Ambrose adds and glances away, his eyes downcast. Then his attention snaps back to the healer. "Can you save him?"

"We will try. Before Argus, I hadn't seen poison like this since the war, and even then, it was rare."

We? Just then, three more fae ran burst into the room, two women and a man, dressed similarly to the master healer. One carries a large basket that clinks with supplies. A lump of cloth sticks out one side.

"We need to get this arrow out," the master healer calls to the new arrivals.

They position themselves about the bed, one crawling atop it with two wicked-looking knives.

I slide my hands from Riven's and make to rise, but a deep voice stops me in my tracks.

"Lia, you stay." The master healer knows my name, though I don't know his. An all-too-common occurrence.

My hands close around Riven's again, across the strong, calloused flesh still covered in grime.

I jump as someone touches my shoulder. I twist to find Sylvie at my side.

"I'll watch your sister," she says. And then she's gone, disappearing through the curtain of vine before I can formulate a response.

"I'll help you hold him," Ambrose offers, clearly reluctant to leave Riven.

In moments, they've cut away his armor and shirt, leaving bloody flesh exposed around the arrow. An apprentice takes the remnants, playing assistant as they hand her ruined sections of clothing and then the knives they'd wielded.

Motion at the doorway catches my attention as Karin hustles into the room with water and more linens. Her feet still on the stonework at the sight of Riven on the bed, but one deep breath has her moving again. An apprentice dips cloth in water before hastily cleaning the wound.

I expect the fae to use medical supplies to remove the arrow. Scalpels, clamps, an IV, but they have none of that. These fae don't even bother to lay cloth across the bed, which already bears new blood stains.

Instead, the master healer places one open palm in the open air behind Riven's back.

Ambrose and the other three hold his body still on the bed.

My brows wrinkle in confusion as I grip Riven's hand, but then the wooden end of the arrow moves, sliding into his chest. His hand tightens on mine as a deep groan rips from his throat. His eyelids flutter.

"I'm here," I croon, my voice shaking with the same tremble gripping my limbs. "You're going to be fine."

Please. Please let it be true.

The shaft disappears completely in his chest. I gag as blood bubbles from the wound, spilling onto the bed, before an assistant presses a cloth to the wound. Riven's hand tightens painfully on mine, bringing tears to my eyes.

I swallow the bile in my throat and try to block out the pain in my hand. "It's almost over," I say, as much for me as for him. "We're right here. It's almost out."

The master healer's magic pulls the rest of the arrow free.

Riven's hand loosens on mine. His eyelids still as unconsciousness claims him once more. A wave of magic zips through the air as the healer's brows crease in concentration, his jaw set firm.

"Bandage the front wound," he grits out. "I have to leave it open for the poison to seep out."

It feels like I've been trapped in this moment a lifetime, whispering silent and spoken prayers and pleas to any god who will listen. Time doesn't matter much when the balance of a life could tip either way in a heartbeat.

The wound on Riven's back has been healed with magic, cleaned, and wrapped for good measure, but the one on the front remains, covered in layers of cloth bandages. They adjust Riven onto his back on the bed. Putrid smells seep from the wound, causing me to gag, as the healers continue to weave their magic into Riven's body, preventing the poison from claiming his life.

Solona rushes into the room. "Where is—"

"Shh," Ambrose replies, but he doesn't need to.

Solona has gone absolutely still. Only her eyes widen as she stares at Riven's unconscious form.

"How bad..." Her words are barely audible.

"Bad, but Iason is doing everything he can," Ambrose says.

Iason, the master healer, sways on the bed. Sweat drips from his forehead. His eyes stare at nothing as he concentrates fully on his magic. His body wobbles again, and this time Ambrose grabs his shoulder, steadying him.

The touch brings the healer back to the moment. "My magic is almost done. But it should be enough, at least for now. Riven's magic is fighting the poison along with my own."

The room breathes a collective sigh of relief at the positive prognosis, though Riven is far from healed, even with the combined power of the master healer, his apprentices, and Riven's own magic.

The apprentice healers help Iason from the room. The dearth of magic causes him to stumble and struggle. They carry the dirtied cloth and supplies out with them.

Karin follows shortly after to acquire clean linens for the bed.

Solona climbs onto the bed next to Riven, brushing sweat-damped hair back from his face with motherly care.

"I'll watch him for a bit if you want to check on your sister," she whispers.

May. I manage a small nod. "Thank you."

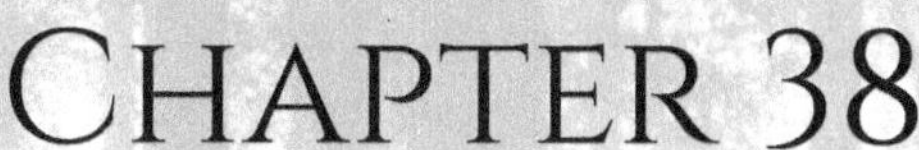

CHAPTER 38

S YLVIE SITS NEXT TO the couch May lies on, rubbing something between her fingers. She drops it as I step into the room and wipes at her face, trying to hide her tears. As I near, the object becomes clear: a golden leaf strung on a cord around her neck. It could be the twin of Galen's earring.

My throat tightens. Yes, I'm almost certain it is. This day has been hard on so many of us.

Sylvie tucks the necklace back down her shirt. "You truly think he didn't want to do it?" she whispers.

"I'm certain. If I'd rejected Sigurd's offer..." I shake my head. "It's my fault Galen ended up in that situation."

Another failure. More pain I've caused.

I sit on the couch next to May and pull her head into my lap. She looks for all the world as if she's just fallen asleep and could wake any moment. Even her skin and clothes are clean as if preserved by whatever magic keeps her slumbering in stasis. I brush a lock of her soft, blond hair back from her face.

You're safe now.

"Do you think he'll come back?" She rubs her chest at about the spot where her necklace would rest.

The hope in Sylvie's voice stills my hand on May's brow.

"I don't know." He betrayed his king. Would he even be welcome? Yet, so did I...

But Riven lied to me too.

So many lies. So much deception. They weigh me down like an anchor, dragging me into the cushions.

"The better question is, will Sigurd have Galen shift him back?" Ambrose joins us in the room. Fatigue drags his steps as he stumbles into a chair across from Sylvie.

"Could he? Even with the wards?" I ask.

"He could. At least until Riven is well enough to adjust them."

Sylvie flinches. Adjusting the wards would bar Galen from the territory...and anyone he planned to bring back with him.

I clutch May tightly to me. "Then we're not safe, even here."

"You'll be safe in this room, as will May. Riven's rooms are specially warded so that only he can shift straight here."

My shoulders droop, but I keep my arms cocooned around my sister.

"How do I wake her?" I ask Ambrose, changing the topic away from Galen for Sylvie's benefit, if nothing else.

"Iason will know how. We'll ask him to do it first thing in the morning after he checks on Riven again." Ambrose cocks his head side to side, staring at May.

His rapt attention stirs up the worries still knotted in my stomach. "What is it?"

He scratches his chin. "Her gift has developed greatly, almost to maturity, yet her body remains young."

I clutch her tighter to me. "How? What does that mean?"

"Maybe some kind of Unseelie magic? I don't know. But she should be able to see our world as you do, to be here without any ill effects."

"Ill effects?" My skin prickles. Way to bring those up now...

"Headaches, confusion, disorientation," Sylvie lists them as though reading from a textbook, her voice empty as the look in her eyes. "Our texts say that young humans have a hard time with our world if their gift is not developed. It would be even worse for the un-gifted, rendering them insane within hours or days."

Her words send a shudder through my body. Gifted humans can improve their magic. My sister can help them. A chill settles in as the shudder subsides.

"She's going home, back where she belongs." I eye the two of them in challenge.

Ambrose raises his hands in the air. "Yes, she is, we promised. But she can visit from time to time if she wants to."

My lips thin.

"And if she doesn't, then that's fine as well," he adds.

Fine. But first, we have to get her home. "Any news from the door? Any sight of my father?"

Riven had used his power to appear to my father in a dream, just as he had me. Or so he said. But would Dad listen to such a thing? It'd taken many times before I truly believed Riven wasn't just some recurring dream I'd concocted in my grief. Honestly, a part of me wasn't totally convinced until I met him again at the circle of trees.

Ambrose shakes his head. "None I've heard, but I will ask the guards again, just to be sure."

I brush my hand through May's hair. We can wake her, but I'm not about to just leave her at the door. I can't leave, and entrusting another fae to return her home is out of the question. Dad *needs* to come to the door, yet with Riven unconscious and unable to send any more dreams...

I swallow my grim thoughts.

May is safe, and no one will take her away again. That's the important thing. Safe and here with me.

"You still have the key?" Ambrose asks.

Between Riven's injury and May's recovery, I'd forgotten about it completely. I reach into the pocket of my dress and wrap my hand around the stone still lingering there. I sigh in relief. "Yes, it's here."

"Good, we should get it back into that protective box. Just in case." He starts to rise, but Sylvie waves him down.

"I'll get it." She stretches and rolls her shoulders before leaving the room to shift back to Arbrean.

A few minutes later, she returns with the box in tow. We secure the key inside. Ambrose tucks it away behind some objects on a bookshelf, out of sight for now until a better solution can be decided upon.

"You don't have a vault?" I ask.

"That's the first place everyone looks for treasure," he replies, a hint of his jovial tone returning. "It's safer here. For now."

Karin returns with several more maids who change the linens of the bed before settling Riven's unconscious form back upon it. They bring food and drink as well, though I can't muster even a bite. Washing the blood from my skin and changing my clothes are the only self-care I have time for. One of the apprentice healers returns, swaying on her feet but determined to stay in case Riven's situation worsens. Sylvie and Solona leave with a promise to return at first light. Ambrose, however, refuses to leave, despite his exhaustion, and settles himself on the couch across a low table from May.

"Are you sure? You need rest," I protest. With all the magic he's used today, combined with the normal need for sleep, he can barely keep his eyes open.

"I'll sleep just fine here," he pats the cushion under him.

"We have another room prepared for you, if you'd like it," Karin offers.

I shake my head. "I'd like to stay as well."

She nods, her face solemn before she leaves us. Ambrose is already half asleep on the sofa. Thank goodness he at least bothered to change clothes. I take one more look at May before walking into the bedroom.

The healer sits in a chair near the bed, attentively watching Riven for any sign of change.

"Do you mind leaving us alone for a bit?" I ask.

The fae rises and bows. "Of course, my lady." The title stings. After all I've done today, it's the very last thing I deserve. "I will be in the other room."

I wait until she leaves before climbing into the bed next to Riven. My hand traces down his strong face, his bare muscled shoulders, and comes to rest atop the bandages on the side of his chest, well away from his wound. The steady rise and fall of his chest and the soft beat of his heart give me some comfort but not near enough.

The mark on my skin has darkened around the edges. A reaction to Riven's pain and illness, Solona told me when I asked about it.

"Please come back to me," I whisper.

His suffering doesn't excuse the pain he caused me, or the fear, the betrayal, the deception. All those things linger between us. They slice at my heart, bleed out on the bed beside him. But I realized something when that arrow slid through his chest, a truth I never had the chance to tell him, one I still struggle to admit to myself.

"I love you too."

Ambrose wakes me at dawn when Iason arrives to check on Riven again. I slept beside him the entire night, curled around one limp arm that I clutched like a lifeline, willing him to return to me.

Low conversations draw to a close as Iason returns to the sitting room.

We all stare at him, waiting for answers.

"The rest of the poison is out, but he's still weak, his magic burned through. It may take a while for his body to recover from its effect."

A sigh ripples through the small crowd of Solona, Ambrose, Sylvie, and the handful of others permitted to gather, eager for news.

"Is he awake?" I need to speak to him, to see him, assure myself that he's okay and not going to leave me.

Iason shakes his head. My heart drops.

His gaze shifts to land again on May's sleeping form in my lap.

"But there is someone else who needs to wake up." A smile pulls his features, the first I've seen on him. It lights up his dark face and paints him as a carefree, loving man rather than the somber one who I'd seen thus far. "May I?"

My lips quirk up at his question. "Please. Should I move her?"

"No, she's fine right there." He kneels beside my sister and me. One wide hand hovers in the air above her face.

She has to wake up, has to be okay.

He closes his eyes, brow furrowed in concentration. Something akin to snowflakes float down and land upon her face, quickly melting into nothingness. The magical snowfall halts when Iason withdraws his palm.

A flutter of eyelashes. A small intake of breath.

I choke in a sob at the small signs of life. Tears blur my eyes. I take her small hand in mine. "May."

"Lia..." May's whispered, sleepy response sends the tears streaming down my face.

"I'm here." I release her hand.

She scrubs at her face and sits up, peering about.

May twists around to stare at me. Her brows wrinkle.

"Where's my bear? And Momma?" She wiggles closer. "Who are they? Lia..." Her voice rises an octave, panic setting in at the unfamiliar surroundings.

Shit. I'd been so preoccupied with saving her, waking her up, and getting her home that I'd never stopped to think of what to tell her.

I hold her close. "They're friends. We're visiting them for a bit, but Mom and Dad will be here soon."

Her head swivels between me and the fae. The wobble of her bottom lip proves just how little she believes my words. A loud sniffle has the fae stepping back.

Solona's eyes widen in alarm.

"Let's give them some space," she whispers, ushering the fae toward the main doors.

May buries her head in my chest, her little fists clutching my shirt. Tears and snot soak into the fabric.

"You're fine. It's fine." I rock her like a much younger child.

After being asleep so long, and with the Unseelie, I can only guess at the emotions surging through her. Even if she remembers none of it, her body no doubt carries phantom memories. And her gift... who knows what that sudden maturation did to her.

"What do you remember?" I need to be sure.

She looks up at me, still sniffling. "Momma read me a bedtime story. The one about the three bears." Her face scrunches up. "Where's Momma? And Daddy?"

"They'll be here soon," I promise again. God, I only hope my words are true.

An animalistic whine at the end of the couch catches my attention. My eyes fly wide. Ambrose stares at us in his bear form, his head tilting to the side then up again.

May goes utterly still in my lap. Even the sniffles turn off abruptly.

"Now is not the—" I start.

She draws in a sharp breath, cutting off my words. "It's a bear!" She swivels her head back to me, golden hair flying behind her. "Just like my story!"

Joy lights her face, the tears forgotten.

Ambrose whines again and rubs his paw over his face.

"It wants to be my friend! Can I play with it? Please?" She bounces in my lap without fear of the large animal only a few feet away.

All the "wild animals are not friends" discussions we've had over the years clearly didn't sink in. I blame all her books about friendly animals.

From the corner of my eye, I catch Ambrose bob his head up and down.

"Fine." I sigh. How am I going to break it to her that not all bears are so friendly?

May squeals, hops to her feet, and goes running over to Ambrose. He lays on the ground as she rubs his fur, wiggles his ears, makes faces at him, and a number of other things entirely inappropriate for a child to do with a wild animal.

But she's happy, laughing, giggling, her terror forgotten, so I don't stop her.

CHAPTER 39

K ARIN BRINGS FOOD, INCLUDING a tray of items that look sus-
piciously like human sandwiches, as well as several small
outfits.

"I found a few things that might fit the girl." She holds up the colorful dresses and lays each one across a nearby table. A dark green sundress reminds me of one of May's favorite outfits. She'll love it, especially since it's her current favorite color.

Iason returns to check on Riven as May lets out a particularly loud yell of laughter while riding bear-form Ambrose like a horse. The healer winces. "I'm glad the girl is happy now, but perhaps they can play outside? Our king will need all the rest he can get in order to recover."

I can barely make out Riven's still form atop the bed in the other room. He hasn't moved. Not a twitch all day.

"I'll have one of the courtyards closed off for us," Solona offers. "They can play out there, and May might find something else more interesting than the captain." A wry smile pulls at her lips as she gazes back over at Ambrose and May. Sylvie plays the dark knight May battles while riding her noble steed. We even had to clear furniture out of the way to form their battlefield.

The thought of leaving Riven alone causes my heart to clench in pain. Even if he's not awake, I want to be with him. But if the noise is harming his recovery... Leaving May's side isn't an option, but we can give him some space, at least for a little while.

"Still no change?" I ask when we return hours later.

Rays of sunset slant through the open balcony, painting the room an array of bright shades.

Iason shakes his head. "I'm afraid not. Not yet." He tilts his head as a smile emerges from his frown. "Though I see the afternoon was a success for someone."

Ambrose, back to his fae self, carries a slumbering May in his arms. The green dress bears the stains of an afternoon of outdoor play. Eventually, all of the excitement of the day caught up with her, and she collapsed into a slumber against the base of a tree. He lays her down on the couch, but as he moves away, she grasps onto his sleeve and mumbles something in her sleep.

"Looks like you made a friend," Solona chuckles.

With considerable care, he unlatches her fingers. May curls up in a ball on the cushions, content to sleep without her new companion. Ambrose drapes a soft, dark blanket over her slumbering form, shielding her from the cool night air that will soon slip into the room.

"He should be through the worst of it by now, but send for me immediately if he wakes or anything changes," Iason says to Ambrose as I exit the bathing room sometime later, dressed in my most conservative nightgown. Night has fallen while I washed up, leaving the room aglow in lamplight and the last remnants of sunset adding traces of fleeting light to the sky.

Ambrose stretches on the couch across from May, his boots cast off the side on the ground. Already a blanket is around his chest.

I shake my head and cross the room toward them.

"Thank you, Iason, we will," I whisper, wary of waking May.

"Goodnight," he calls quietly and strides for the exit.

My attention shifts to Ambrose, who stifles a long yawn. "Are you sure you want to sleep on the couch again?"

"I'll be fine. Besides, one of us should be here if she wakes." He nods toward May. "I assume you'll be keeping Riven company?" Humor dances in his eyes.

Heat rises to my cheeks at his words. He'd hit the nail on the head.

"My presence helped him before," I say, recalling the last time he'd been thoroughly drained of magic.

"I'm sorry I was harsh with you in the forest." Humor leeches from his face. "When I thought you'd given away the key..." He shakes his head.

"Don't be sorry. I'd have been angry with me too."

The silent agreement of forgiveness passes between us.

"There's something else I want to ask you about," I whisper, conscious of May's sleeping form. "Evelyn was human."

Ambrose nods, his eyes widening ever so slightly.

"So Riven is half-fae?"

He scratches his beard and inhales in a deep breath that ruffles the blanket over him. "No. Half-fae do not exist."

My brow wrinkles. "But how..."

"Humans amplify our magic. So, a human mother passes on even greater gifts to her fae children."

My legs wobble. I sit down heavily in the chair next to him. My hand flies to my stomach as panic threatens to swallow me whole. "Could I..."

"Unlikely," Ambrose says, catching my meaning.

A relieved sigh bursts free as I sink into the cushions. Thank goodness for that.

"Children are rare for us," Ambrose continues. "Even more so with human women, but such a child would be powerful." He looks away before his gaze settles on me again. "All the current Seelie monarchs are children of human mothers."

Even Sigurd.

A strange sorrow leaks in like ink spreading through water. I'm everything they need. For now, and for the generations to come. But those thoughts send my head spinning in a direction I can't begin to follow. Not now. Maybe not for a long time.

"Why did no one tell me?" Another secret. Not a lie exactly but one more thing I didn't know.

"Would it have put you at ease?"

A small, humorless laugh tries to break free. "No."

Hell, I'd have definitely run for the woods and never come back.

"Then you know why. But we would have once the girl was safe. Once you were happier. So many things didn't go as we'd have preferred." He shakes his head. "We'll do better, if you give us a chance."

Despite all the pain and revelations of recent days, I believe him. "No more secrets."

"None. Anything you want to know, we'll tell you. And then some."

My heart lurches every time I see Riven lying still and motionless on the bed. Iason closed the wound on his chest after determining that all the poison was out. Only a round, puckered scar remains, close, far too close, to his heart. Another inch to the left, and even Iason's powerful magic wouldn't have saved him.

I trace the circle of that scar, the pale flesh that almost glimmers in the moonlight. The maids washed him earlier, cleaning away the last of the blood and dirt, fitting him in new pants on freshly cleaned linens. The familiar scent of honeysuckle clings to him again, wrapping around me too as I snuggle next to him on the bed. I tug a thick fur over us to shield us from the slight chill of night.

The pleasant warmth of his skin, the soft set of his lips, the way his hair trails around his face and over the pillows...the serenity of it all belies the internal struggle he still fights to heal the ravages of the poison.

"Come back to me," I whisper, adding another kiss to his cheek. My nightly prayer. Last night's had not been answered, but maybe tonight's will be.

Faint sensation tickles my cheek, waking me. I blink in the darkness as the feeling comes again—a hand caressing my cheek. I gasp and shove myself upright in bed. The sight before me causes my heart to skip and stumble.

Riven stares up at me in the dark, a soft smile playing about his face.

My mouth opens in a soundless scream of joy, but his finger over my lips cuts off any words before I can utter them.

"Let me be alone with you, just for a little while." His hand moves to cup my cheek.

My brows draw together. "How—"

"I can hear Ambrose's snores from here."

Funny, I can't. The curtain of vine blocks a surprising amount of sound. Likely magic at work, but none of that matters.

He's alive! Tears blur his night-darkened form.

"Your wound. The poison." My hand trails along his chest, over the circular scar.

"It still burns, worse than I could have imagined, but I think I'll live." His lips quirk up. A calloused thumb wipes away the tears leaking down my face. "I take it this means you don't completely hate me."

A small huff of laughter bubbles from my lips. I return a wobbly smile. "Not completely."

"Good. If you did, I'd be tempted to lie back and let the poison take me."

My eyes widen as I hold back the urge to swat his grinning face.

"Don't say that," I hiss in a whisper.

"May is safe?"

"Asleep—a natural sleep—in the other room."

"Good."

I settle down next to him again, our faces only inches apart as he tilts his to the side to stare at me in the dark. The heat soaks from his body into mine, stirring up the pool of warmth that stretches from my chest, down through my stomach and between my legs.

It lay dormant, iced over, since Sigurd revealed Riven's deception to me.

But here, lying closely with him in the dark, all our secrets bared, the hurt and the pain melt away.

Well, almost all of our secrets.

"I love you too." My truth. The one he didn't have.

His breath hitches. He searches me, strips my soul bare. "Lia—"

I don't wait for him to finish. His words are lost against my mouth when I close the space between us, sealing my truth with a kiss.

All my love. All my pain. All my passion.

I pour it out to him, taking all the emotion his hungry mouth gives back. Our bodies melt together, two twined souls embracing their lost other half.

Everywhere he touches comes alight in a spark of life. I need to touch him, to remind myself he's real, alive. My hands are everywhere, on his chest, down his back, in his hair. We're a tangle of limbs and desires. No words are needed, and none can convey all that we say as we cling together.

Joy floods my veins as we part—a happy, bubbling spring of hope, filling in and binding the cracks amidst my broken heart.

Our foreheads press together. Heavy breaths mingle.

If only I could freeze this moment and hold onto it forever.

The tangled web of secrets and bitter deception almost tore us apart. But the sharp edge of truth, a knife meant to cut the threads that bound us, welds us together instead, solidifying the tenuous bond between us.

"The wound, the poison, is worth it just to hear those words." His chest rises and falls with heavy breaths as I lay pressed against him. "You truly mean it? Despite everything?"

"I do." I add another kiss to his shoulder. "If you died without knowing..." I bite my lip, unable to continue as the tears well up again.

"It feels like a dream. If it is, never wake me."

"I should be letting you rest."

"Stay with me. Please." His eyes beg right along with his words.

"I'm not going anywhere."

"My Ciela." The words float across me like a caress before his lips claim mine again. Soft. Delicate. A promise more than anything else.

"What does that mean?"

"I don't know the human translation, but it's our word for chosen mate. Your destined one."

My breath hitches. "Soulmate."

"Soulmate," His smile is broad as he tests the words. "Yes, that sounds perfect."

We cling together until exhaustion pulls into slumber once more.

This night holds everything we need.

Acceptance of truth. Forgiveness of sins. Recognition of the fate we almost destroyed.

CHAPTER 40

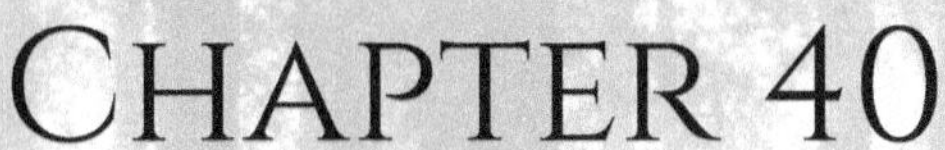

"**S**o, are you my sister's boyfriend?"

I gape at May where she sits on the foot of Riven's bed, staring over at him where we've propped him up with pillows behind his back. Leave it to her to skip introductions and go straight for the jugular.

Riven chuckles and looks to me, his eyebrows raised.

"He is," I confirm.

"Does he get to come over to our house to play then?"

I rub the edge of the sheets between my fingers. May knows nothing of my bargain. I've avoided that, the magic, and the fact that we're in a different world. Basically everything I can in an attempt not to frighten her. Oddly enough, she hasn't asked any of the questions I expected. Nothing about the pointed ears, the clothing that doesn't resemble anything we normally wear, or even the odd foods.

May fits in Faery like a fish in water, much more than me, and even more than I expected.

"We'll have to see," I say.

She frowns. "When do I get to play with the bear again?"

So quickly her attention shifts. She's been asking for him all morning, having no idea that Ambrose, who's been no more than twenty-five feet from her the entire time, is her bear friend.

"You might have worn him out." I wink at her.

Her shoulders drop. "I did ride him a lot."

Riven lets out a bellow of laughter, throwing back his head in mirth. "I missed all the fun."

Voices tease my ears from the other room, but I can't quite make them out.

Riven's smile dims as he wraps his hand around mine and squeezes.

"What—" I begin, but just then, Ambrose steps into the room.

"Lia," he says then pauses. "There's someone to see you at the door. *That* door."

My hand squeezes Riven's in return. Joy lights me up from the inside out.

Dad. He's come after all.

But the light burning within me fades when my eyes catch on May, still sitting at the end of the bed and looking between us all. She can go home.

It's the goal I've worked for, my whole purpose in coming here, so why does the thought sit so heavily on my heart?

"He's not particularly happy. Made some comment about *raisin' hell*," Ambrose adds.

Yeah. I swallow a huff of laughter. That sounds like Dad.

"Can you take us?" I ask Ambrose.

"Do I get to go?" May jumps into the conversation and bounces off the bed onto the floor.

"Yes, you get to go." I look over my shoulder at Riven. His sad smile mirrors my own. "Daddy is waiting for us."

It's a victory, what I've worked for, so why does it hurt?

"Daddy!" She bounces on the balls of her feet. "Let's go now."

"I'm coming too." Riven slides from the bed.

"You can barely stand," Ambrose protests.

Riven shrugs and stretches his stiff limbs. At least he put a shirt on before my sister came in. "I need to make my apologies at some point. Might as well start today."

Ambrose groans. "Fine. I'll shift you all, but if you collapse, I'm finding someone else to carry you back."

We make a square between us all, holding hands to connect us to Ambrose's magic.

"This will feel weird," I tell May. "But don't let go, okay?"

The magic stirs around us. May's eyes widen, but they contain excitement more than fear. Her hand tightens on mine, holding on like she's been told.

"—my girls now!" The familiar voice reaches my ears before I see him.

Dad. I close my eyes against the tears that fill them. How I've ached for this moment, for him to know we're safe.

"Daddy!"

My eyes snap open at May's ecstatic cry. The magic pops, planting us firmly outside near the door to Earth. May tears her hand from mine and bolts. I spin around, following her movement. My knees wobble as I stare at my dad.

His mouth gapes. Overgrown stubble clings to his chin.

My heart shatters in a flurry of fireworks and heartache. He charges toward his youngest daughter as she flies to him, knocking two fae guards out of the way in the process.

"May," he calls, over and over in his strong, gruff voice, one that breaks and cracks around her name.

With all my focus on the scene unfolding before me, I don't realize I've been holding Riven's hand in a death grip until he squeezes mine in return.

Dad kneels as May launches herself into his arms and hugs him around his neck. His embrace encircles her, pulling her close, as he heaves a sob into her hair. They hold each other, their entwined forms a portrait of relief and love against the solemn stone monoliths behind them.

Bittersweet joy sweeps through me. Dad found us. May can go home, even if I can't. Not yet.

Dad looks up at me over May's head.

"Lia?" he croaks.

I release Riven's hand and run to him like a child. He peels one arm away from May and holds open his embrace for me to join it.

I do, sliding home next to my sister. A sob rips from my throat as he pulls me in tight and kisses my forehead.

"My girls." He draws back just enough to look at us. "How? Where—"

"It's a long story." I sniffle, trying to halt my tears. God, I've cried so much recently. You'd think I'd have run out of tears by now. "How did you find us?"

"I had the craziest dream a few nights ago. I thought that's all it was, but I just couldn't get it out of my head. It took me days to find that damn tree circle again."

Barely contained laughter shakes my chest. The dreams had affected me the same way.

"This is real, isn't it?" he asks me.

I nod. "This is Faery."

"That's what they told me. I saw the ears but still." He shakes his head. "Your mother's been so worried. Damn near had to sedate her. Time to get you girls home."

About that...

May wiggles in his grip. "It's only been a day. Can I stay and play more?"

Dad's eyes widen and cut to me in a silent question.

"Like I said, really long story." And about to get longer.

His gaze shifts past me now, at the two imposing fae males still likely lurking behind us. His jaw stiffens, a hard edge to his voice as he says, "Friends of yours?"

"They helped me find—"

"That one is Lia's boyfriend," May exclaims and points to Riven.

Oh, my God. I want to die. To sink beneath the ground and hide forever.

The feeling only intensifies when Dad's flat gaze settles on me, demanding answers. Nothing I can say will make him feel any better about this situation. Dad pushes to his feet as Riven and Ambrose approach.

Riven holds out his hand in an oddly human gesture of greeting. "It's nice to meet you."

Dad just blinks at it and then at me.

Shit. *Say something, Lia. Anything.*

I swallow. "As I was saying, they helped me find May."

Now it's May's turn to look confused as she stares up at us all, her lips pursed.

A sigh of relief slips through my lips when Dad finally grips Riven's hand in return and gives it one, hard shake. "Thank you for my daughters, but we'll be leaving now."

"Dad..."

"No buts," he says, "You can explain it all later, but now we're going home." He takes May's hand and strides for the stones.

"Should I talk to him?" Riven whispers and wraps his arm around my shoulder.

Someone has to but not Riven. "No, I'll do it. Wait for me."

"Forever."

It wasn't a question, but his answer sends my pulse racing any-way.

May protests as Dad practically drags her into the circle of stones.

"How's this damn thing work?" he says.

"I can show you, but I can't go with you," I reply.

Dad goes utterly still before turning to gaze at me, expression full of barely concealed panic. "You've both been missing for days." His voice is icy, the false calm concealing the emotions surging across his face. "We didn't know if you were alive, and now I find you both in this place that shouldn't exist."

May whimpers, the tears coming again.

I drop down next to her and wipe at her face. "It's okay. Don't cry. You want to go see Momma, right?"

She nods. My hands slide to cover her ears. "I made a magical promise to stay for a year. It was the price to save her."

Dad's mouth drops open. His eyes slide from me to the fae lurking outside the stone circle. A muscle ticks in his jaw.

I release May and stand, attempting to position myself in his line of sight.

"But I would want to stay even if I hadn't promised to. I want to be here, Dad. I belong here." The words ring true in my heart as soon as I speak them.

His head snaps back to me now, eyes shining with unshed tears.

"You know how hard a time I've had since..." I glance at May, fleeting. "But I fit here. It's right here. *I'm* all right here. I want to stay, and I'm old enough to make my own choices about life. More than old enough."

"Are they even human?" The silent plea laced in his words doesn't pull me the way it might once have.

"In the ways that matter."

He sucks in a ragged breath. "I don't like it. I don't like it at all. Come home."

May sniffles again. This time, Dad lifts her into his arms with a grunt and holds her against his chest.

Tears glaze my eyes, accompanying the sad smile on my face. "I can't, but you can come visit me. I'd like that. I think they'd all like that." I motion behind me. "Take May home, tell Elise I love and miss her, and then come back tomorrow. I'll explain everything."

I wipe away my own tears.

I haven't run any of my plans, my offers, by Riven, but I don't expect him to mind. More gifted humans will help their magic. How can he protest?

"How do we get home?" he asks. "Or back here?"

I place one hand on his arm and another on May. "You just have to *want* to be there."

May gasps. Her tears dry in an instant as the stones around us transform into trees.

Dad swears.

"Where'd they go?" May asks as she squirms in his arms, trying to find the fae who reside on the other side of the door.

"I can't leave here." I gesture to the trees. "But come here, and you can find me."

"And I can play with the bear again?"

I giggle, more at Dad's look of horror than May's question. "Yes, I'm sure you can."

"You'll be here tomorrow?" Dad questions again. "And you'll be safe with those...people?"

"I will," I promise to both questions.

"If they do anything to you, I'm coming through that door and—" He bites off his own words with a glance at May, but I get the picture. He can truly raise hell when he wants to, and nothing, no fae or otherwise, will stop him if anything happens to his girls again.

It takes a few more promises and assurances to convince Dad to leave with May. Even then, he stops just outside the circle and looks back at me, maybe expecting I'll change my mind.

But I don't. Even when the tears form again—Jesus, they really never end—and roll down my cheeks as they walk away. I keep my feet rooted to the ground, standing in the doorway between worlds. May waves at me over Dad's shoulder where he still carries her. I bite back a sob and wave back, trying everything I can to hold my smile in place until they're out of sight.

Strong arms wrap around me from behind, holding me tight. Their strength and support break the dam holding in my sobs.

May is safe. Finally, she's on her way home.

I've done it.

We've done it.

Riven holds me until the tears subside and my family has traveled far out of sight.

Tomorrow, I'll be better. Stronger. With Riven at my side, I know it's true. Plus, I need to let Dad in on my idea to save the cabin, pay off May's medical bills, and maybe a little extra. The fae love giving gifts, and I know there are plenty of pawn shops that would love to buy some, uh, *well-maintained family heirlooms.*

"There is one other thing Sigurd told me that I need to understand." The memory tugs at my thoughts, refusing to let me be at peace.

"Of course," Riven says. "What is it?"

"He said that Faery would steal my humanity, make it harder for me to remember my family, my past, my world."

Riven stiffens.

I twist in his arms to look up into his face, one that pulls down into a frown.

"It does."

A hard, dark knot twists in my stomach. Another hidden truth only Sigurd revealed.

"However," Riven continues, "A few months is far too short a time for it to affect you very much, if at all, and certainly not permanently."

The knot loosens, a little.

"I'm sorry. It's been too long since we've had experience with new humans. I didn't consider the effects of Faery. You will not forget your family or your life while you are here. In fact, I vow that I, Rivenean Lutheon Silvanus, will remind you of your family every day that we are together. I ask nothing in return."

I suck in a breath as a chill runs up my spine. The air around us squeezes tight, a warm blanket of thick magic cocooning us in. It pops as suddenly as it came, slithering off and away from us.

I know the feeling of that magic. I felt it once before, on the first day I came to Faery.

"A magical bargain. Why?" I gape at the now smiling face before me.

"Not a bargain." Long fingers caress my face. "A vow is one-sided. Consider it a step toward re-earning your trust."

The knots in my stomach loosen completely. He made a magical vow, for me, for my benefit alone, asking nothing in return. The magic would hold him to that promise, as it holds us to our bargain.

I lean forward and place a quick kiss on his lips.

"Accepted," I whisper. "And I have an excellent idea for how to show my gratitude once we return home."

His eyes widen on the last word. The surprise melts into a wicked smile. "Are you ready to go home?"

Not here, not the human world I'd been born in. Staring into his loving eyes, another truth locks into place, no longer just the murmur of possibility. I love my family—I always will—but the home of my heart exists elsewhere.

We're fated, Riven and I, a truth I hadn't realized until almost too late. A part of my heart is irrevocably his. Our love is a balm to each other's wounds, the answer to the questions that plagued our lives, and a new beginning for the Court of the Forest.

My heart knows only one answer to give him.

"Yes."

Thank you for reading *A Bargain with the Fae King*!
Reviews are so important for authors, so I hope you'll take a
moment to share your thoughts on this book.

Anxious for more books in the Courts of Faery series? Sign-up for
my newsletter to stay in the loop on all major updates:
www.authormeganvandyke.com/newsletter/

ALSO BY MEGAN VAN DYKE

The Castamar Duology

The Musician and the Monster (Beauty and the Beast)
The Artist and the Dragon (Sleeping Beauty)

Reimagined Fairy Tales Collection

Second Star to the Left (Peter Pan)
The Ugly Stepsister (Cinderella & Snow White)
The Alice Curse (Alice in Wonderland)

The Courts of Faery

A Gift for a Fae Warrior (Optional Prequel)
A Bargain with the Fae King (Book 1)
Bound to the Fae King (Book 2)
Forgiving a Fae Warrior (Book 2.5 - Optional Novella)
Destined for the Fae King (Book 3)
Marked by the Fae King (Book 4)

Stolen Empire

Captive of the Stolen Empire (Book 1)

ACKNOWLEDGEMENTS

First off, thank you to my family. My life would be nothing without you all. You are the best anyone could wish for, and I truly don't know what I would do without all of your continual love and support. Whether near or far, you mean the world to me, and your support of my books is such an incredible gift.

A huge thank you to my editor Jeni Chappelle. Not only did you help me finally understand deep POV, but you helped me sort out the opening to this book which I'd been struggling with for YEARS! I really appreciate you helping me revise and polish this book baby so that it could venture out into the world at last.

To all my friends in the writing world who have supported my journey with this book (and it's been a long one), I am eternally thankful for you. Special shoutout to my Oceans11 ladies, my Street Team, and my publishing sisters at Portal World Publishing. I would never have made it this far in my publishing journey without you, and this book certainly wouldn't be what it is today.

To my readers, you all are the best! Every review, recommendation, blog article, and social media post that I see about my books brightens my day more than you can know. They matter. You matter. I am so thankful.

About the Author

Megan Van Dyke is a fantasy romance author with a love for all things that include magic and romance, especially fairy tales and anything with a happily ever after. Many of her stories include themes of family (whether born into or found) and a sense of home and belonging, which are important aspects of her life as well. When not writing, Megan loves to cook, play video games, explore the great outdoors, and spend time with her family. A southerner by birth and at heart, Megan currently lives with her family in Florida.

Connect with Megan
www.authormeganvandyke.com
www.authormeganvandyke.com/newsletter/
facebook.com/AuthorMeganVanDyke
instagram.com/authormeganvandyke
tiktok.com/@authormeganvandyke
bookbub.com/authors/megan-van-dyke